SCARY SUMMER

R.L. STINE
GOOSEBUMPS

SCARY SUMMER

graphix

AN IMPRINT OF

SCHOLASTIC

NEW YORK   TORONTO   LONDON   AUCKLAND   SYDNEY   MEXICO CITY   NEW DELHI   HONG KONG   BUENOS AIRES

The Goosebumps book series created by Parachute Press, Inc.

Library of Congress Cataloging-in-Publication Data is available.

ISBN-13: ISBN 978-0-439-85782-6 / ISBN-10: 0-439-85782-1

12 11 12 13 14/0

First edition, July 2007

Edited by Sheila Keenan

Book design by Richard Amari

Creative Director: David Saylor

Printed in the United States of America 23

REVENGE OF THE LAWN GNOMES

ADAPTED AND ILLUSTRATED BY

Dean Haspiel

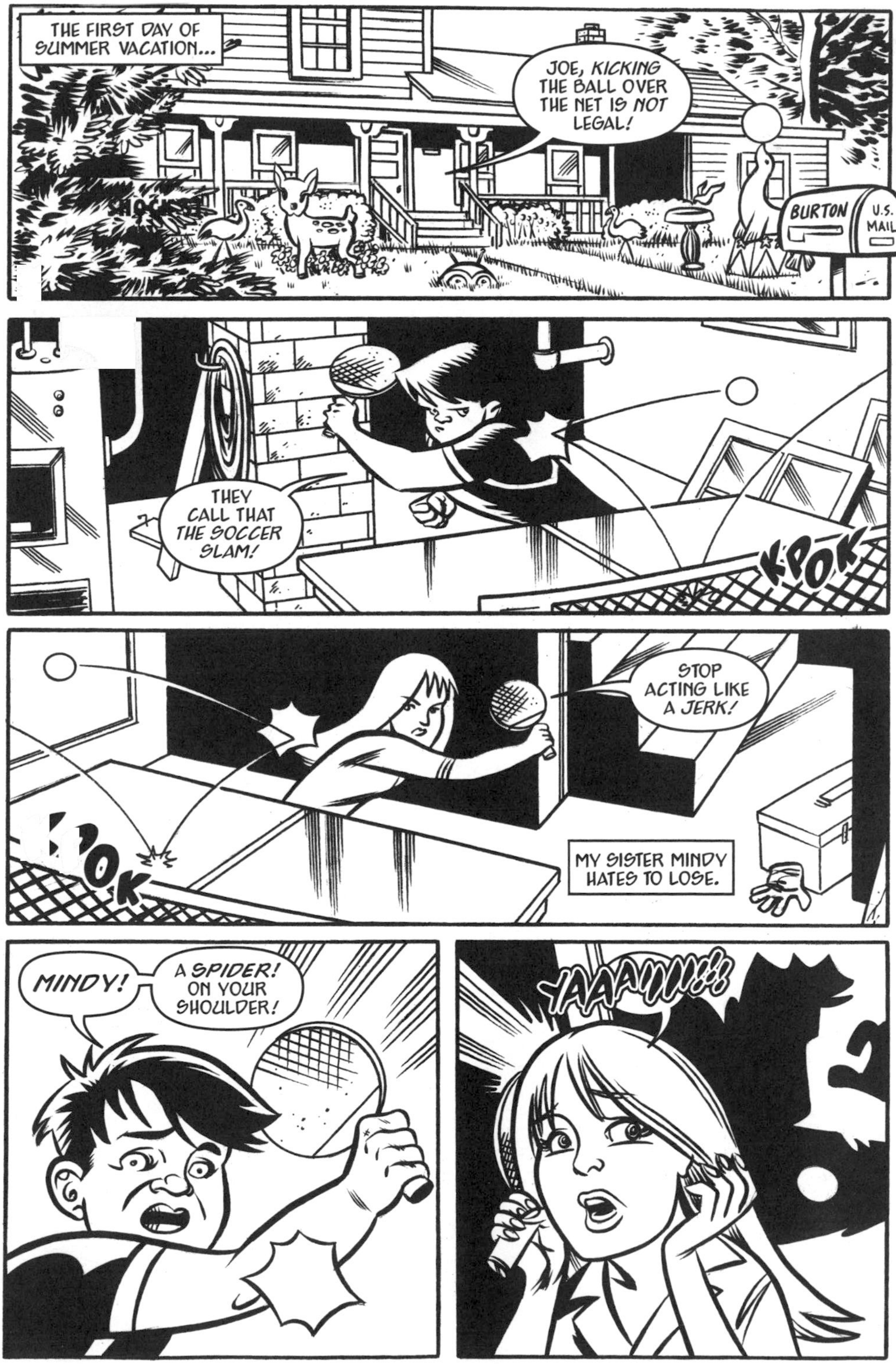
THE FIRST DAY OF SUMMER VACATION...
JOE, KICKING THE BALL OVER THE NET IS NOT LEGAL!
BURTON
U.S. MAIL
THEY CALL THAT THE SOCCER SLAM!
K-POK
STOP ACTING LIKE A JERK!
MY SISTER MINDY HATES TO LOSE.
MINDY!
A SPIDER! ON YOUR SHOULDER!
YAAAIIII!!

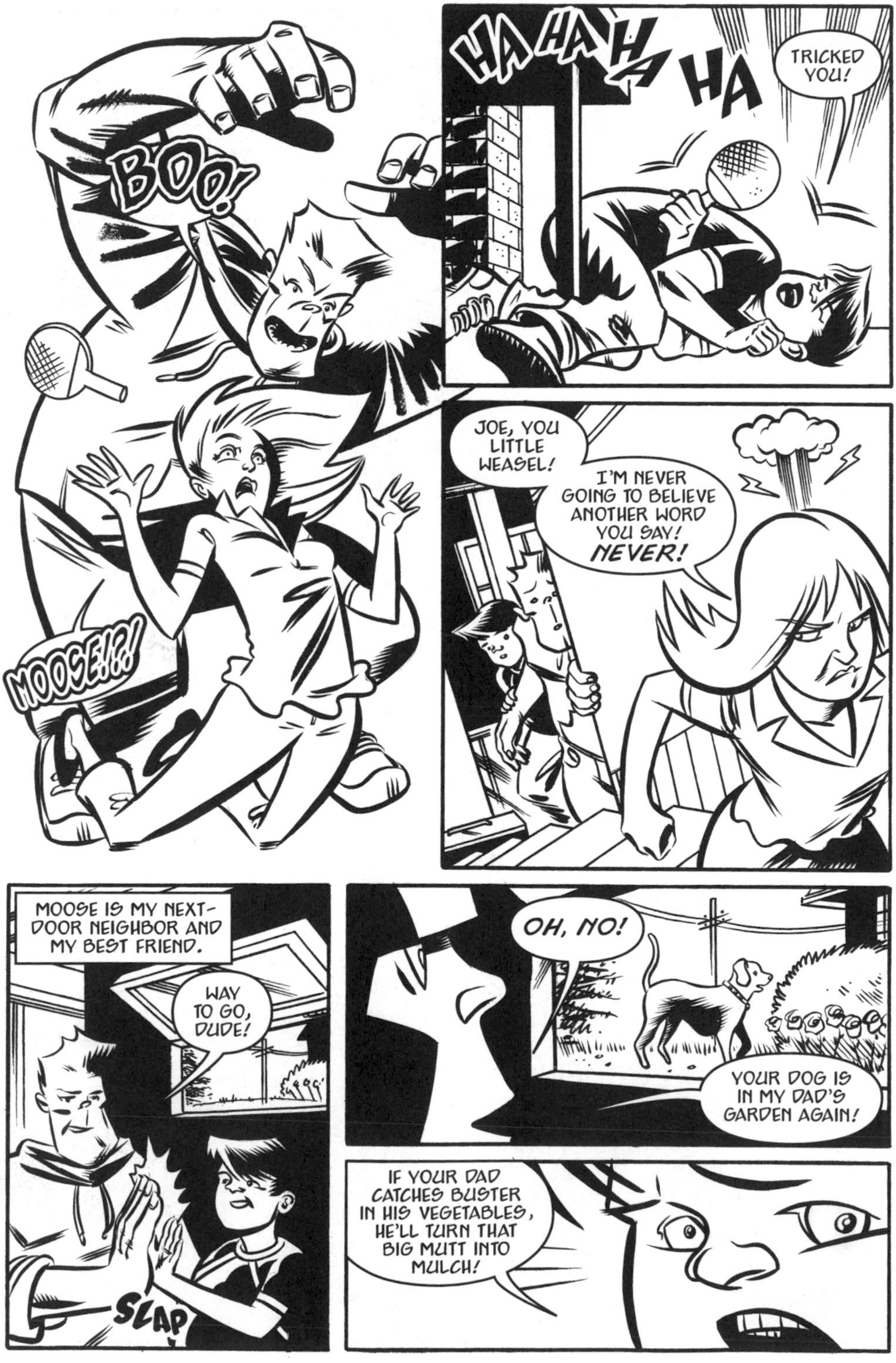
BOO!
MOOSE!?!
HA HA HA HA
TRICKED YOU!
JOE, YOU LITTLE WEASEL!
I'M NEVER GOING TO BELIEVE ANOTHER WORD YOU SAY! NEVER!
MOOSE IS MY NEXT-DOOR NEIGHBOR AND MY BEST FRIEND.
WAY TO GO, DUDE!
SLAP
OH, NO!
YOUR DOG IS IN MY DAD'S GARDEN AGAIN!
IF YOUR DAD CATCHES BUSTER IN HIS VEGETABLES, HE'LL TURN THAT BIG MUTT INTO MULCH!

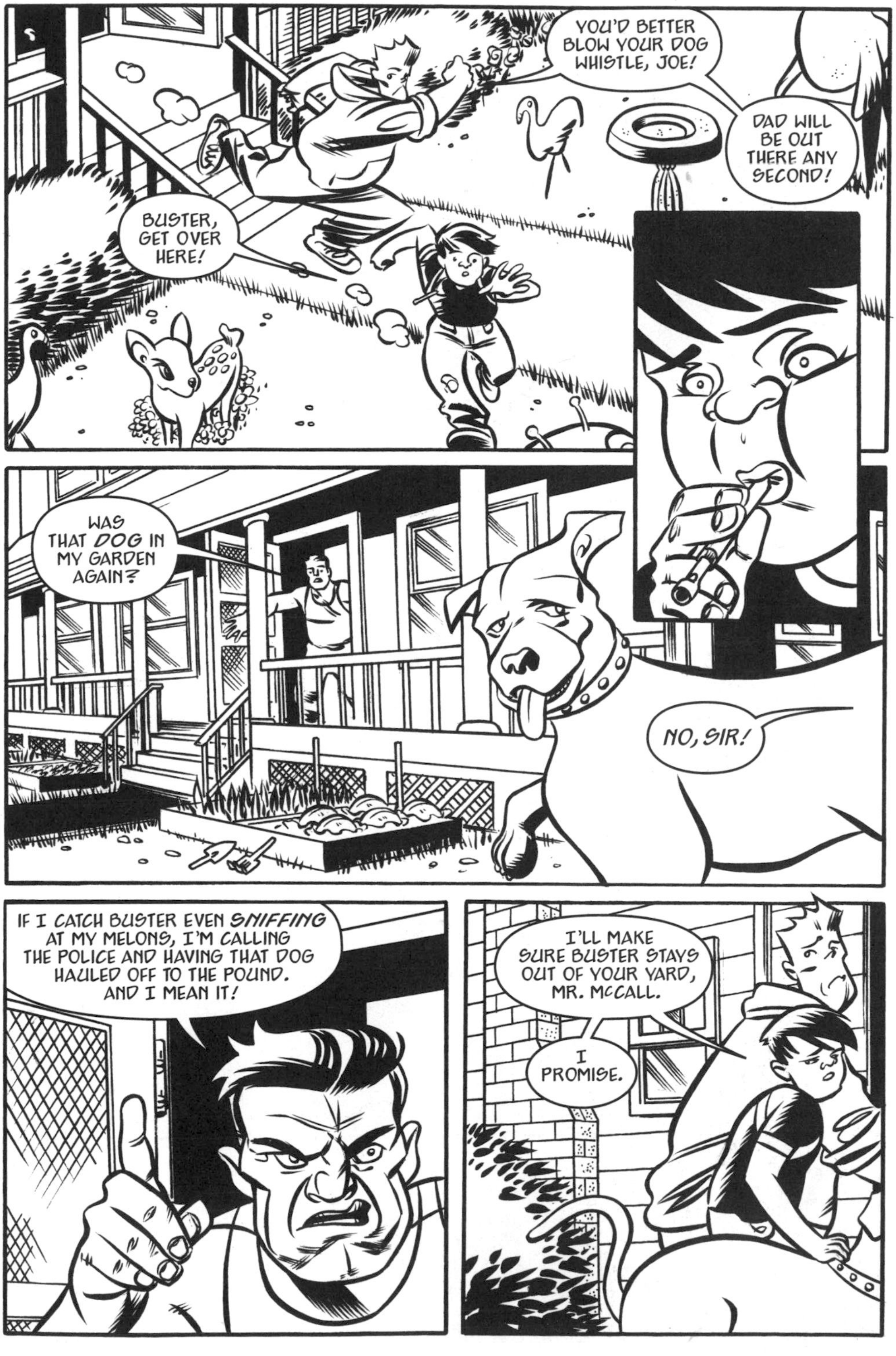
YOU'D BETTER BLOW YOUR DOG WHISTLE, JOE!
DAD WILL BE OUT THERE ANY SECOND!
BUSTER, GET OVER HERE!
WAS THAT DOG IN MY GARDEN AGAIN?
NO, SIR!
IF I CATCH BUSTER EVEN SNIFFING AT MY MELONS, I'M CALLING THE POLICE AND HAVING THAT DOG HAULED OFF TO THE POUND. AND I MEAN IT!
I'LL MAKE SURE BUSTER STAYS OUT OF YOUR YARD, MR. McCALL.
I PROMISE.

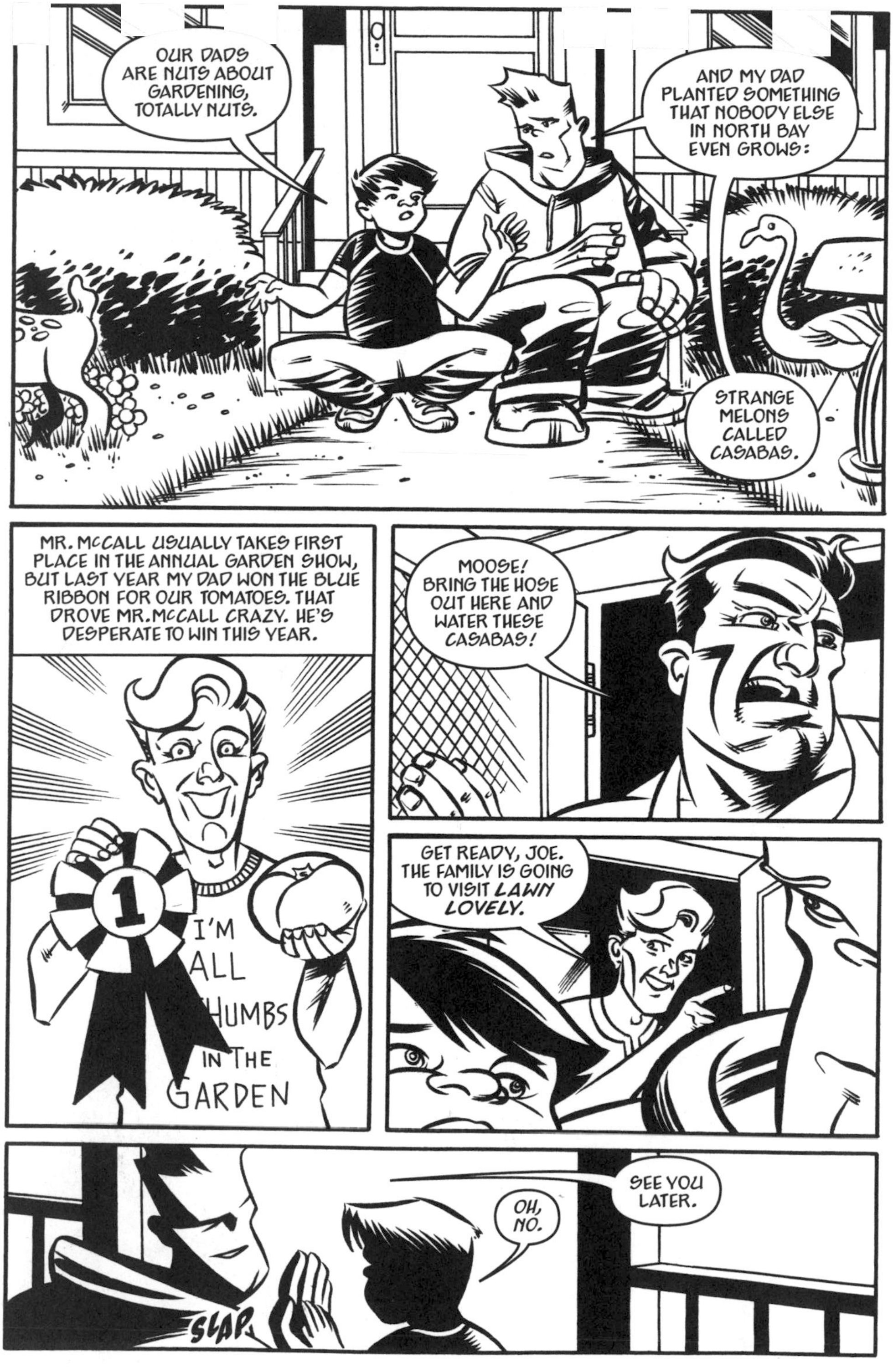
OUR DADS ARE NUTS ABOUT GARDENING, TOTALLY NUTS.
AND MY DAD PLANTED SOMETHING THAT NOBODY ELSE IN NORTH BAY EVEN GROWS:
STRANGE MELONS CALLED CASABAS.
MR. McCALL USUALLY TAKES FIRST PLACE IN THE ANNUAL GARDEN SHOW, BUT LAST YEAR MY DAD WON THE BLUE RIBBON FOR OUR TOMATOES. THAT DROVE MR. McCALL CRAZY. HE'S DESPERATE TO WIN THIS YEAR.
1
I'M ALL THUMBS IN THE GARDEN
MOOSE! BRING THE HOSE OUT HERE AND WATER THESE CASABAS!
GET READY, JOE. THE FAMILY IS GOING TO VISIT *LAWN LOVELY.*
SLAP
SEE YOU LATER.
OH, NO.

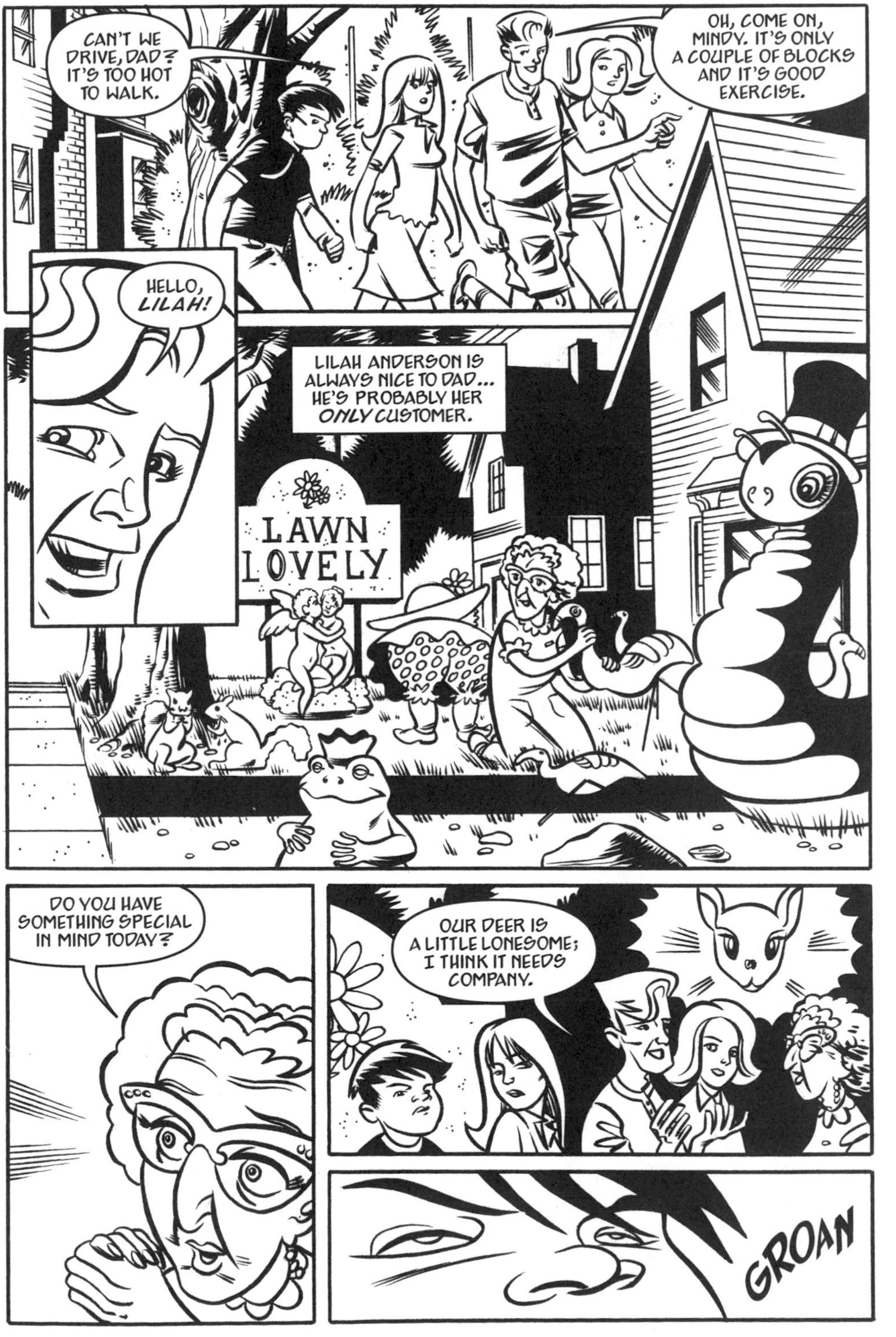
CAN'T WE DRIVE, DAD? IT'S TOO HOT TO WALK.
OH, COME ON, MINDY. IT'S ONLY A COUPLE OF BLOCKS AND IT'S GOOD EXERCISE.
HELLO, *LILAH!*
LILAH ANDERSON IS ALWAYS NICE TO DAD... HE'S PROBABLY HER *ONLY* CUSTOMER.
LAWN LOVELY
DO YOU HAVE SOMETHING SPECIAL IN MIND TODAY?
OUR DEER IS A LITTLE LONESOME; I THINK IT NEEDS COMPANY.
GROAN

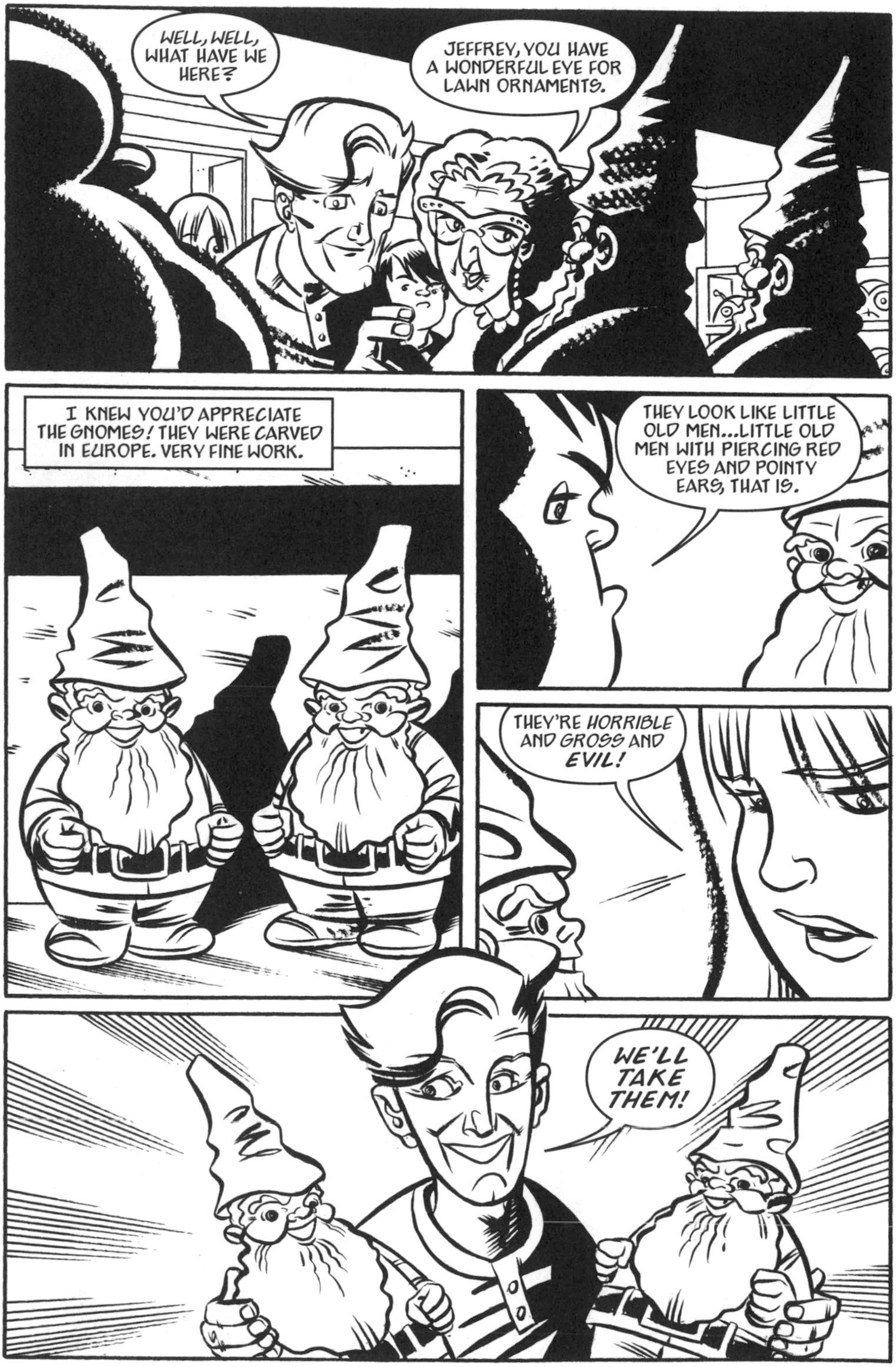
WELL, WELL, WHAT HAVE WE HERE?
JEFFREY, YOU HAVE A WONDERFUL EYE FOR LAWN ORNAMENTS.
I KNEW YOU'D APPRECIATE THE GNOMES! THEY WERE CARVED IN EUROPE. VERY FINE WORK.
THEY LOOK LIKE LITTLE OLD MEN...LITTLE OLD MEN WITH PIERCING RED EYES AND POINTY EARS, THAT IS.
THEY'RE *HORRIBLE* AND *GROSS* AND **EVIL!**
WE'LL TAKE THEM!

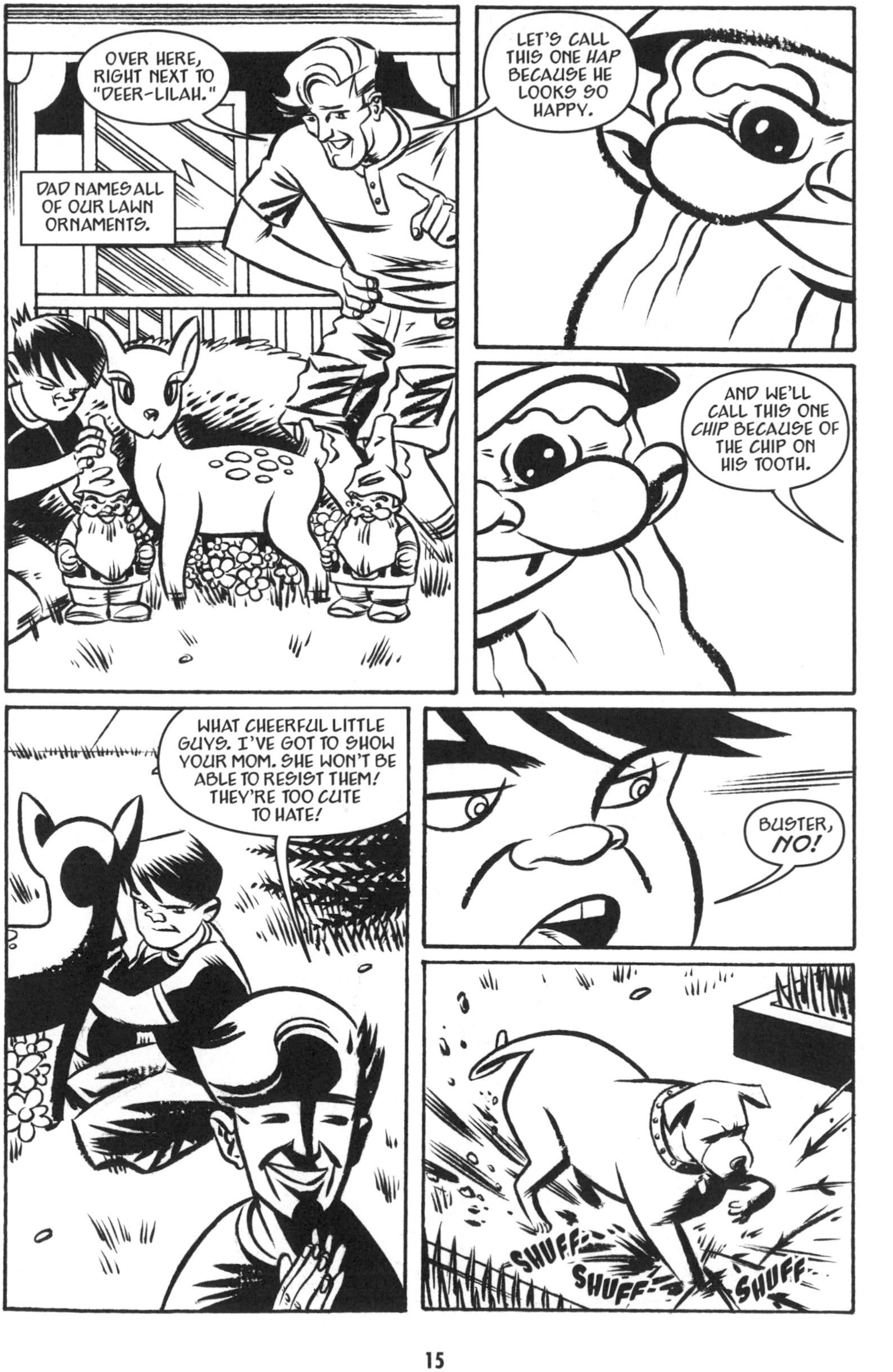
OVER HERE, RIGHT NEXT TO "DEER-LILAH."
DAD NAMES ALL OF OUR LAWN ORNAMENTS.
LET'S CALL THIS ONE HAP BECAUSE HE LOOKS SO HAPPY.
AND WE'LL CALL THIS ONE CHIP BECAUSE OF THE CHIP ON HIS TOOTH.
WHAT CHEERFUL LITTLE GUYS. I'VE GOT TO SHOW YOUR MOM. SHE WON'T BE ABLE TO RESIST THEM! THEY'RE TOO CUTE TO HATE!
BUSTER, NO!
SHUFF SHUFF SHUFF

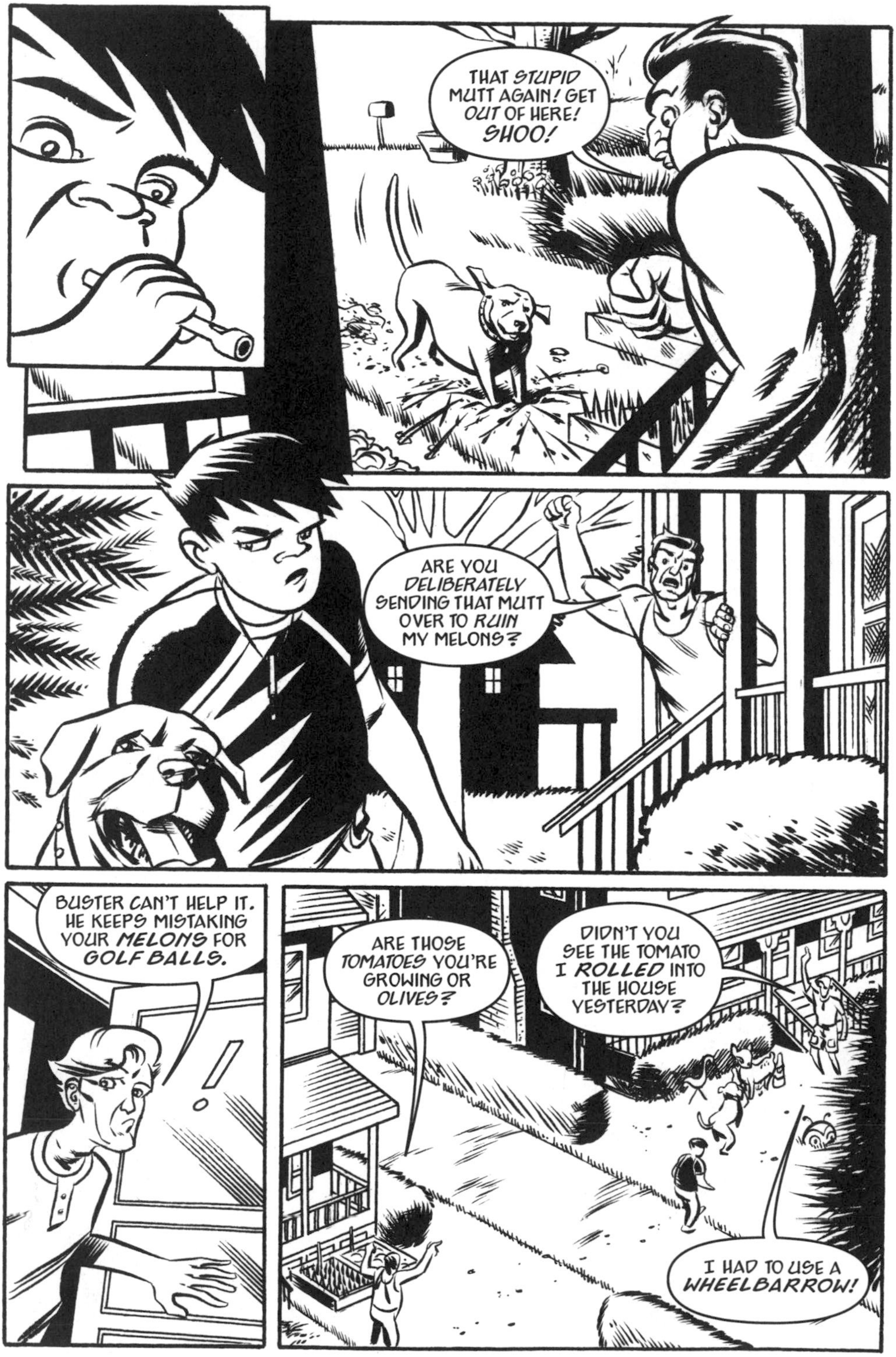
THAT *STUPID* MUTT AGAIN! GET *OUT* OF HERE! ***SHOO!***
ARE YOU *DELIBERATELY* SENDING THAT MUTT OVER TO *RUIN* MY MELONS?
BUSTER CAN'T HELP IT. HE KEEPS MISTAKING YOUR ***MELONS*** FOR ***GOLF BALLS.***
!
ARE THOSE *TOMATOES* YOU'RE GROWING OR *OLIVES*?
DIDN'T YOU SEE THE TOMATO I ***ROLLED*** INTO THE HOUSE YESTERDAY?
I HAD TO USE A ***WHEELBARROW!***

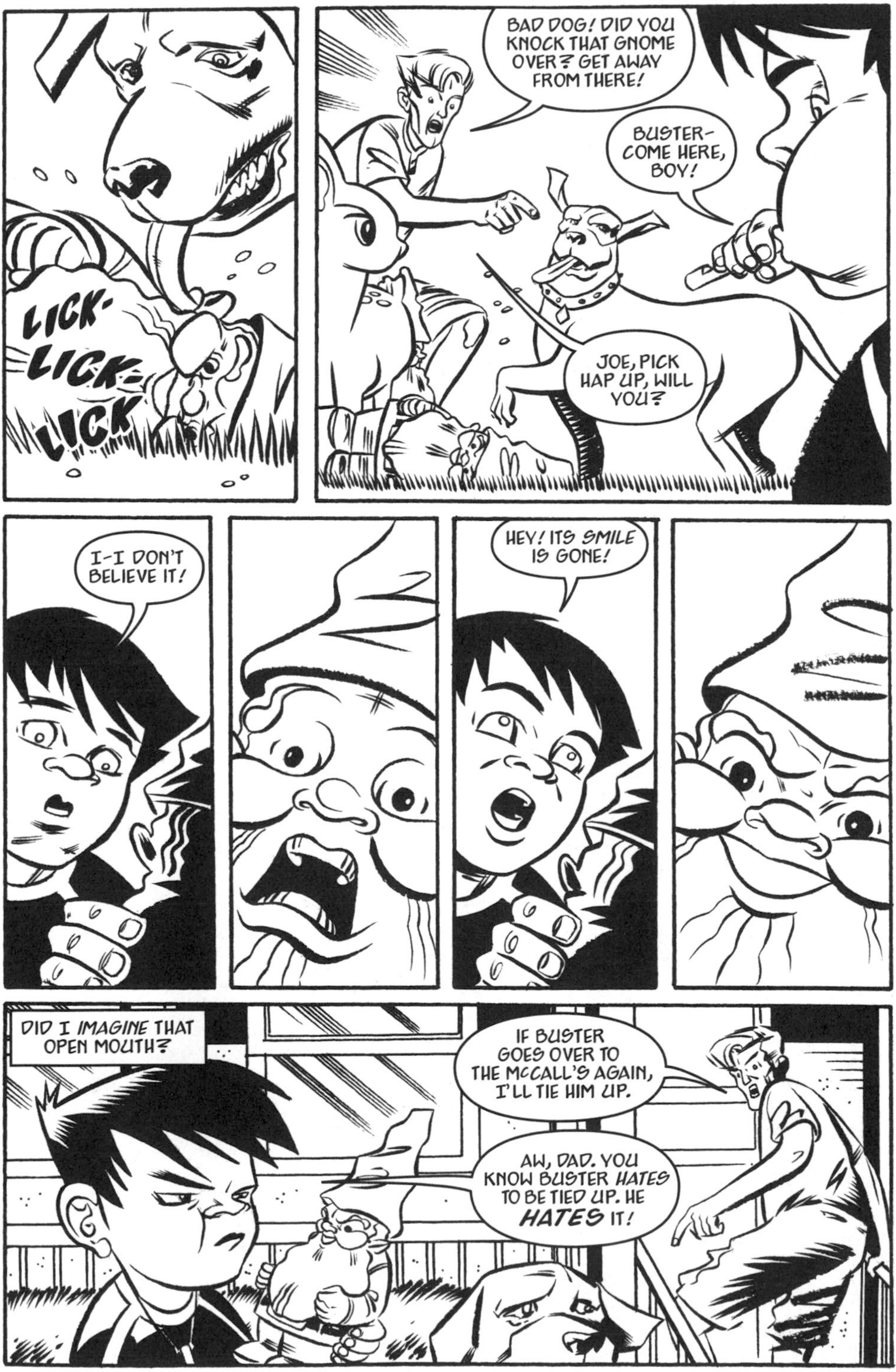
LICK-
LICK-
LICK
BAD DOG! DID YOU KNOCK THAT GNOME OVER? GET AWAY FROM THERE!
BUSTER- COME HERE, BOY!
JOE, PICK HAP UP, WILL YOU?
I-I DON'T BELIEVE IT!
HEY! ITS SMILE IS GONE!
DID I IMAGINE THAT OPEN MOUTH?
IF BUSTER GOES OVER TO THE McCALL'S AGAIN, I'LL TIE HIM UP.
AW, DAD. YOU KNOW BUSTER HATES TO BE TIED UP. HE HATES IT!

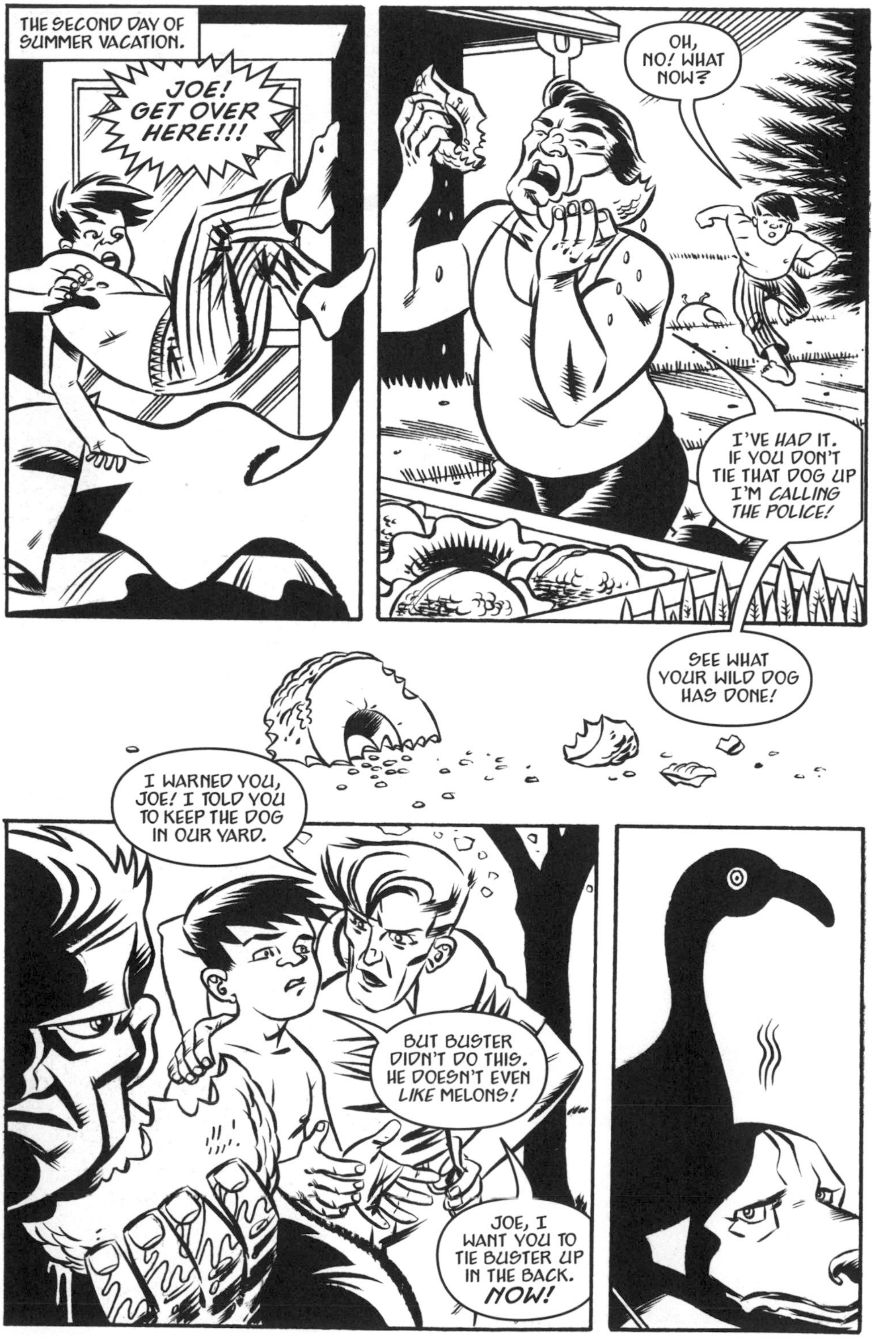
THE SECOND DAY OF SUMMER VACATION.
JOE! GET OVER HERE!!!
OH, NO! WHAT NOW?
I'VE HAD IT. IF YOU DON'T TIE THAT DOG UP I'M CALLING THE POLICE!
SEE WHAT YOUR WILD DOG HAS DONE!
I WARNED YOU, JOE! I TOLD YOU TO KEEP THE DOG IN OUR YARD.
BUT BUSTER DIDN'T DO THIS. HE DOESN'T EVEN LIKE MELONS!
JOE, I WANT YOU TO TIE BUSTER UP IN THE BACK. NOW!

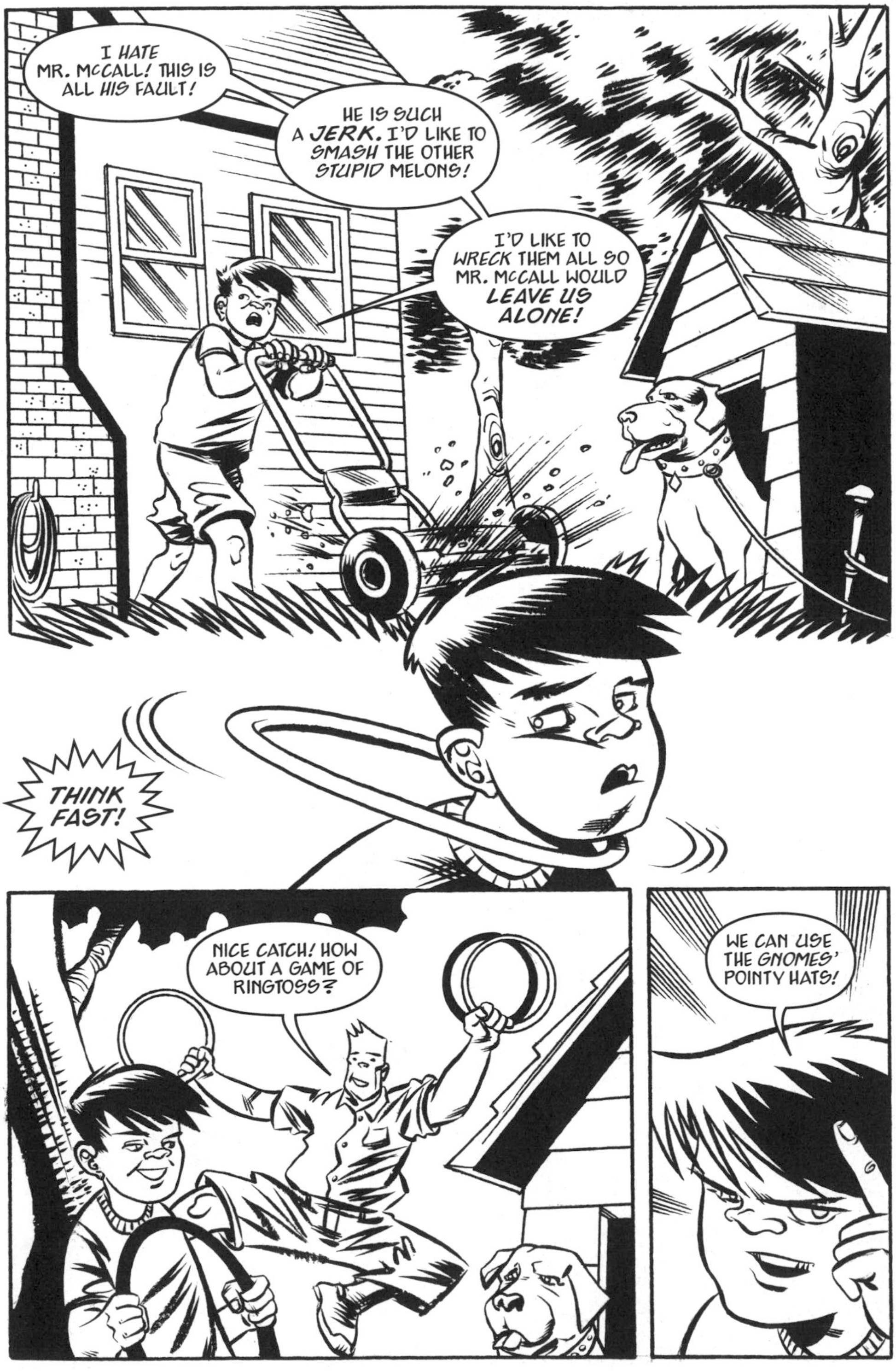
I HATE MR. McCALL! THIS IS ALL HIS FAULT!
HE IS SUCH A JERK. I'D LIKE TO SMASH THE OTHER STUPID MELONS!
I'D LIKE TO WRECK THEM ALL SO MR. McCALL WOULD LEAVE US ALONE!
THINK FAST!
NICE CATCH! HOW ABOUT A GAME OF RINGTOSS?
WE CAN USE THE GNOMES' POINTY HATS!

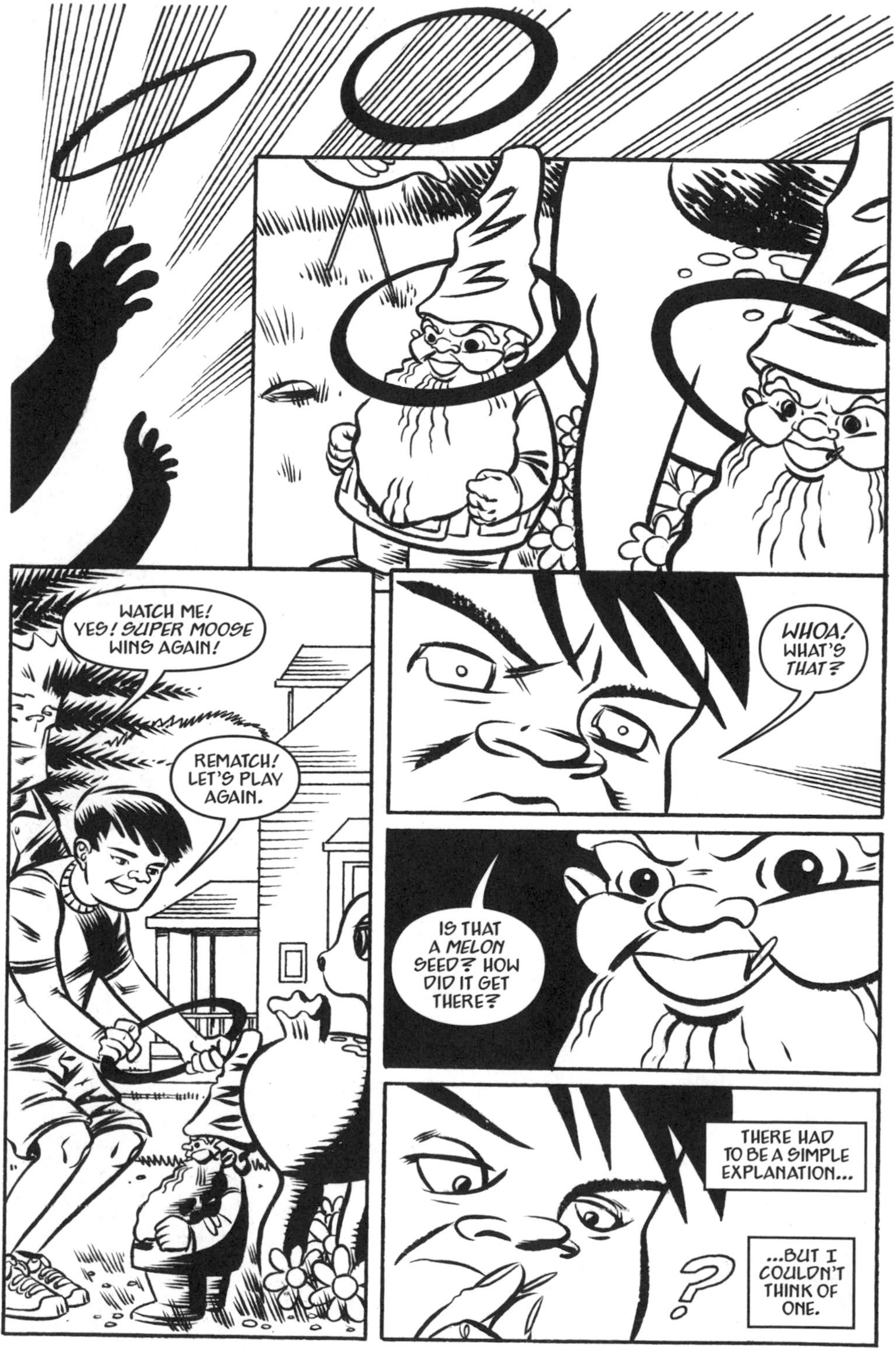
WATCH ME! YES! SUPER MOOSE WINS AGAIN!
REMATCH! LET'S PLAY AGAIN.
WHOA! WHAT'S THAT?
IS THAT A MELON SEED? HOW DID IT GET THERE?
THERE HAD TO BE A SIMPLE EXPLANATION...
?
...BUT I COULDN'T THINK OF ONE.

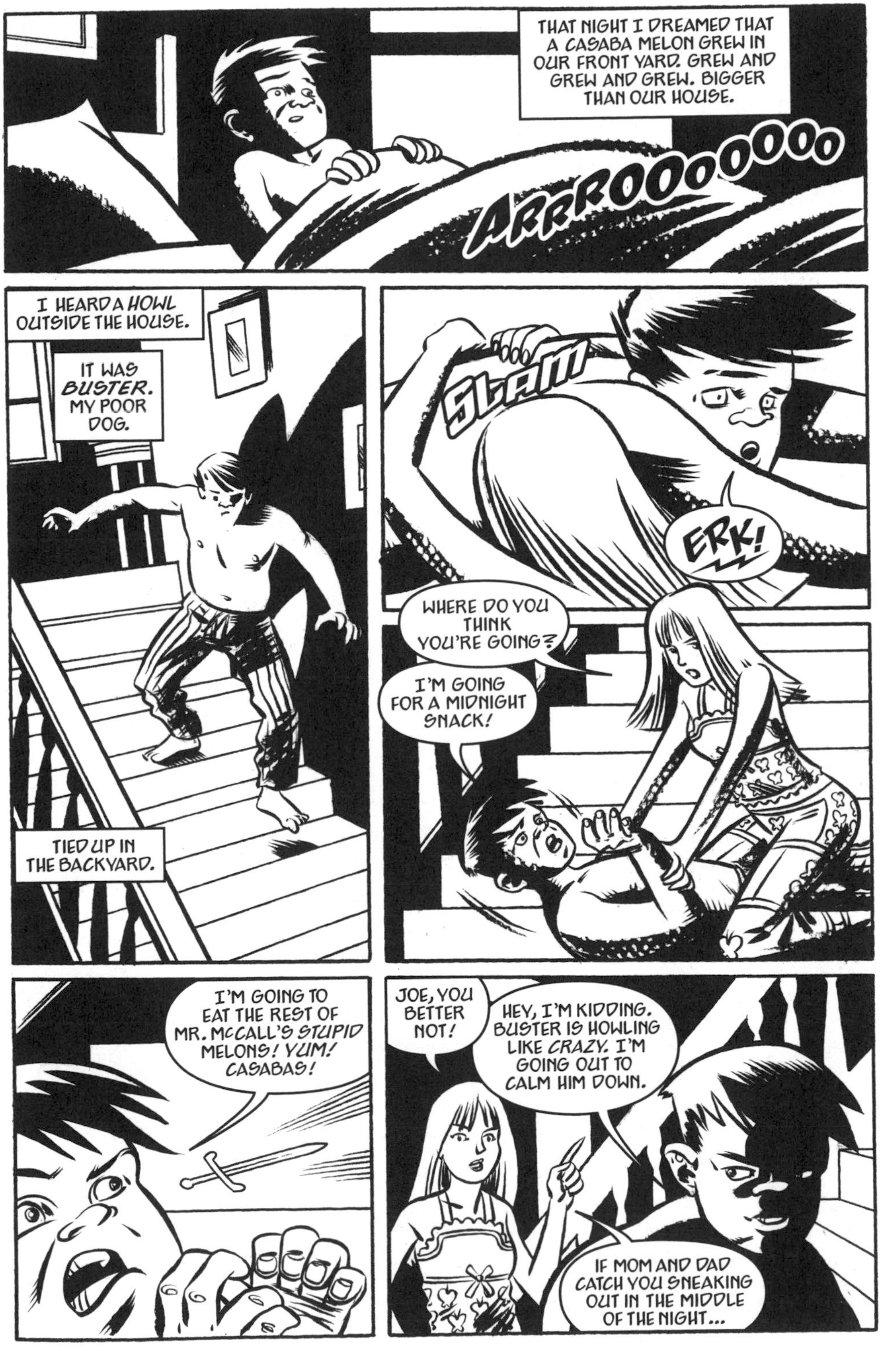
THAT NIGHT I DREAMED THAT A CASABA MELON GREW IN OUR FRONT YARD. GREW AND GREW AND GREW. BIGGER THAN OUR HOUSE.
ARRROOOOOOOO
I HEARD A HOWL OUTSIDE THE HOUSE.
IT WAS BUSTER. MY POOR DOG.
TIED UP IN THE BACKYARD.
SLAM
ERK!
WHERE DO YOU THINK YOU'RE GOING?
I'M GOING FOR A MIDNIGHT SNACK!
I'M GOING TO EAT THE REST OF MR. McCALL'S STUPID MELONS! YUM! CASABAS!
JOE, YOU BETTER NOT!
HEY, I'M KIDDING. BUSTER IS HOWLING LIKE CRAZY. I'M GOING OUT TO CALM HIM DOWN.
IF MOM AND DAD CATCH YOU SNEAKING OUT IN THE MIDDLE OF THE NIGHT...

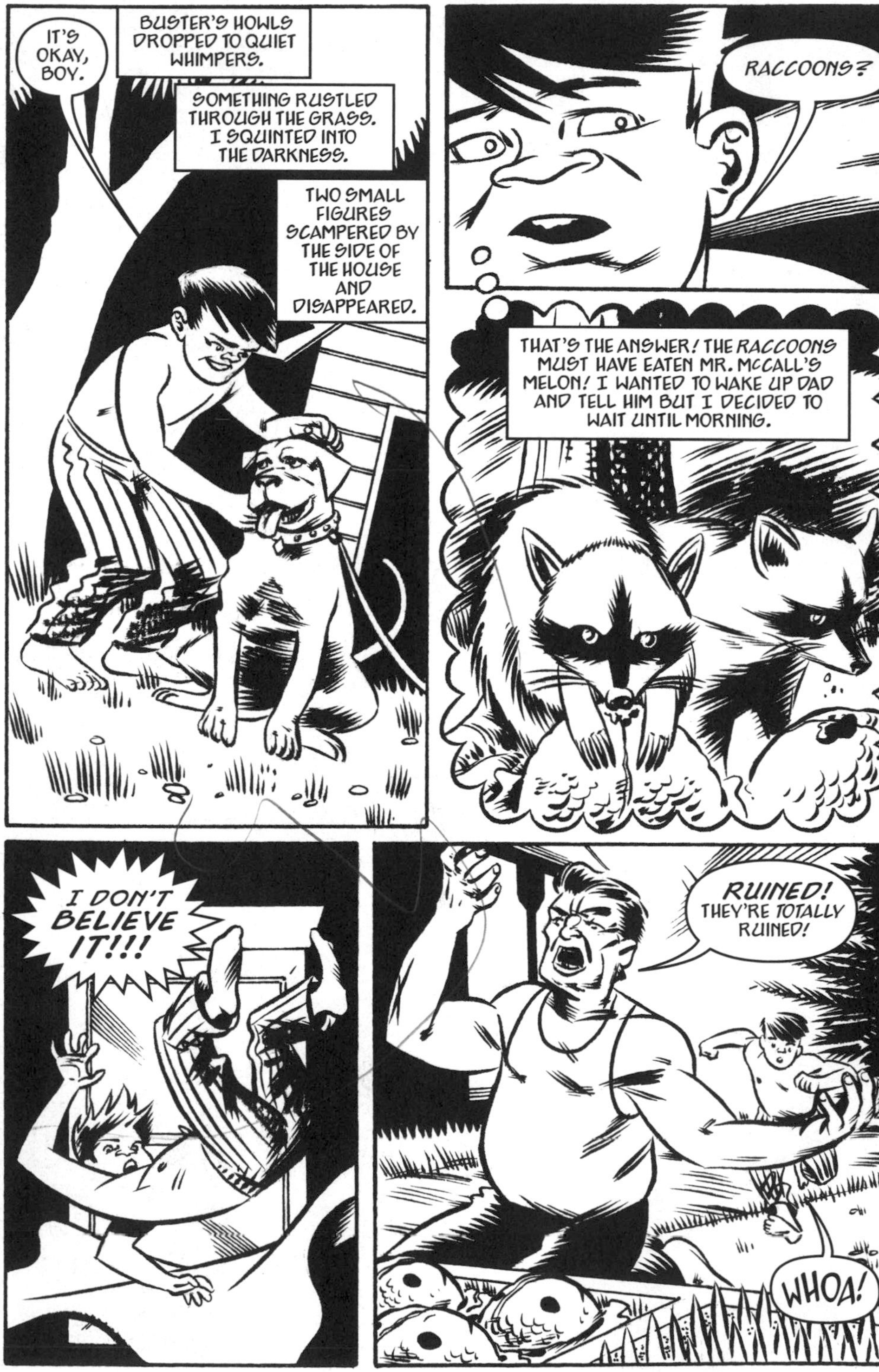

IT'S OKAY, BOY.
BUSTER'S HOWLS DROPPED TO QUIET WHIMPERS.
SOMETHING RUSTLED THROUGH THE GRASS. I SQUINTED INTO THE DARKNESS.
TWO SMALL FIGURES SCAMPERED BY THE SIDE OF THE HOUSE AND DISAPPEARED.
RACCOONS?
THAT'S THE ANSWER! THE RACCOONS MUST HAVE EATEN MR. McCALL'S MELON! I WANTED TO WAKE UP DAD AND TELL HIM BUT I DECIDED TO WAIT UNTIL MORNING.
I DON'T BELIEVE IT!!!
RUINED! THEY'RE TOTALLY RUINED!
WHOA!

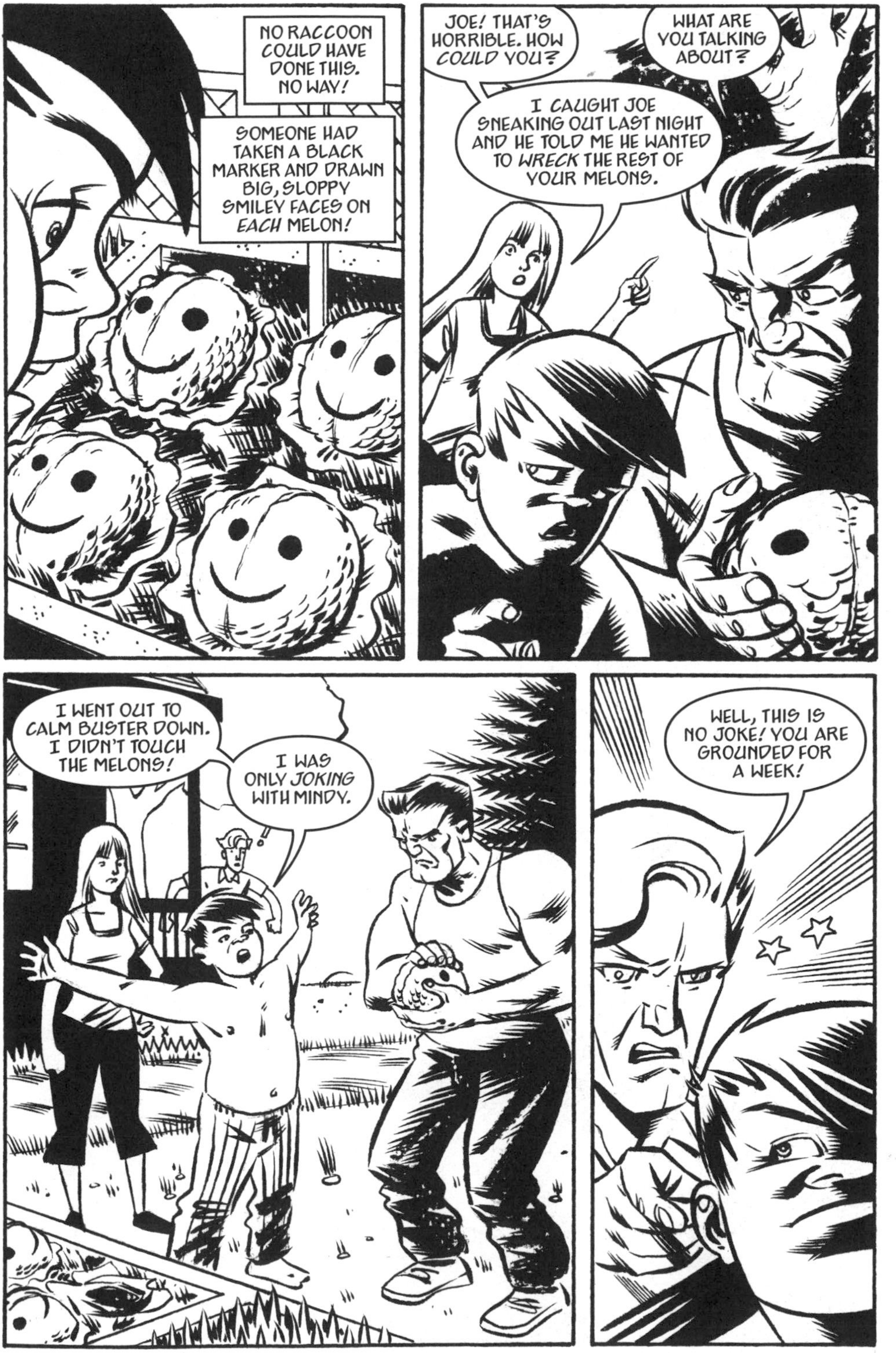
NO RACCOON COULD HAVE DONE THIS. NO WAY!
SOMEONE HAD TAKEN A BLACK MARKER AND DRAWN BIG, SLOPPY SMILEY FACES ON EACH MELON!
JOE! THAT'S HORRIBLE. HOW COULD YOU?
WHAT ARE YOU TALKING ABOUT?
I CAUGHT JOE SNEAKING OUT LAST NIGHT AND HE TOLD ME HE WANTED TO WRECK THE REST OF YOUR MELONS.
I WENT OUT TO CALM BUSTER DOWN. I DIDN'T TOUCH THE MELONS!
I WAS ONLY JOKING WITH MINDY.
WELL, THIS IS NO JOKE! YOU ARE GROUNDED FOR A WEEK!

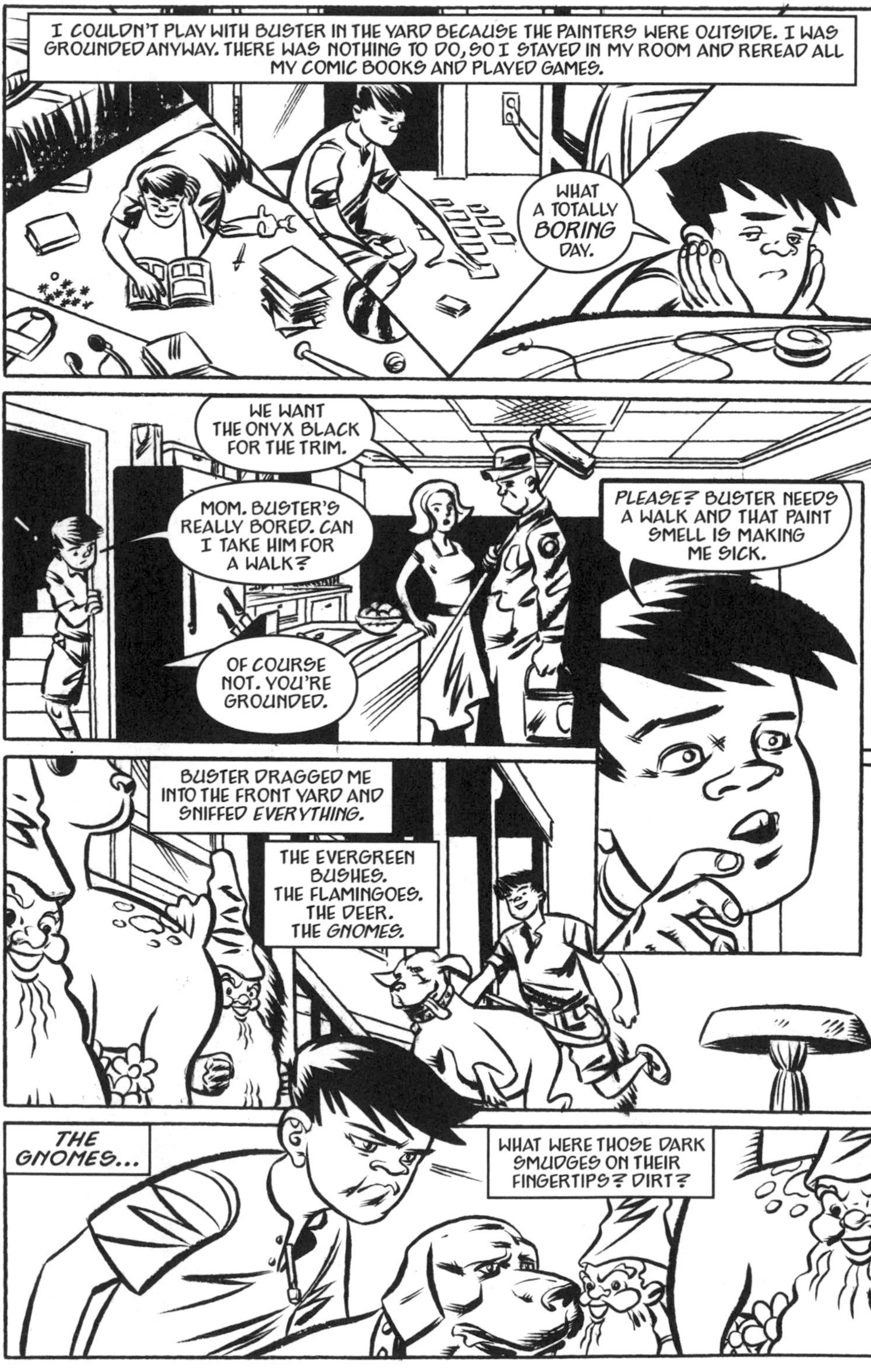
I COULDN'T PLAY WITH BUSTER IN THE YARD BECAUSE THE PAINTERS WERE OUTSIDE. I WAS GROUNDED ANYWAY. THERE WAS NOTHING TO DO, SO I STAYED IN MY ROOM AND REREAD ALL MY COMIC BOOKS AND PLAYED GAMES.
WHAT A TOTALLY *BORING* DAY.
WE WANT THE ONYX BLACK FOR THE TRIM.
MOM. BUSTER'S REALLY BORED. CAN I TAKE HIM FOR A WALK?
OF COURSE NOT. YOU'RE GROUNDED.
PLEASE? BUSTER NEEDS A WALK AND THAT PAINT SMELL IS MAKING ME SICK.
BUSTER DRAGGED ME INTO THE FRONT YARD AND SNIFFED *EVERYTHING.*
THE EVERGREEN BUSHES. THE FLAMINGOES. THE DEER. THE *GNOMES.*
THE GNOMES...
WHAT WERE THOSE DARK SMUDGES ON THEIR FINGERTIPS? DIRT?

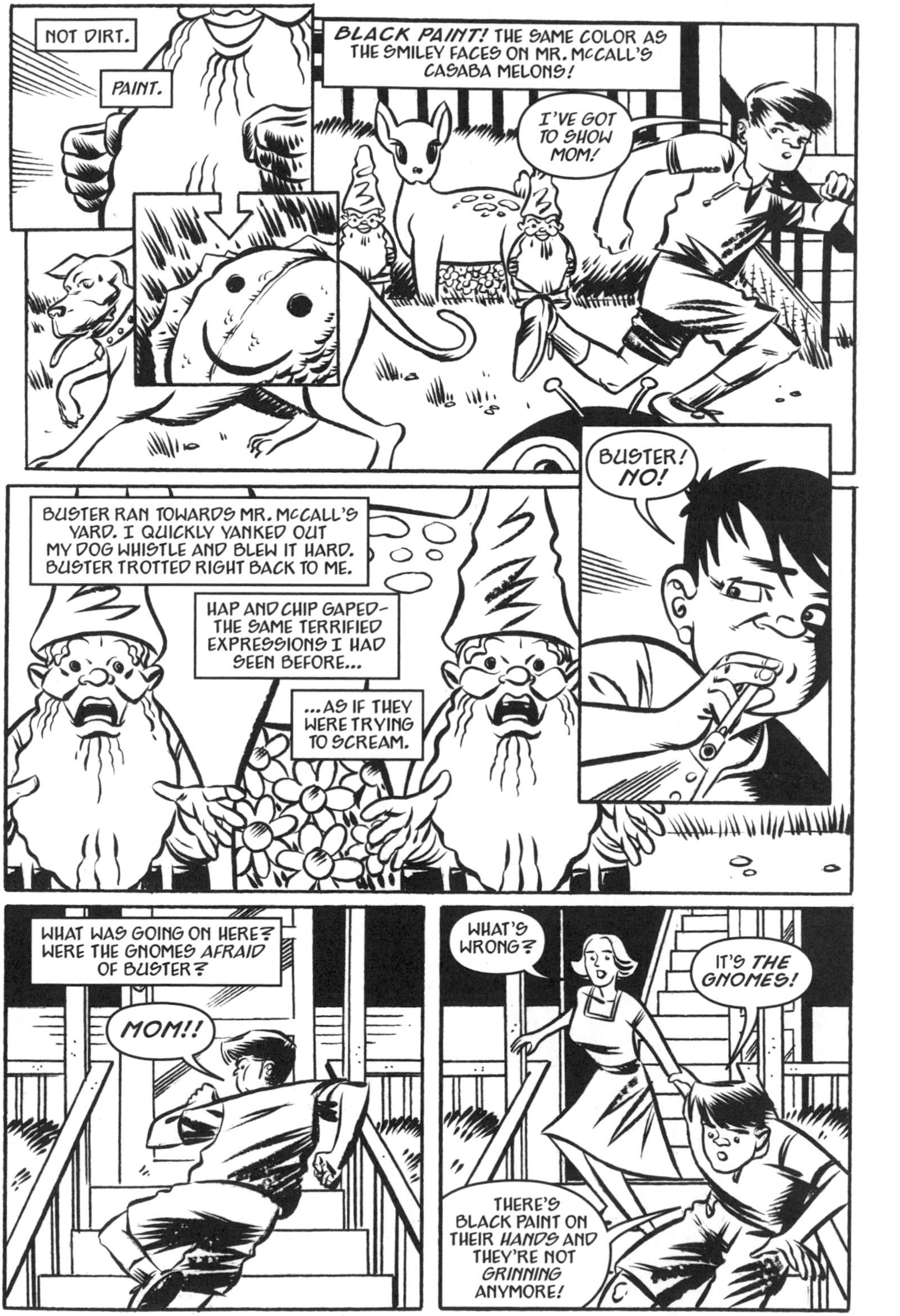
NOT DIRT.
PAINT.
BLACK PAINT! THE SAME COLOR AS THE SMILEY FACES ON MR. McCALL'S CASABA MELONS!
I'VE GOT TO SHOW MOM!
BUSTER RAN TOWARDS MR. McCALL'S YARD. I QUICKLY YANKED OUT MY DOG WHISTLE AND BLEW IT HARD. BUSTER TROTTED RIGHT BACK TO ME.
HAP AND CHIP GAPED-THE SAME TERRIFIED EXPRESSIONS I HAD SEEN BEFORE...
...AS IF THEY WERE TRYING TO SCREAM.
BUSTER! NO!
WHAT WAS GOING ON HERE? WERE THE GNOMES AFRAID OF BUSTER?
MOM!!
WHAT'S WRONG?
IT'S THE GNOMES!
THERE'S BLACK PAINT ON THEIR HANDS AND THEY'RE NOT GRINNING ANYMORE!

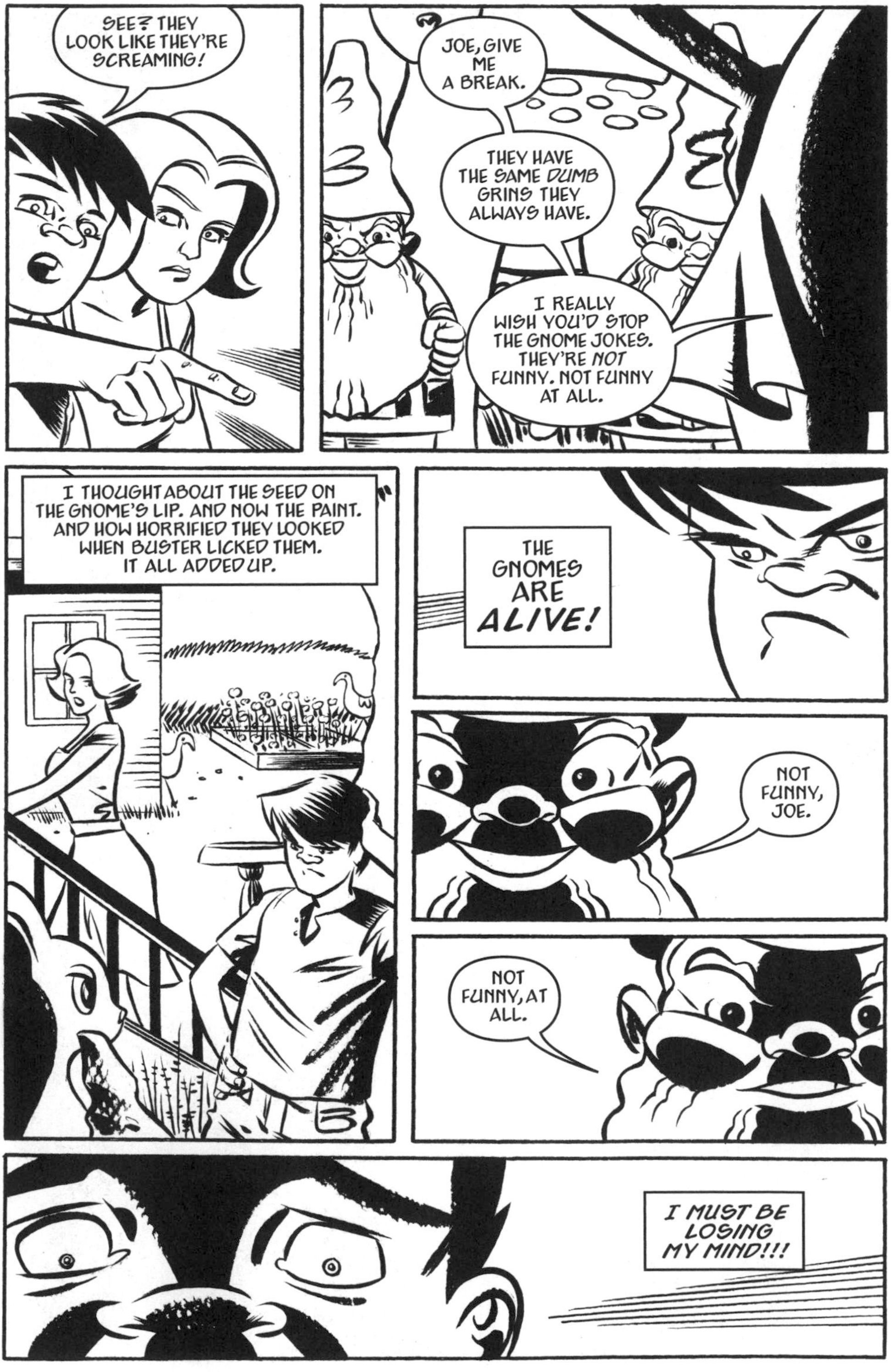
SEE? THEY LOOK LIKE THEY'RE SCREAMING!
JOE, GIVE ME A BREAK.
THEY HAVE THE SAME DUMB GRINS THEY ALWAYS HAVE.
I REALLY WISH YOU'D STOP THE GNOME JOKES. THEY'RE NOT FUNNY. NOT FUNNY AT ALL.
I THOUGHT ABOUT THE SEED ON THE GNOME'S LIP. AND NOW THE PAINT. AND HOW HORRIFIED THEY LOOKED WHEN BUSTER LICKED THEM. IT ALL ADDED UP.
THE GNOMES ARE ALIVE!
NOT FUNNY, JOE.
NOT FUNNY, AT ALL.
I MUST BE LOSING MY MIND!!!

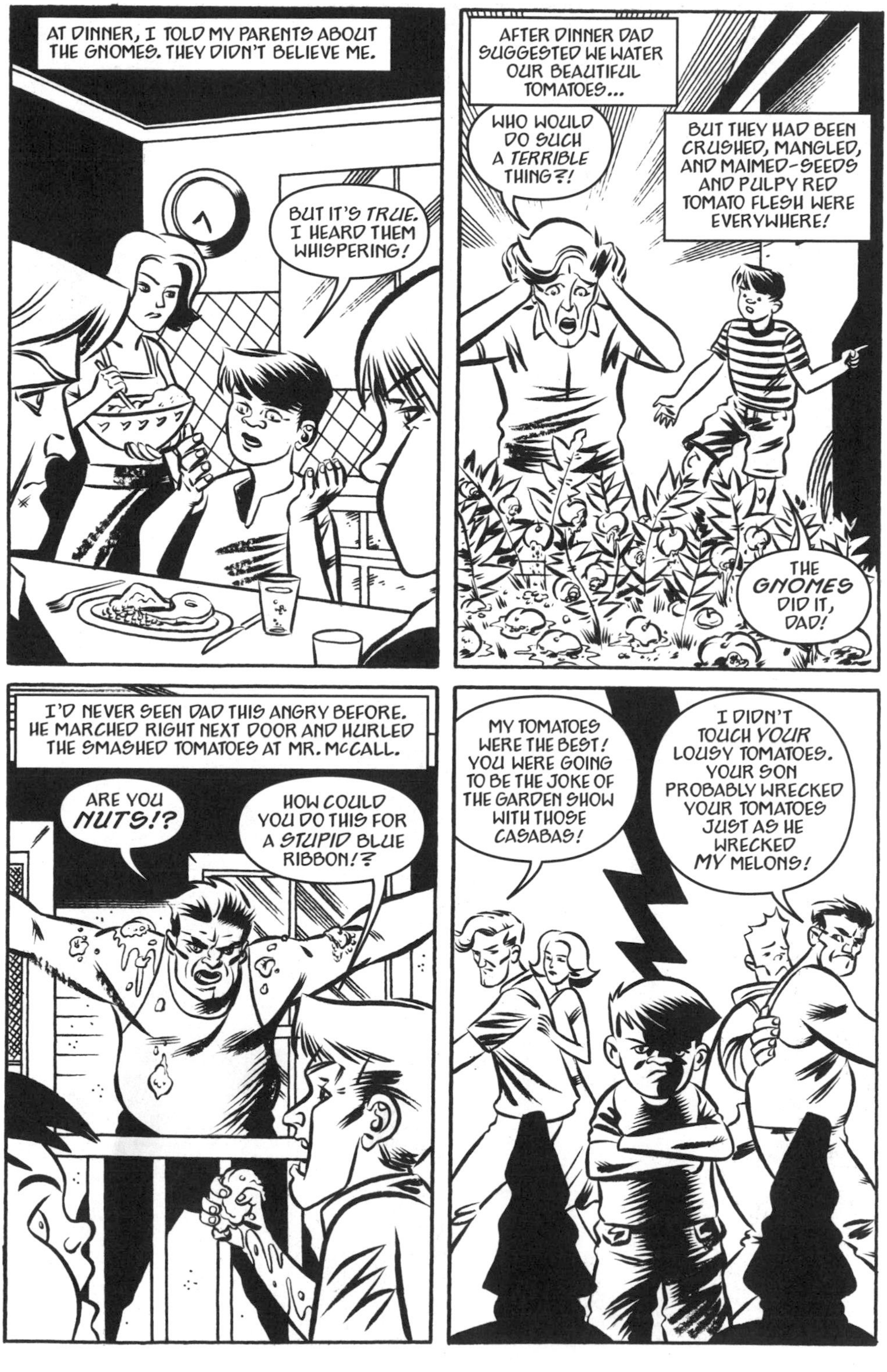
AT DINNER, I TOLD MY PARENTS ABOUT THE GNOMES. THEY DIDN'T BELIEVE ME.
BUT IT'S TRUE. I HEARD THEM WHISPERING!
AFTER DINNER DAD SUGGESTED WE WATER OUR BEAUTIFUL TOMATOES...
WHO WOULD DO SUCH A TERRIBLE THING?!
BUT THEY HAD BEEN CRUSHED, MANGLED, AND MAIMED—SEEDS AND PULPY RED TOMATO FLESH WERE EVERYWHERE!
THE GNOMES DID IT, DAD!
I'D NEVER SEEN DAD THIS ANGRY BEFORE. HE MARCHED RIGHT NEXT DOOR AND HURLED THE SMASHED TOMATOES AT MR. McCALL.
ARE YOU NUTS!?
HOW COULD YOU DO THIS FOR A STUPID BLUE RIBBON!?
MY TOMATOES WERE THE BEST! YOU WERE GOING TO BE THE JOKE OF THE GARDEN SHOW WITH THOSE CASABAS!
I DIDN'T TOUCH YOUR LOUSY TOMATOES. YOUR SON PROBABLY WRECKED YOUR TOMATOES JUST AS HE WRECKED MY MELONS!

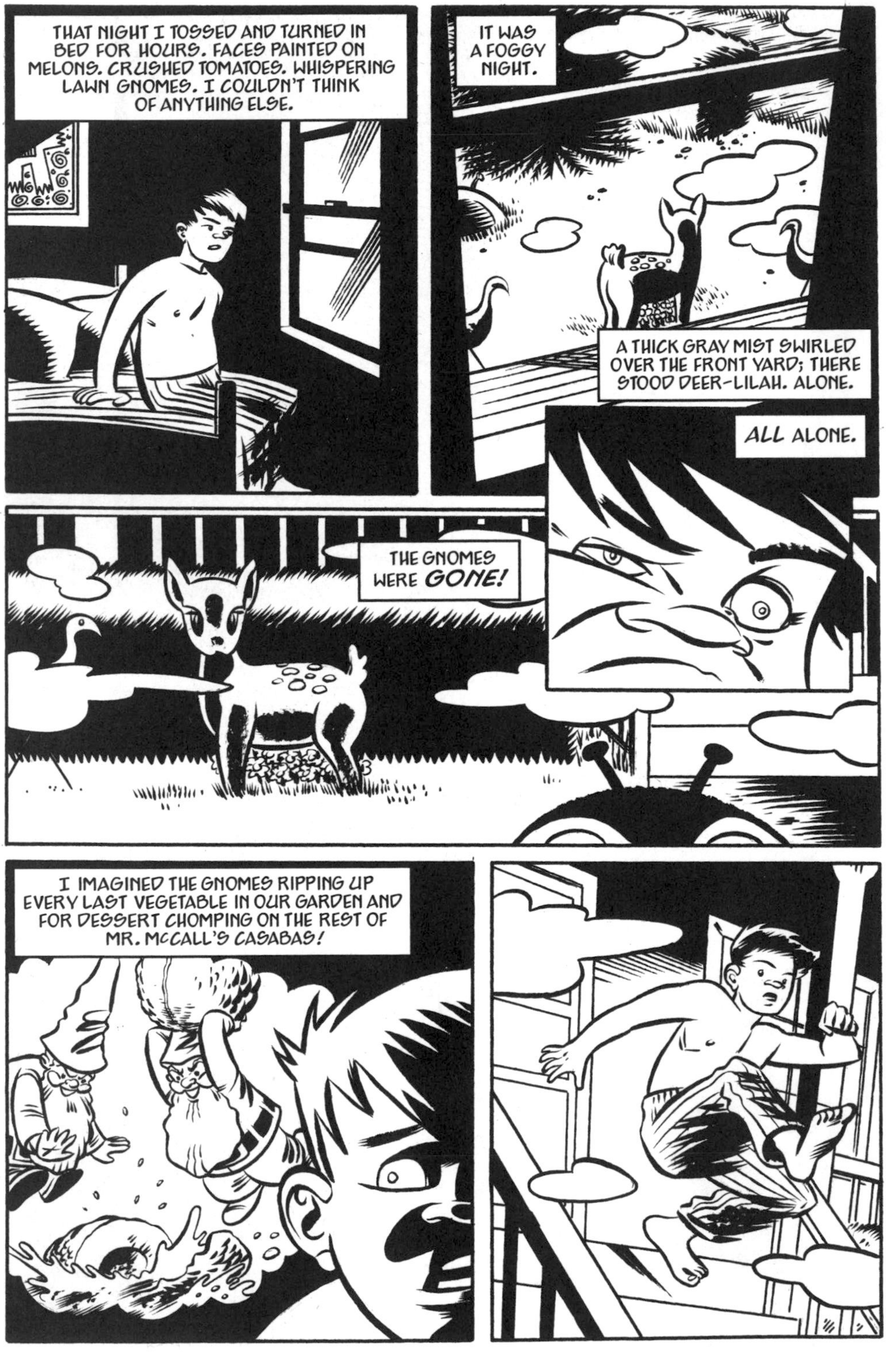
THAT NIGHT I TOSSED AND TURNED IN BED FOR HOURS. FACES PAINTED ON MELONS. CRUSHED TOMATOES. WHISPERING LAWN GNOMES. I COULDN'T THINK OF ANYTHING ELSE.
IT WAS A FOGGY NIGHT.
A THICK GRAY MIST SWIRLED OVER THE FRONT YARD; THERE STOOD DEER-LILAH. ALONE.
ALL ALONE.
THE GNOMES WERE GONE!
I IMAGINED THE GNOMES RIPPING UP EVERY LAST VEGETABLE IN OUR GARDEN AND FOR DESSERT CHOMPING ON THE REST OF MR. McCALL'S CASABAS!

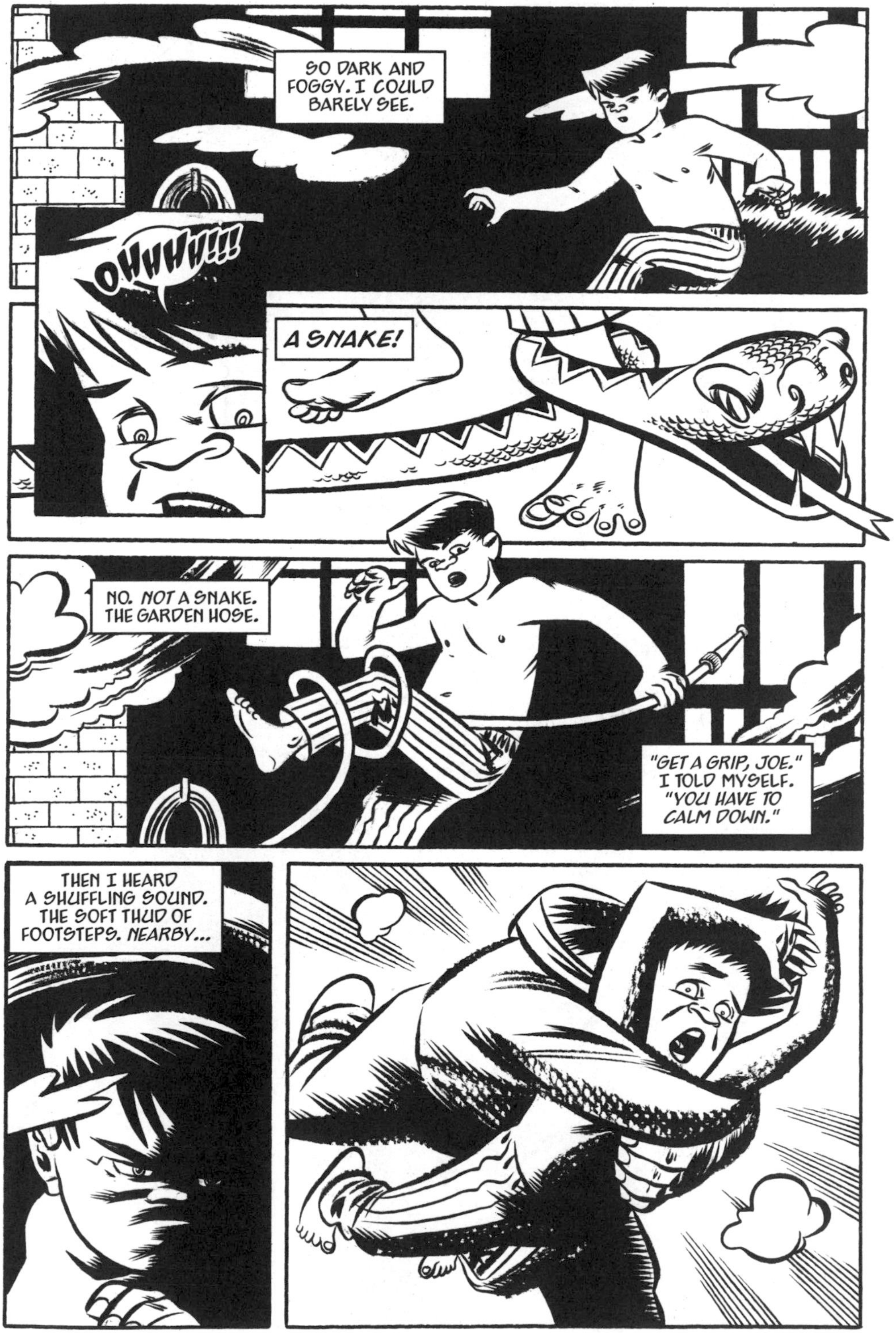
SO DARK AND FOGGY. I COULD BARELY SEE.
OHHHH!!!
A SNAKE!
NO. *NOT* A SNAKE. THE GARDEN HOSE.
"GET A GRIP, JOE." I TOLD MYSELF. "YOU HAVE TO CALM DOWN."
THEN I HEARD A SHUFFLING SOUND. THE SOFT THUD OF FOOTSTEPS. *NEARBY*...

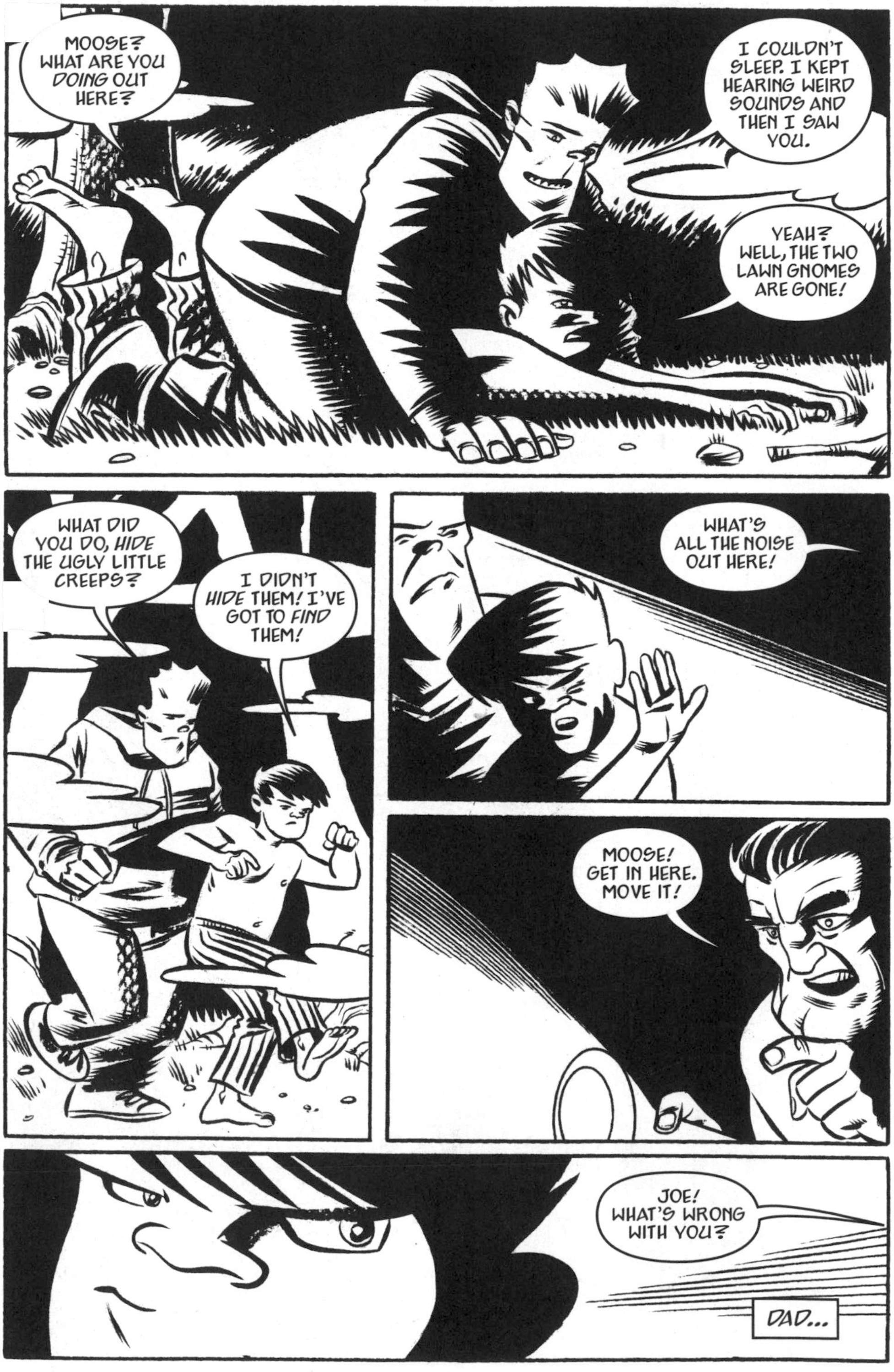
MOOSE? WHAT ARE YOU DOING OUT HERE?
I COULDN'T SLEEP. I KEPT HEARING WEIRD SOUNDS AND THEN I SAW YOU.
YEAH? WELL, THE TWO LAWN GNOMES ARE GONE!
WHAT DID YOU DO, HIDE THE UGLY LITTLE CREEPS?
I DIDN'T HIDE THEM! I'VE GOT TO FIND THEM!
WHAT'S ALL THE NOISE OUT HERE!
MOOSE! GET IN HERE. MOVE IT!
JOE! WHAT'S WRONG WITH YOU?
DAD...

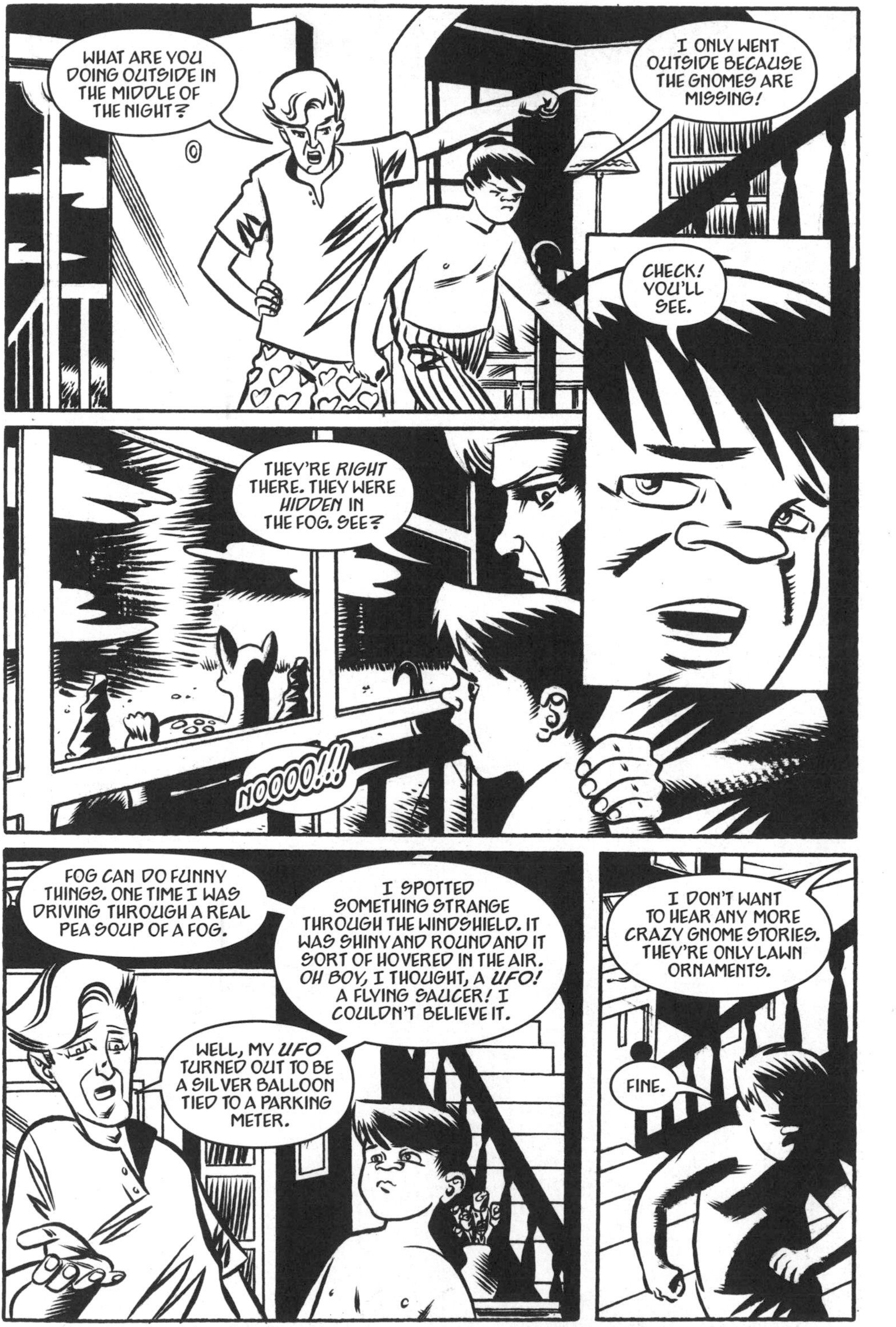
WHAT ARE YOU DOING OUTSIDE IN THE MIDDLE OF THE NIGHT?
I ONLY WENT OUTSIDE BECAUSE THE GNOMES ARE MISSING!
CHECK! YOU'LL SEE.
THEY'RE *RIGHT* THERE. THEY WERE *HIDDEN* IN THE FOG. SEE?
NOOOO!!!
FOG CAN DO FUNNY THINGS. ONE TIME I WAS DRIVING THROUGH A REAL PEA SOUP OF A FOG.
I SPOTTED SOMETHING STRANGE THROUGH THE WINDSHIELD. IT WAS SHINY AND ROUND AND IT SORT OF HOVERED IN THE AIR. *OH BOY,* I THOUGHT, *A UFO!* A FLYING SAUCER! I COULDN'T BELIEVE IT.
WELL, MY *UFO* TURNED OUT TO BE A SILVER BALLOON TIED TO A PARKING METER.
I DON'T WANT TO HEAR ANY MORE CRAZY GNOME STORIES. THEY'RE ONLY LAWN ORNAMENTS.
FINE.

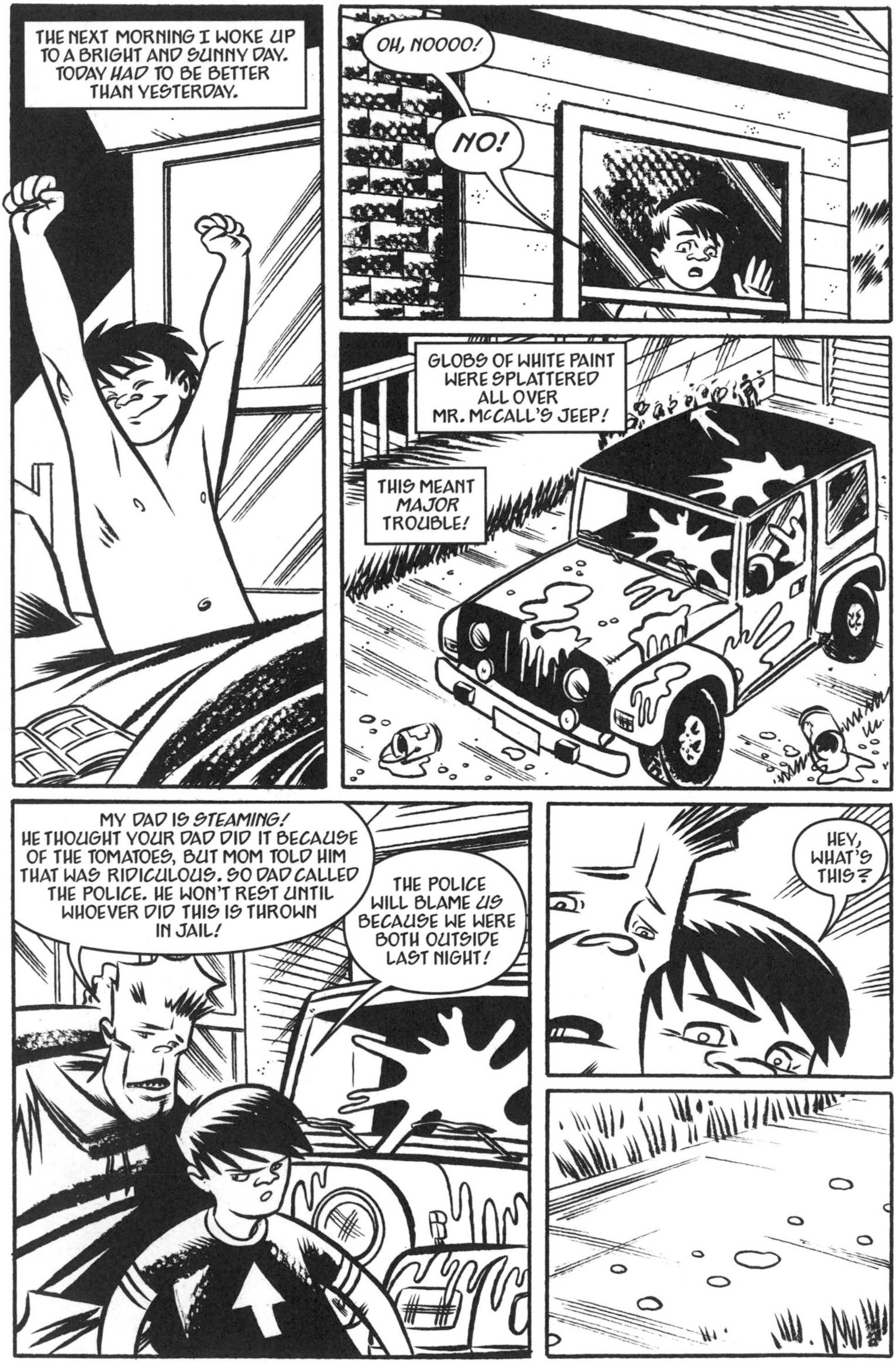
THE NEXT MORNING I WOKE UP TO A BRIGHT AND SUNNY DAY. TODAY HAD TO BE BETTER THAN YESTERDAY.
OH, NOOOO!
NO!
GLOBS OF WHITE PAINT WERE SPLATTERED ALL OVER MR. McCALL'S JEEP!
THIS MEANT MAJOR TROUBLE!
MY DAD IS STEAMING! HE THOUGHT YOUR DAD DID IT BECAUSE OF THE TOMATOES, BUT MOM TOLD HIM THAT WAS RIDICULOUS. SO DAD CALLED THE POLICE. HE WON'T REST UNTIL WHOEVER DID THIS IS THROWN IN JAIL!
THE POLICE WILL BLAME US BECAUSE WE WERE BOTH OUTSIDE LAST NIGHT!
HEY, WHAT'S THIS?

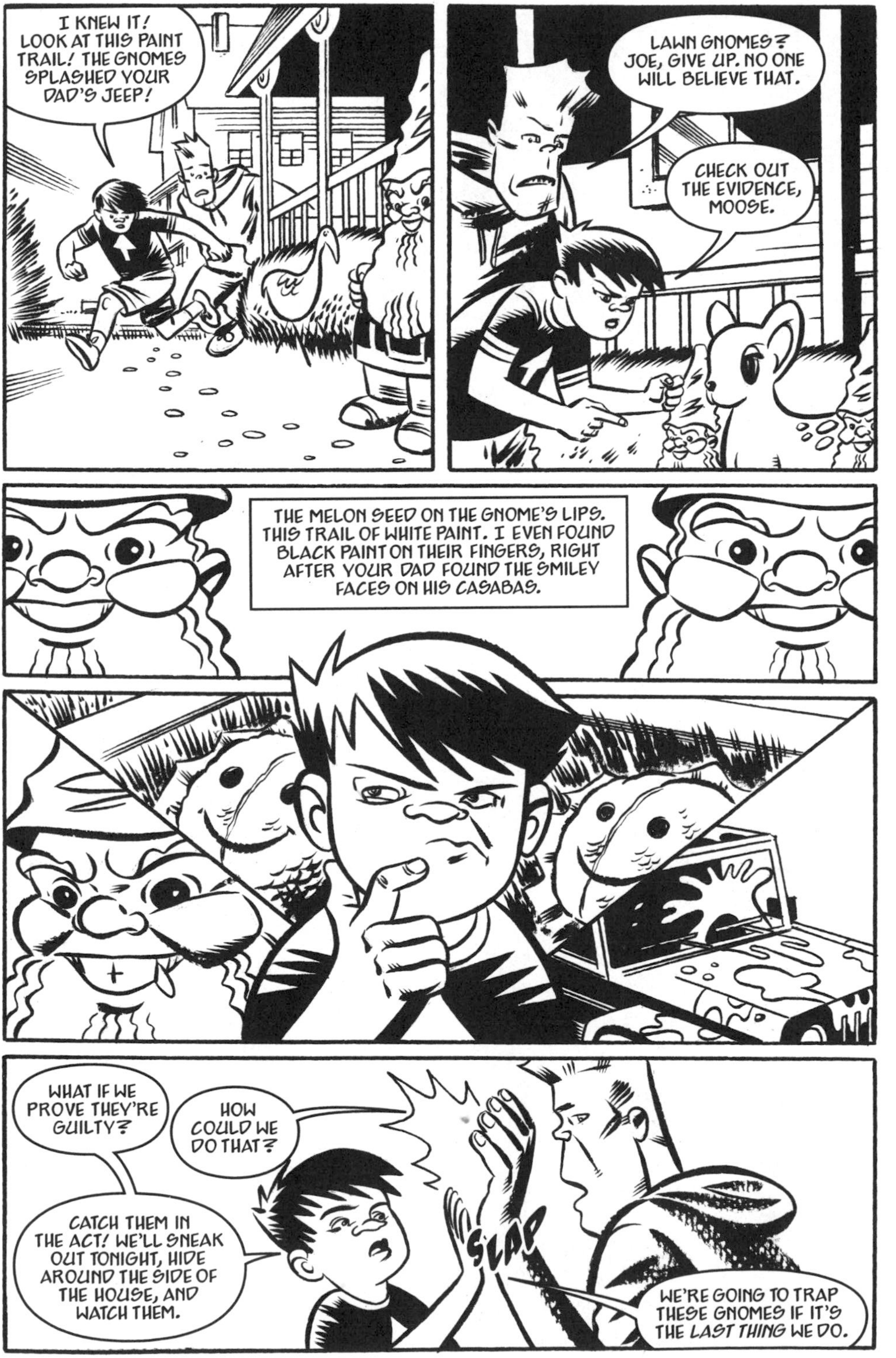
I KNEW IT! LOOK AT THIS PAINT TRAIL! THE GNOMES SPLASHED YOUR DAD'S JEEP!
LAWN GNOMES? JOE, GIVE UP. NO ONE WILL BELIEVE THAT.
CHECK OUT THE EVIDENCE, MOOSE.
THE MELON SEED ON THE GNOME'S LIPS. THIS TRAIL OF WHITE PAINT. I EVEN FOUND BLACK PAINT ON THEIR FINGERS, RIGHT AFTER YOUR DAD FOUND THE SMILEY FACES ON HIS CASABAS.
WHAT IF WE PROVE THEY'RE GUILTY?
HOW COULD WE DO THAT?
CATCH THEM IN THE ACT! WE'LL SNEAK OUT TONIGHT, HIDE AROUND THE SIDE OF THE HOUSE, AND WATCH THEM.
SLAP
WE'RE GOING TO TRAP THESE GNOMES IF IT'S THE *LAST THING* WE DO.

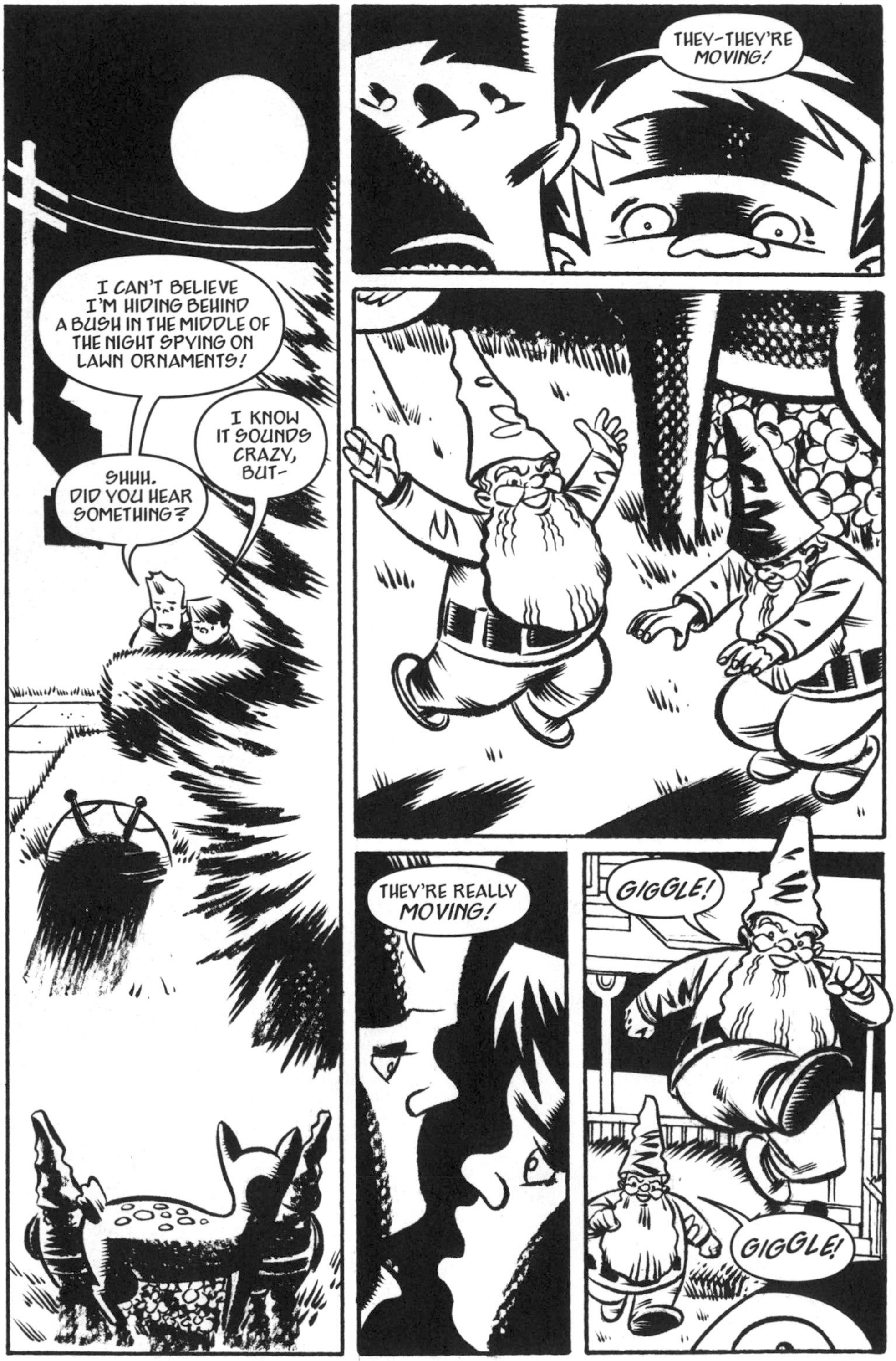
I CAN'T BELIEVE I'M HIDING BEHIND A BUSH IN THE MIDDLE OF THE NIGHT SPYING ON LAWN ORNAMENTS!
I KNOW IT SOUNDS CRAZY, BUT-
SHHH. DID YOU HEAR SOMETHING?
THEY-THEY'RE MOVING!
THEY'RE REALLY MOVING!
GIGGLE!
GIGGLE!

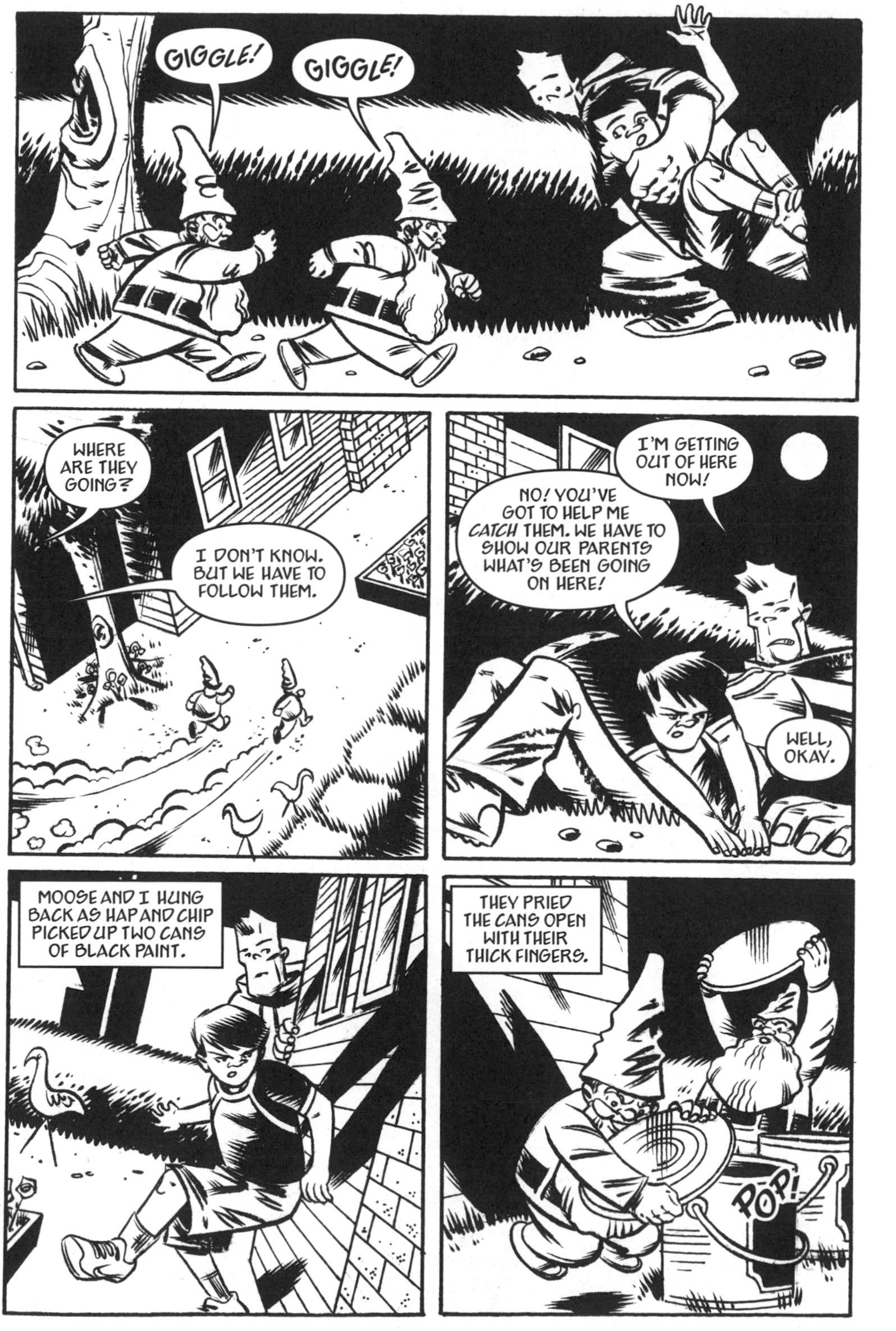
GIGGLE!
GIGGLE!
WHERE ARE THEY GOING?
I DON'T KNOW. BUT WE HAVE TO FOLLOW THEM.
I'M GETTING OUT OF HERE NOW!
NO! YOU'VE GOT TO HELP ME CATCH THEM. WE HAVE TO SHOW OUR PARENTS WHAT'S BEEN GOING ON HERE!
WELL, OKAY.
MOOSE AND I HUNG BACK AS HAP AND CHIP PICKED UP TWO CANS OF BLACK PAINT.
THEY PRIED THE CANS OPEN WITH THEIR THICK FINGERS.
POP!

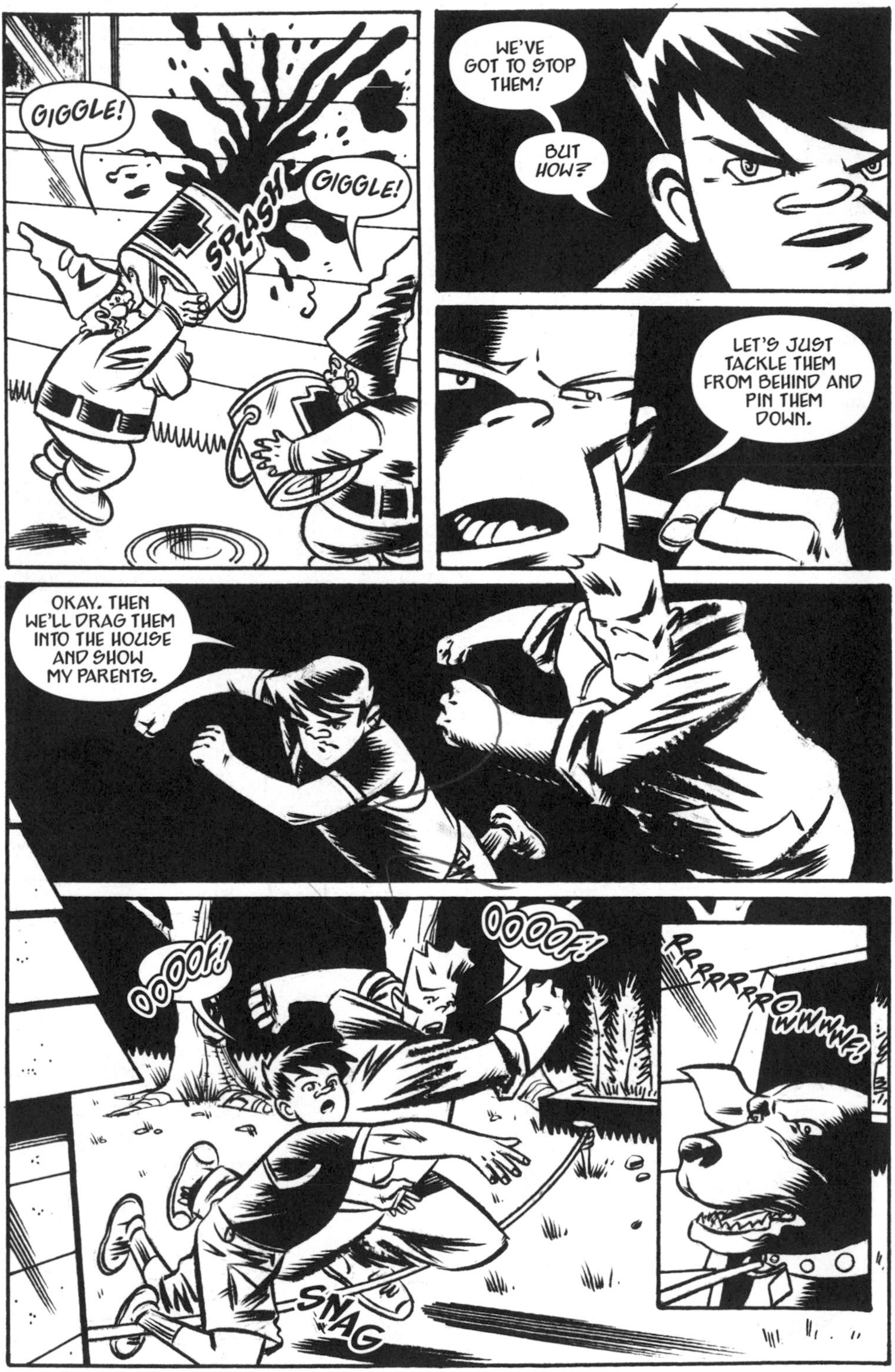
GIGGLE!
SPLASH!
GIGGLE!
WE'VE GOT TO STOP THEM!
BUT HOW?
LET'S JUST TACKLE THEM FROM BEHIND AND PIN THEM DOWN.
OKAY. THEN WE'LL DRAG THEM INTO THE HOUSE AND SHOW MY PARENTS.
OOOOF!
OOOOF!
SNAG
RRRRRRROWWWWF!

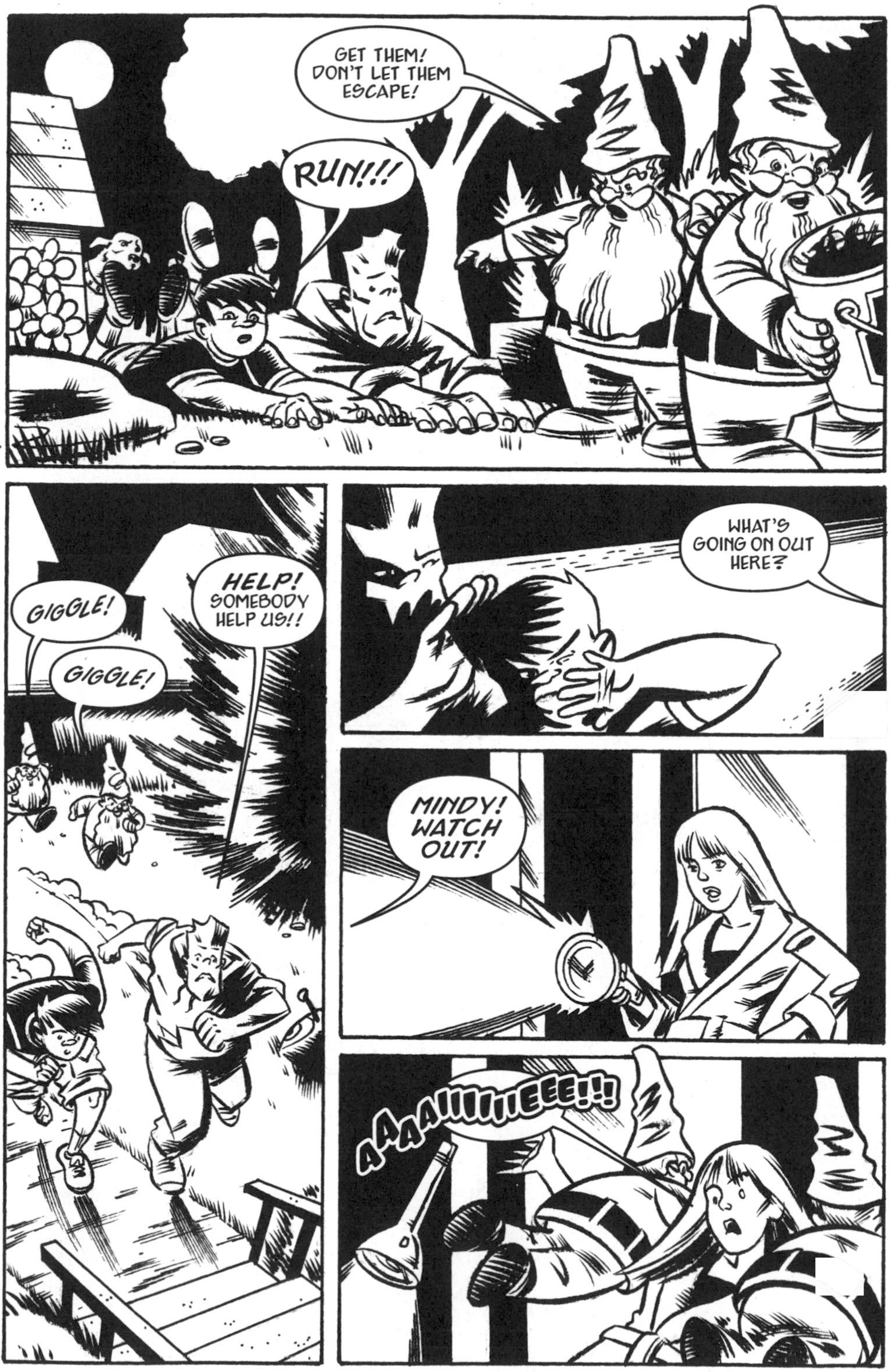
GET THEM! DON'T LET THEM ESCAPE!
RUN!!!
GIGGLE!
GIGGLE!
HELP! SOMEBODY HELP US!!
WHAT'S GOING ON OUT HERE?
MINDY! WATCH OUT!
AAAAIIIIIIEEE!!!

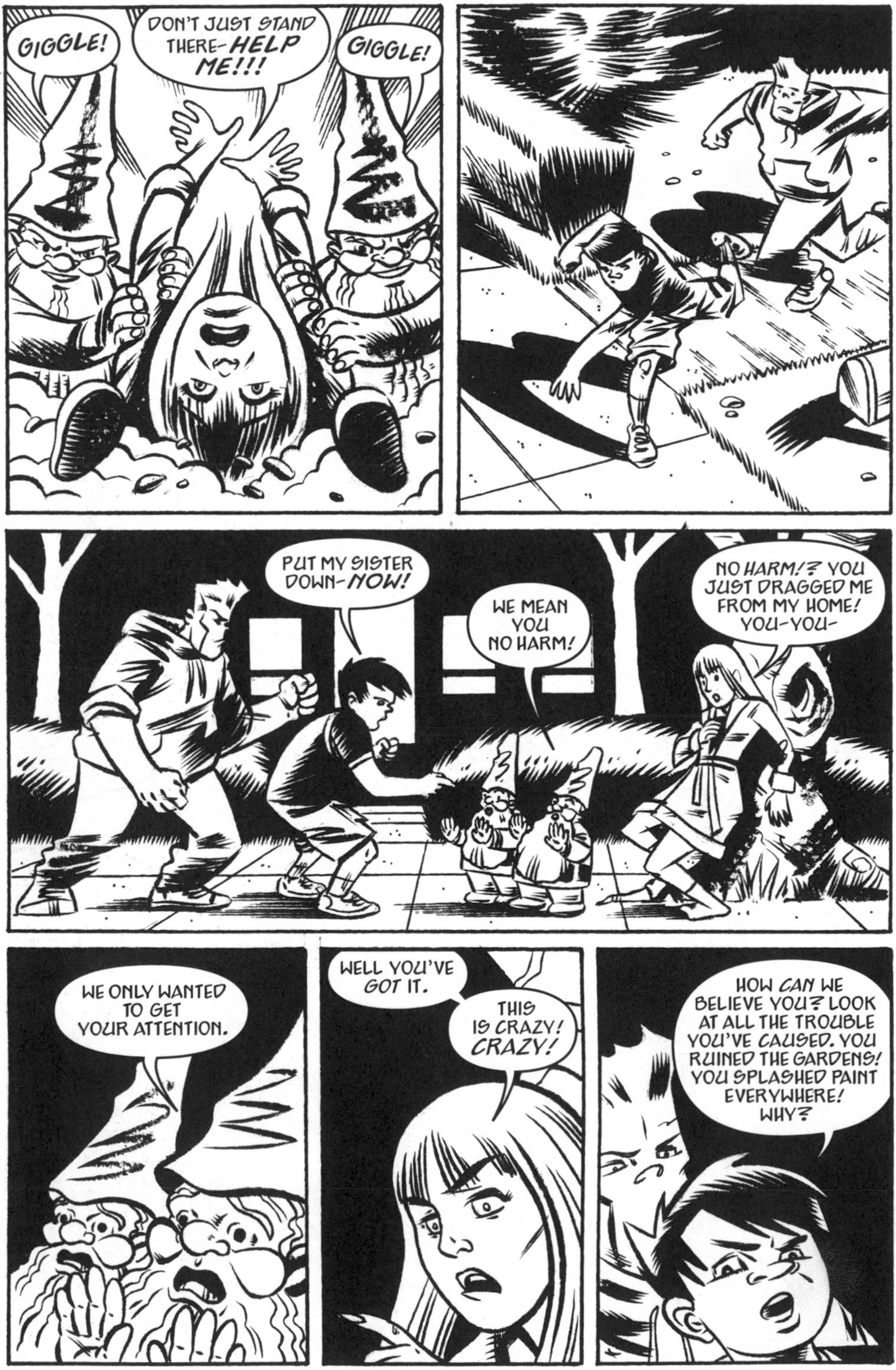
GIGGLE!
DON'T JUST STAND THERE-HELP ME!!!
GIGGLE!
PUT MY SISTER DOWN-NOW!
WE MEAN YOU NO HARM!
NO HARM!? YOU JUST DRAGGED ME FROM MY HOME! YOU-YOU-
WE ONLY WANTED TO GET YOUR ATTENTION.
WELL YOU'VE GOT IT.
THIS IS CRAZY! CRAZY!
HOW CAN WE BELIEVE YOU? LOOK AT ALL THE TROUBLE YOU'VE CAUSED. YOU RUINED THE GARDENS! YOU SPLASHED PAINT EVERYWHERE! WHY?

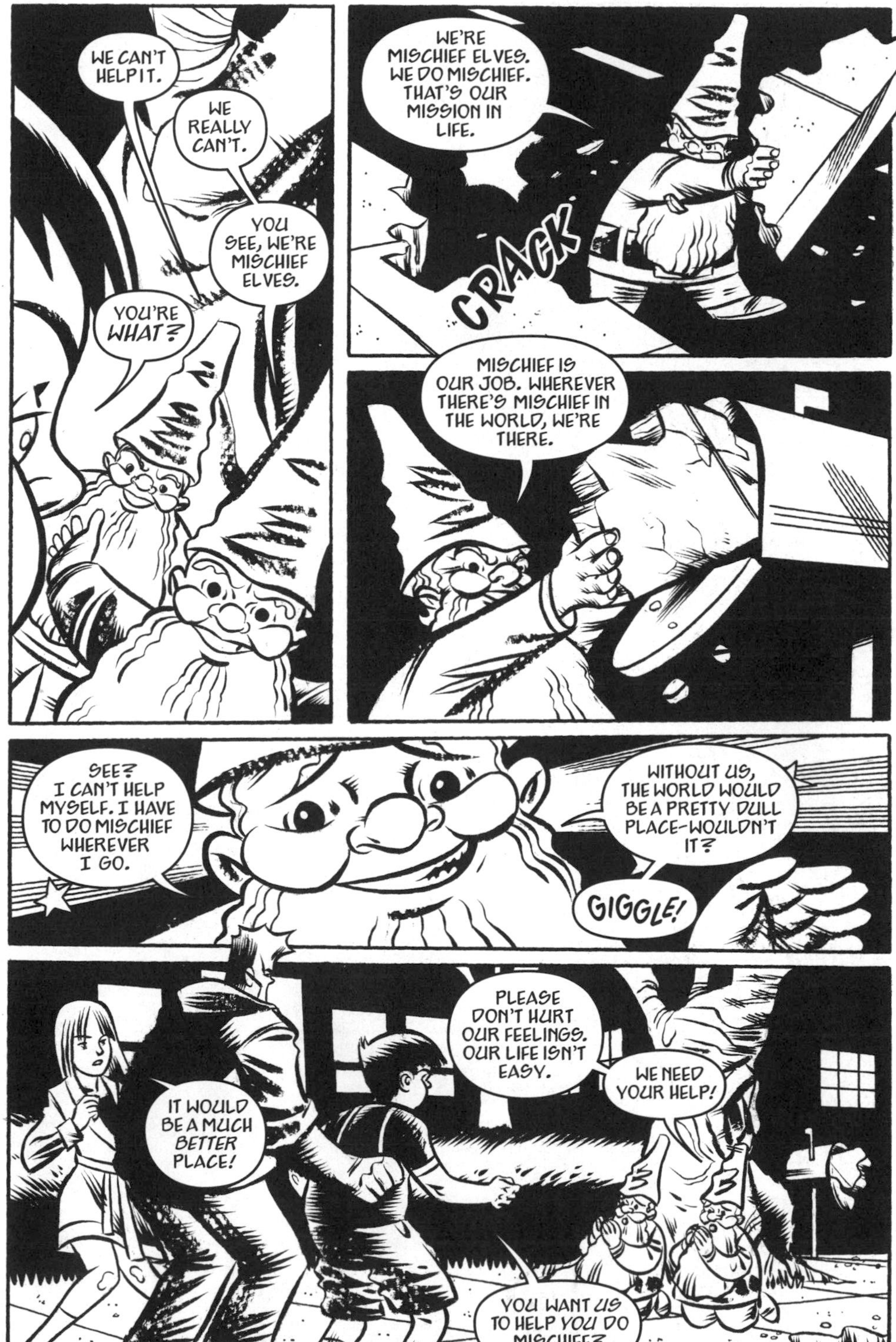
WE CAN'T HELP IT.
WE REALLY CAN'T.
YOU SEE, WE'RE MISCHIEF ELVES.
YOU'RE *WHAT*?
WE'RE MISCHIEF ELVES. WE DO MISCHIEF. THAT'S OUR MISSION IN LIFE.
CRACK
MISCHIEF IS OUR JOB. WHEREVER THERE'S MISCHIEF IN THE WORLD, WE'RE THERE.
SEE? I CAN'T HELP MYSELF. I HAVE TO DO MISCHIEF WHEREVER I GO.
WITHOUT US, THE WORLD WOULD BE A PRETTY DULL PLACE–WOULDN'T IT?
GIGGLE!
IT WOULD BE A MUCH *BETTER* PLACE!
PLEASE DON'T HURT OUR FEELINGS. OUR LIFE ISN'T EASY.
WE NEED YOUR HELP!
YOU WANT *US* TO HELP *YOU* DO MISCHIEF?

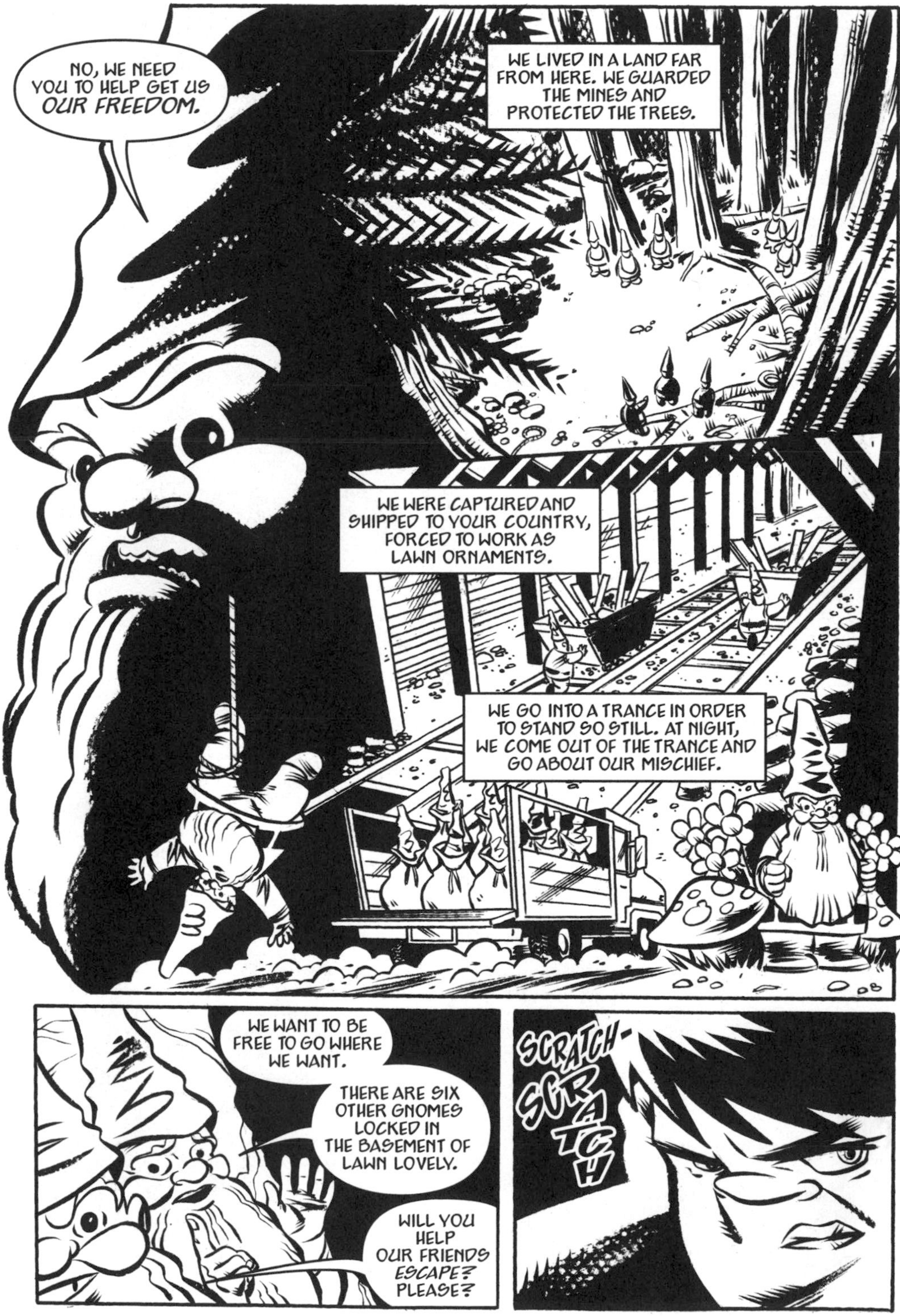
NO, WE NEED YOU TO HELP GET US OUR FREEDOM.
WE LIVED IN A LAND FAR FROM HERE. WE GUARDED THE MINES AND PROTECTED THE TREES.
WE WERE CAPTURED AND SHIPPED TO YOUR COUNTRY, FORCED TO WORK AS LAWN ORNAMENTS.
WE GO INTO A TRANCE IN ORDER TO STAND SO STILL. AT NIGHT, WE COME OUT OF THE TRANCE AND GO ABOUT OUR MISCHIEF.
WE WANT TO BE FREE TO GO WHERE WE WANT.
THERE ARE SIX OTHER GNOMES LOCKED IN THE BASEMENT OF LAWN LOVELY.
WILL YOU HELP OUR FRIENDS ESCAPE? PLEASE?
SCRATCH-
SCRATCH

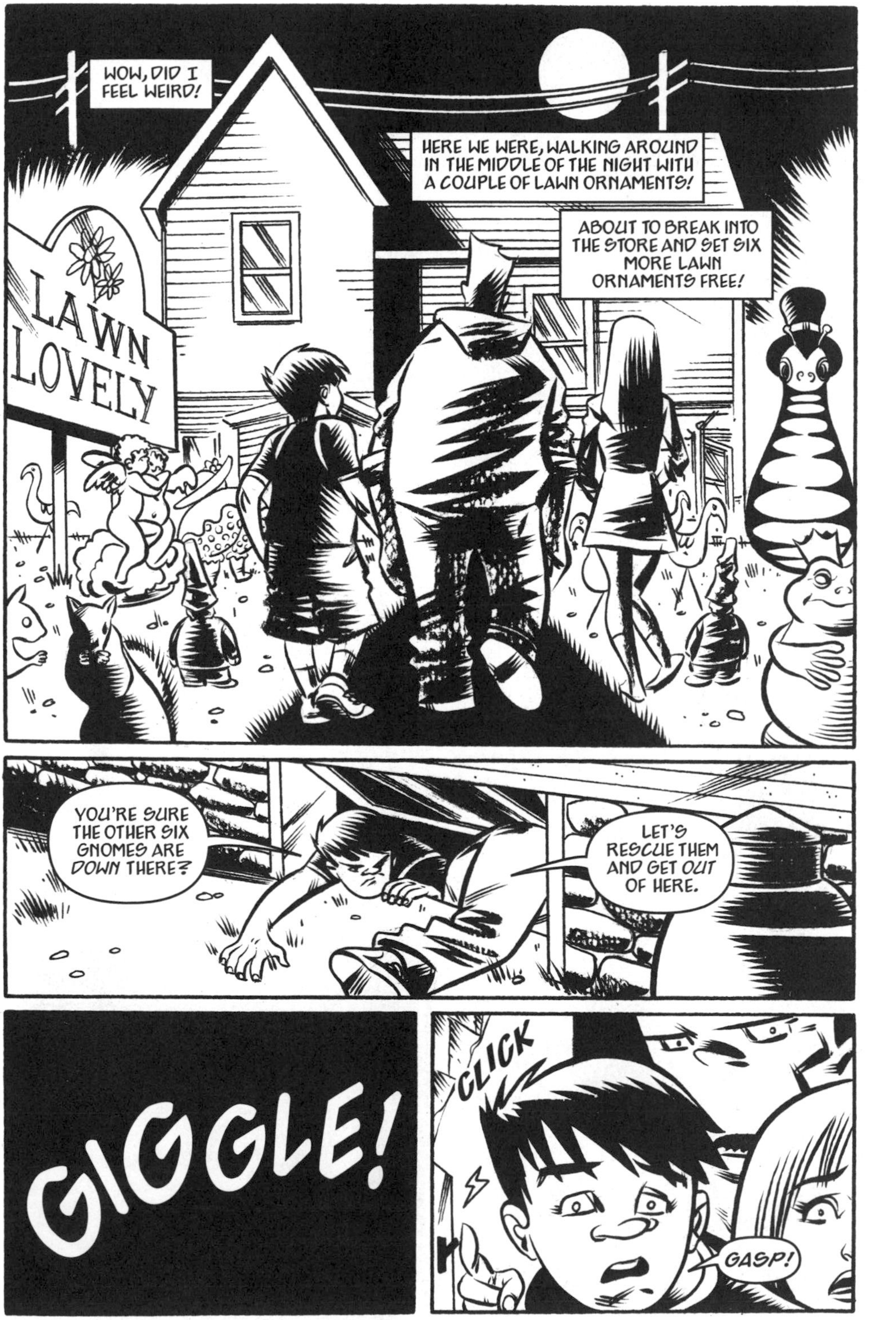
WOW, DID I FEEL WEIRD!
HERE WE WERE, WALKING AROUND IN THE MIDDLE OF THE NIGHT WITH A COUPLE OF LAWN ORNAMENTS!
ABOUT TO BREAK INTO THE STORE AND SET SIX MORE LAWN ORNAMENTS FREE!
LAWN LOVELY
YOU'RE SURE THE OTHER SIX GNOMES ARE DOWN THERE?
LET'S RESCUE THEM AND GET OUT OF HERE.
GIGGLE!
CLICK
GASP!

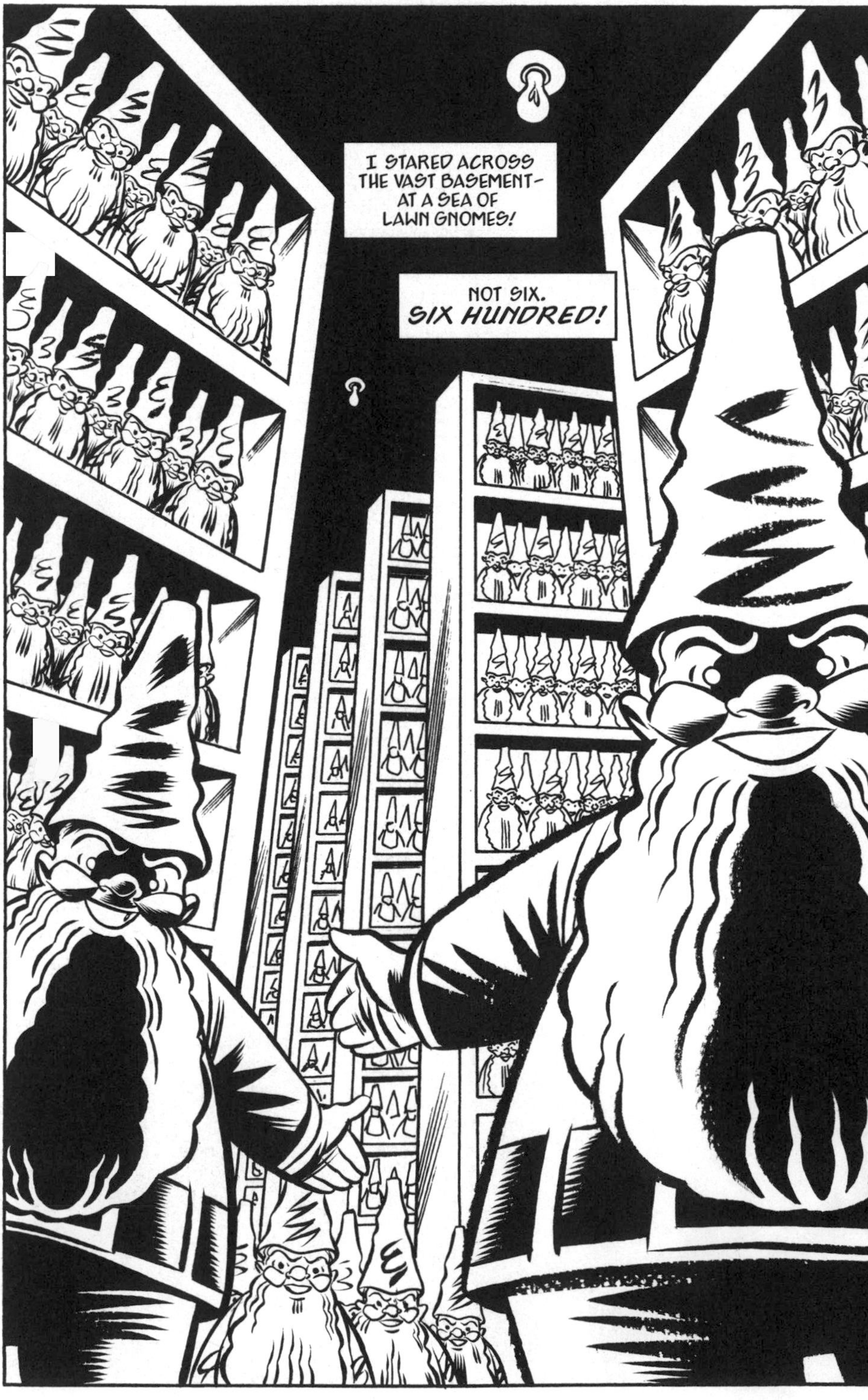
I STARED ACROSS THE VAST BASEMENT– AT A SEA OF LAWN GNOMES!
NOT SIX. SIX HUNDRED!

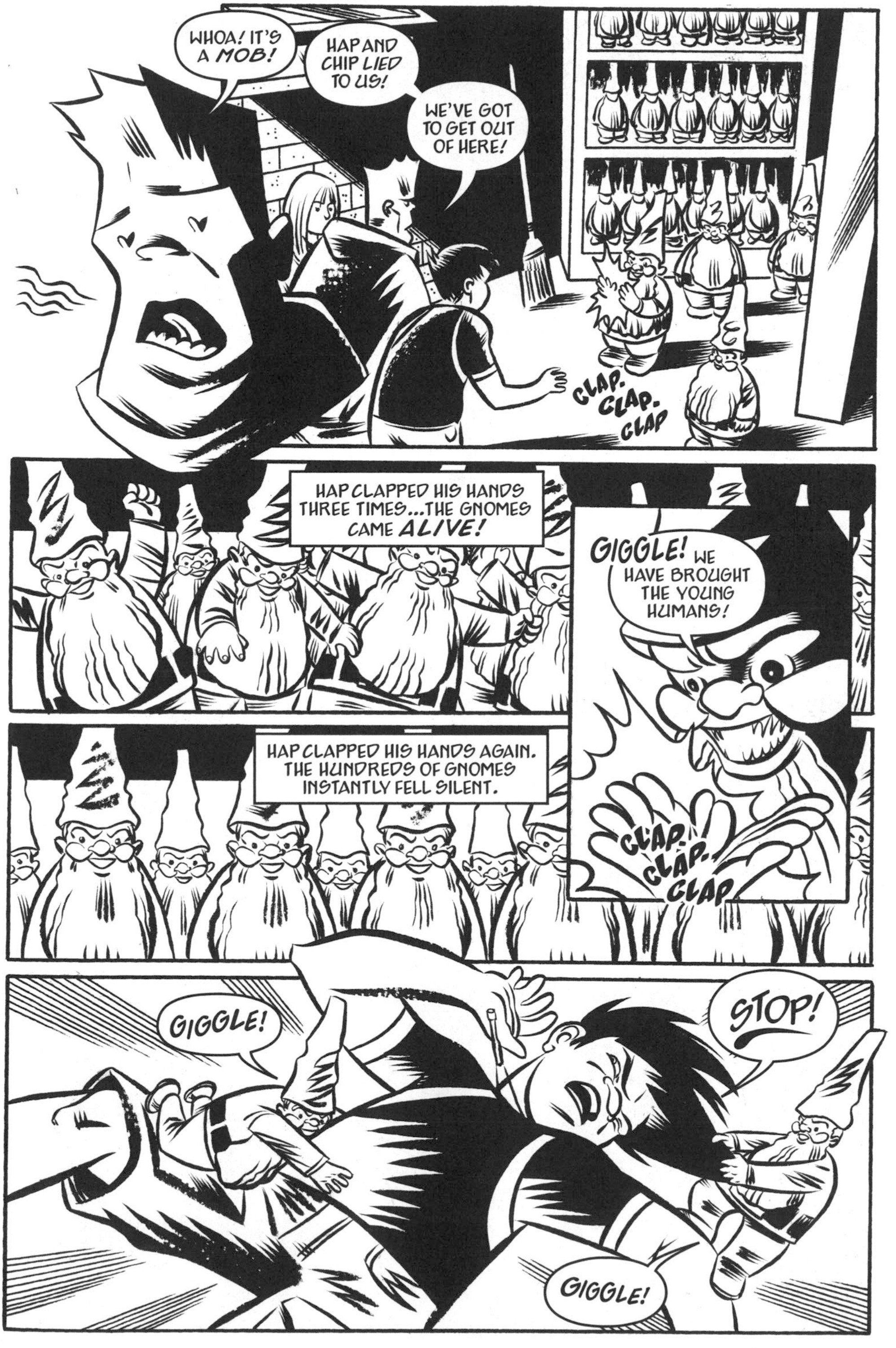
WHOA! IT'S A MOB!
HAP AND CHIP LIED TO US!
WE'VE GOT TO GET OUT OF HERE!
CLAP. CLAP. CLAP
HAP CLAPPED HIS HANDS THREE TIMES...THE GNOMES CAME ALIVE!
GIGGLE! WE HAVE BROUGHT THE YOUNG HUMANS!
CLAP. CLAP. CLAP
HAP CLAPPED HIS HANDS AGAIN. THE HUNDREDS OF GNOMES INSTANTLY FELL SILENT.
GIGGLE!
STOP!
GIGGLE!

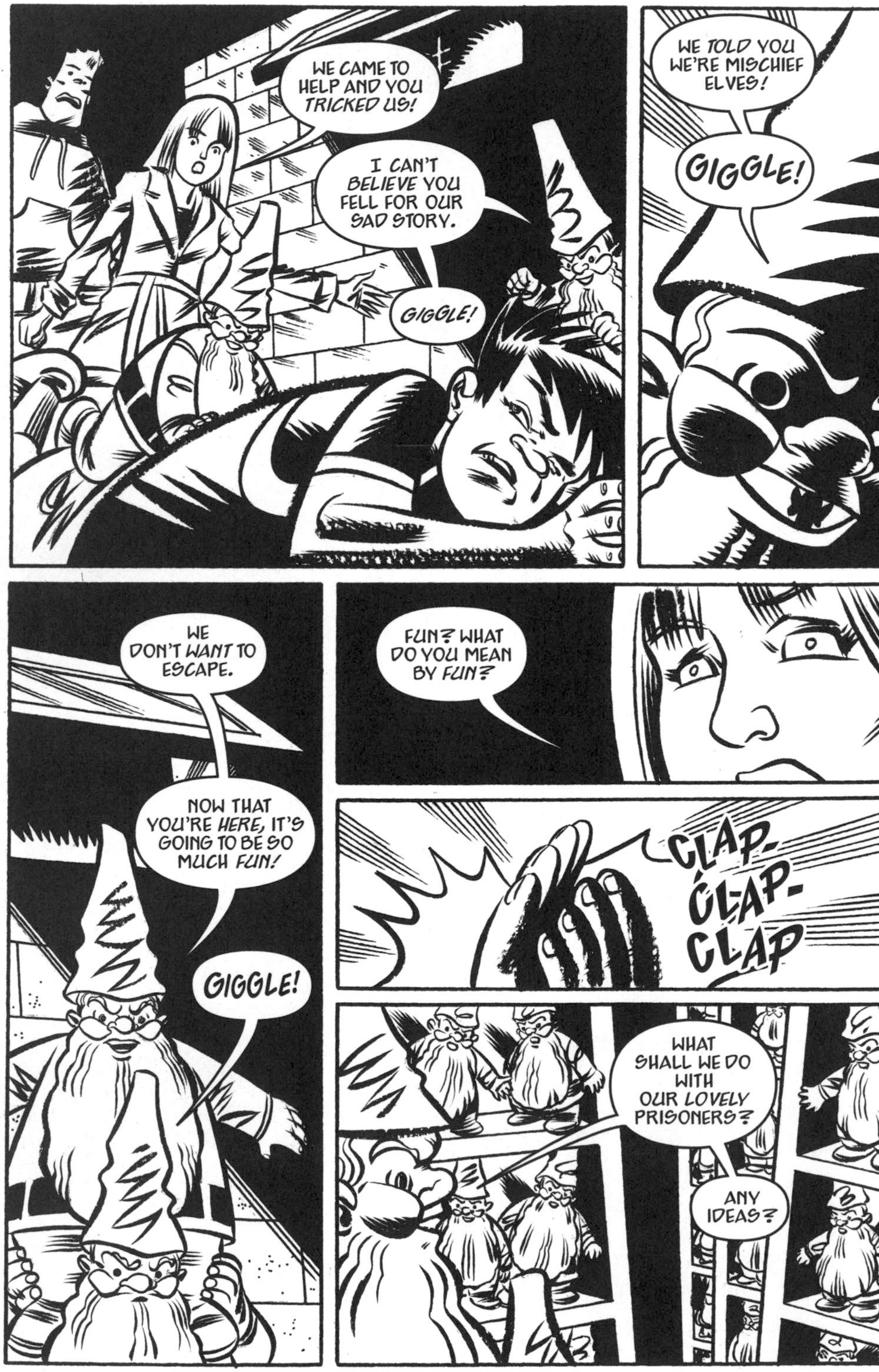
WE CAME TO HELP AND YOU TRICKED US!
I CAN'T BELIEVE YOU FELL FOR OUR SAD STORY.
GIGGLE!
WE TOLD YOU WE'RE MISCHIEF ELVES!
GIGGLE!
WE DON'T WANT TO ESCAPE.
NOW THAT YOU'RE HERE, IT'S GOING TO BE SO MUCH FUN!
GIGGLE!
FUN? WHAT DO YOU MEAN BY FUN?
CLAP-CLAP-CLAP
WHAT SHALL WE DO WITH OUR LOVELY PRISONERS?
ANY IDEAS?

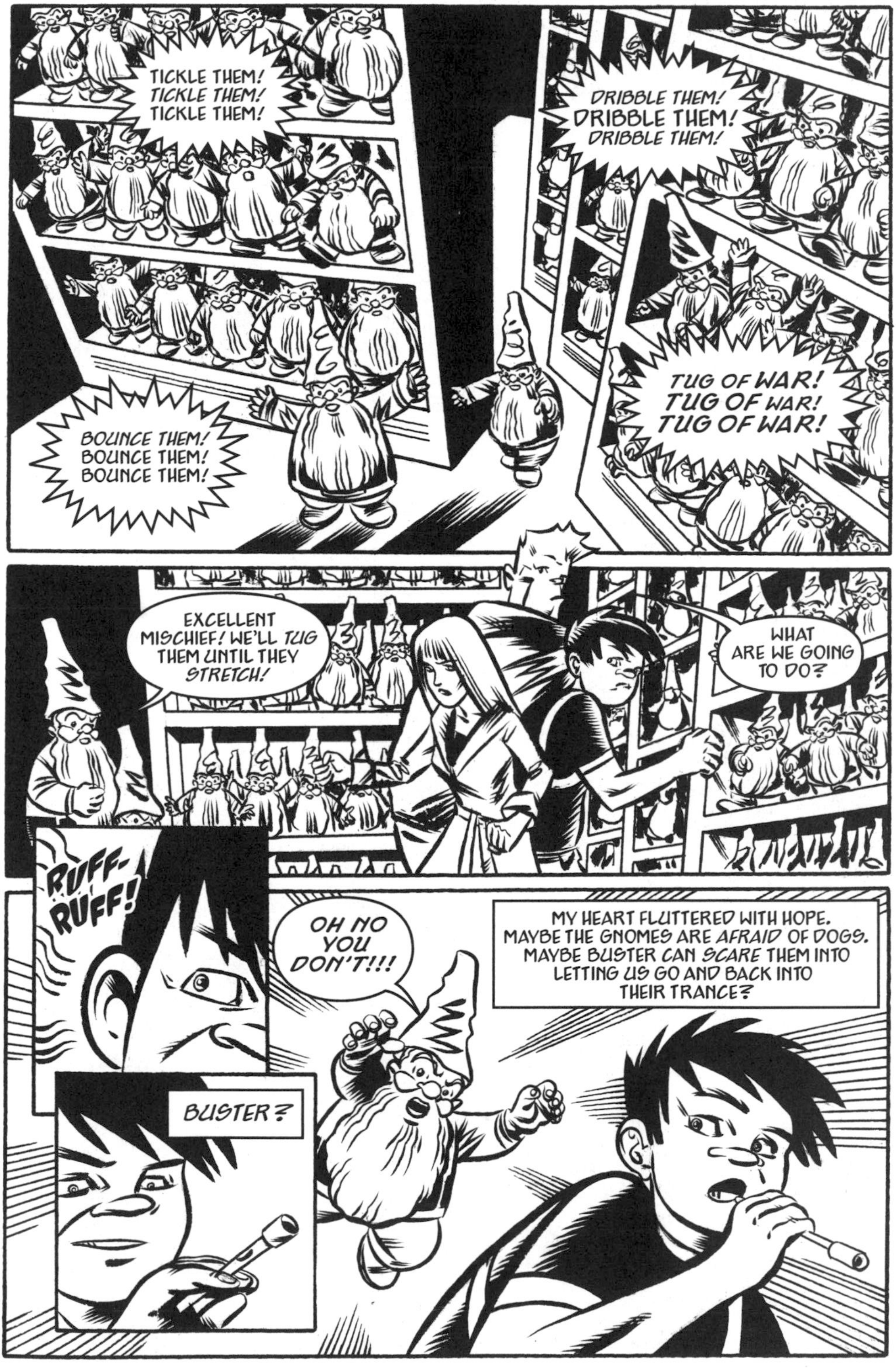
TICKLE THEM! TICKLE THEM! TICKLE THEM!
DRIBBLE THEM! DRIBBLE THEM! DRIBBLE THEM!
BOUNCE THEM! BOUNCE THEM! BOUNCE THEM!
TUG OF WAR! TUG OF WAR! TUG OF WAR!
EXCELLENT MISCHIEF! WE'LL TUG THEM UNTIL THEY STRETCH!
WHAT ARE WE GOING TO DO?
RUFF-RUFF!
OH NO YOU DON'T!!!
MY HEART FLUTTERED WITH HOPE. MAYBE THE GNOMES ARE AFRAID OF DOGS. MAYBE BUSTER CAN SCARE THEM INTO LETTING US GO AND BACK INTO THEIR TRANCE?
BUSTER?

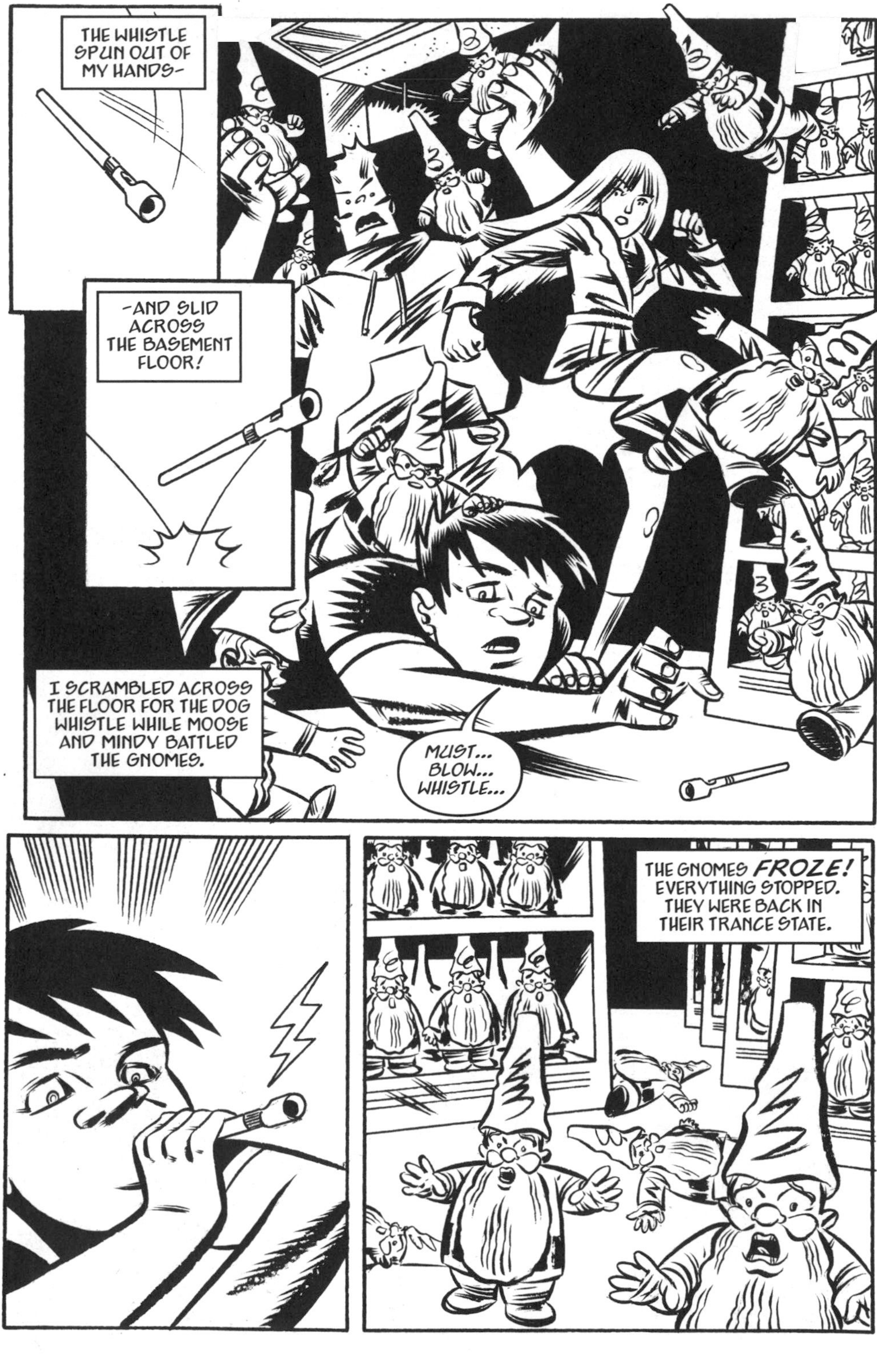
THE WHISTLE SPUN OUT OF MY HANDS-
-AND SLID ACROSS THE BASEMENT FLOOR!
I SCRAMBLED ACROSS THE FLOOR FOR THE DOG WHISTLE WHILE MOOSE AND MINDY BATTLED THE GNOMES.
MUST... BLOW... WHISTLE...
THE GNOMES FROZE! EVERYTHING STOPPED. THEY WERE BACK IN THEIR TRANCE STATE.

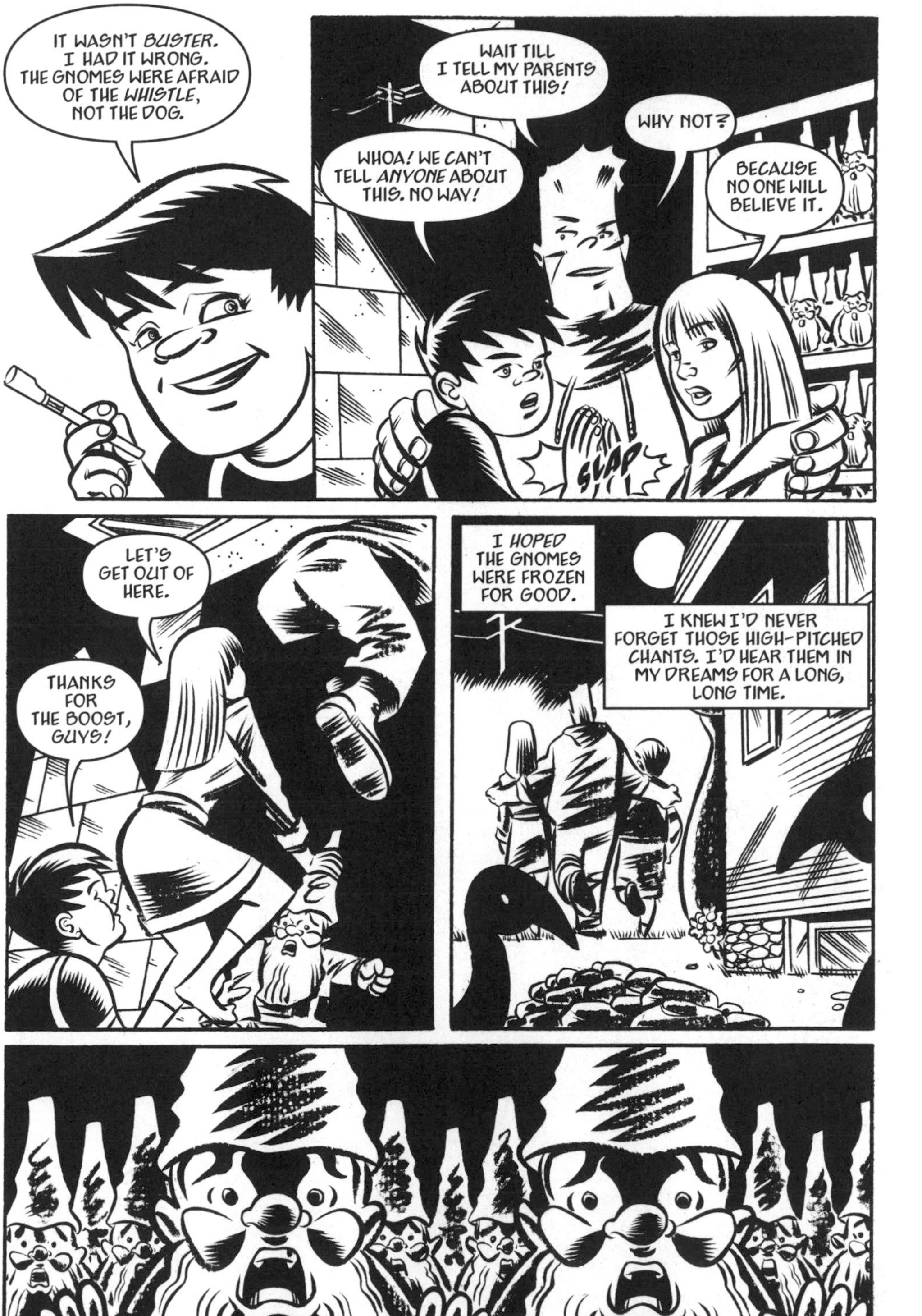
IT WASN'T BUSTER. I HAD IT WRONG. THE GNOMES WERE AFRAID OF THE WHISTLE, NOT THE DOG.
WAIT TILL I TELL MY PARENTS ABOUT THIS!
WHOA! WE CAN'T TELL ANYONE ABOUT THIS. NO WAY!
WHY NOT?
BECAUSE NO ONE WILL BELIEVE IT.
SLAP
LET'S GET OUT OF HERE.
THANKS FOR THE BOOST, GUYS!
I HOPED THE GNOMES WERE FROZEN FOR GOOD.
I KNEW I'D NEVER FORGET THOSE HIGH-PITCHED CHANTS. I'D HEAR THEM IN MY DREAMS FOR A LONG, LONG TIME.

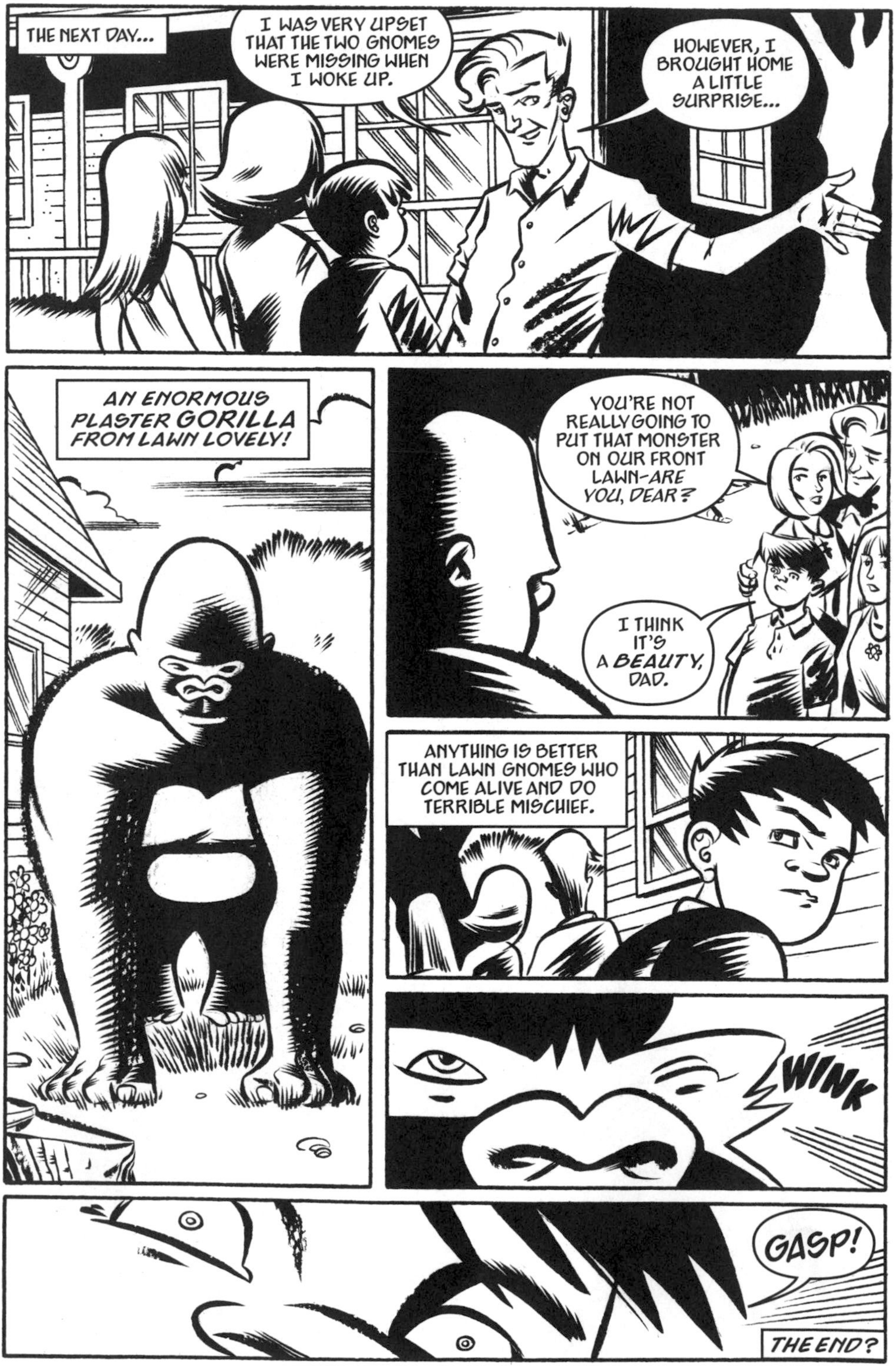
THE NEXT DAY...
I WAS VERY UPSET THAT THE TWO GNOMES WERE MISSING WHEN I WOKE UP.
HOWEVER, I BROUGHT HOME A LITTLE SURPRISE...
AN ENORMOUS PLASTER GORILLA FROM LAWN LOVELY!
YOU'RE NOT REALLY GOING TO PUT THAT MONSTER ON OUR FRONT LAWN–ARE YOU, DEAR?
I THINK IT'S A BEAUTY, DAD.
ANYTHING IS BETTER THAN LAWN GNOMES WHO COME ALIVE AND DO TERRIBLE MISCHIEF.
WINK
GASP!
THE END?

GHOST BEACH

ADAPTED AND ILLUSTRATED BY

Ted Naifeh

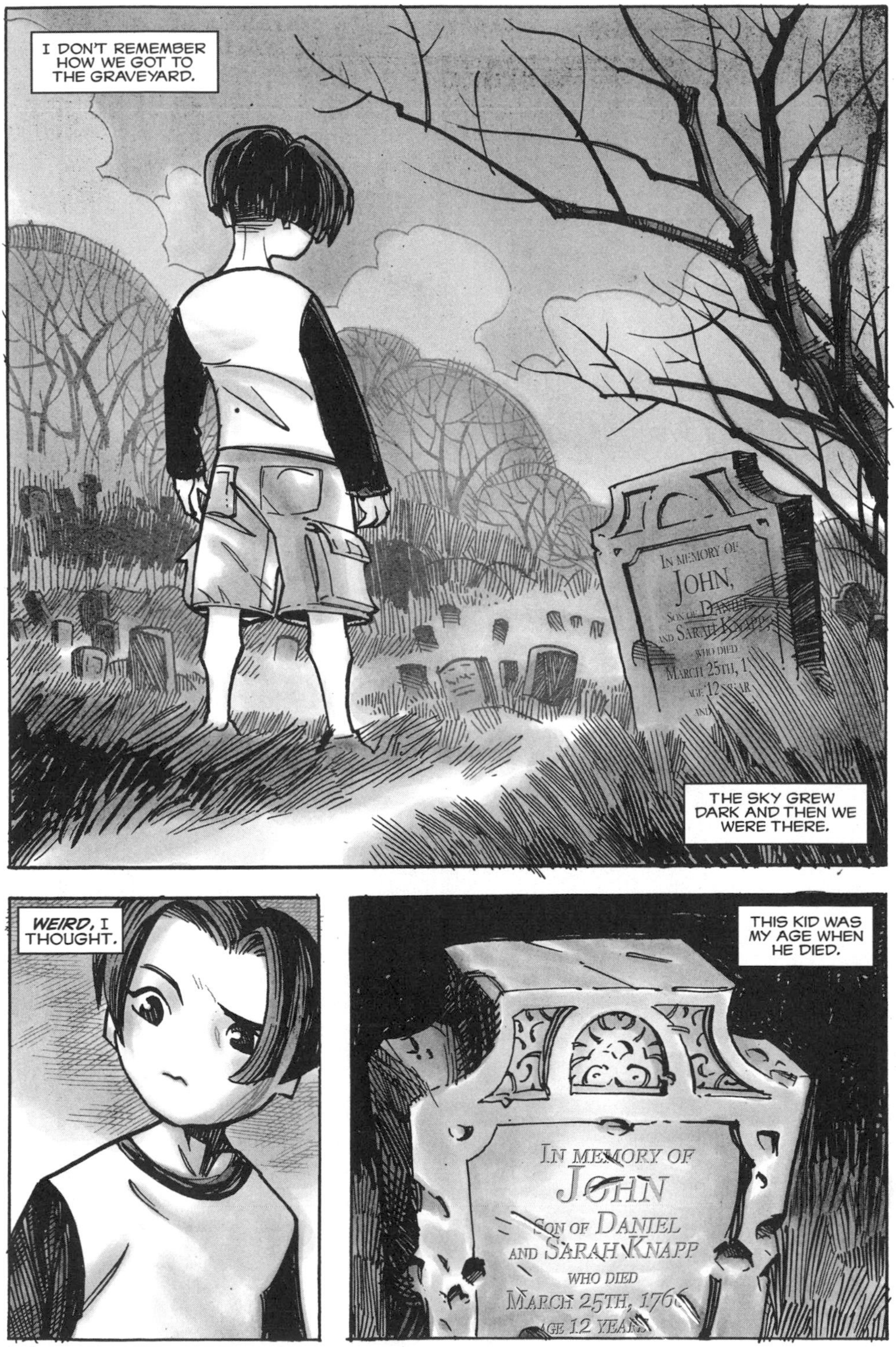
I DON'T REMEMBER HOW WE GOT TO THE GRAVEYARD.
THE SKY GREW DARK AND THEN WE WERE THERE.
WEIRD, I THOUGHT.
THIS KID WAS MY AGE WHEN HE DIED.
IN MEMORY OF
JOHN
SON OF DANIEL
AND SARAH KNAPP
WHO DIED
MARCH 25TH, 176

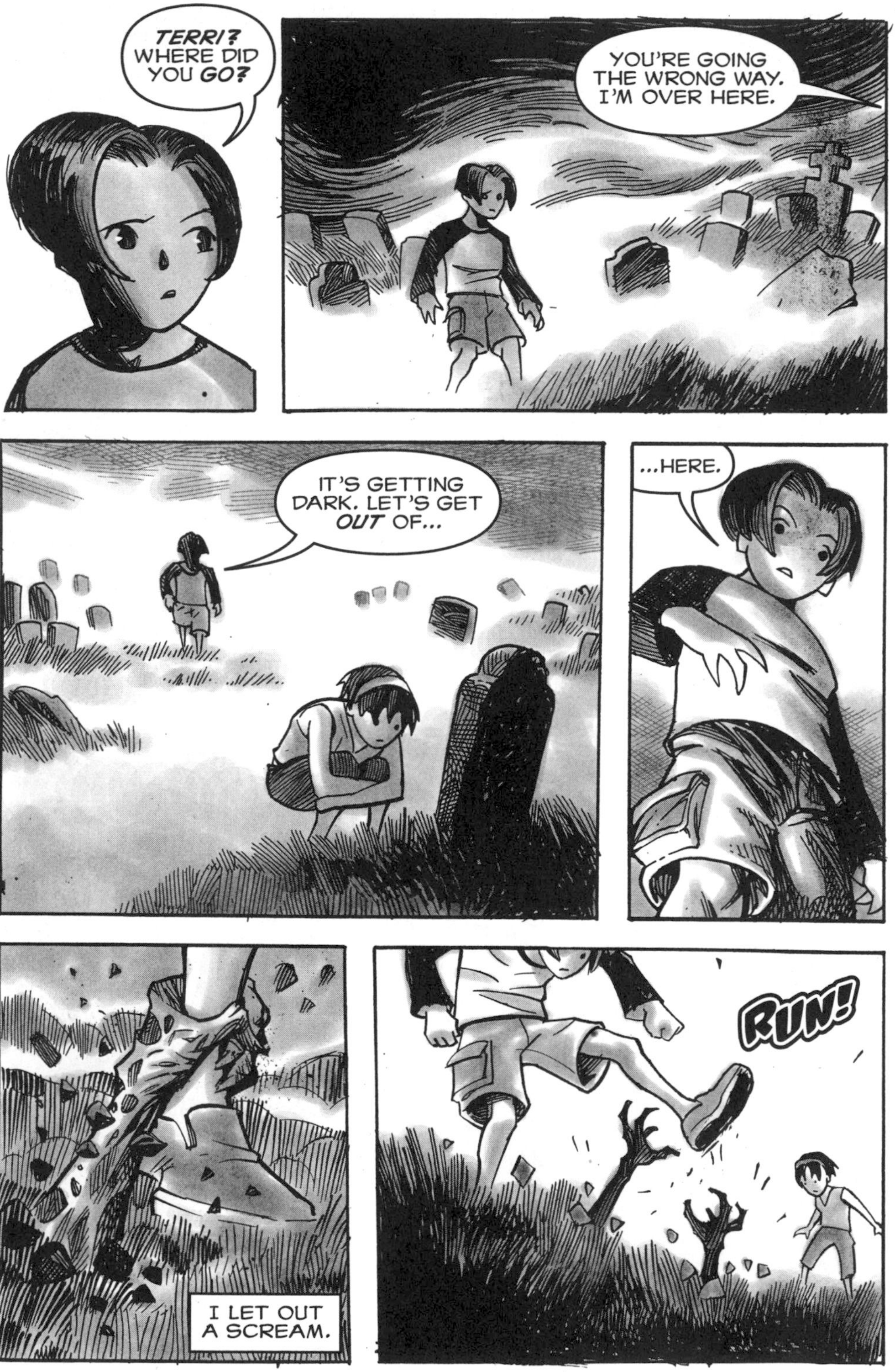
TERRI? WHERE DID YOU GO?
YOU'RE GOING THE WRONG WAY. I'M OVER HERE.
IT'S GETTING DARK. LET'S GET OUT OF...
...HERE.
I LET OUT A SCREAM.
RUN!

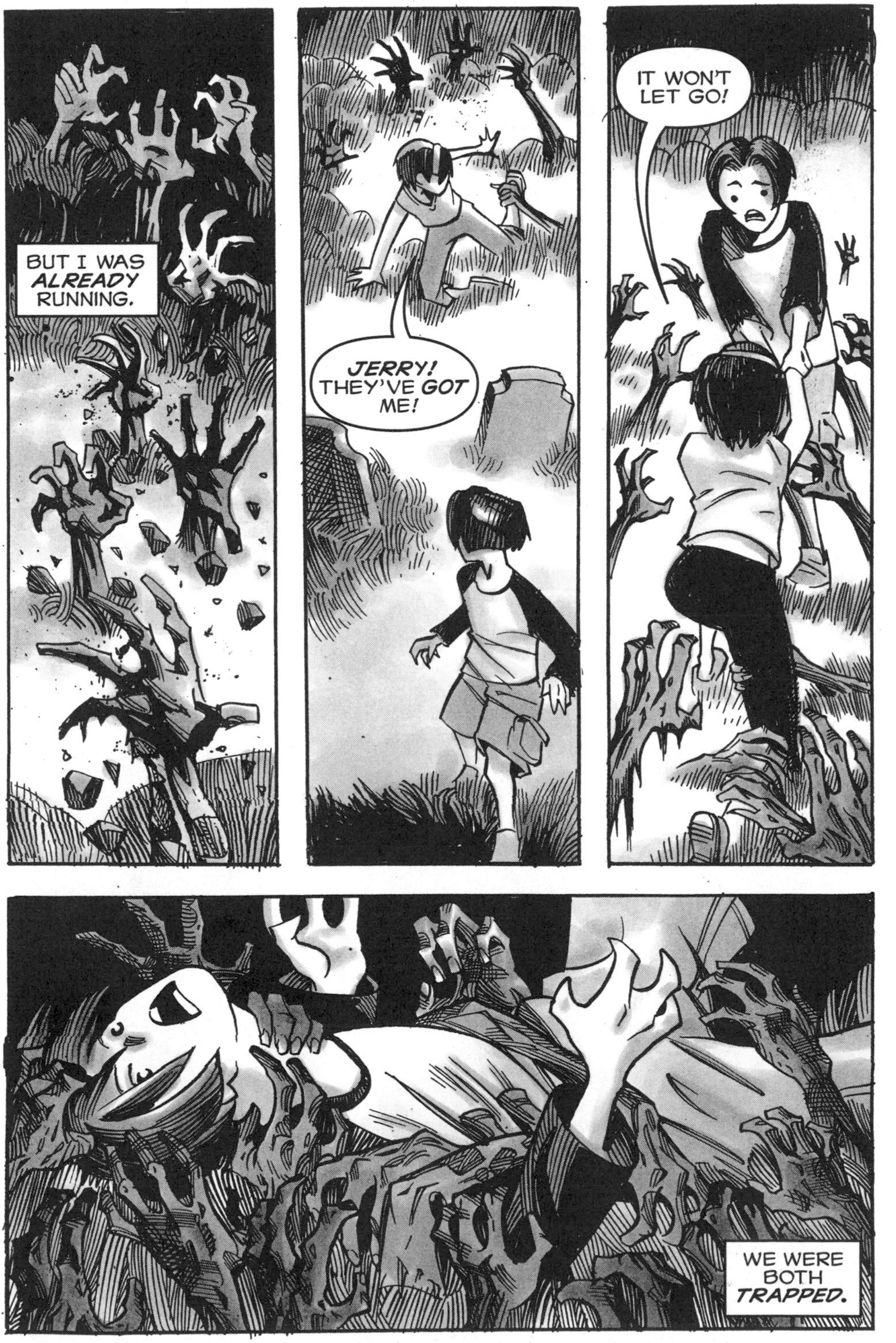
BUT I WAS *ALREADY* RUNNING.
JERRY! THEY'VE *GOT* ME!
IT WON'T LET GO!
WE WERE BOTH *TRAPPED*.

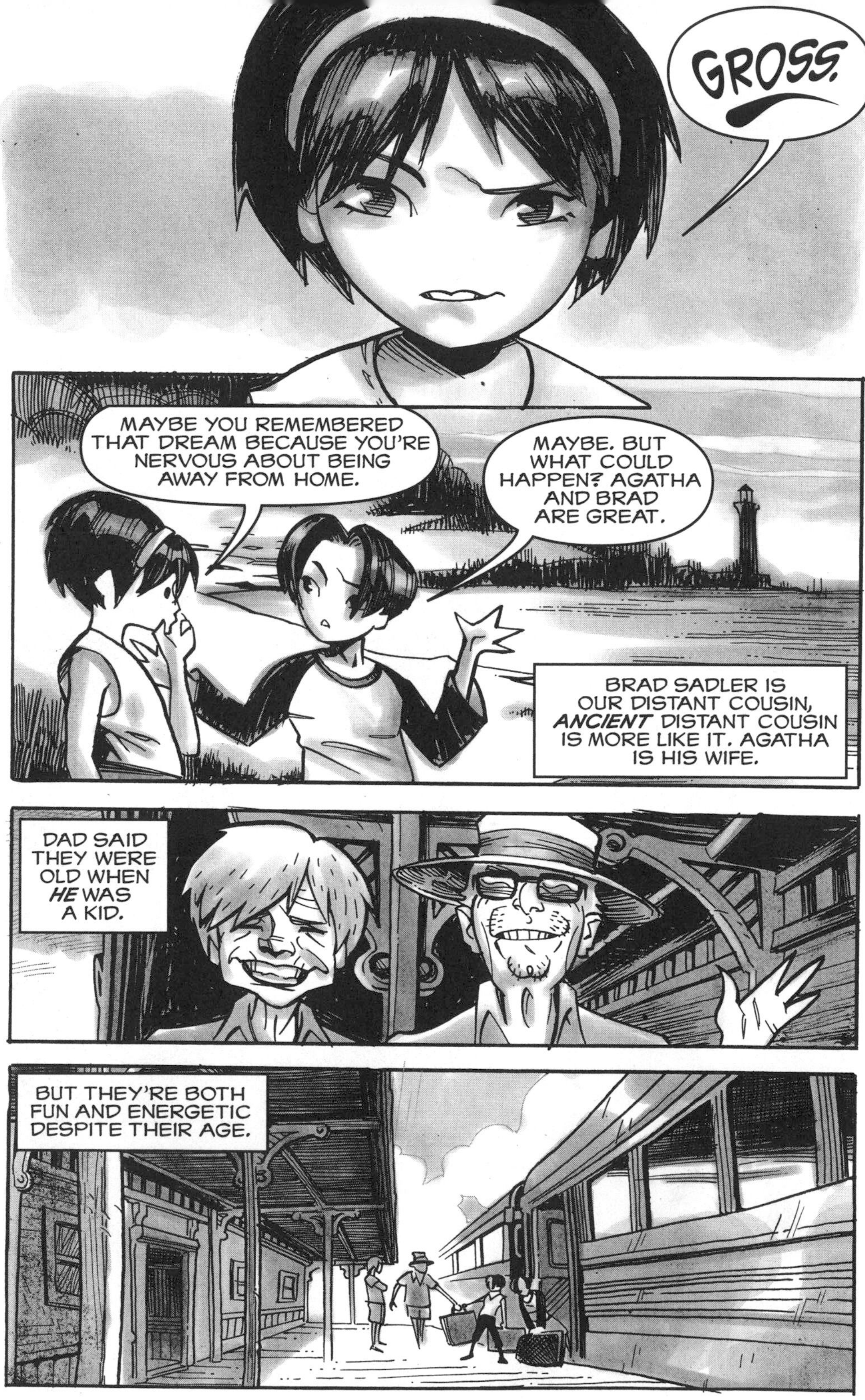
GROSS.
MAYBE YOU REMEMBERED THAT DREAM BECAUSE YOU'RE NERVOUS ABOUT BEING AWAY FROM HOME.
MAYBE. BUT WHAT COULD HAPPEN? AGATHA AND BRAD ARE GREAT.
BRAD SADLER IS OUR DISTANT COUSIN, *ANCIENT* DISTANT COUSIN IS MORE LIKE IT. AGATHA IS HIS WIFE.
DAD SAID THEY WERE OLD WHEN *HE* WAS A KID.
BUT THEY'RE BOTH FUN AND ENERGETIC DESPITE THEIR AGE.

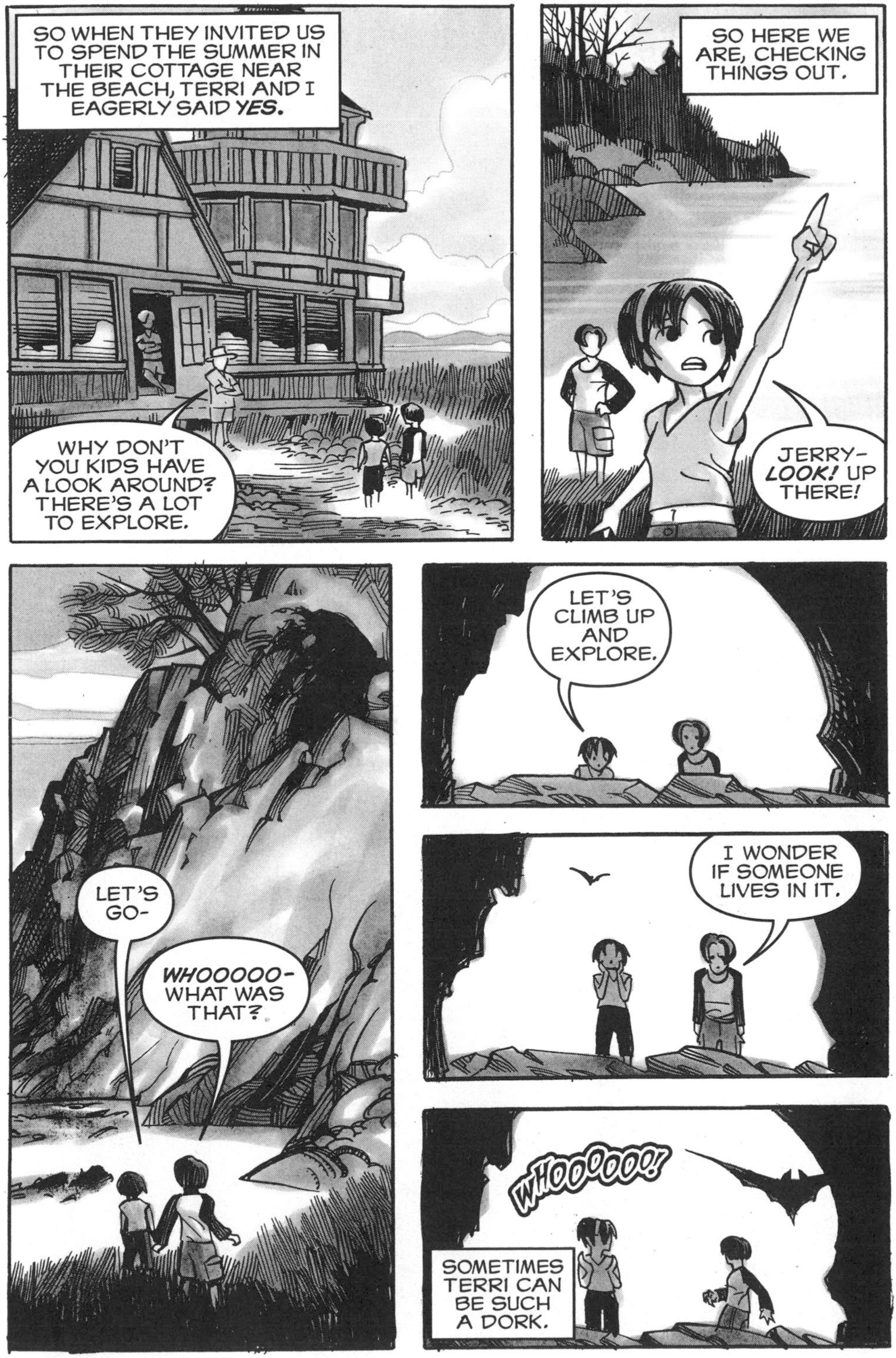
SO WHEN THEY INVITED US TO SPEND THE SUMMER IN THEIR COTTAGE NEAR THE BEACH, TERRI AND I EAGERLY SAID YES.
WHY DON'T YOU KIDS HAVE A LOOK AROUND? THERE'S A LOT TO EXPLORE.
SO HERE WE ARE, CHECKING THINGS OUT.
JERRY- LOOK! UP THERE!
LET'S GO-
WHOOOOO- WHAT WAS THAT?
LET'S CLIMB UP AND EXPLORE.
I WONDER IF SOMEONE LIVES IN IT.
WHOOOOOO!
SOMETIMES TERRI CAN BE SUCH A DORK.

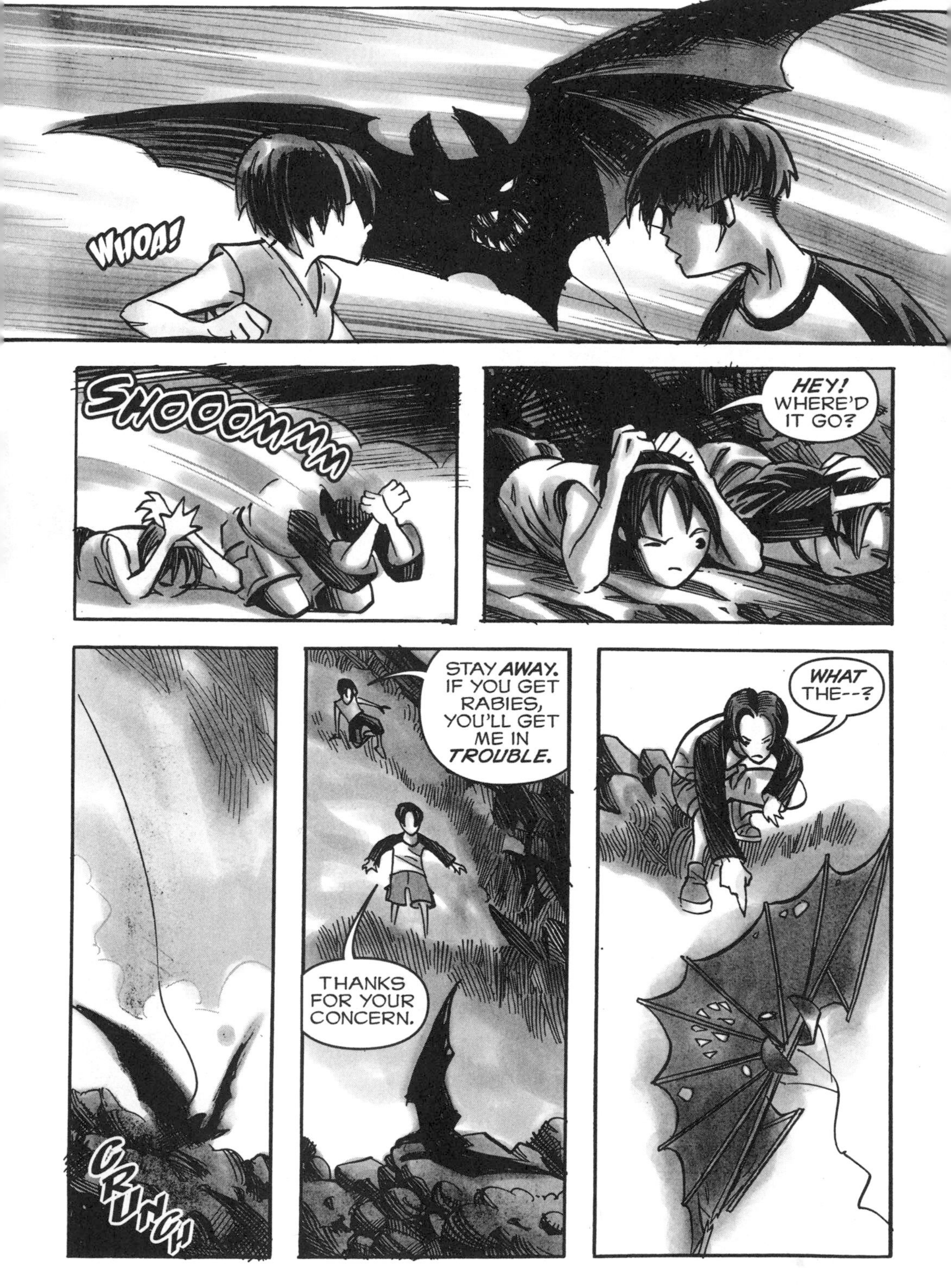
WHOA!
SHOOOMMM
HEY! WHERE'D IT GO?
CRUNCH
STAY AWAY. IF YOU GET RABIES, YOU'LL GET ME IN TROUBLE.
THANKS FOR YOUR CONCERN.
WHAT THE--?

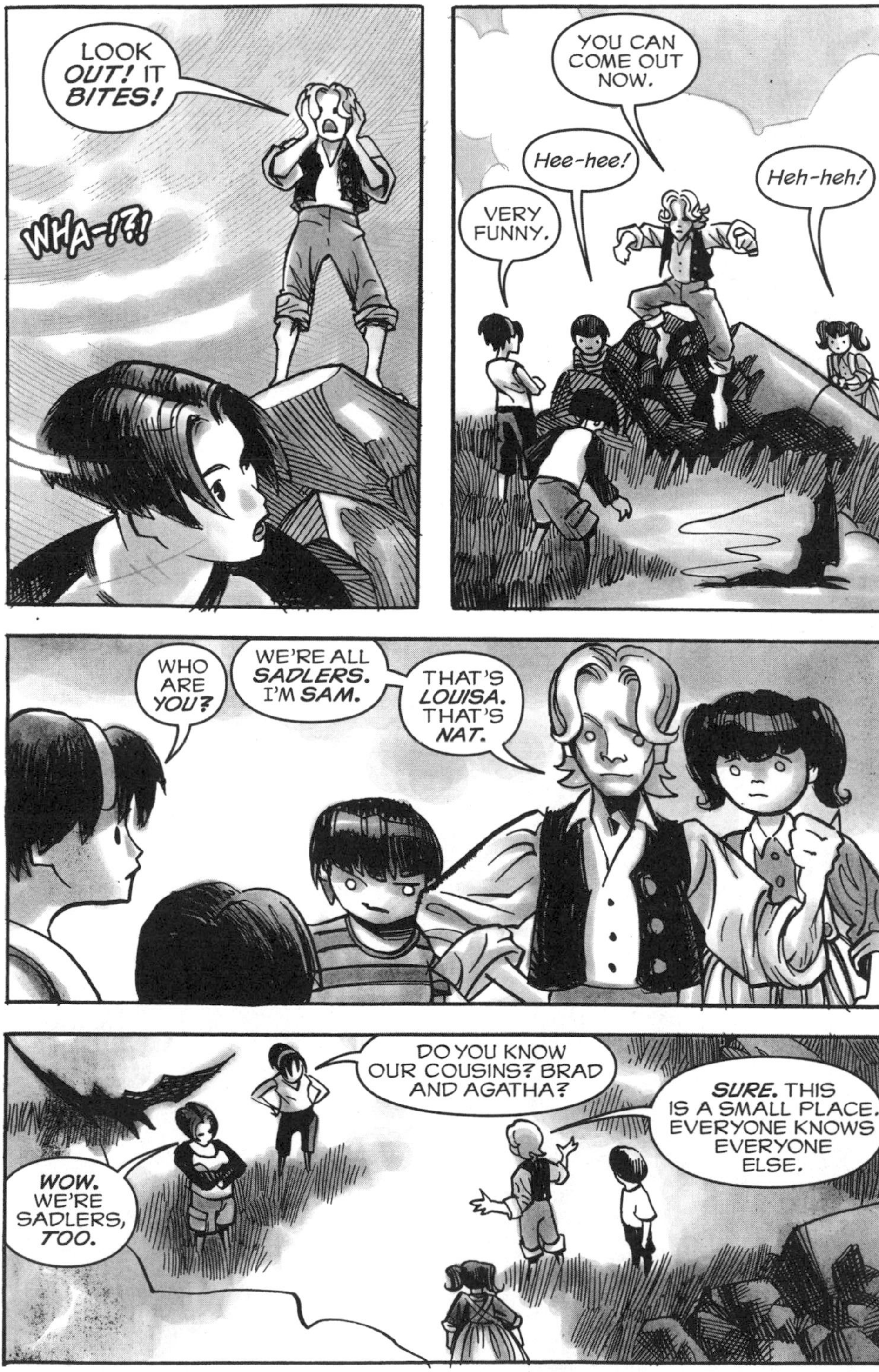
LOOK OUT! IT BITES!
WHA-!?!
YOU CAN COME OUT NOW.
Hee-hee!
Heh-heh!
VERY FUNNY.
WHO ARE YOU?
WE'RE ALL SADLERS. I'M SAM.
THAT'S LOUISA. THAT'S NAT.
DO YOU KNOW OUR COUSINS? BRAD AND AGATHA?
SURE. THIS IS A SMALL PLACE. EVERYONE KNOWS EVERYONE ELSE.
WOW. WE'RE SADLERS, TOO.

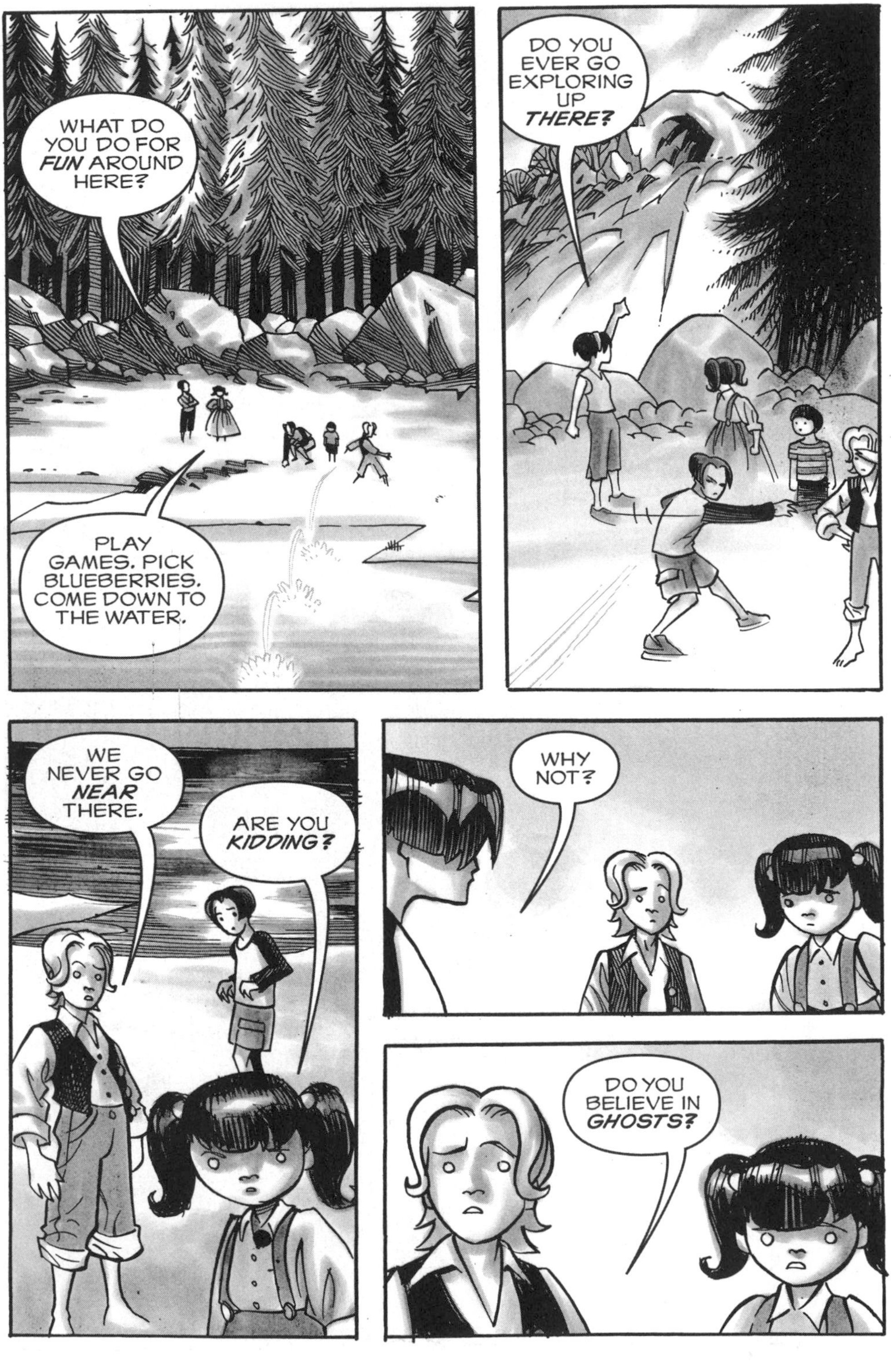
WHAT DO YOU DO FOR *FUN* AROUND HERE?
PLAY GAMES. PICK BLUEBERRIES. COME DOWN TO THE WATER.
DO YOU EVER GO EXPLORING UP *THERE?*
WE NEVER GO *NEAR* THERE.
ARE YOU *KIDDING?*
WHY NOT?
DO YOU BELIEVE IN *GHOSTS?*

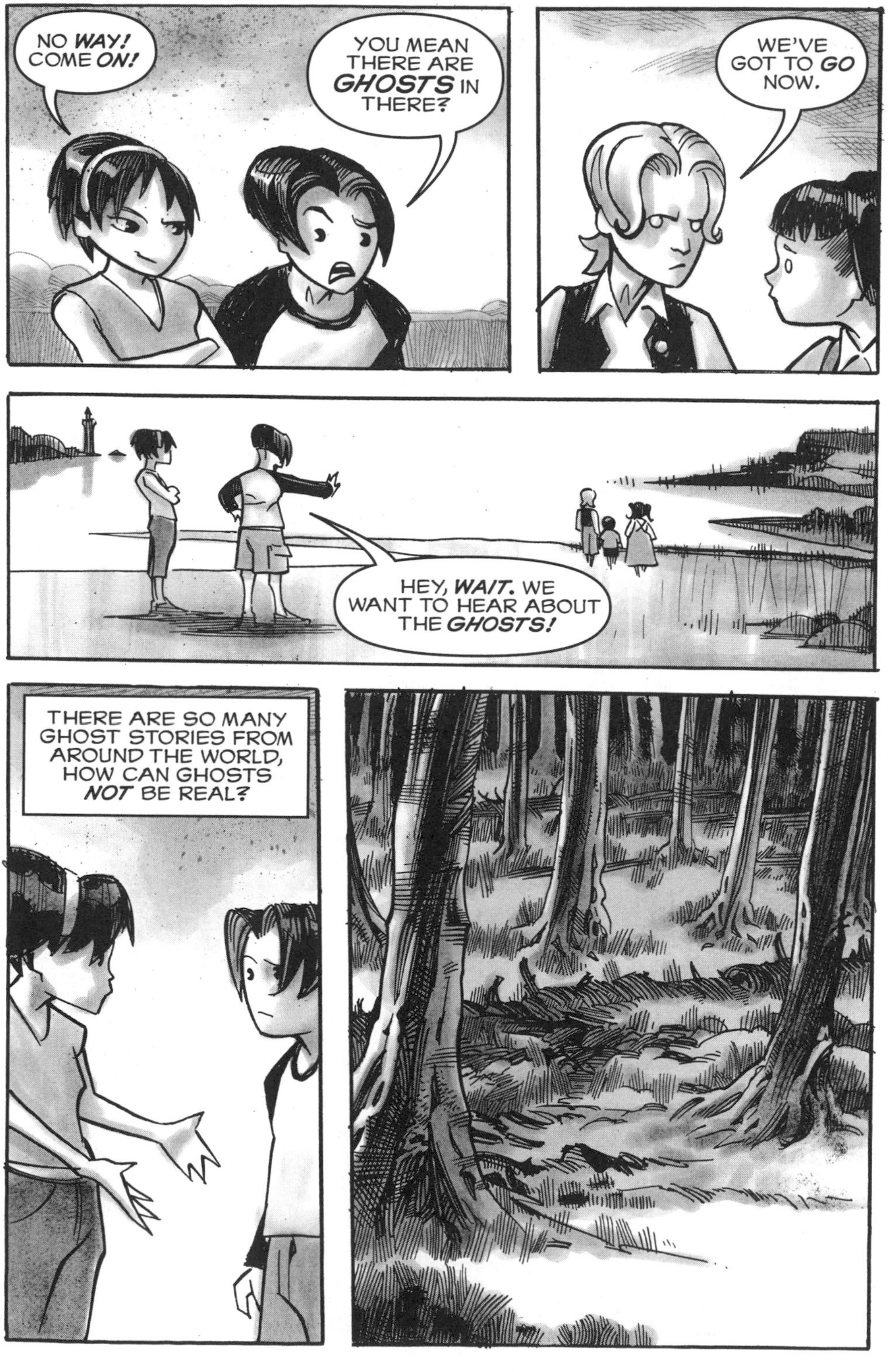
NO WAY! COME ON!
YOU MEAN THERE ARE GHOSTS IN THERE?
WE'VE GOT TO GO NOW.
HEY, WAIT. WE WANT TO HEAR ABOUT THE GHOSTS!
THERE ARE SO MANY GHOST STORIES FROM AROUND THE WORLD, HOW CAN GHOSTS NOT BE REAL?

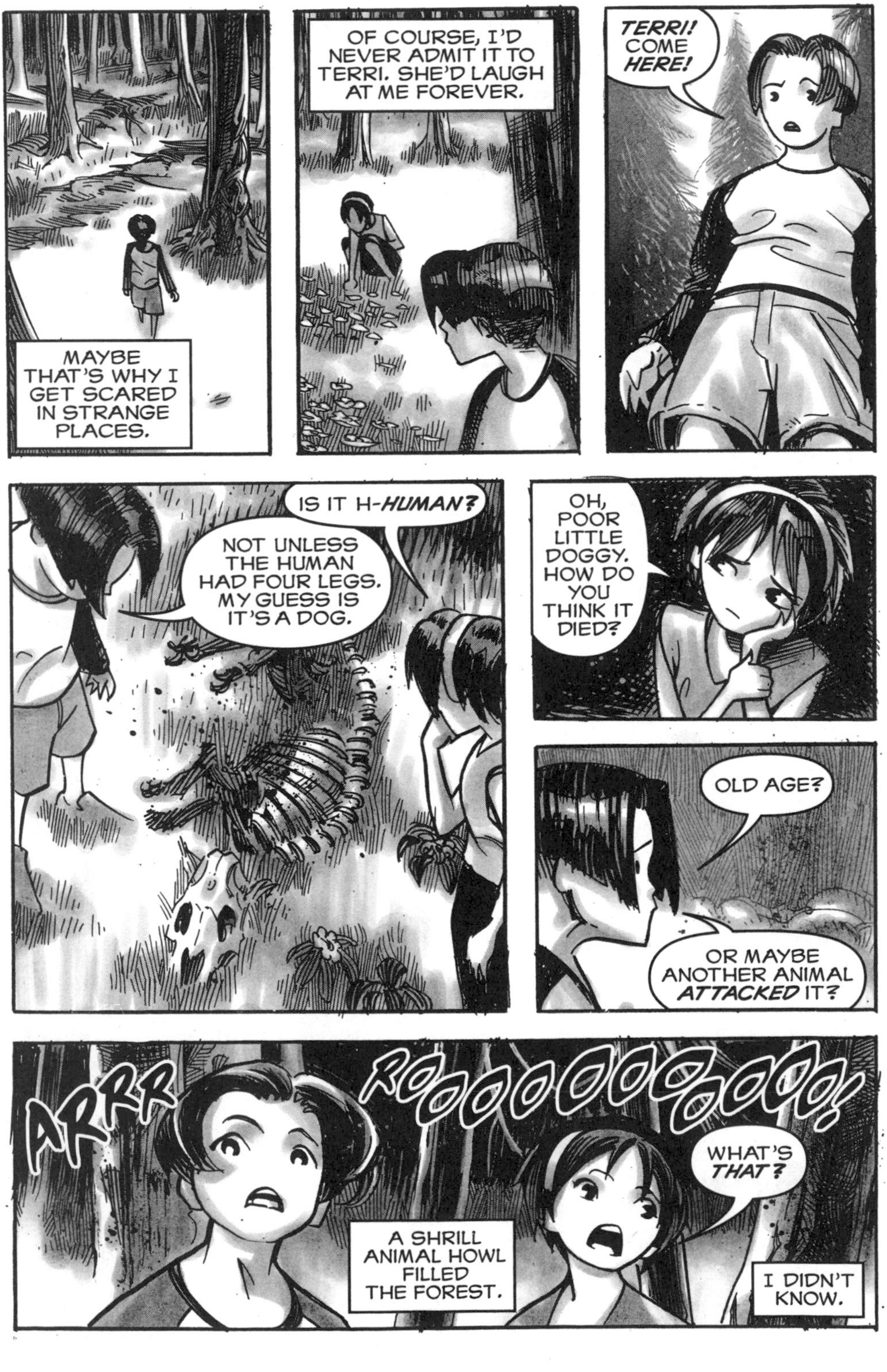
MAYBE THAT'S WHY I GET SCARED IN STRANGE PLACES.
OF COURSE, I'D NEVER ADMIT IT TO TERRI. SHE'D LAUGH AT ME FOREVER.
TERRI! COME HERE!
IS IT H-HUMAN?
NOT UNLESS THE HUMAN HAD FOUR LEGS. MY GUESS IS IT'S A DOG.
OH, POOR LITTLE DOGGY. HOW DO YOU THINK IT DIED?
OLD AGE?
OR MAYBE ANOTHER ANIMAL ATTACKED IT?
ARRR
ROOOOOOOOOOOOO!
A SHRILL ANIMAL HOWL FILLED THE FOREST.
WHAT'S THAT?
I DIDN'T KNOW.

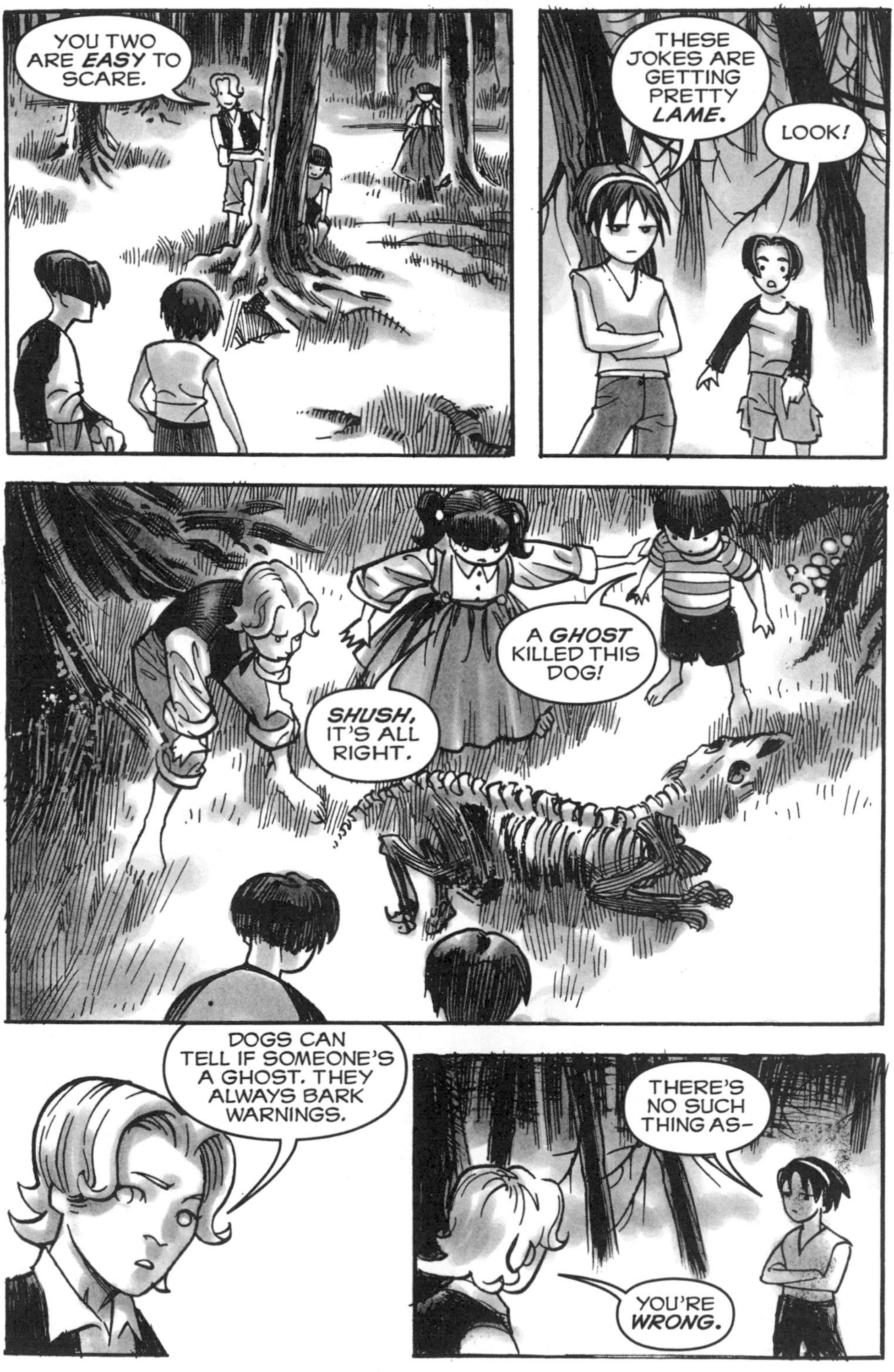
YOU TWO ARE *EASY* TO SCARE.
THESE JOKES ARE GETTING PRETTY *LAME*.
LOOK!
A *GHOST* KILLED THIS DOG!
SHUSH, IT'S ALL RIGHT.
DOGS CAN TELL IF SOMEONE'S A GHOST. THEY ALWAYS BARK WARNINGS.
THERE'S NO SUCH THING AS-
YOU'RE *WRONG*.

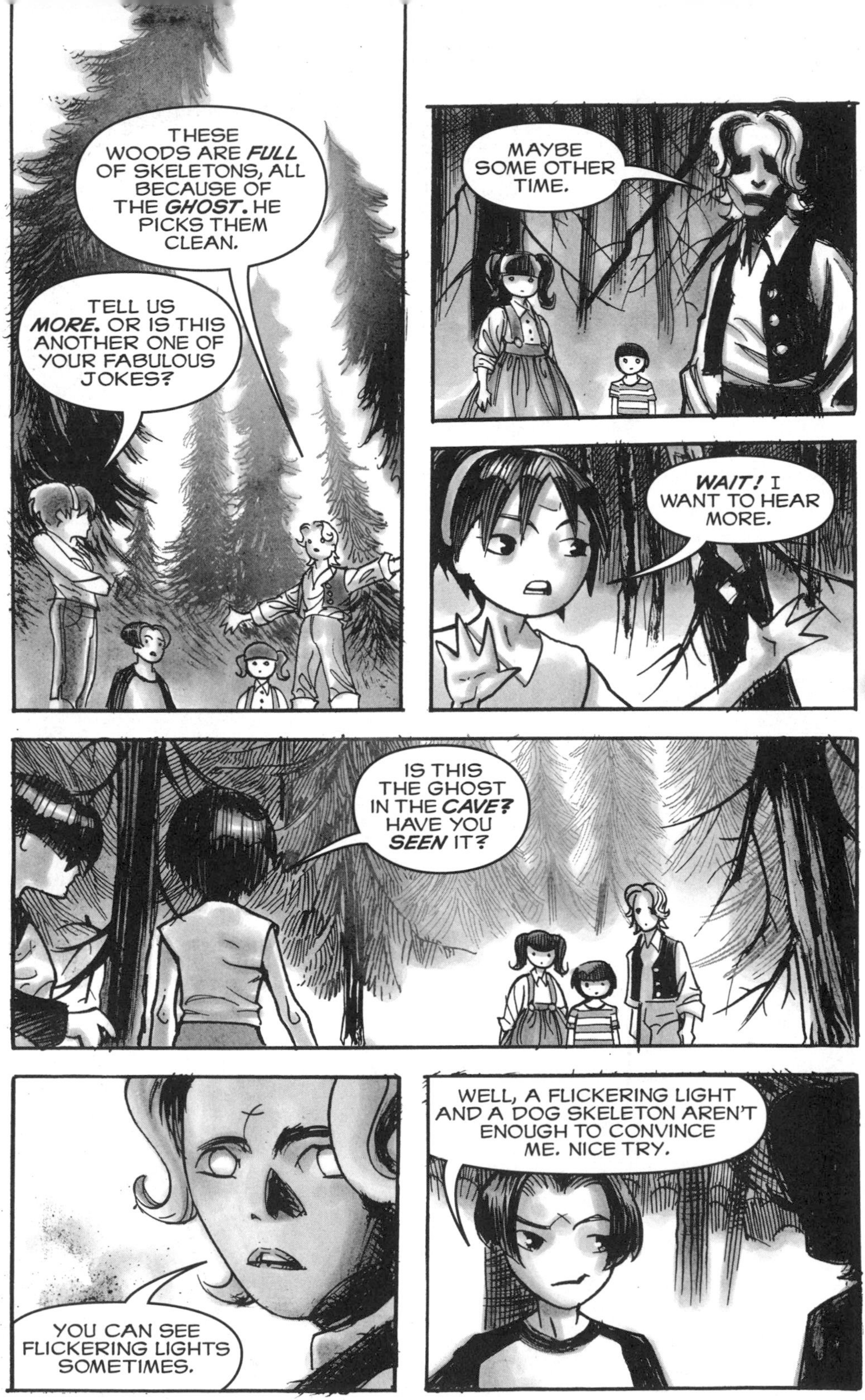
THESE WOODS ARE *FULL* OF SKELETONS, ALL BECAUSE OF THE *GHOST*. HE PICKS THEM CLEAN.
TELL US *MORE*. OR IS THIS ANOTHER ONE OF YOUR FABULOUS JOKES?
MAYBE SOME OTHER TIME.
WAIT! I WANT TO HEAR MORE.
IS THIS THE GHOST IN THE *CAVE?* HAVE YOU *SEEN* IT?
YOU CAN SEE FLICKERING LIGHTS SOMETIMES.
WELL, A FLICKERING LIGHT AND A DOG SKELETON AREN'T ENOUGH TO CONVINCE ME. NICE TRY.

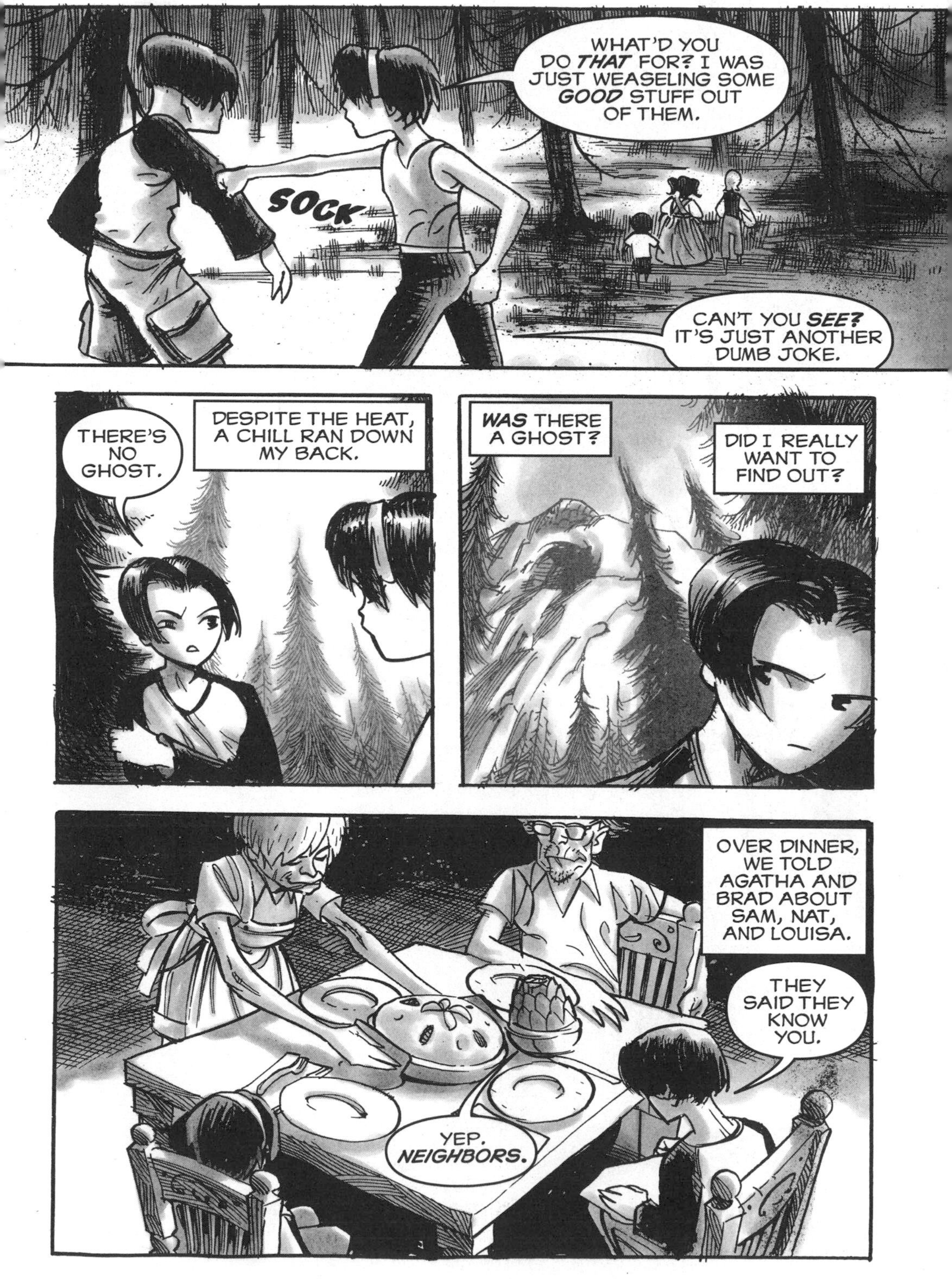
WHAT'D YOU DO *THAT* FOR? I WAS JUST WEASELING SOME *GOOD* STUFF OUT OF THEM.
SOCK
CAN'T YOU *SEE?* IT'S JUST ANOTHER DUMB JOKE.
THERE'S NO GHOST.
DESPITE THE HEAT, A CHILL RAN DOWN MY BACK.
WAS THERE A GHOST?
DID I REALLY WANT TO FIND OUT?
OVER DINNER, WE TOLD AGATHA AND BRAD ABOUT SAM, NAT, AND LOUISA.
THEY SAID THEY KNOW YOU.
YEP. *NEIGHBORS.*

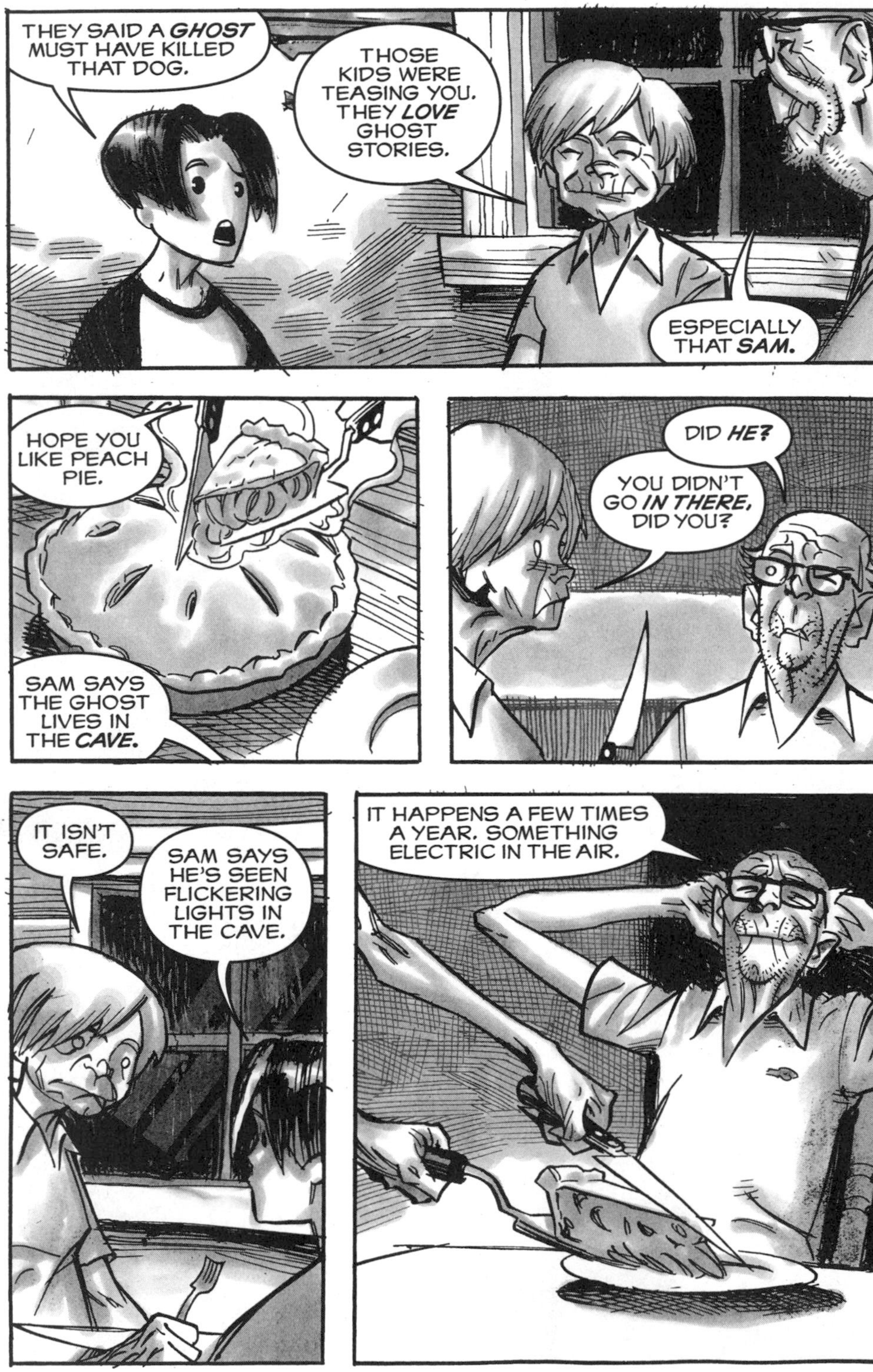
THEY SAID A *GHOST* MUST HAVE KILLED THAT DOG.
THOSE KIDS WERE TEASING YOU. THEY *LOVE* GHOST STORIES.
ESPECIALLY THAT *SAM.*
HOPE YOU LIKE PEACH PIE.
SAM SAYS THE GHOST LIVES IN THE *CAVE.*
DID *HE?*
YOU DIDN'T GO *IN THERE,* DID YOU?
IT ISN'T SAFE.
SAM SAYS HE'S SEEN FLICKERING LIGHTS IN THE CAVE.
IT HAPPENS A FEW TIMES A YEAR. SOMETHING ELECTRIC IN THE AIR.

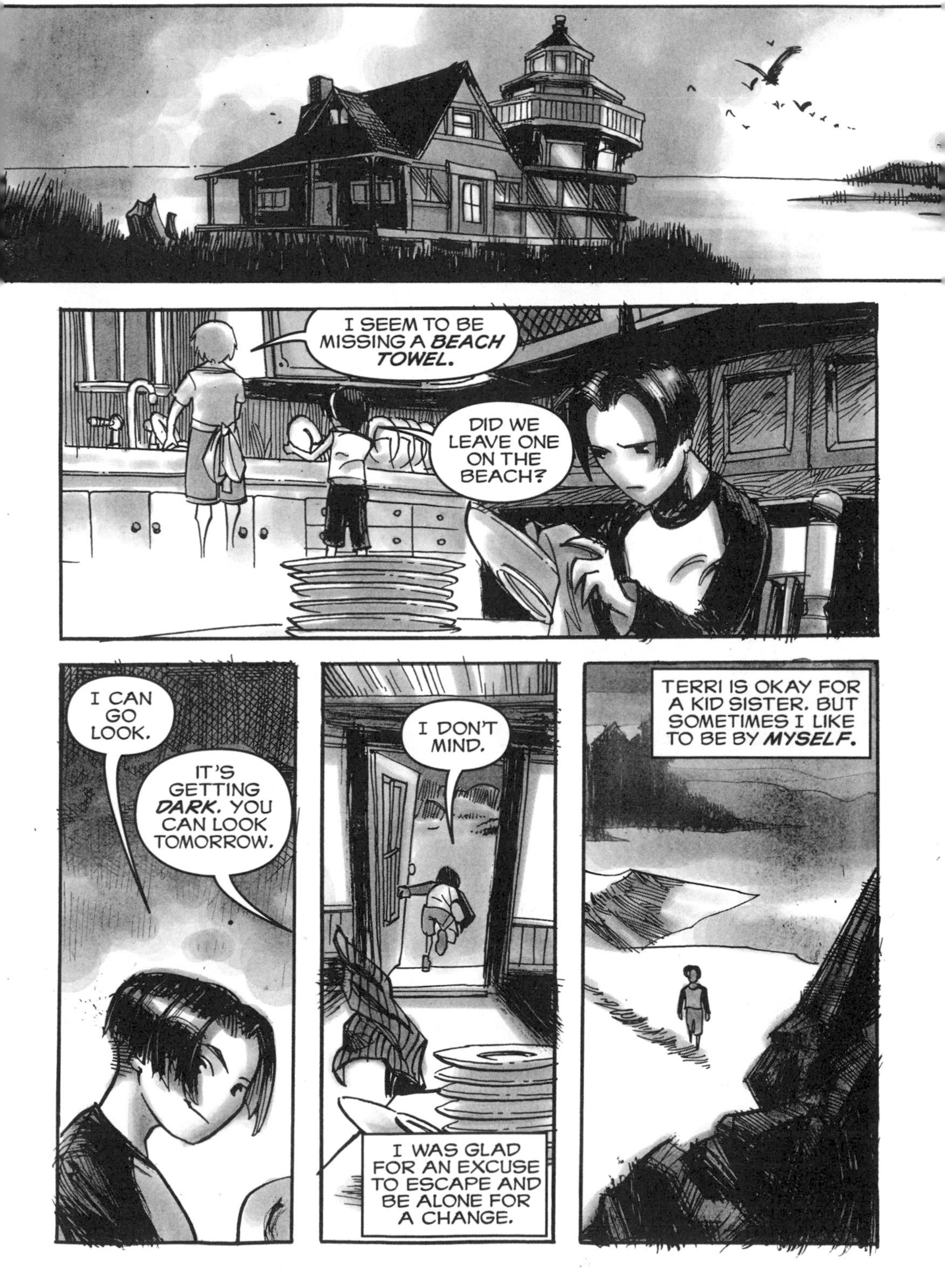
I SEEM TO BE MISSING A *BEACH TOWEL.*
DID WE LEAVE ONE ON THE BEACH?
I CAN GO LOOK.
IT'S GETTING *DARK.* YOU CAN LOOK TOMORROW.
I DON'T MIND.
I WAS GLAD FOR AN EXCUSE TO ESCAPE AND BE ALONE FOR A CHANGE.
TERRI IS OKAY FOR A KID SISTER. BUT SOMETIMES I LIKE TO BE BY *MYSELF.*

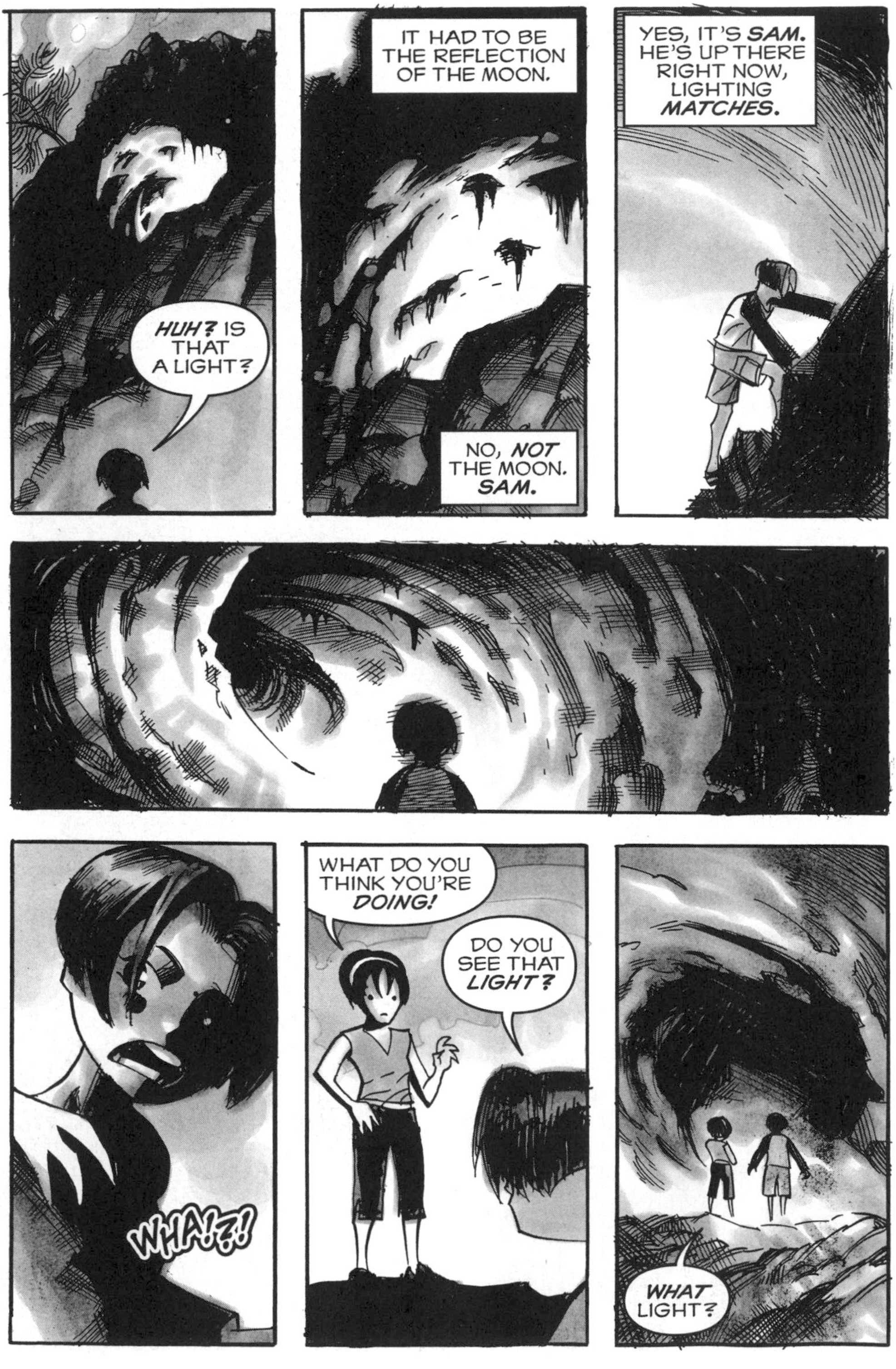
HUH? IS THAT A LIGHT?
IT HAD TO BE THE REFLECTION OF THE MOON.
NO, NOT THE MOON. SAM.
YES, IT'S SAM. HE'S UP THERE RIGHT NOW, LIGHTING MATCHES.
WHA!?!
WHAT DO YOU THINK YOU'RE DOING!
DO YOU SEE THAT LIGHT?
WHAT LIGHT?

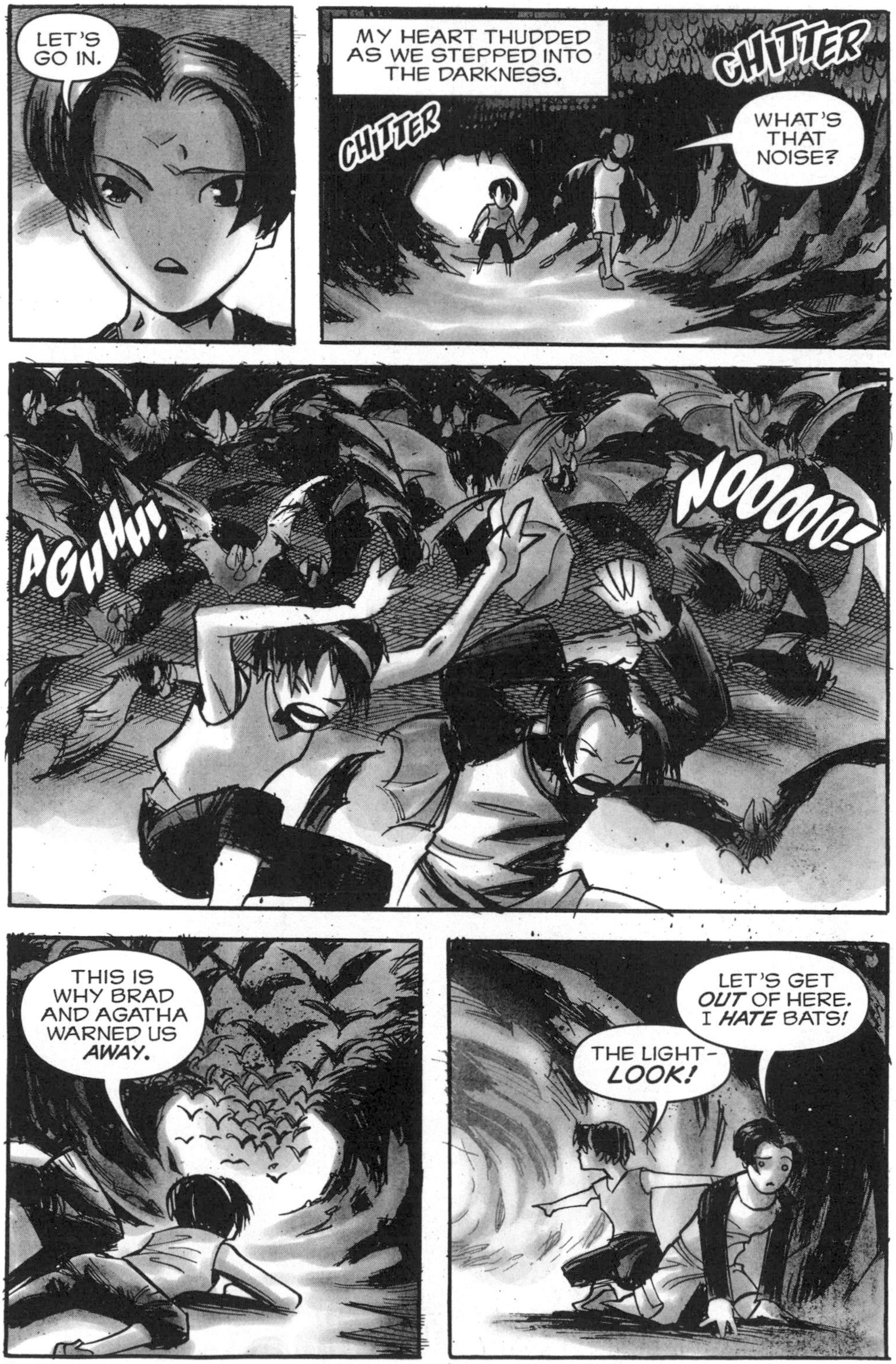
LET'S GO IN.
MY HEART THUDDED AS WE STEPPED INTO THE DARKNESS.
CHITTER
CHITTER
WHAT'S THAT NOISE?
AGHHH!
NOOOOO!
THIS IS WHY BRAD AND AGATHA WARNED US AWAY.
LET'S GET OUT OF HERE. I HATE BATS!
THE LIGHT-LOOK!

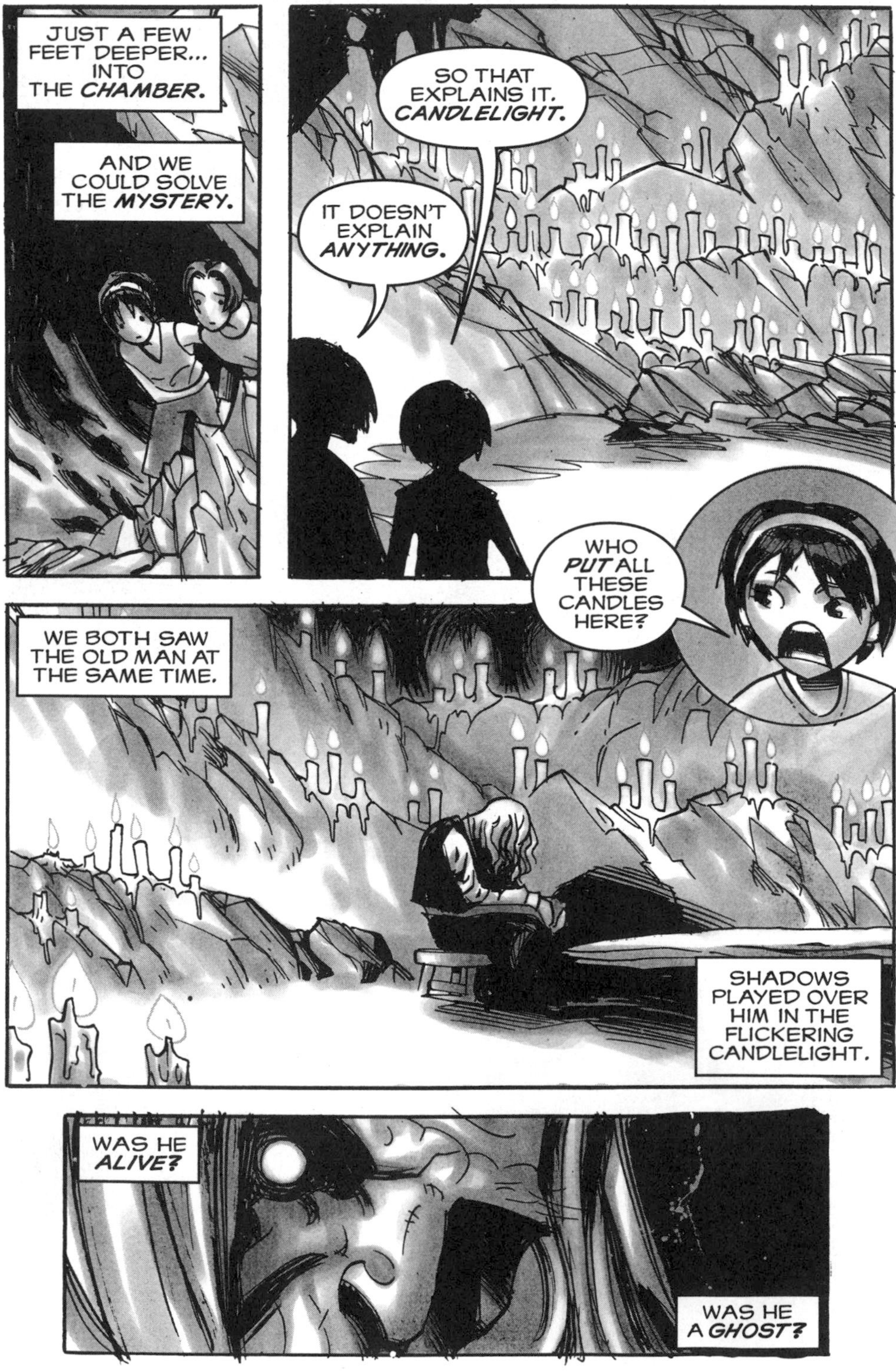
JUST A FEW FEET DEEPER... INTO THE CHAMBER.
AND WE COULD SOLVE THE MYSTERY.
SO THAT EXPLAINS IT. CANDLELIGHT.
IT DOESN'T EXPLAIN ANYTHING.
WHO PUT ALL THESE CANDLES HERE?
WE BOTH SAW THE OLD MAN AT THE SAME TIME.
SHADOWS PLAYED OVER HIM IN THE FLICKERING CANDLELIGHT.
WAS HE ALIVE?
WAS HE A GHOST?

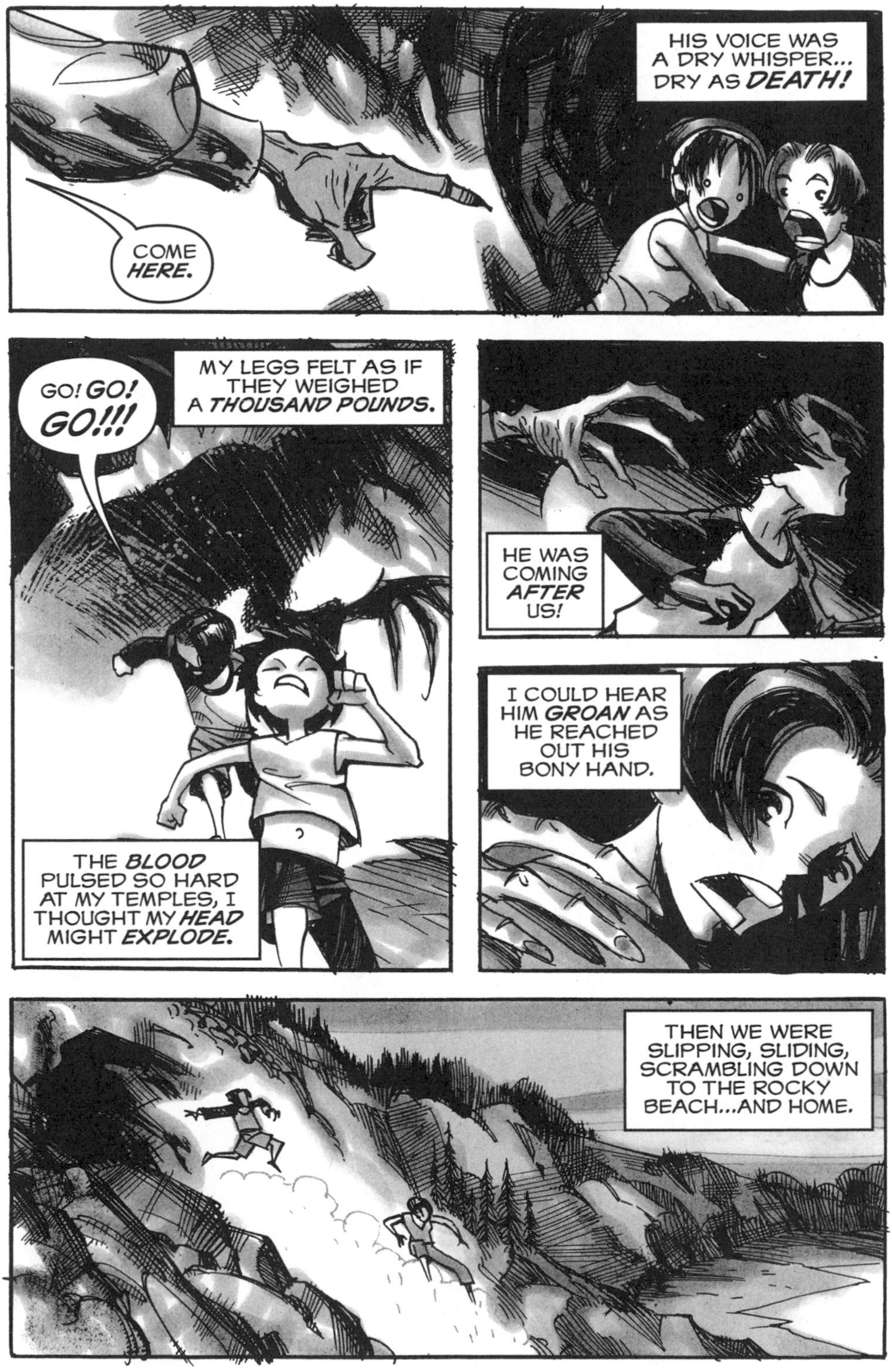
HIS VOICE WAS A DRY WHISPER... DRY AS *DEATH!*
COME *HERE.*
GO! *GO! GO!!!*
MY LEGS FELT AS IF THEY WEIGHED A *THOUSAND POUNDS.*
HE WAS COMING *AFTER* US!
THE *BLOOD* PULSED SO HARD AT MY TEMPLES, I THOUGHT MY *HEAD* MIGHT *EXPLODE.*
I COULD HEAR HIM *GROAN* AS HE REACHED OUT HIS BONY HAND.
THEN WE WERE SLIPPING, SLIDING, SCRAMBLING DOWN TO THE ROCKY BEACH...AND HOME.

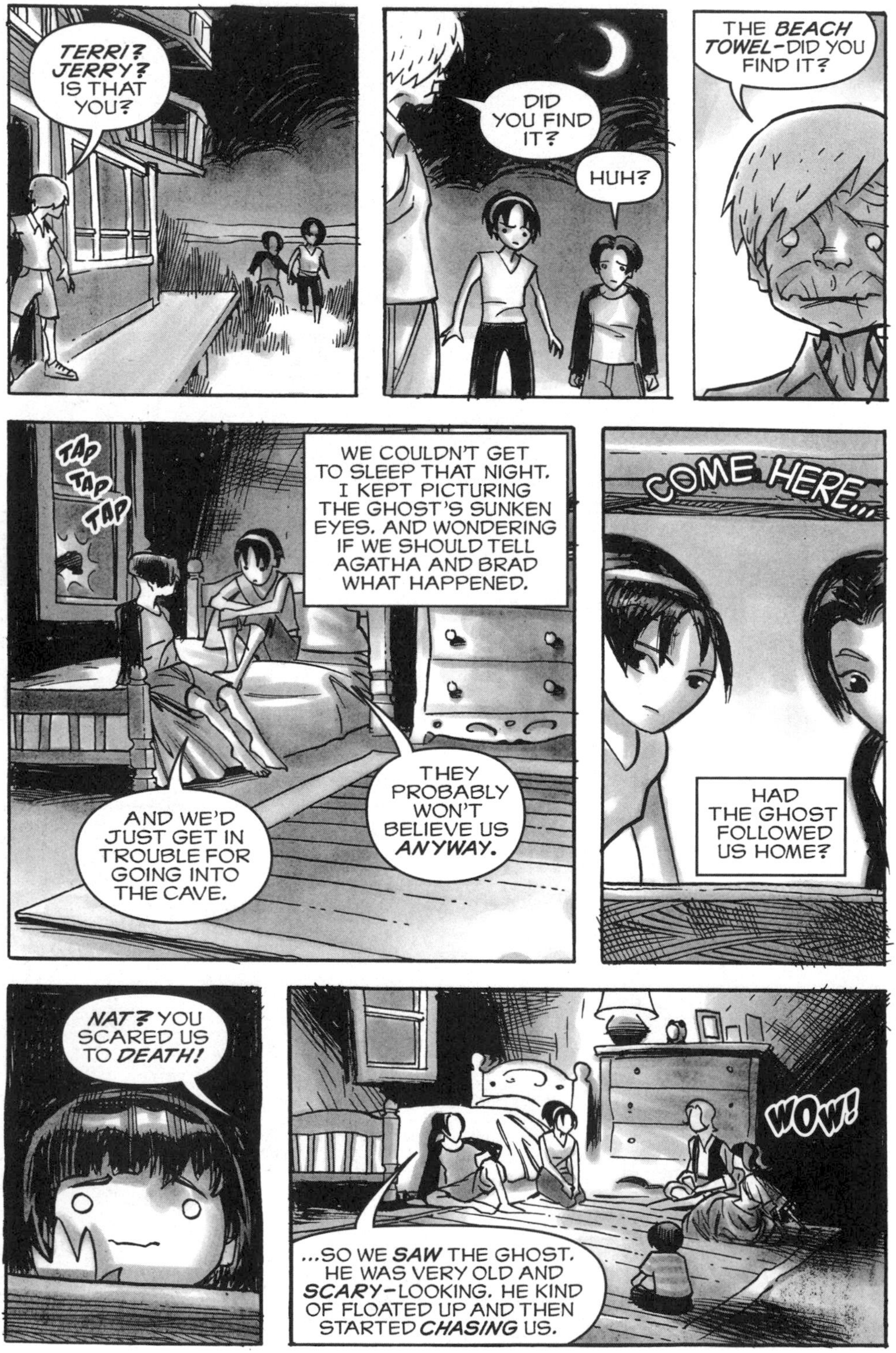
TERRI? JERRY? IS THAT YOU?
DID YOU FIND IT?
HUH?
THE BEACH TOWEL-DID YOU FIND IT?
TAP TAP TAP
WE COULDN'T GET TO SLEEP THAT NIGHT. I KEPT PICTURING THE GHOST'S SUNKEN EYES. AND WONDERING IF WE SHOULD TELL AGATHA AND BRAD WHAT HAPPENED.
THEY PROBABLY WON'T BELIEVE US ANYWAY.
AND WE'D JUST GET IN TROUBLE FOR GOING INTO THE CAVE.
COME HERE...
HAD THE GHOST FOLLOWED US HOME?
NAT? YOU SCARED US TO DEATH!
WOW!
...SO WE SAW THE GHOST. HE WAS VERY OLD AND SCARY-LOOKING. HE KIND OF FLOATED UP AND THEN STARTED CHASING US.

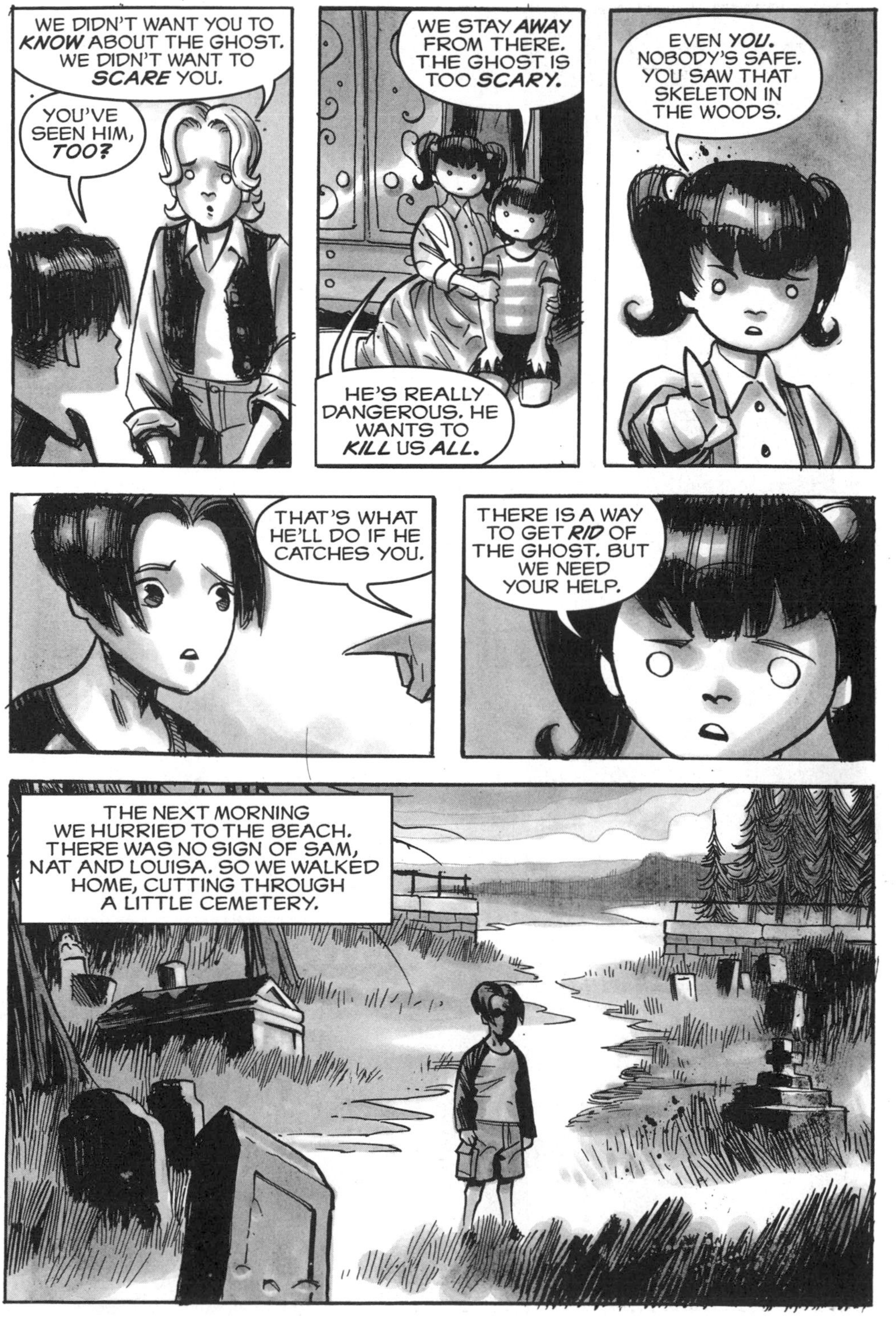
WE DIDN'T WANT YOU TO KNOW ABOUT THE GHOST. WE DIDN'T WANT TO SCARE YOU.
YOU'VE SEEN HIM, TOO?
WE STAY AWAY FROM THERE. THE GHOST IS TOO SCARY.
HE'S REALLY DANGEROUS. HE WANTS TO KILL US ALL.
EVEN YOU. NOBODY'S SAFE. YOU SAW THAT SKELETON IN THE WOODS.
THAT'S WHAT HE'LL DO IF HE CATCHES YOU.
THERE IS A WAY TO GET RID OF THE GHOST. BUT WE NEED YOUR HELP.
THE NEXT MORNING WE HURRIED TO THE BEACH. THERE WAS NO SIGN OF SAM, NAT AND LOUISA. SO WE WALKED HOME, CUTTING THROUGH A LITTLE CEMETERY.

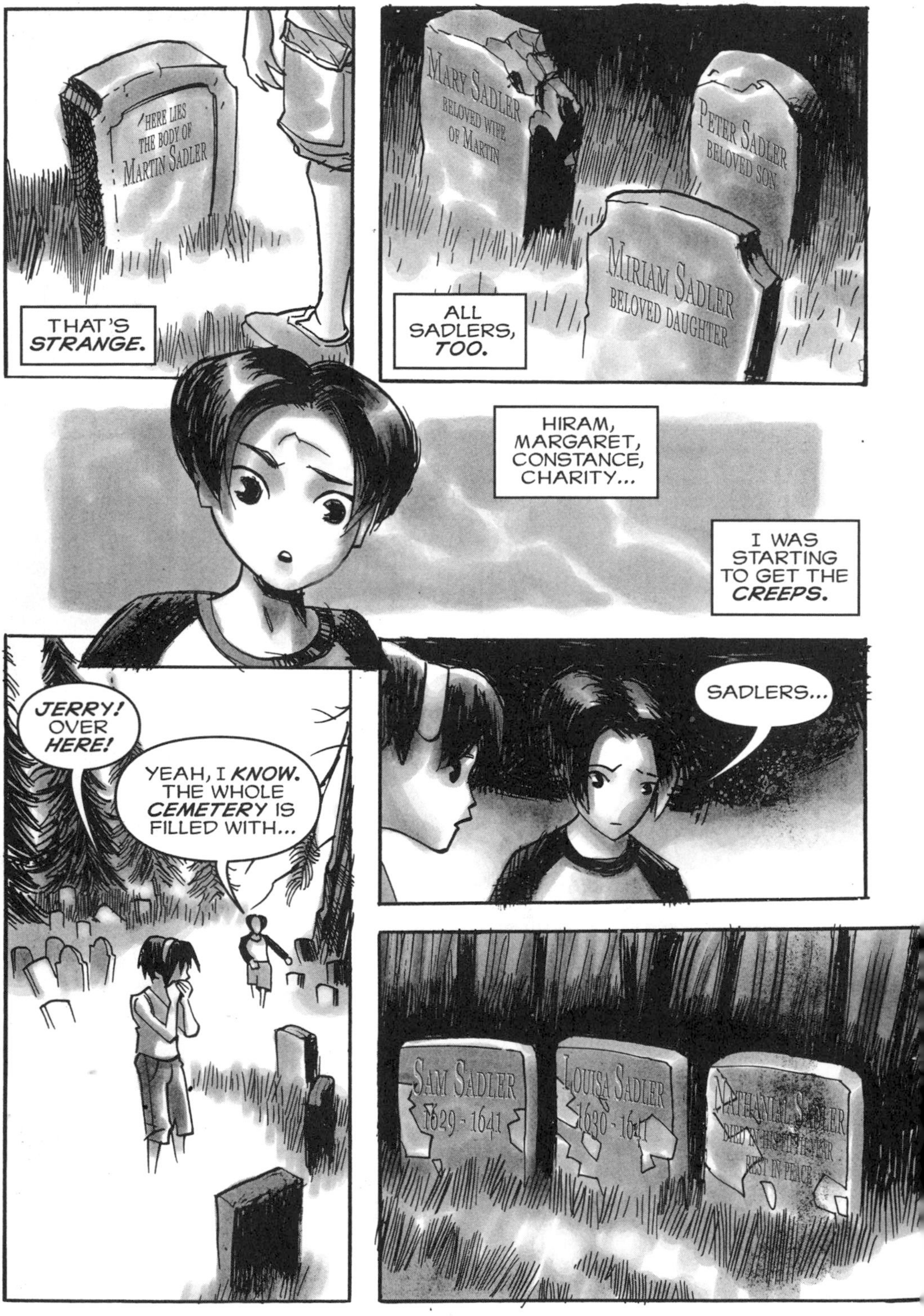
HERE LIES
THE BODY OF
MARTIN SADLER
THAT'S *STRANGE.*
MARY SADLER
BELOVED WIFE
OF MARTIN
PETER SADLER
BELOVED SON
MIRIAM SADLER
BELOVED DAUGHTER
ALL SADLERS, *TOO.*
HIRAM, MARGARET, CONSTANCE, CHARITY...
I WAS STARTING TO GET THE *CREEPS.*
JERRY! OVER *HERE!*
YEAH, I *KNOW.* THE WHOLE *CEMETERY* IS FILLED WITH...
SADLERS...
SAM SADLER
1629 - 1641
LOUISA SADLER
1630 - 1641

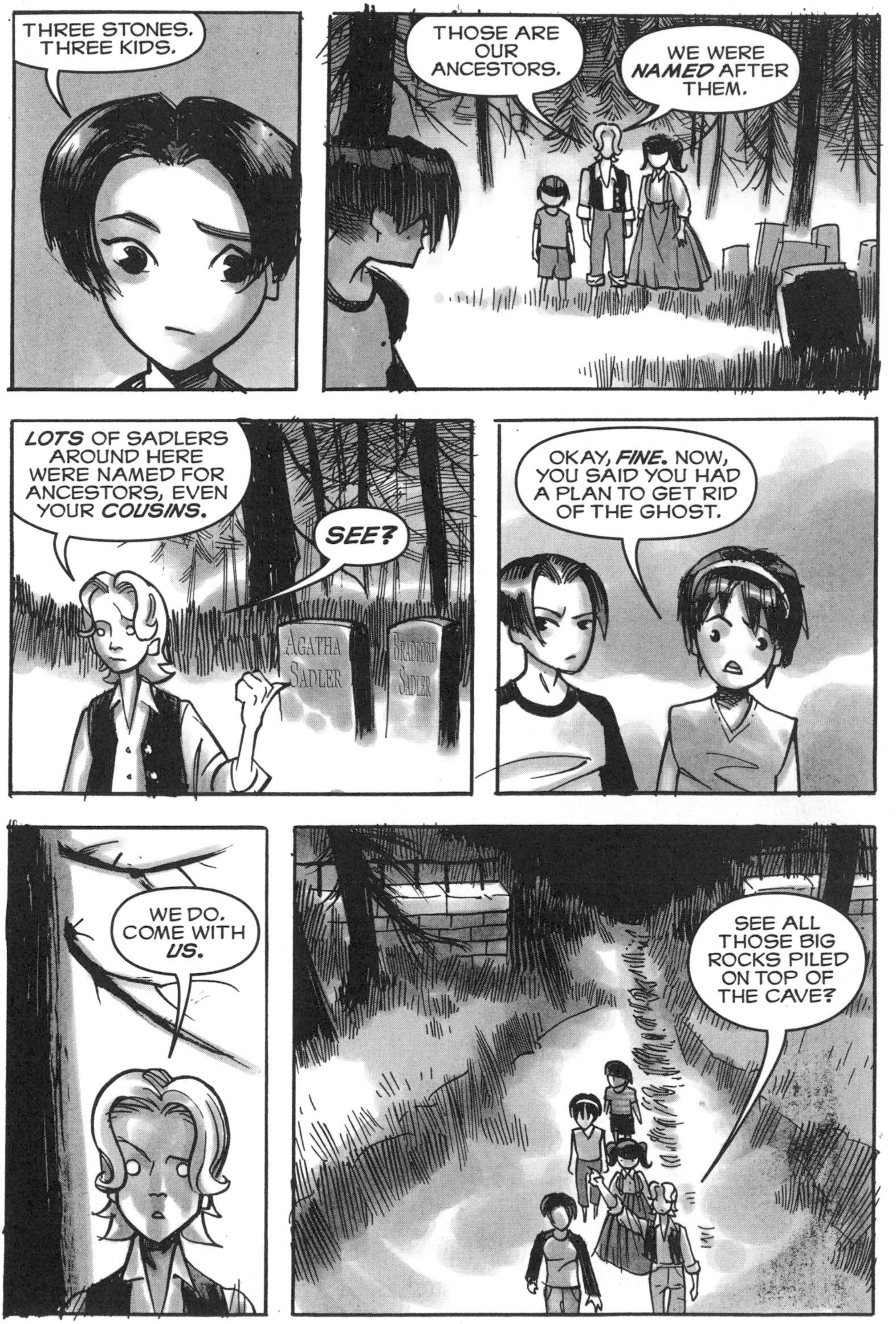
THREE STONES. THREE KIDS.
THOSE ARE OUR ANCESTORS.
WE WERE NAMED AFTER THEM.
LOTS OF SADLERS AROUND HERE WERE NAMED FOR ANCESTORS, EVEN YOUR COUSINS.
SEE?
AGATHA SADLER
BRADFORD SADLER
OKAY, FINE. NOW, YOU SAID YOU HAD A PLAN TO GET RID OF THE GHOST.
WE DO. COME WITH US.
SEE ALL THOSE BIG ROCKS PILED ON TOP OF THE CAVE?

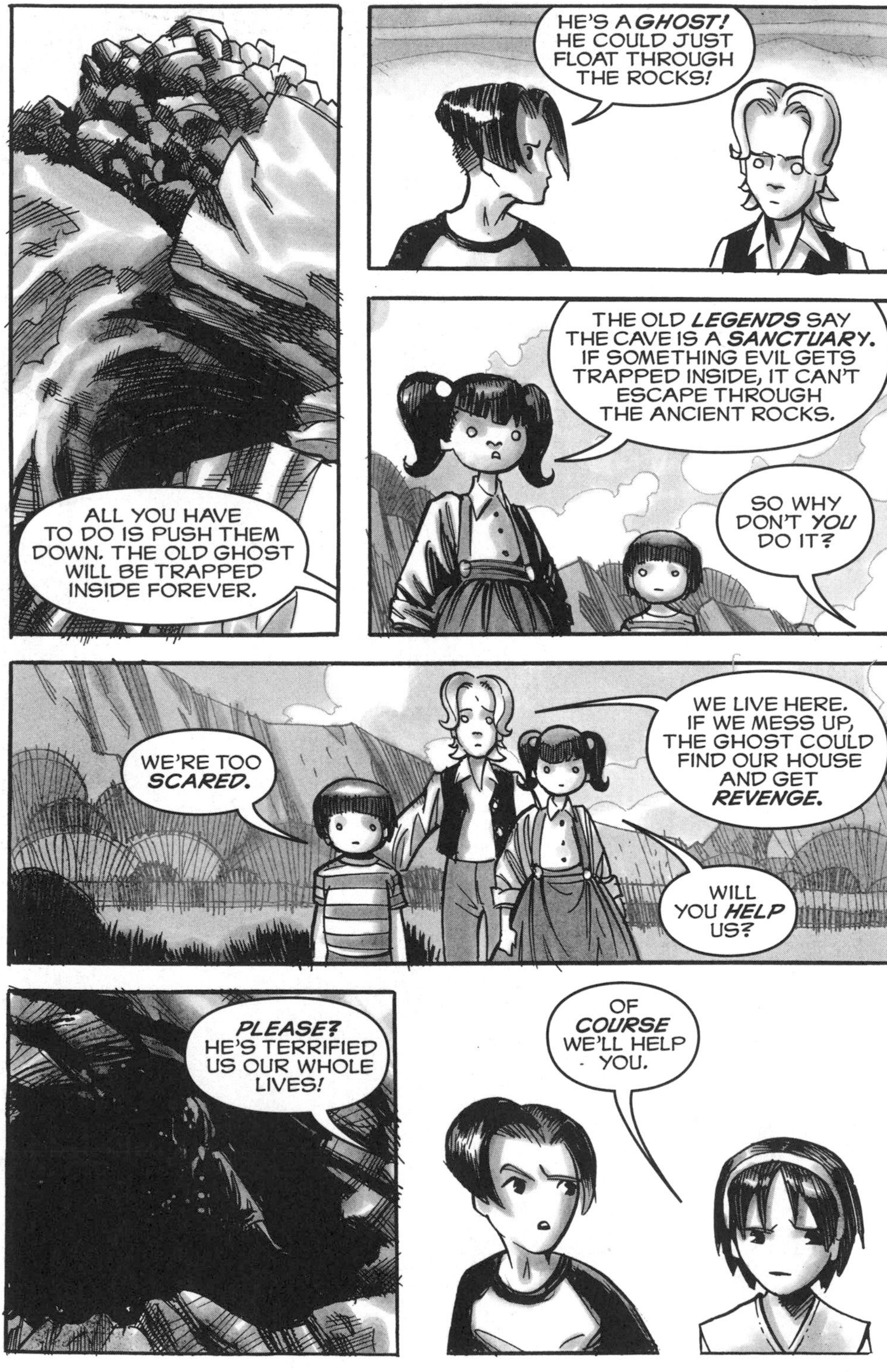
HE'S A GHOST! HE COULD JUST FLOAT THROUGH THE ROCKS!
THE OLD LEGENDS SAY THE CAVE IS A SANCTUARY. IF SOMETHING EVIL GETS TRAPPED INSIDE, IT CAN'T ESCAPE THROUGH THE ANCIENT ROCKS.
ALL YOU HAVE TO DO IS PUSH THEM DOWN. THE OLD GHOST WILL BE TRAPPED INSIDE FOREVER.
SO WHY DON'T YOU DO IT?
WE'RE TOO SCARED.
WE LIVE HERE. IF WE MESS UP, THE GHOST COULD FIND OUR HOUSE AND GET REVENGE.
WILL YOU HELP US?
PLEASE? HE'S TERRIFIED US OUR WHOLE LIVES!
OF COURSE WE'LL HELP YOU.

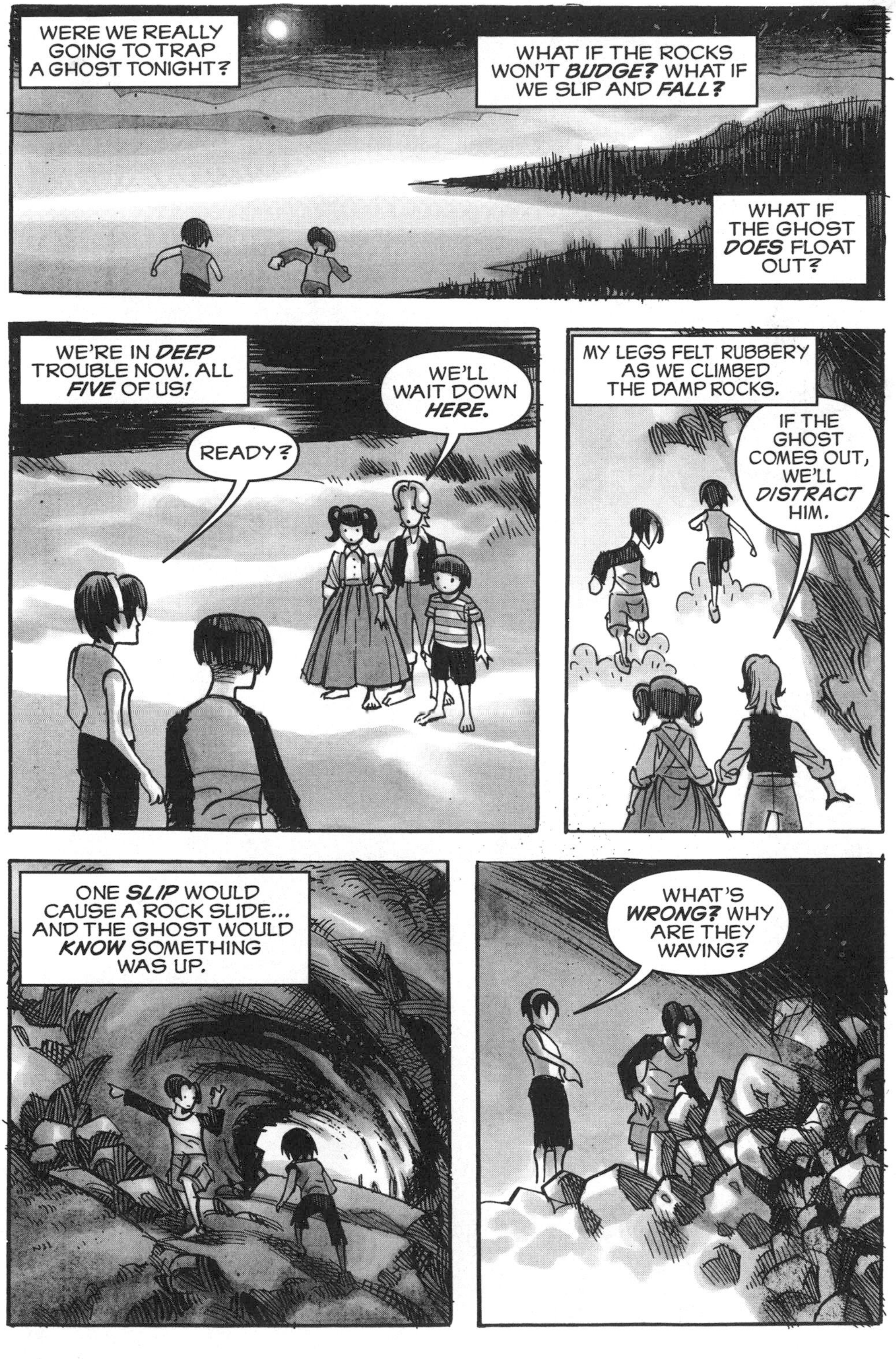
WERE WE REALLY GOING TO TRAP A GHOST TONIGHT?
WHAT IF THE ROCKS WON'T BUDGE? WHAT IF WE SLIP AND FALL?
WHAT IF THE GHOST DOES FLOAT OUT?
WE'RE IN DEEP TROUBLE NOW. ALL FIVE OF US!
WE'LL WAIT DOWN HERE.
READY?
MY LEGS FELT RUBBERY AS WE CLIMBED THE DAMP ROCKS.
IF THE GHOST COMES OUT, WE'LL DISTRACT HIM.
ONE SLIP WOULD CAUSE A ROCK SLIDE... AND THE GHOST WOULD KNOW SOMETHING WAS UP.
WHAT'S WRONG? WHY ARE THEY WAVING?

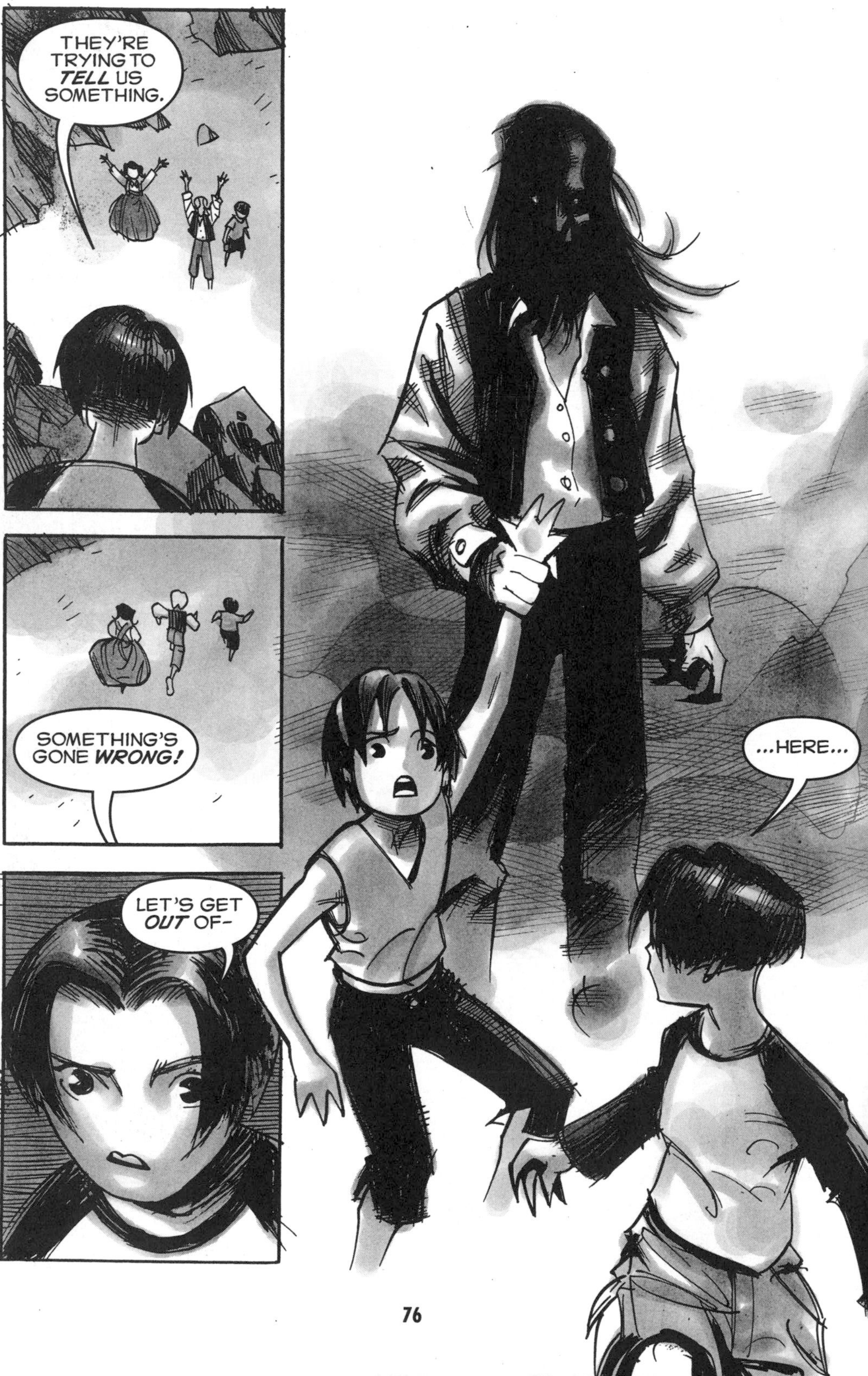
THEY'RE TRYING TO *TELL* US SOMETHING.
SOMETHING'S GONE *WRONG!*
LET'S GET *OUT* OF-
...HERE...

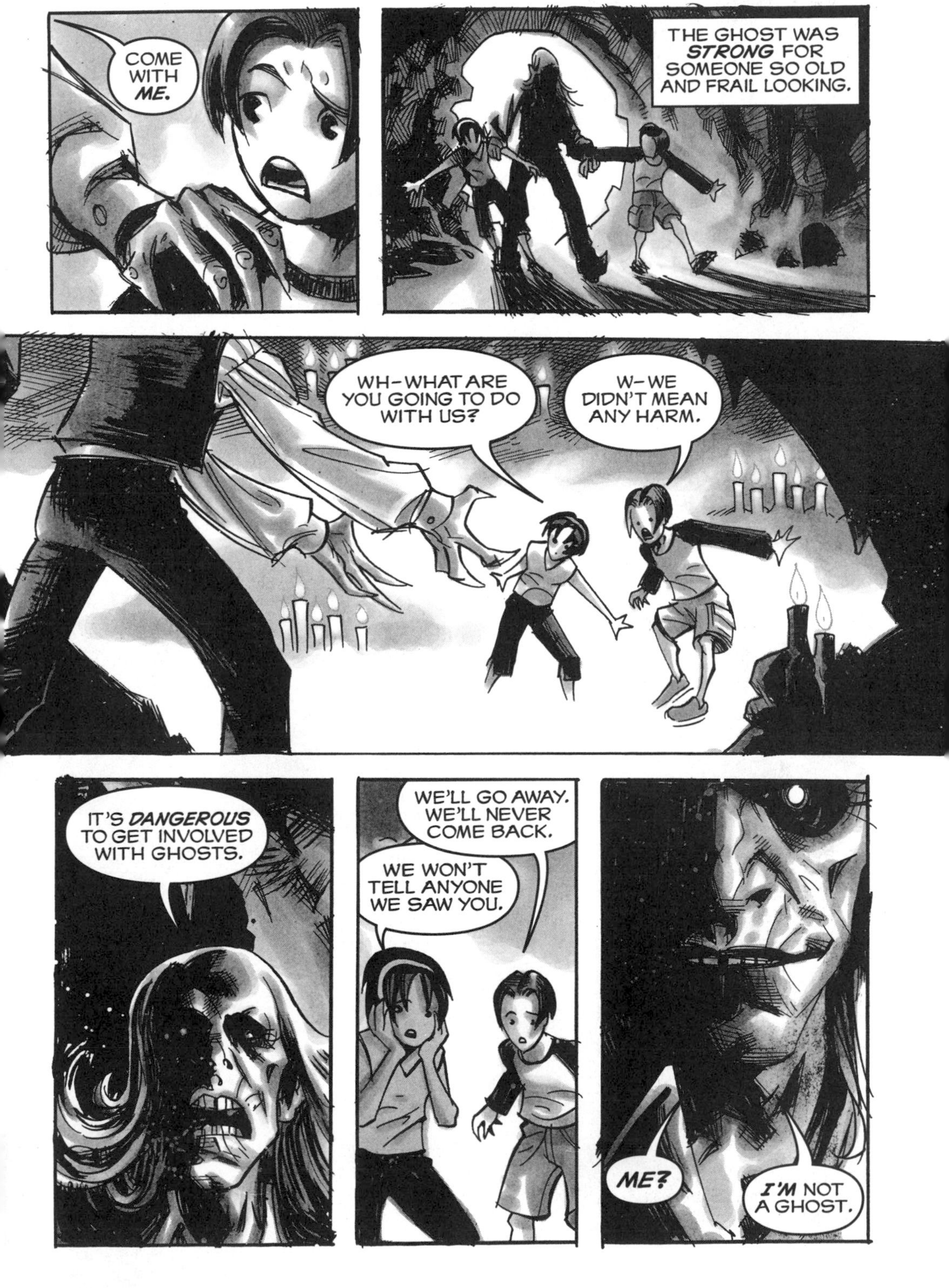
COME WITH ME.
THE GHOST WAS STRONG FOR SOMEONE SO OLD AND FRAIL LOOKING.
WH-WHAT ARE YOU GOING TO DO WITH US?
W-WE DIDN'T MEAN ANY HARM.
IT'S DANGEROUS TO GET INVOLVED WITH GHOSTS.
WE'LL GO AWAY. WE'LL NEVER COME BACK.
WE WON'T TELL ANYONE WE SAW YOU.
ME?
I'M NOT A GHOST.

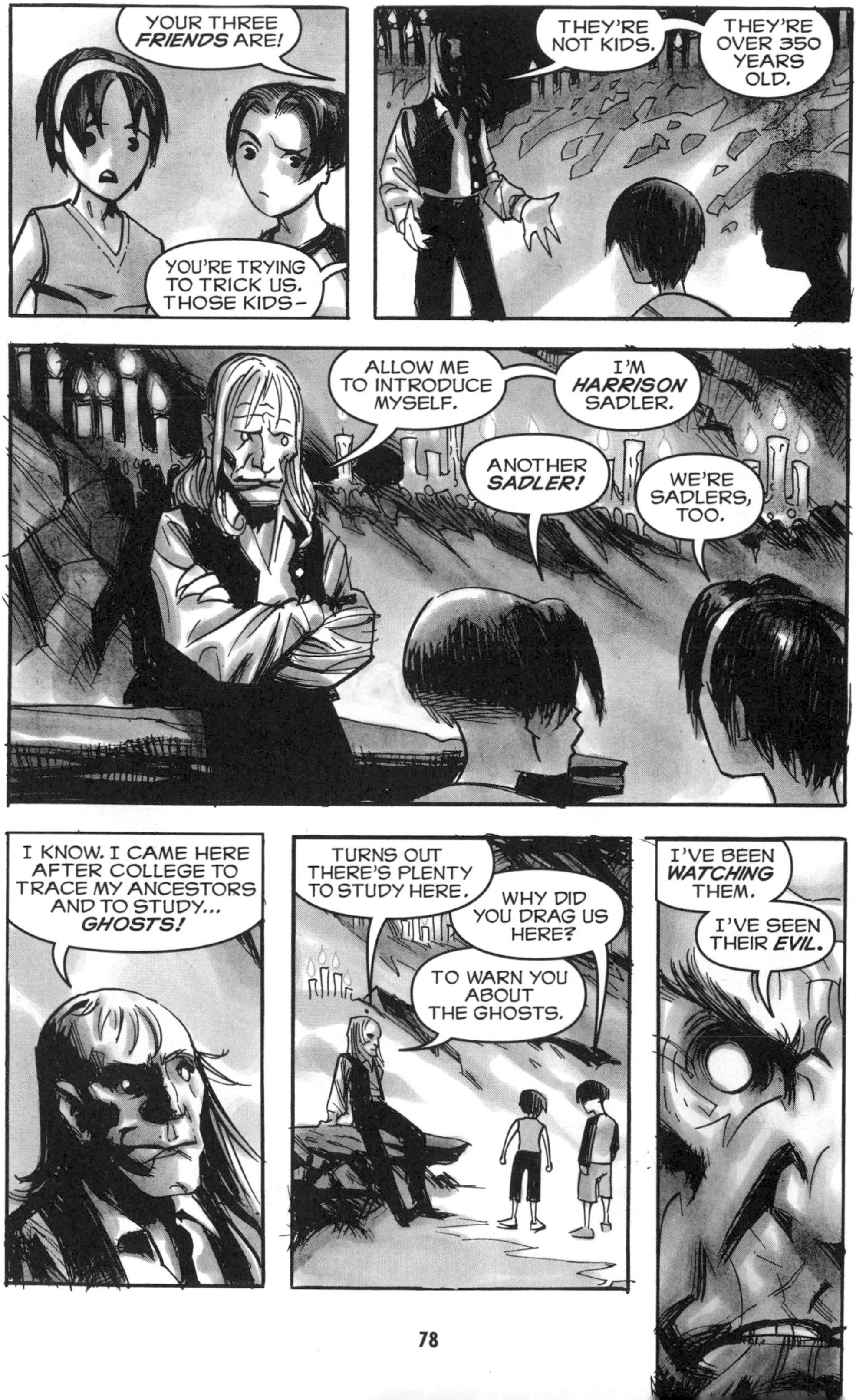
YOUR THREE FRIENDS ARE!
YOU'RE TRYING TO TRICK US. THOSE KIDS–
THEY'RE NOT KIDS.
THEY'RE OVER 350 YEARS OLD.
ALLOW ME TO INTRODUCE MYSELF.
I'M HARRISON SADLER.
ANOTHER SADLER!
WE'RE SADLERS, TOO.
I KNOW. I CAME HERE AFTER COLLEGE TO TRACE MY ANCESTORS AND TO STUDY... GHOSTS!
TURNS OUT THERE'S PLENTY TO STUDY HERE.
WHY DID YOU DRAG US HERE?
TO WARN YOU ABOUT THE GHOSTS.
I'VE BEEN WATCHING THEM.
I'VE SEEN THEIR EVIL.

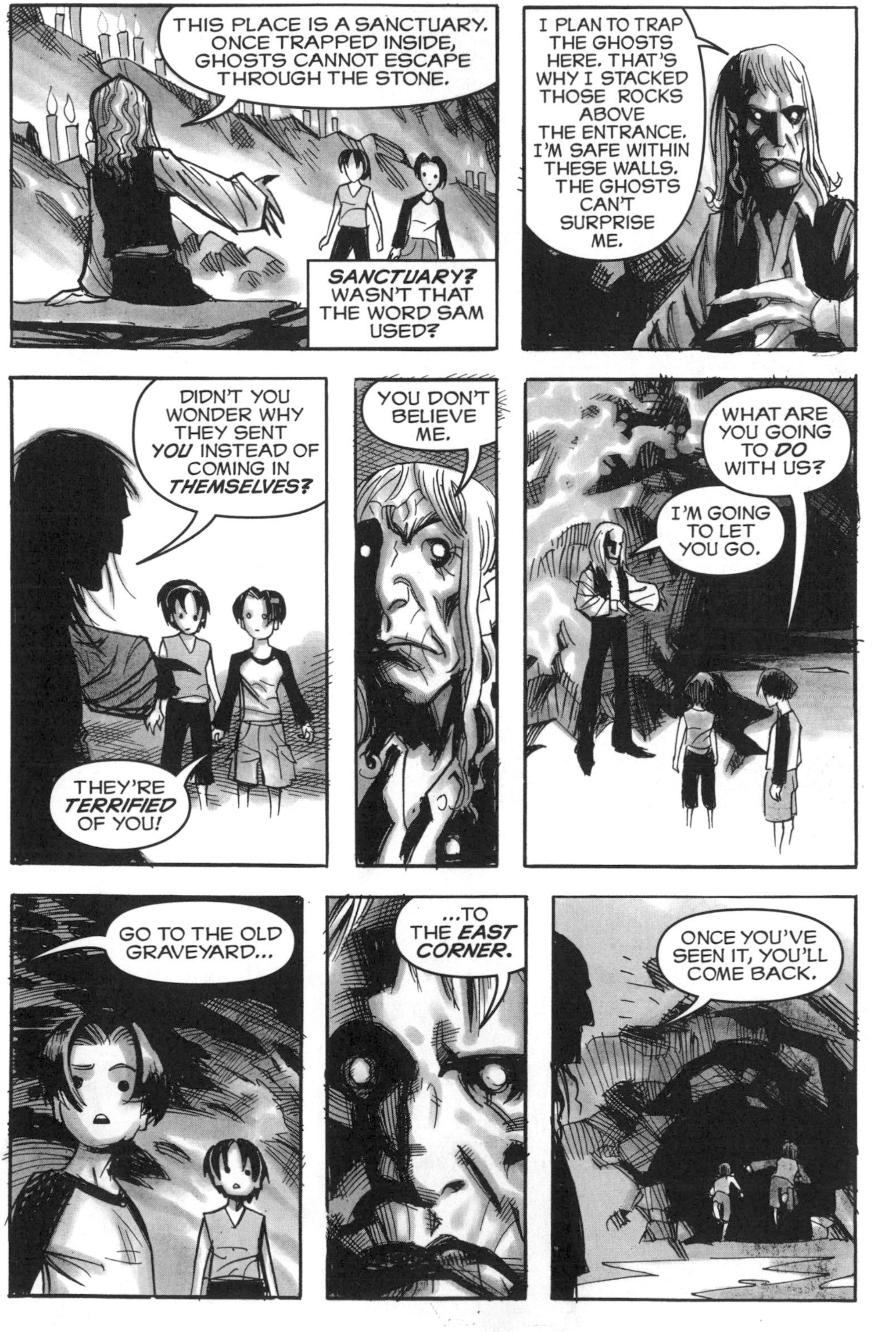
THIS PLACE IS A SANCTUARY. ONCE TRAPPED INSIDE, GHOSTS CANNOT ESCAPE THROUGH THE STONE.
SANCTUARY? WASN'T THAT THE WORD SAM USED?
I PLAN TO TRAP THE GHOSTS HERE. THAT'S WHY I STACKED THOSE ROCKS ABOVE THE ENTRANCE. I'M SAFE WITHIN THESE WALLS. THE GHOSTS CAN'T SURPRISE ME.
DIDN'T YOU WONDER WHY THEY SENT YOU INSTEAD OF COMING IN THEMSELVES?
THEY'RE TERRIFIED OF YOU!
YOU DON'T BELIEVE ME.
WHAT ARE YOU GOING TO DO WITH US?
I'M GOING TO LET YOU GO.
GO TO THE OLD GRAVEYARD...
...TO THE EAST CORNER.
ONCE YOU'VE SEEN IT, YOU'LL COME BACK.

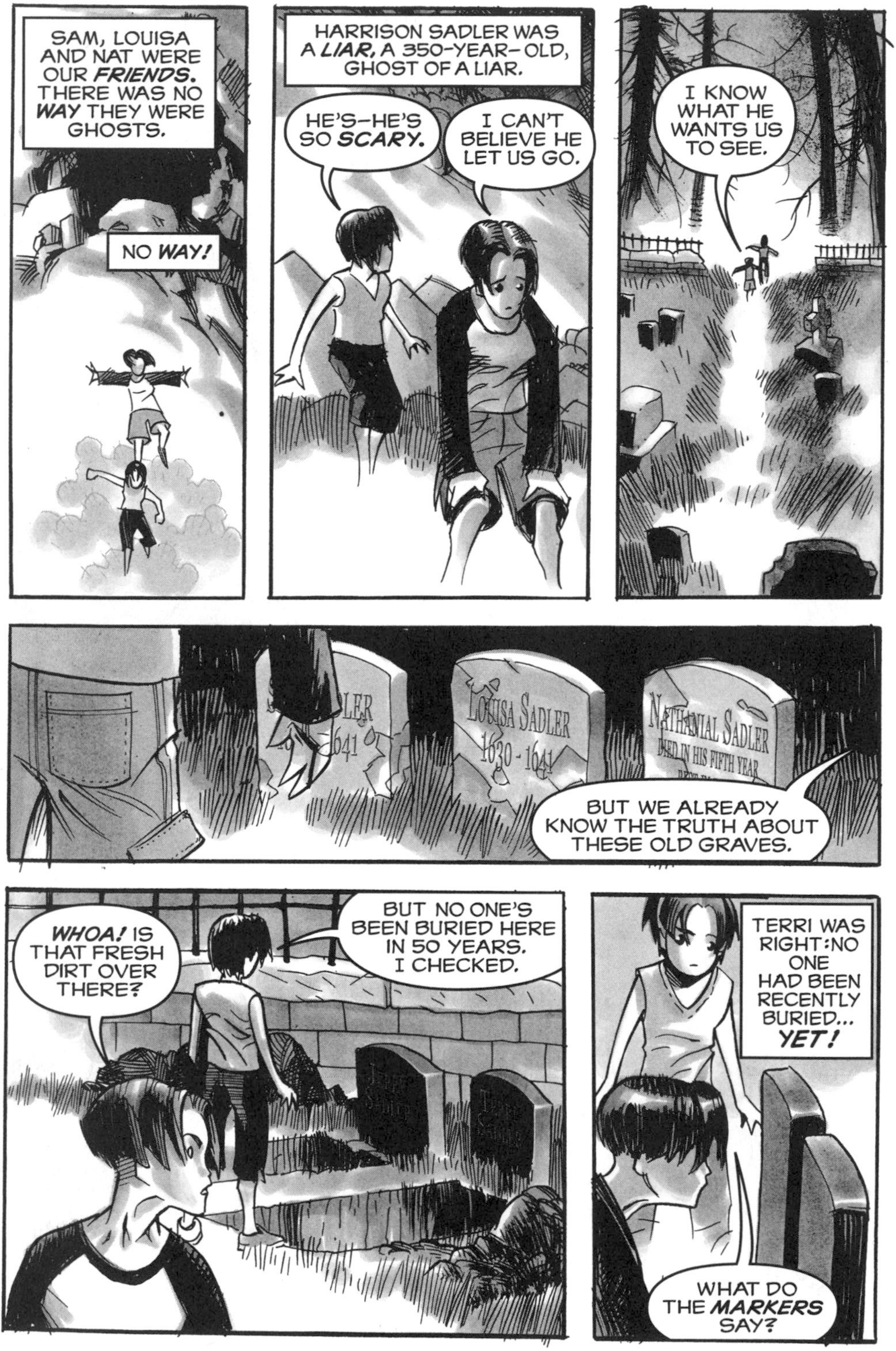
SAM, LOUISA AND NAT WERE OUR FRIENDS. THERE WAS NO WAY THEY WERE GHOSTS.
NO WAY!
HARRISON SADLER WAS A LIAR, A 350-YEAR-OLD, GHOST OF A LIAR.
HE'S—HE'S SO SCARY.
I CAN'T BELIEVE HE LET US GO.
I KNOW WHAT HE WANTS US TO SEE.
LOUISA SADLER
1630 - 1641
NATHANIAL SADLER
DIED IN HIS FIFTH YEAR
BUT WE ALREADY KNOW THE TRUTH ABOUT THESE OLD GRAVES.
WHOA! IS THAT FRESH DIRT OVER THERE?
BUT NO ONE'S BEEN BURIED HERE IN 50 YEARS. I CHECKED.
TERRI WAS RIGHT: NO ONE HAD BEEN RECENTLY BURIED... YET!
WHAT DO THE MARKERS SAY?

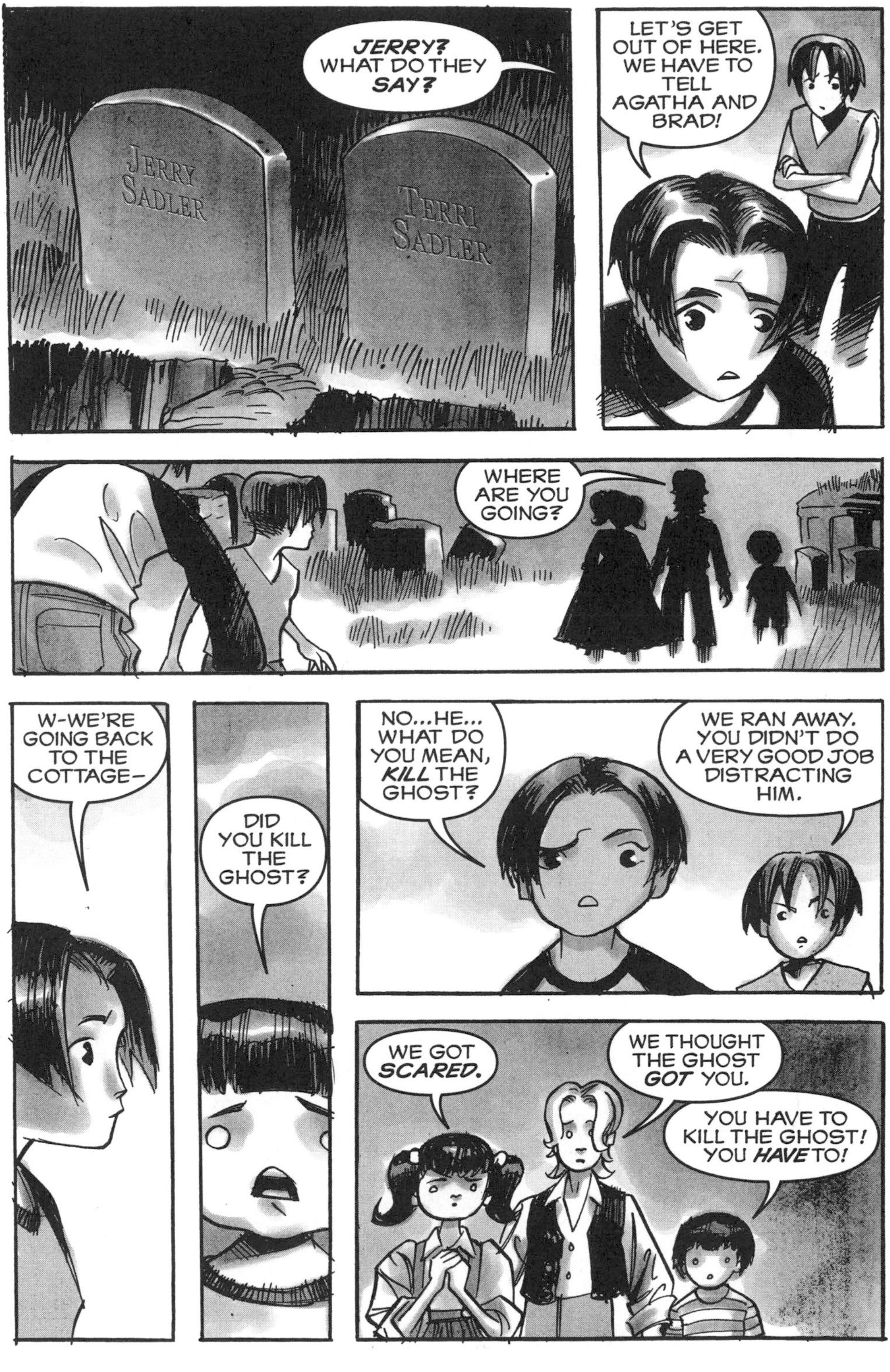
JERRY? WHAT DO THEY SAY?
JERRY SADLER
TERRI SADLER
LET'S GET OUT OF HERE. WE HAVE TO TELL AGATHA AND BRAD!
WHERE ARE YOU GOING?
W-WE'RE GOING BACK TO THE COTTAGE-
DID YOU KILL THE GHOST?
NO...HE... WHAT DO YOU MEAN, KILL THE GHOST?
WE RAN AWAY. YOU DIDN'T DO A VERY GOOD JOB DISTRACTING HIM.
WE GOT SCARED.
WE THOUGHT THE GHOST GOT YOU.
YOU HAVE TO KILL THE GHOST! YOU HAVE TO!

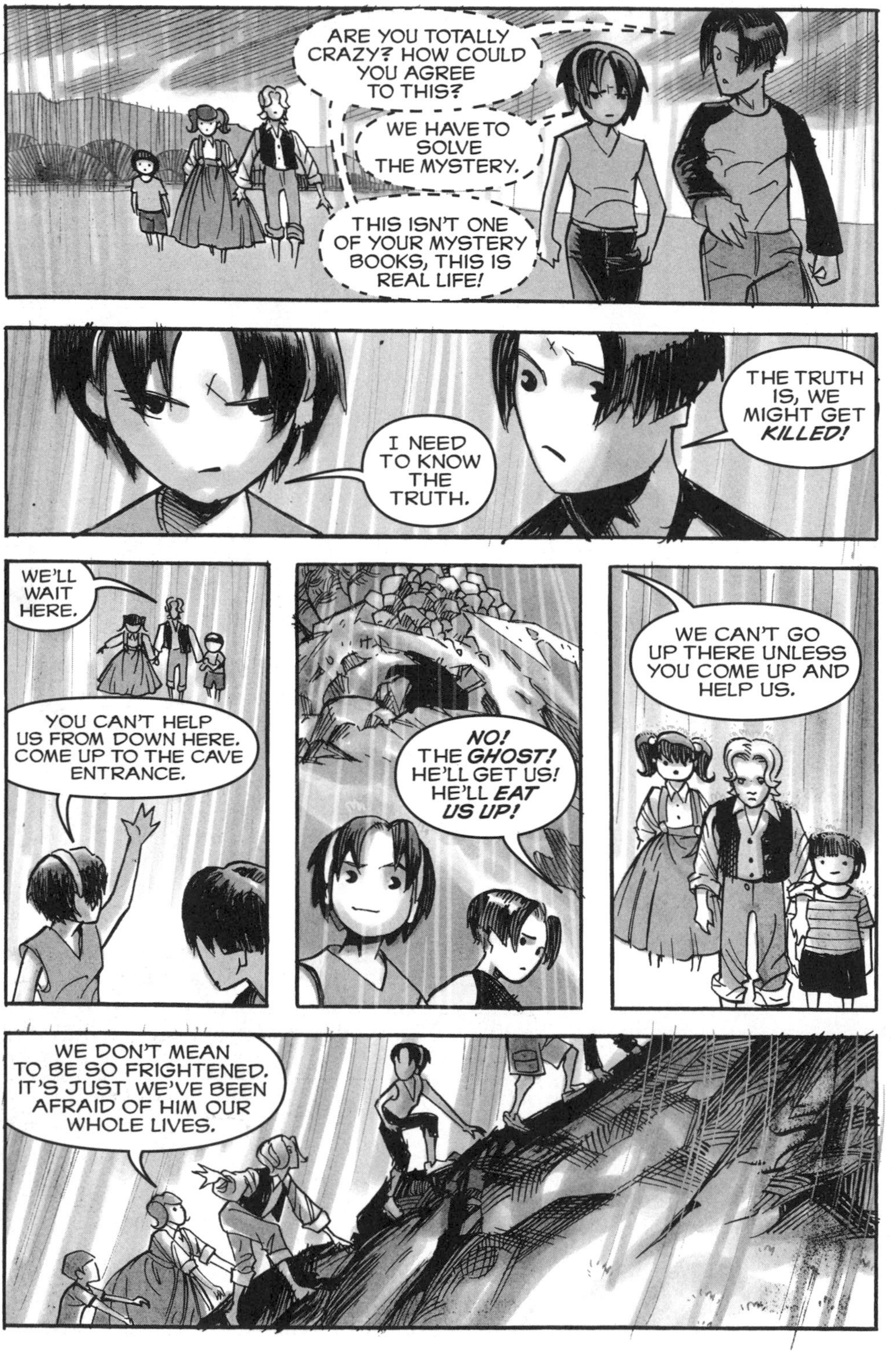
ARE YOU TOTALLY CRAZY? HOW COULD YOU AGREE TO THIS?
WE HAVE TO SOLVE THE MYSTERY.
THIS ISN'T ONE OF YOUR MYSTERY BOOKS, THIS IS REAL LIFE!
I NEED TO KNOW THE TRUTH.
THE TRUTH IS, WE MIGHT GET KILLED!
WE'LL WAIT HERE.
YOU CAN'T HELP US FROM DOWN HERE. COME UP TO THE CAVE ENTRANCE.
NO! THE GHOST! HE'LL GET US! HE'LL EAT US UP!
WE CAN'T GO UP THERE UNLESS YOU COME UP AND HELP US.
WE DON'T MEAN TO BE SO FRIGHTENED. IT'S JUST WE'VE BEEN AFRAID OF HIM OUR WHOLE LIVES.

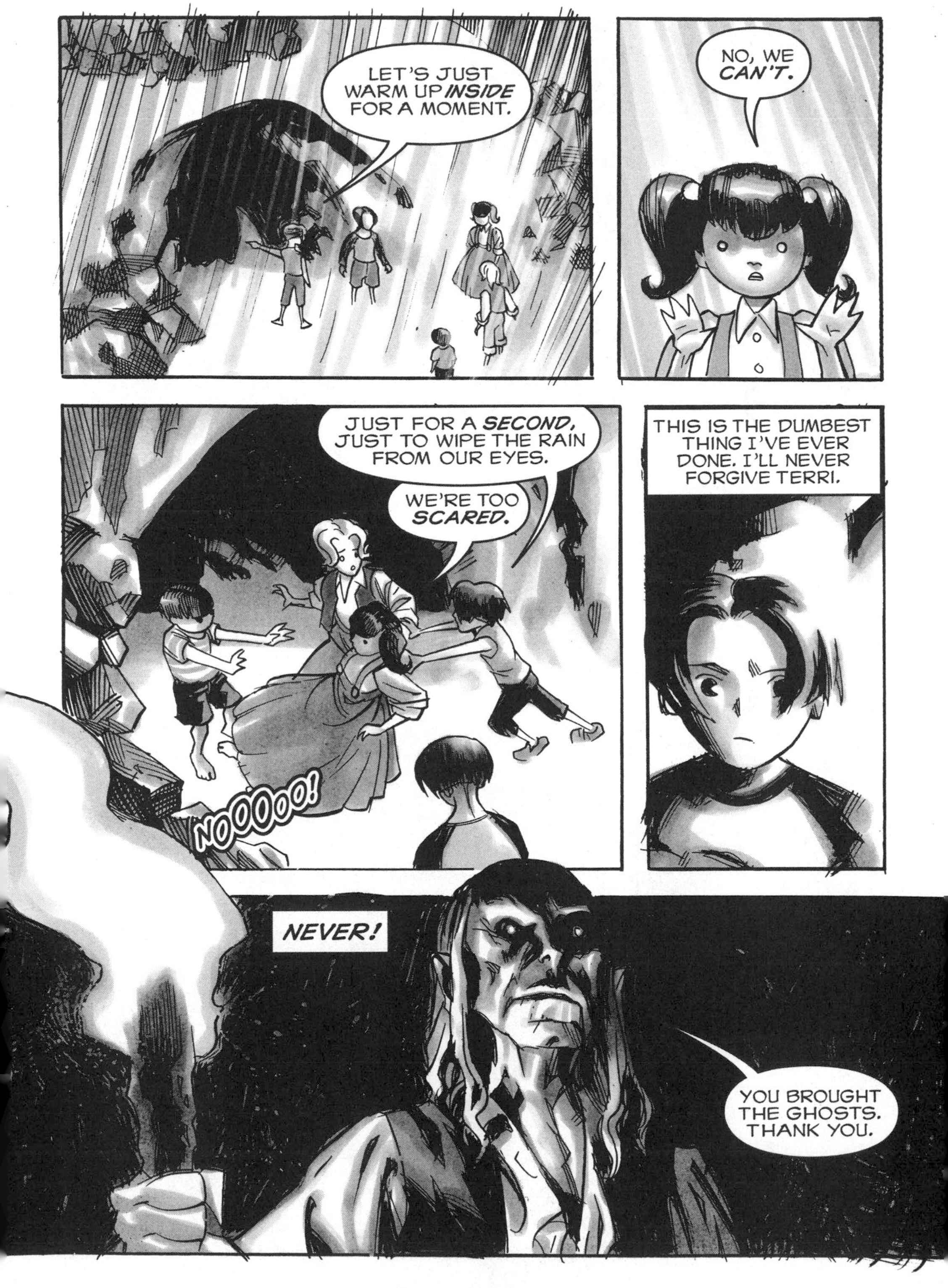
LET'S JUST WARM UP INSIDE FOR A MOMENT.
NO, WE CAN'T.
JUST FOR A SECOND, JUST TO WIPE THE RAIN FROM OUR EYES.
WE'RE TOO SCARED.
NOOOoo!
THIS IS THE DUMBEST THING I'VE EVER DONE. I'LL NEVER FORGIVE TERRI.
NEVER!
YOU BROUGHT THE GHOSTS. THANK YOU.

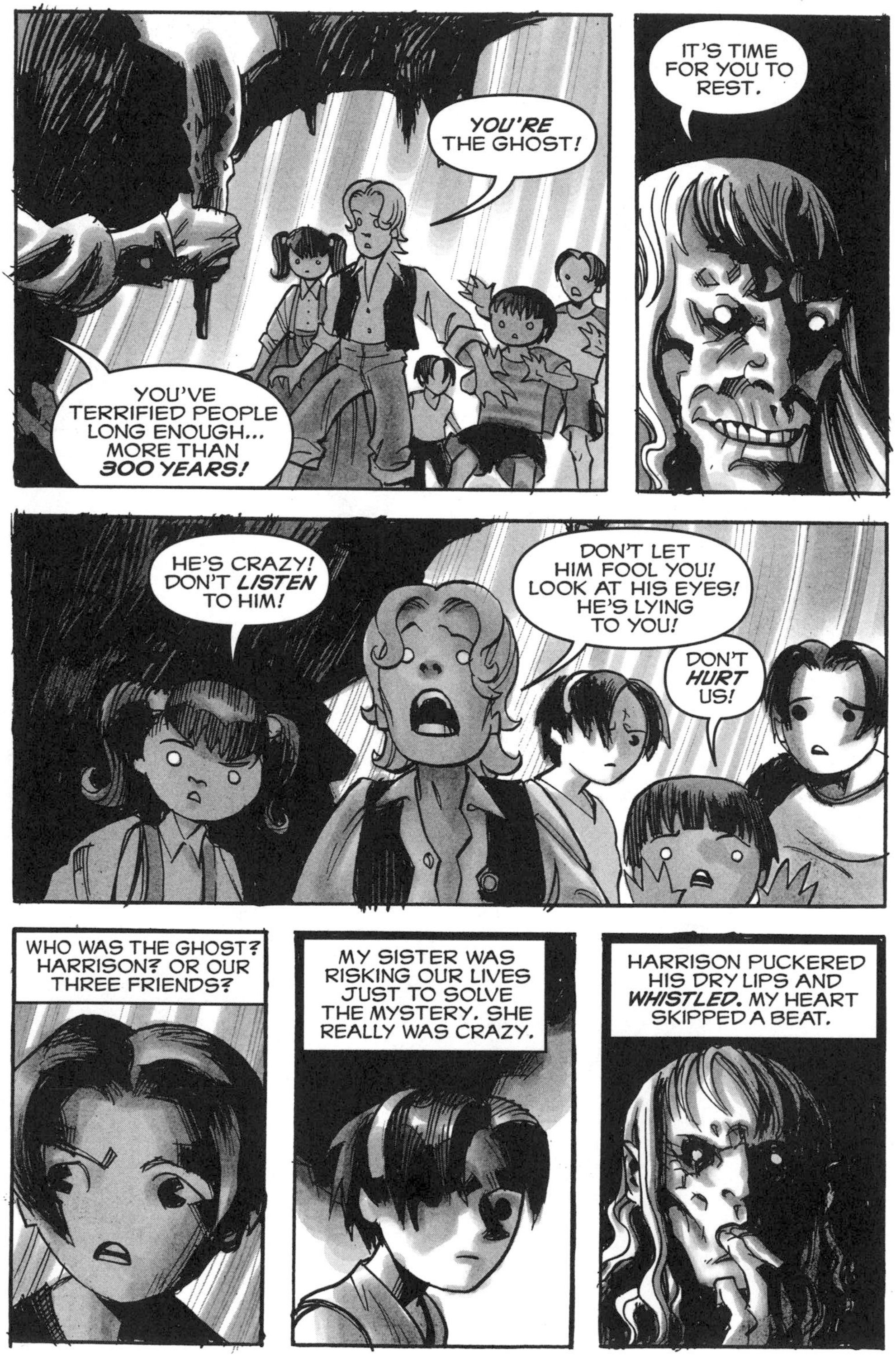
YOU'RE THE GHOST!
YOU'VE TERRIFIED PEOPLE LONG ENOUGH... MORE THAN 300 YEARS!
IT'S TIME FOR YOU TO REST.
HE'S CRAZY! DON'T LISTEN TO HIM!
DON'T LET HIM FOOL YOU! LOOK AT HIS EYES! HE'S LYING TO YOU!
DON'T HURT US!
WHO WAS THE GHOST? HARRISON? OR OUR THREE FRIENDS?
MY SISTER WAS RISKING OUR LIVES JUST TO SOLVE THE MYSTERY. SHE REALLY WAS CRAZY.
HARRISON PUCKERED HIS DRY LIPS AND WHISTLED. MY HEART SKIPPED A BEAT.

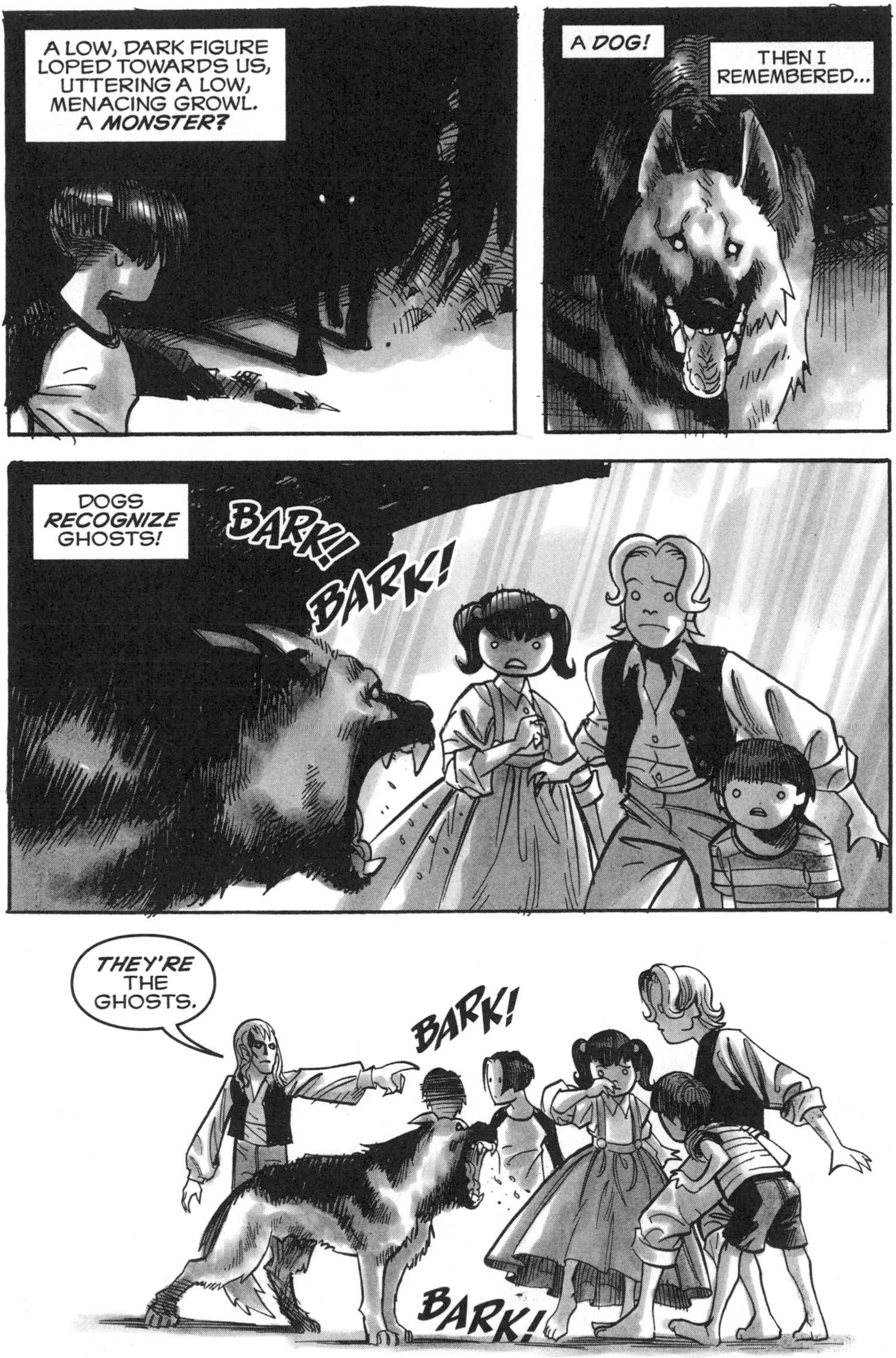
A LOW, DARK FIGURE LOPED TOWARDS US, UTTERING A LOW, MENACING GROWL. A MONSTER?
A DOG!
THEN I REMEMBERED...
DOGS RECOGNIZE GHOSTS!
BARK!
BARK!
THEY'RE THE GHOSTS.
BARK!
BARK!

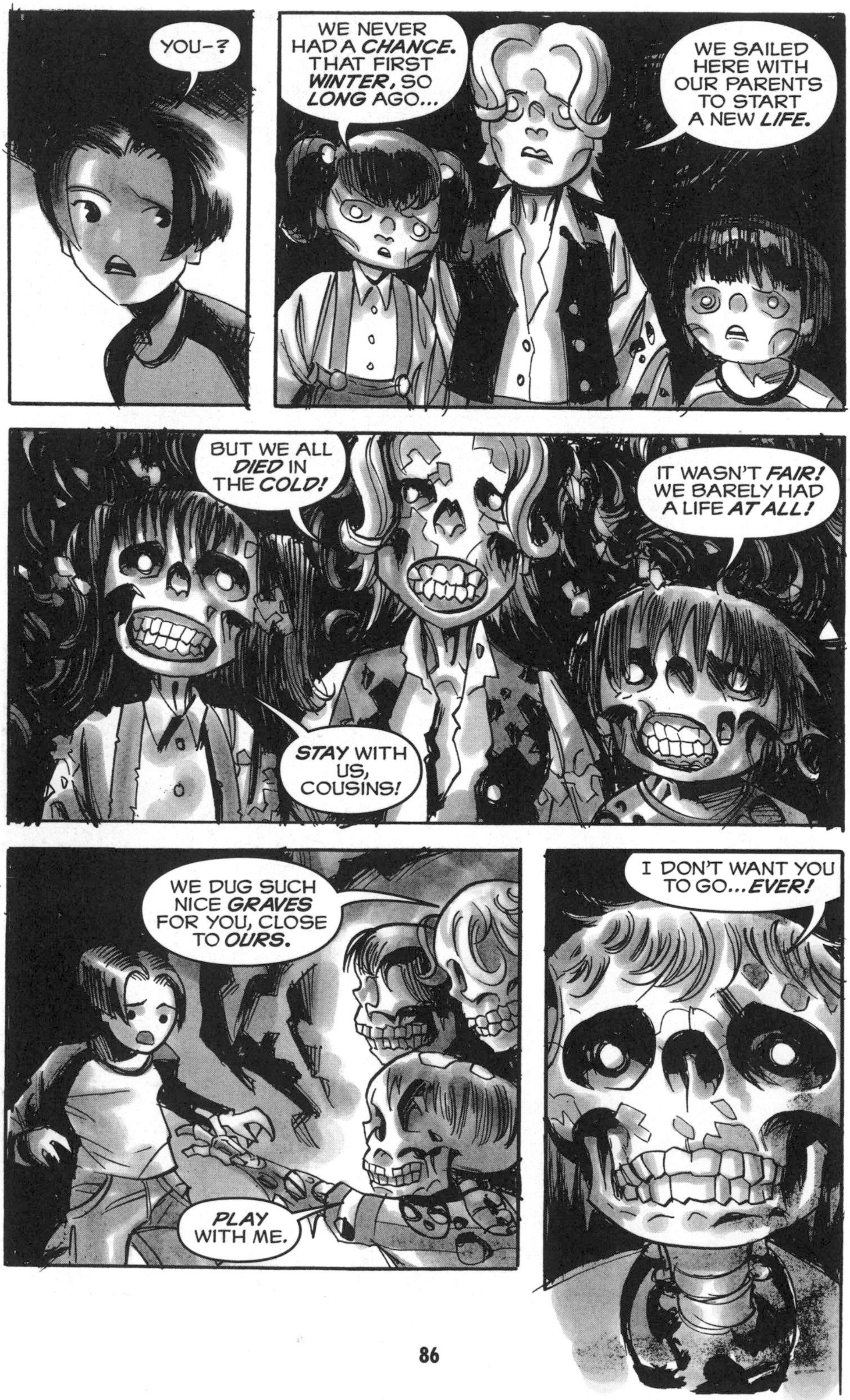
YOU-?
WE NEVER HAD A CHANCE. THAT FIRST WINTER, SO LONG AGO...
WE SAILED HERE WITH OUR PARENTS TO START A NEW LIFE.
BUT WE ALL DIED IN THE COLD!
IT WASN'T FAIR! WE BARELY HAD A LIFE AT ALL!
STAY WITH US, COUSINS!
WE DUG SUCH NICE GRAVES FOR YOU, CLOSE TO OURS.
PLAY WITH ME.
I DON'T WANT YOU TO GO...EVER!

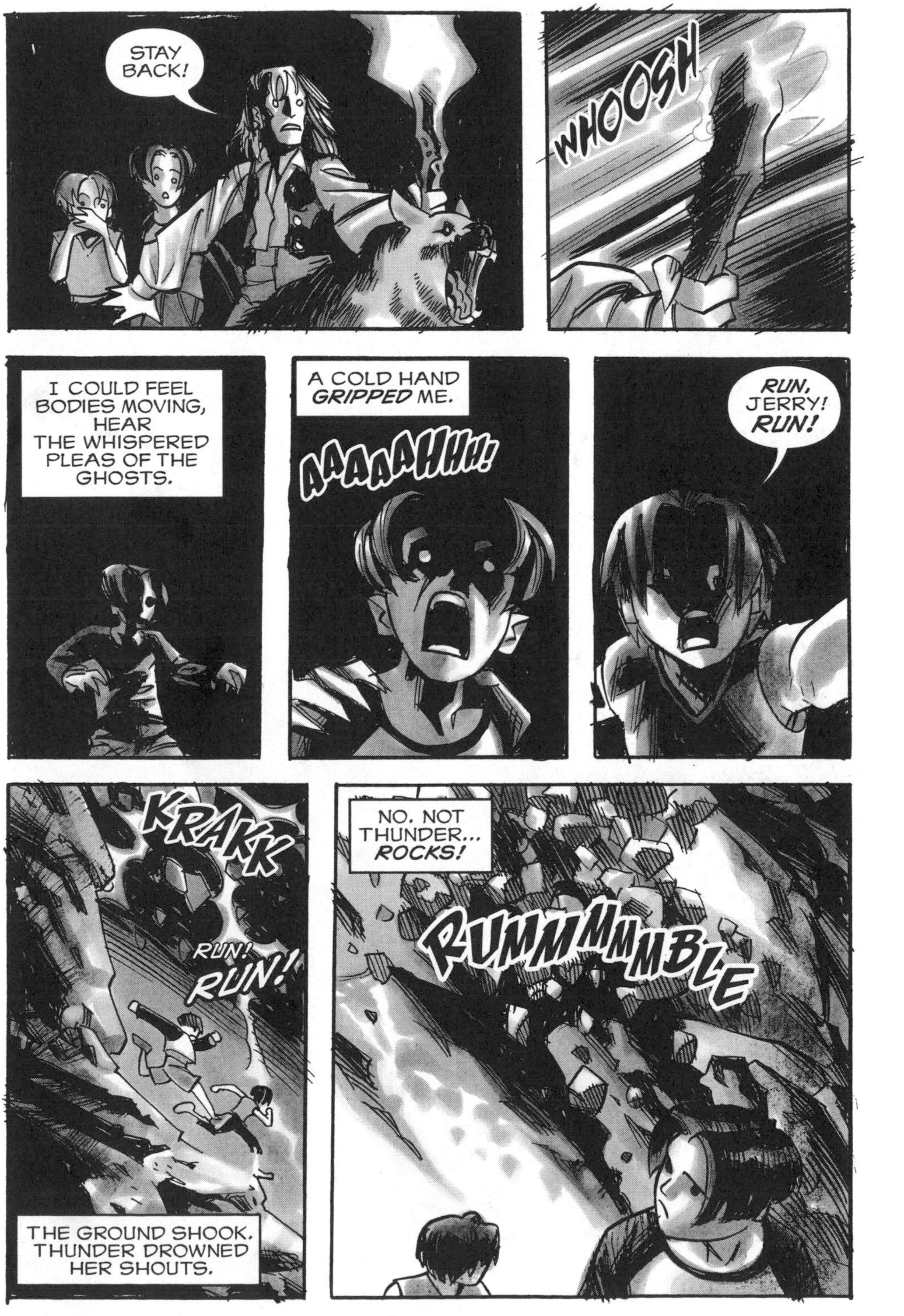
STAY BACK!
WHOOSH
I COULD FEEL BODIES MOVING, HEAR THE WHISPERED PLEAS OF THE GHOSTS.
A COLD HAND GRIPPED ME.
AAAAAHHH!
RUN, JERRY! RUN!
KRAKK
RUN! RUN!
THE GROUND SHOOK. THUNDER DROWNED HER SHOUTS.
NO. NOT THUNDER... ROCKS!
RUMMMMMMBLE

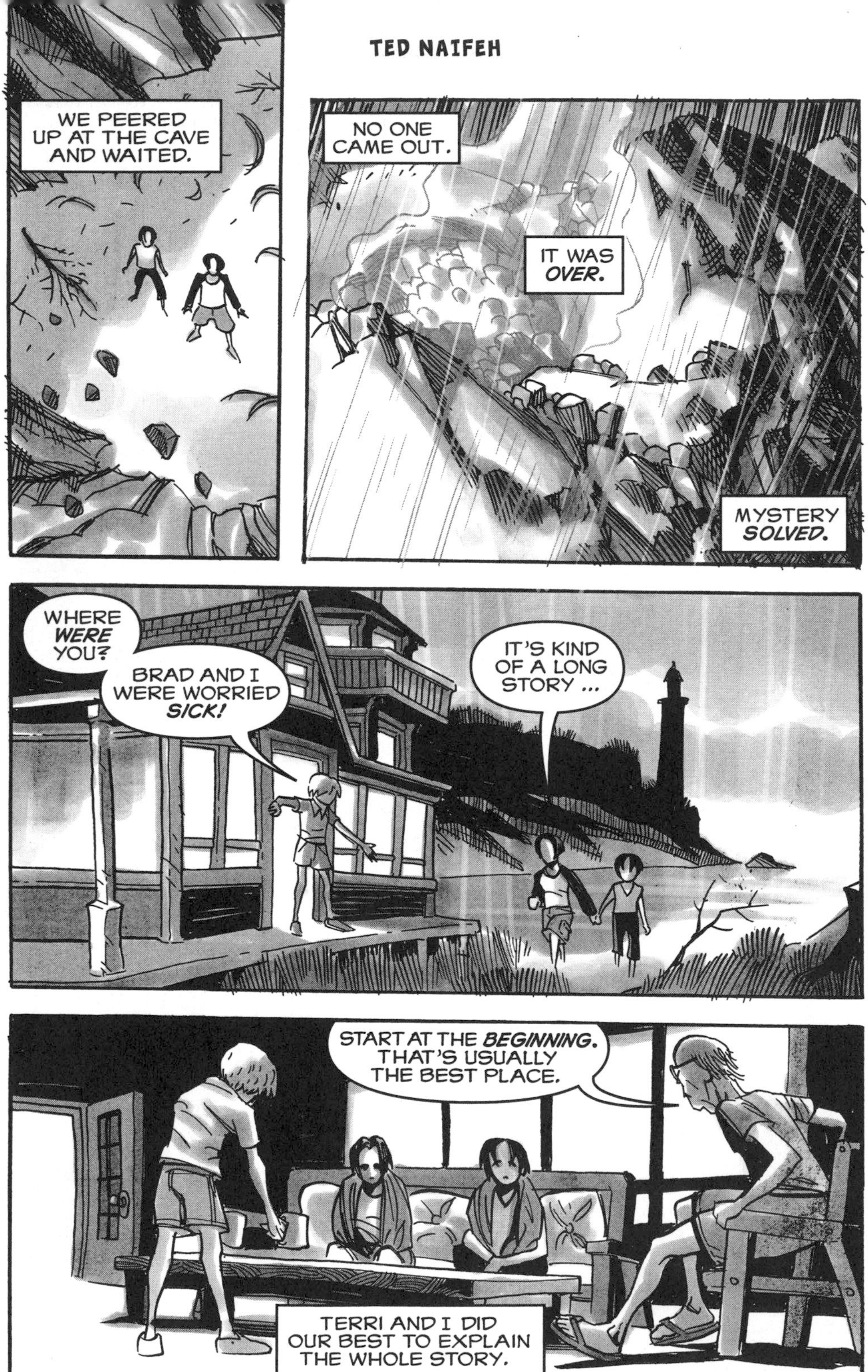
WE PEERED UP AT THE CAVE AND WAITED.
NO ONE CAME OUT.
IT WAS *OVER*.
MYSTERY *SOLVED*.
WHERE *WERE* YOU?
BRAD AND I WERE WORRIED *SICK!*
IT'S KIND OF A LONG STORY ...
START AT THE *BEGINNING*. THAT'S USUALLY THE BEST PLACE.
TERRI AND I DID OUR BEST TO EXPLAIN THE WHOLE STORY.

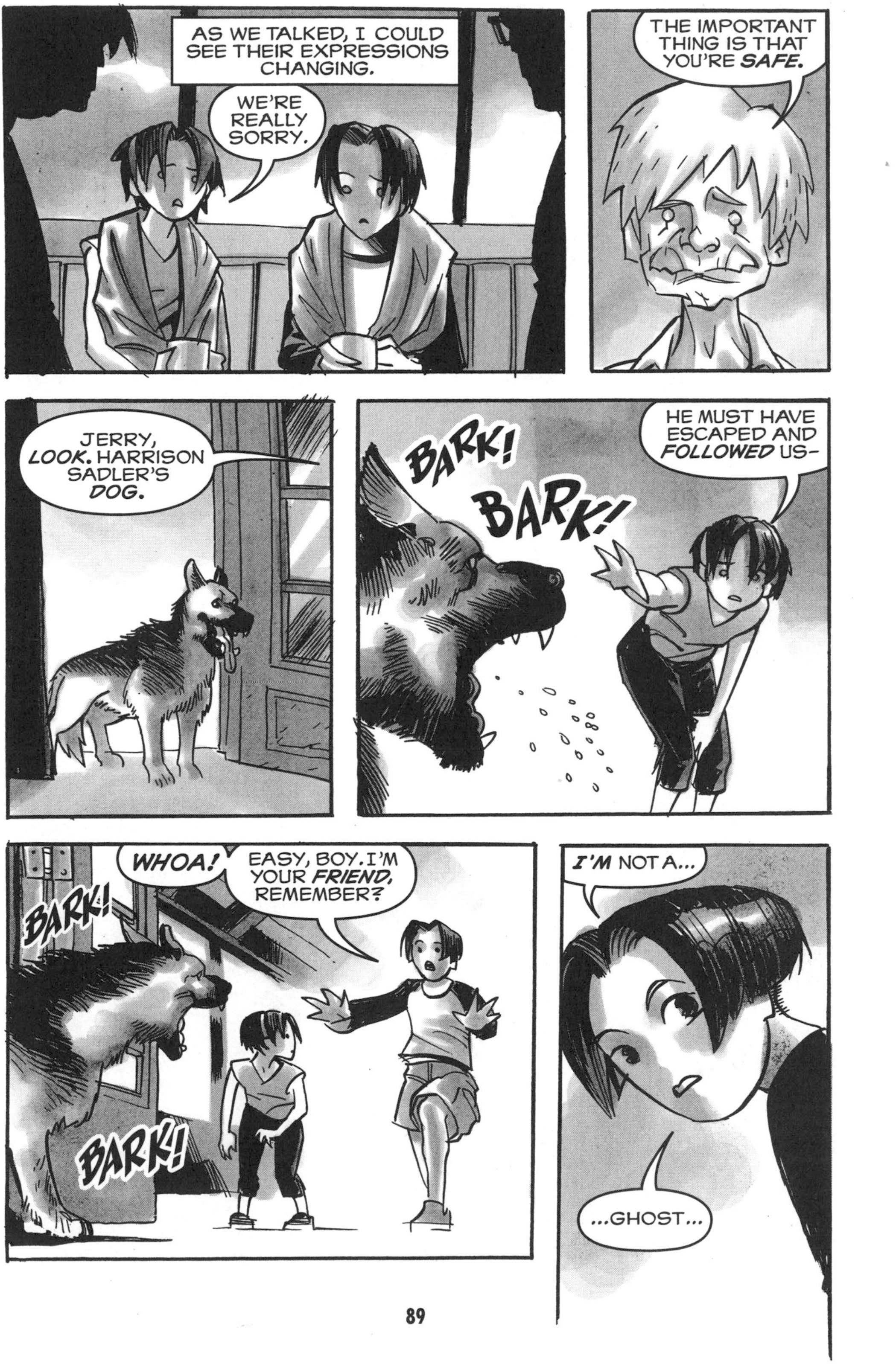
AS WE TALKED, I COULD SEE THEIR EXPRESSIONS CHANGING.
WE'RE REALLY SORRY.
THE IMPORTANT THING IS THAT YOU'RE SAFE.
JERRY, LOOK. HARRISON SADLER'S DOG.
BARK!
BARK!
HE MUST HAVE ESCAPED AND FOLLOWED US–
BARK!
WHOA!
EASY, BOY. I'M YOUR FRIEND, REMEMBER?
BARK!
I'M NOT A...
...GHOST...

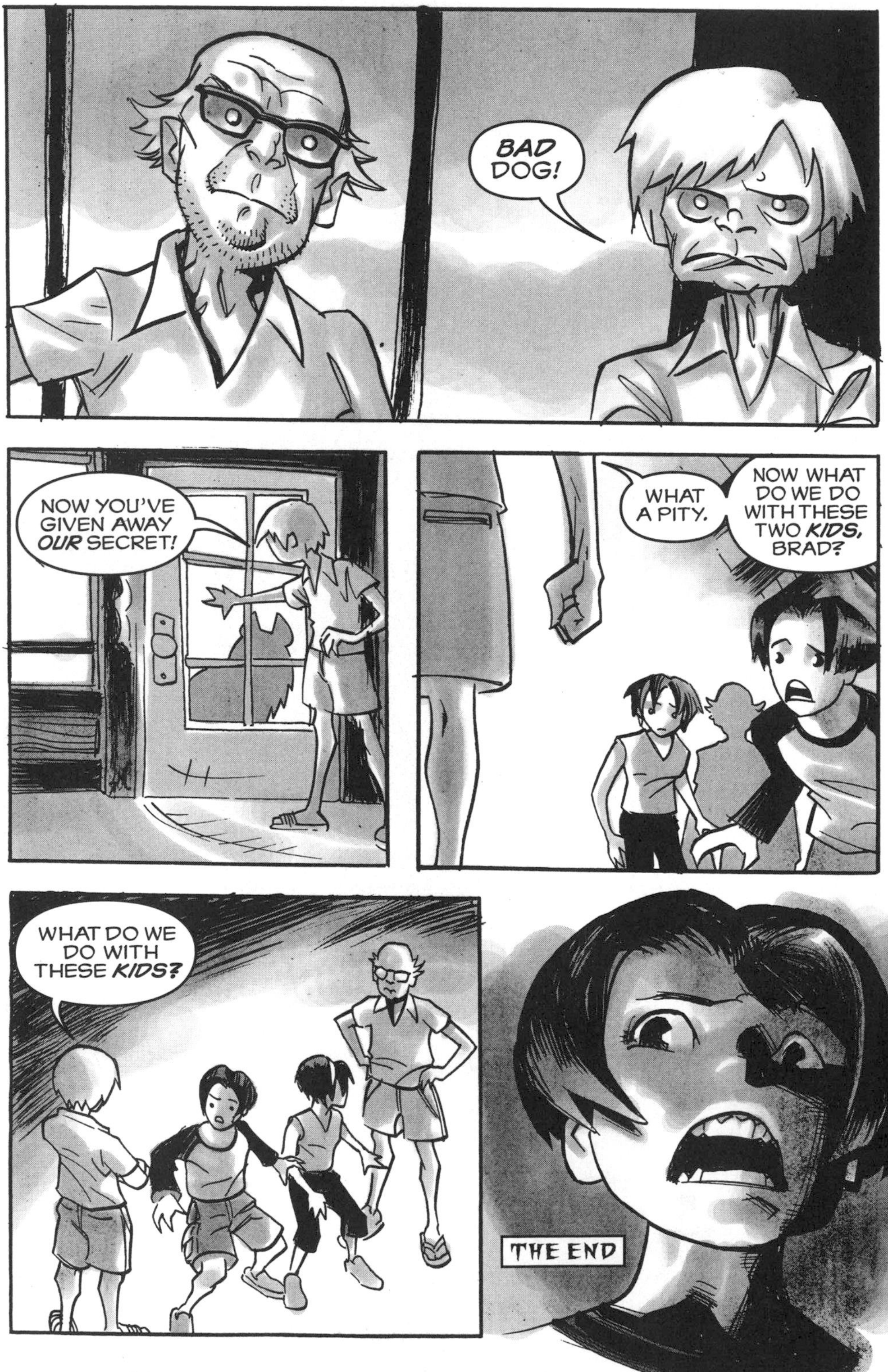
BAD DOG!
NOW YOU'VE GIVEN AWAY OUR SECRET!
WHAT A PITY.
NOW WHAT DO WE DO WITH THESE TWO KIDS, BRAD?
WHAT DO WE DO WITH THESE KIDS?
THE END

THE HORROR AT CAMP JELLYJAM

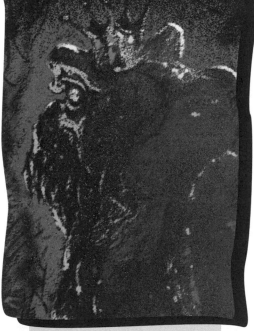

ADAPTED AND ILLUSTRATED BY

Kyle Baker

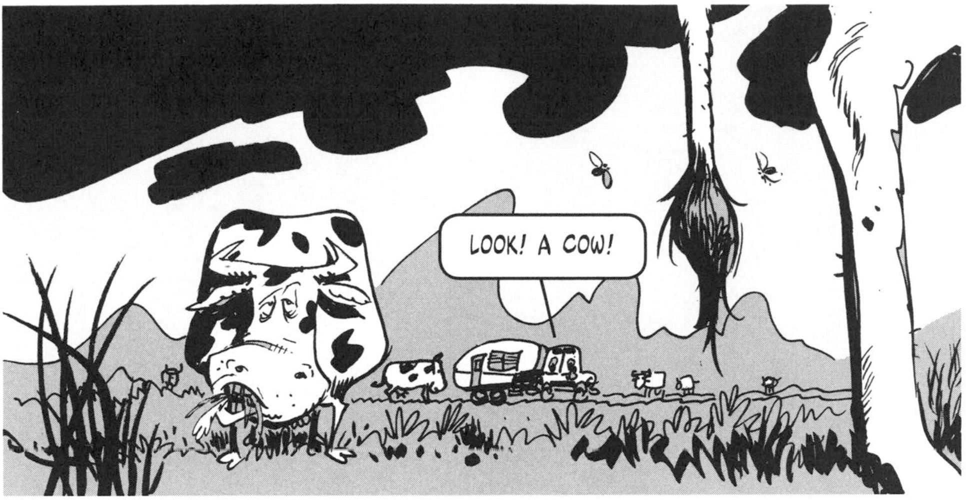
LOOK! A COW!

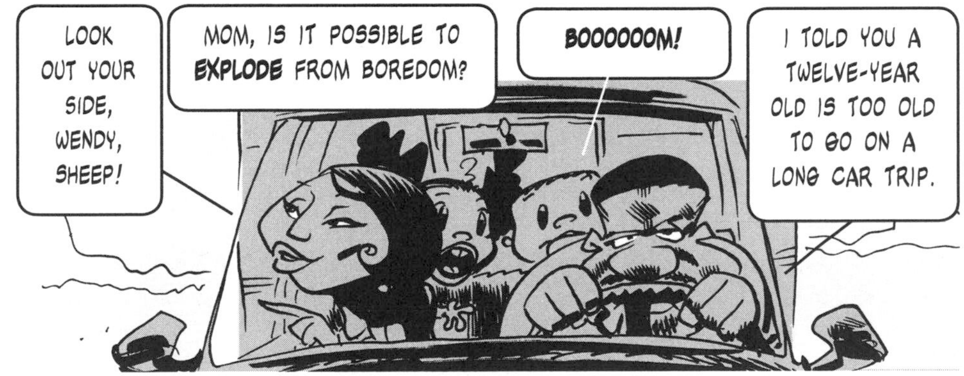
LOOK OUT YOUR SIDE, WENDY, SHEEP!
MOM, IS IT POSSIBLE TO **EXPLODE** FROM BOREDOM?
BOOOOOOM!
I TOLD YOU A TWELVE-YEAR OLD IS TOO OLD TO GO ON A LONG CAR TRIP.

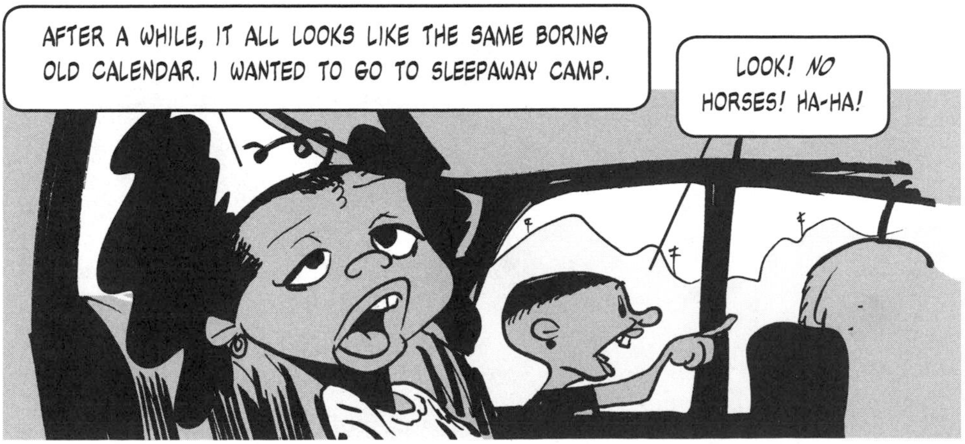
AFTER A WHILE, IT ALL LOOKS LIKE THE SAME BORING OLD CALENDAR. I WANTED TO GO TO SLEEPAWAY CAMP.
LOOK! *NO* HORSES! HA-HA!

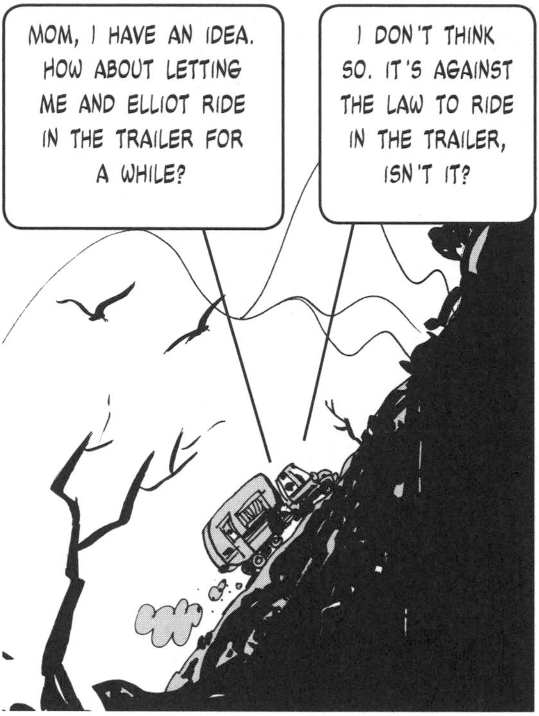
MOM, I HAVE AN IDEA. HOW ABOUT LETTING ME AND ELLIOT RIDE IN THE TRAILER FOR A WHILE?
I DON'T THINK SO. IT'S AGAINST THE LAW TO RIDE IN THE TRAILER, ISN'T IT?

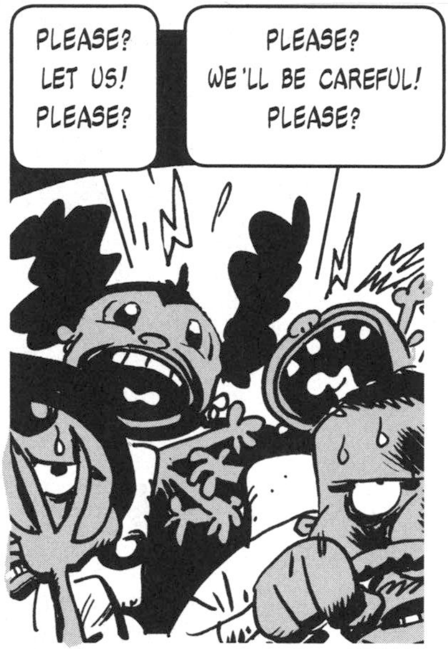
PLEASE? LET US! PLEASE?
PLEASE? WE'LL BE CAREFUL! PLEASE?

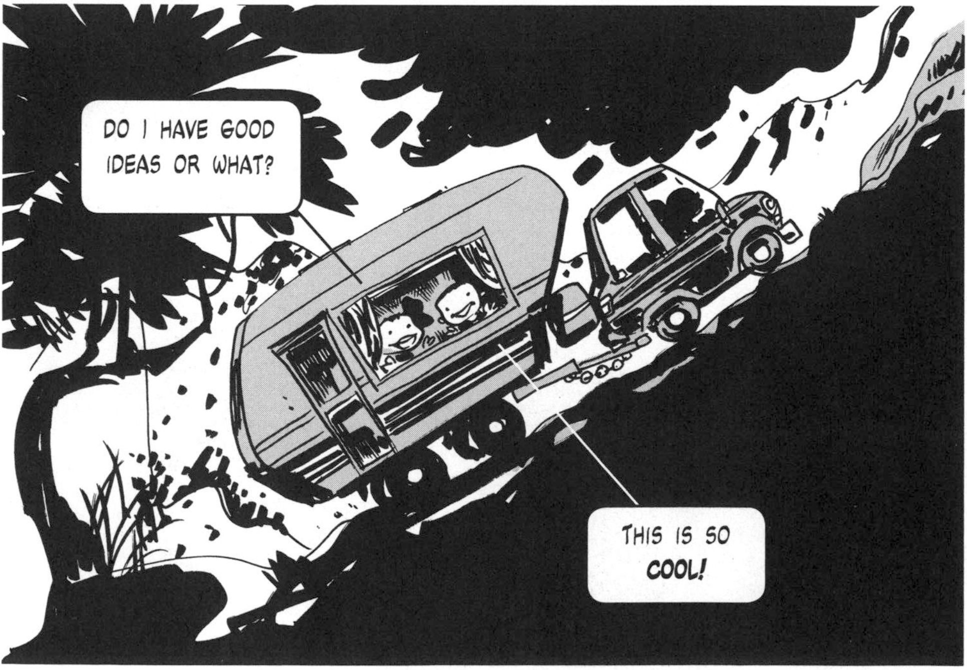
DO I HAVE GOOD IDEAS OR WHAT?
THIS IS SO COOL!

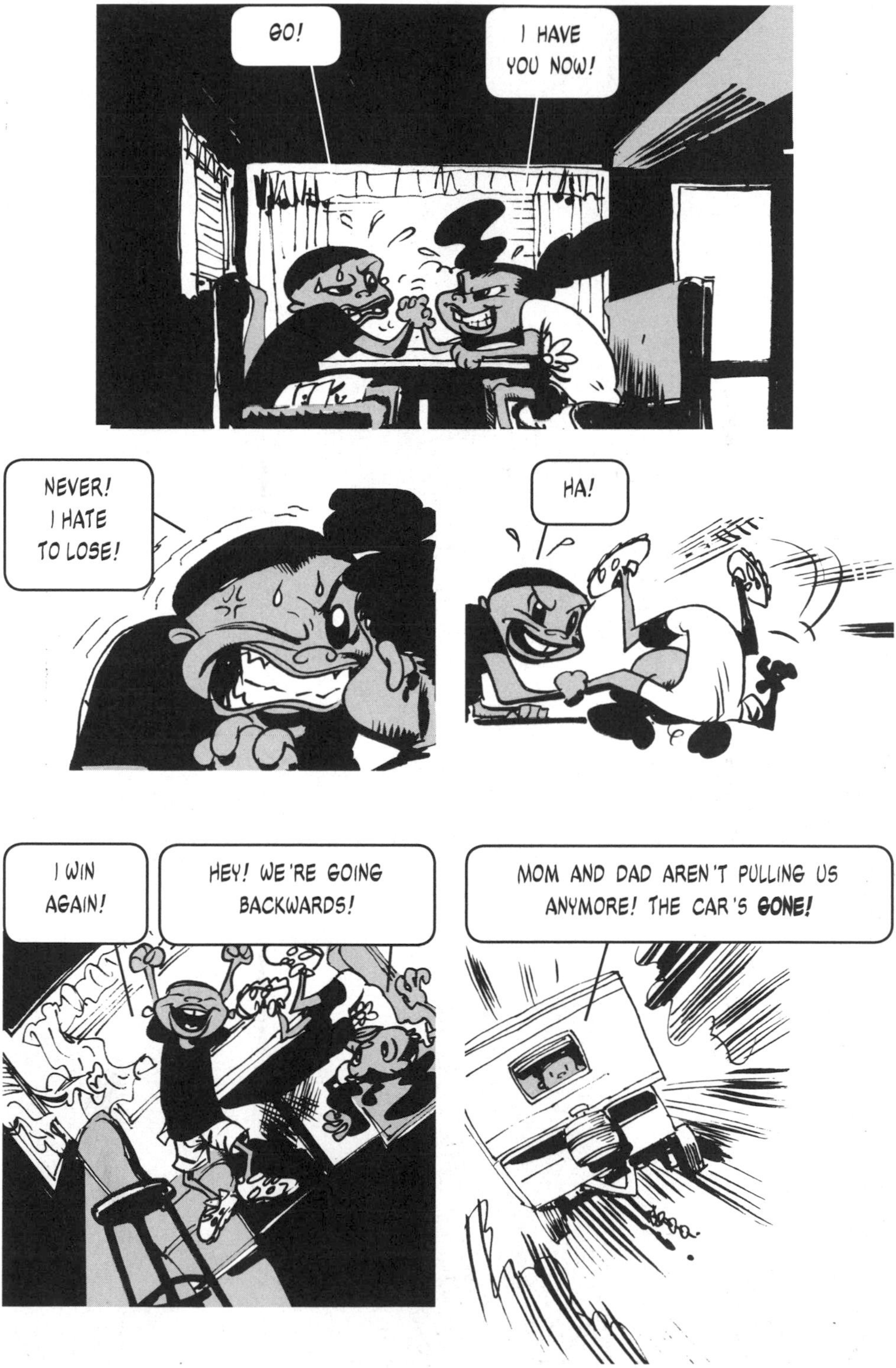
GO!
I HAVE YOU NOW!
NEVER! I HATE TO LOSE!
HA!
I WIN AGAIN!
HEY! WE'RE GOING BACKWARDS!
MOM AND DAD AREN'T PULLING US ANYMORE! THE CAR'S **GONE!**

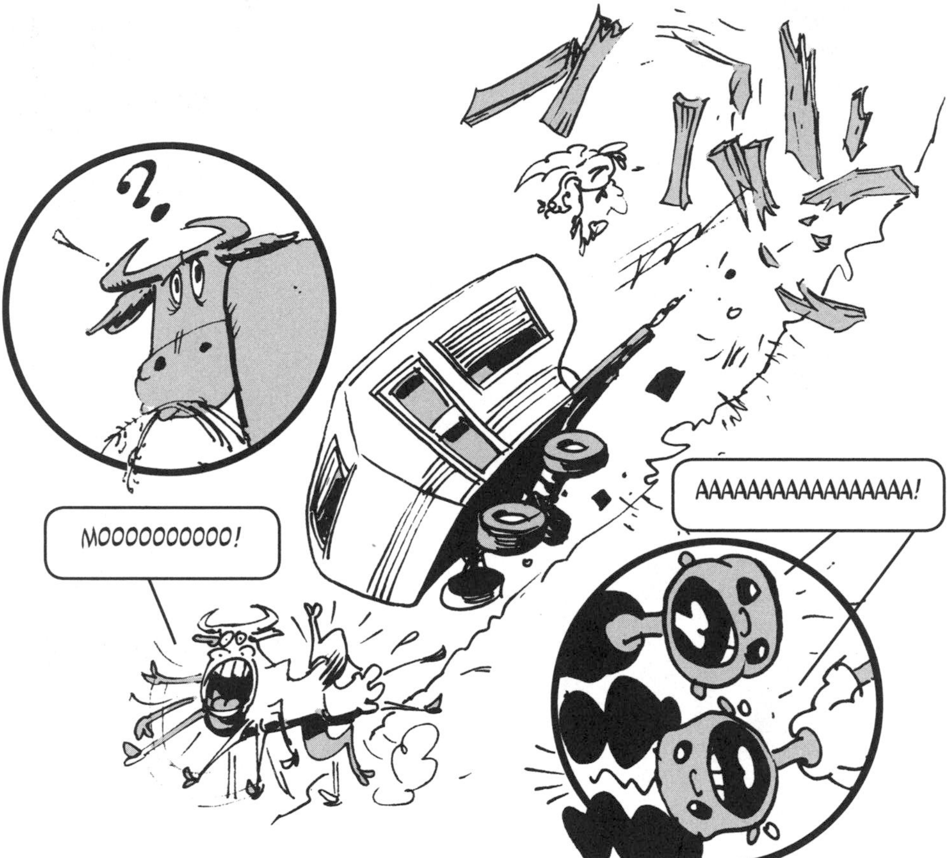
MOOOOOOOOOO!
AAAAAAAAAAAAAAAAAA!

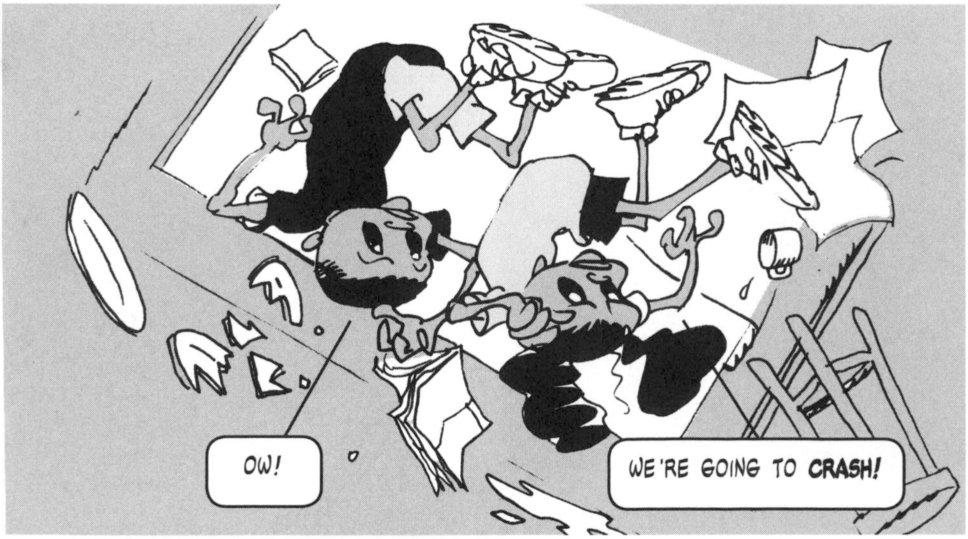
OW!
WE'RE GOING TO **CRASH!**

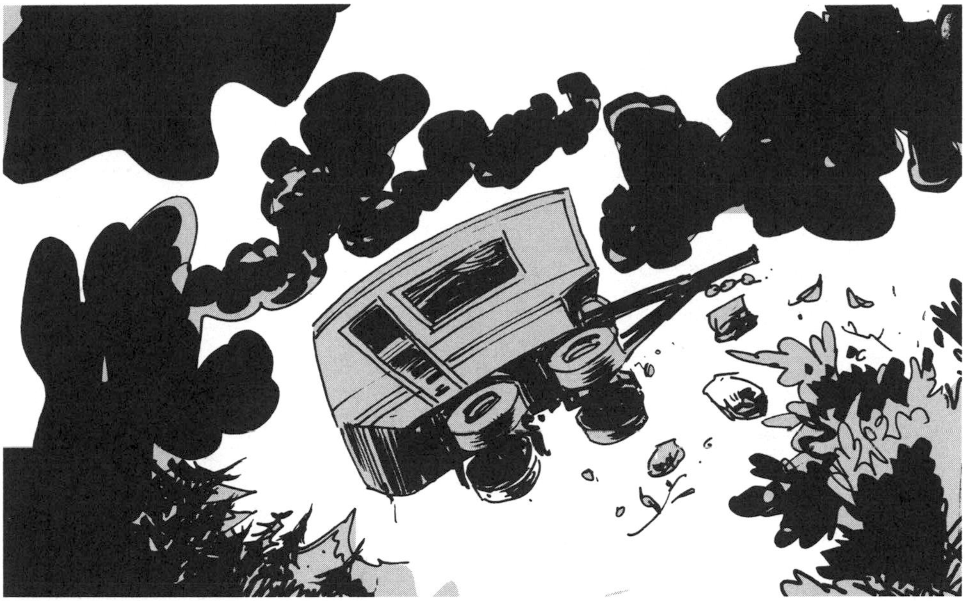

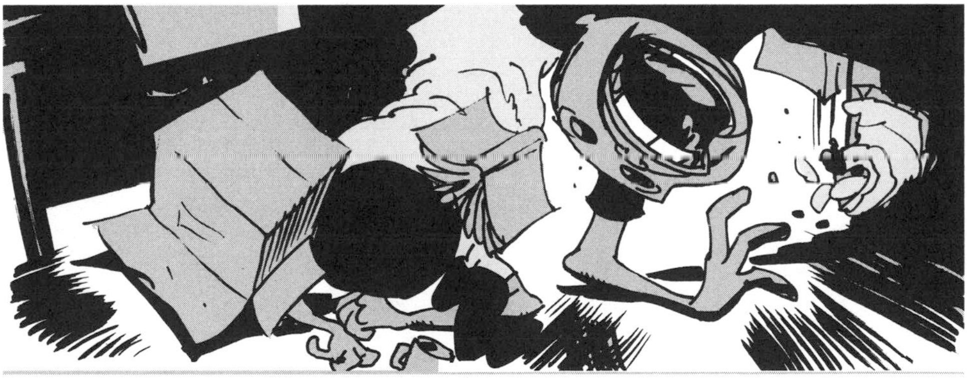

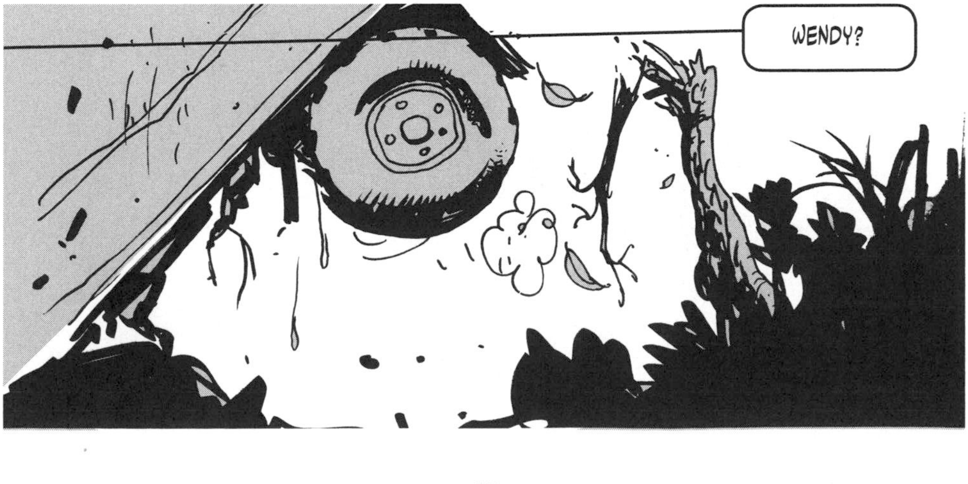
WENDY?

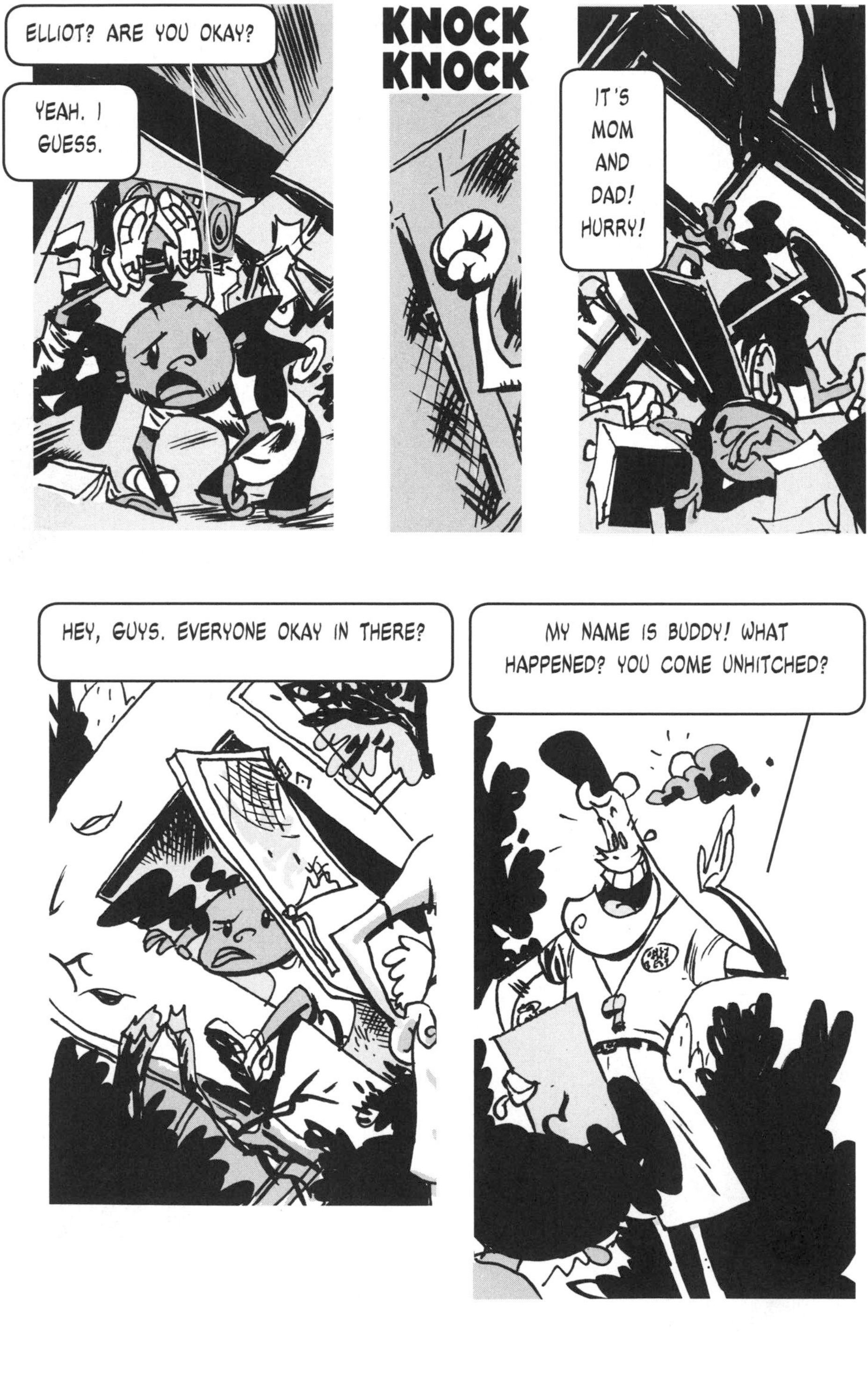
ELLIOT? ARE YOU OKAY?
YEAH. I GUESS.
KNOCK KNOCK
IT'S MOM AND DAD! HURRY!
HEY, GUYS. EVERYONE OKAY IN THERE?
MY NAME IS BUDDY! WHAT HAPPENED? YOU COME UNHITCHED?

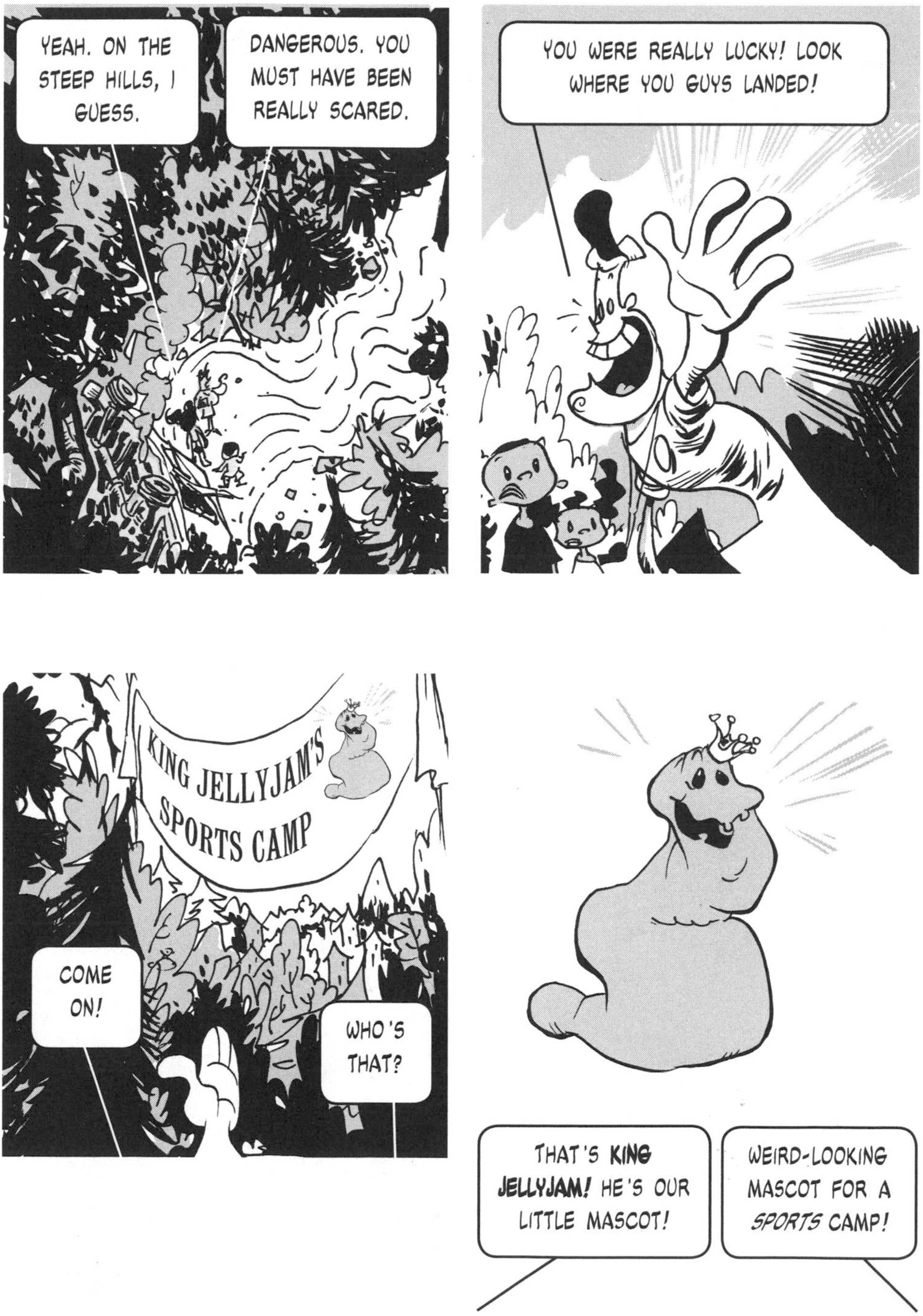
YEAH. ON THE STEEP HILLS, I GUESS.
DANGEROUS. YOU MUST HAVE BEEN REALLY SCARED.
YOU WERE REALLY LUCKY! LOOK WHERE YOU GUYS LANDED!
KING JELLYJAM'S SPORTS CAMP
COME ON!
WHO'S THAT?
THAT'S KING JELLYJAM! HE'S OUR LITTLE MASCOT!
WEIRD-LOOKING MASCOT FOR A SPORTS CAMP!

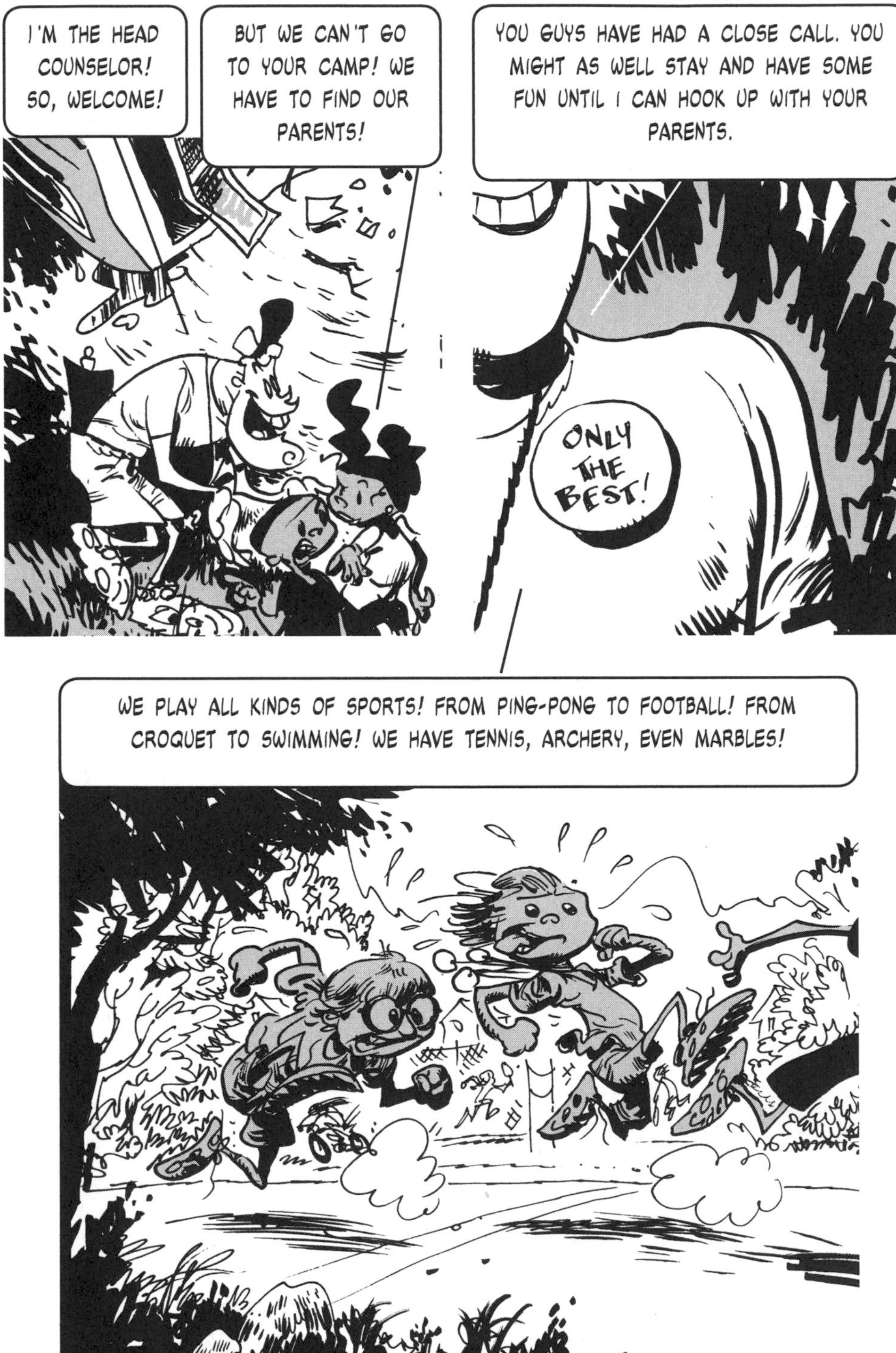
I'M THE HEAD COUNSELOR! SO, WELCOME!
BUT WE CAN'T GO TO YOUR CAMP! WE HAVE TO FIND OUR PARENTS!
YOU GUYS HAVE HAD A CLOSE CALL. YOU MIGHT AS WELL STAY AND HAVE SOME FUN UNTIL I CAN HOOK UP WITH YOUR PARENTS.
ONLY THE BEST!
WE PLAY ALL KINDS OF SPORTS! FROM PING-PONG TO FOOTBALL! FROM CROQUET TO SWIMMING! WE HAVE TENNIS, ARCHERY, EVEN MARBLES!

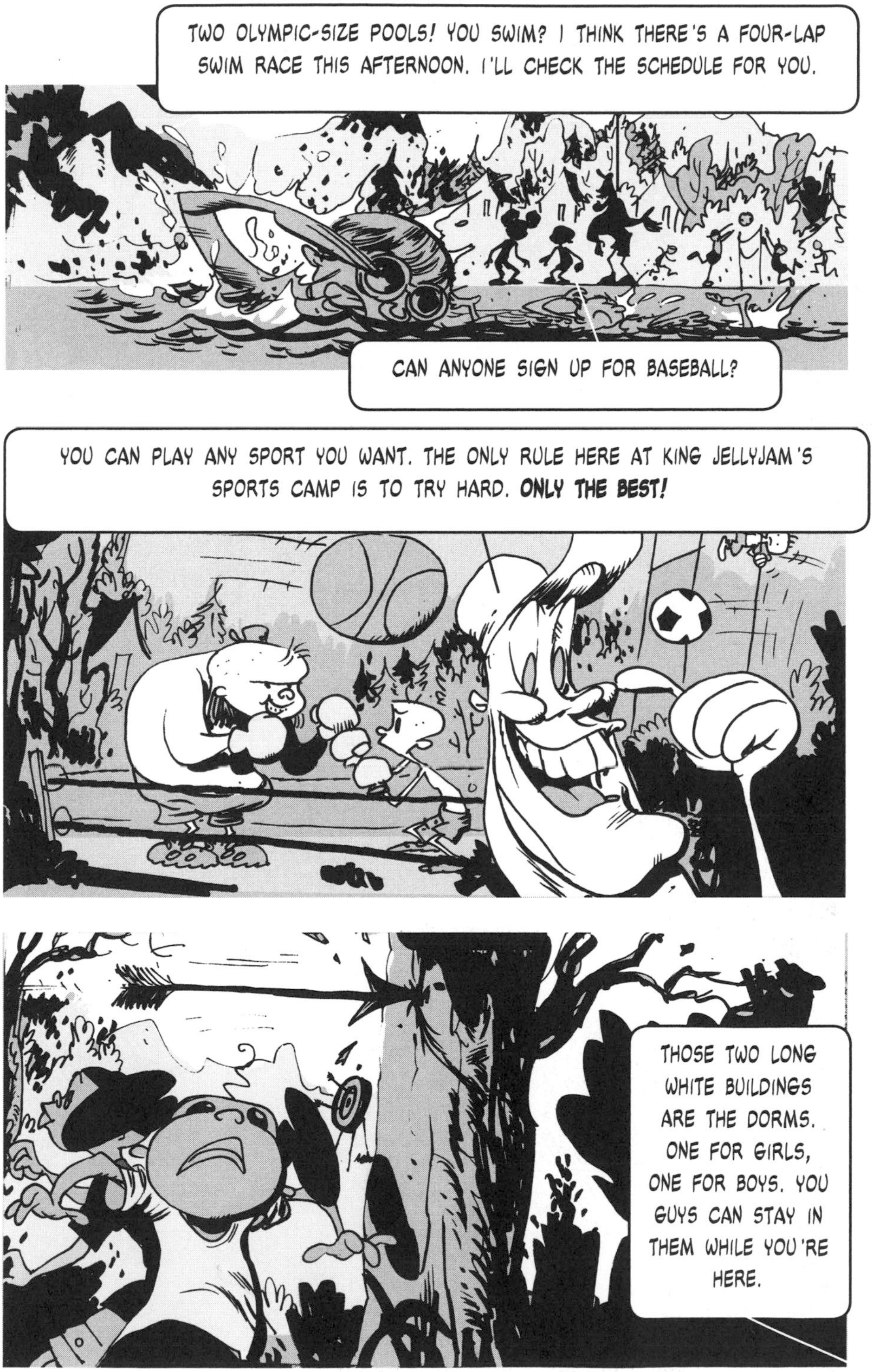
TWO OLYMPIC-SIZE POOLS! YOU SWIM? I THINK THERE'S A FOUR-LAP SWIM RACE THIS AFTERNOON. I'LL CHECK THE SCHEDULE FOR YOU.
CAN ANYONE SIGN UP FOR BASEBALL?
YOU CAN PLAY ANY SPORT YOU WANT. THE ONLY RULE HERE AT KING JELLYJAM'S SPORTS CAMP IS TO TRY HARD. **ONLY THE BEST!**
THOSE TWO LONG WHITE BUILDINGS ARE THE DORMS. ONE FOR GIRLS, ONE FOR BOYS. YOU GUYS CAN STAY IN THEM WHILE YOU'RE HERE.

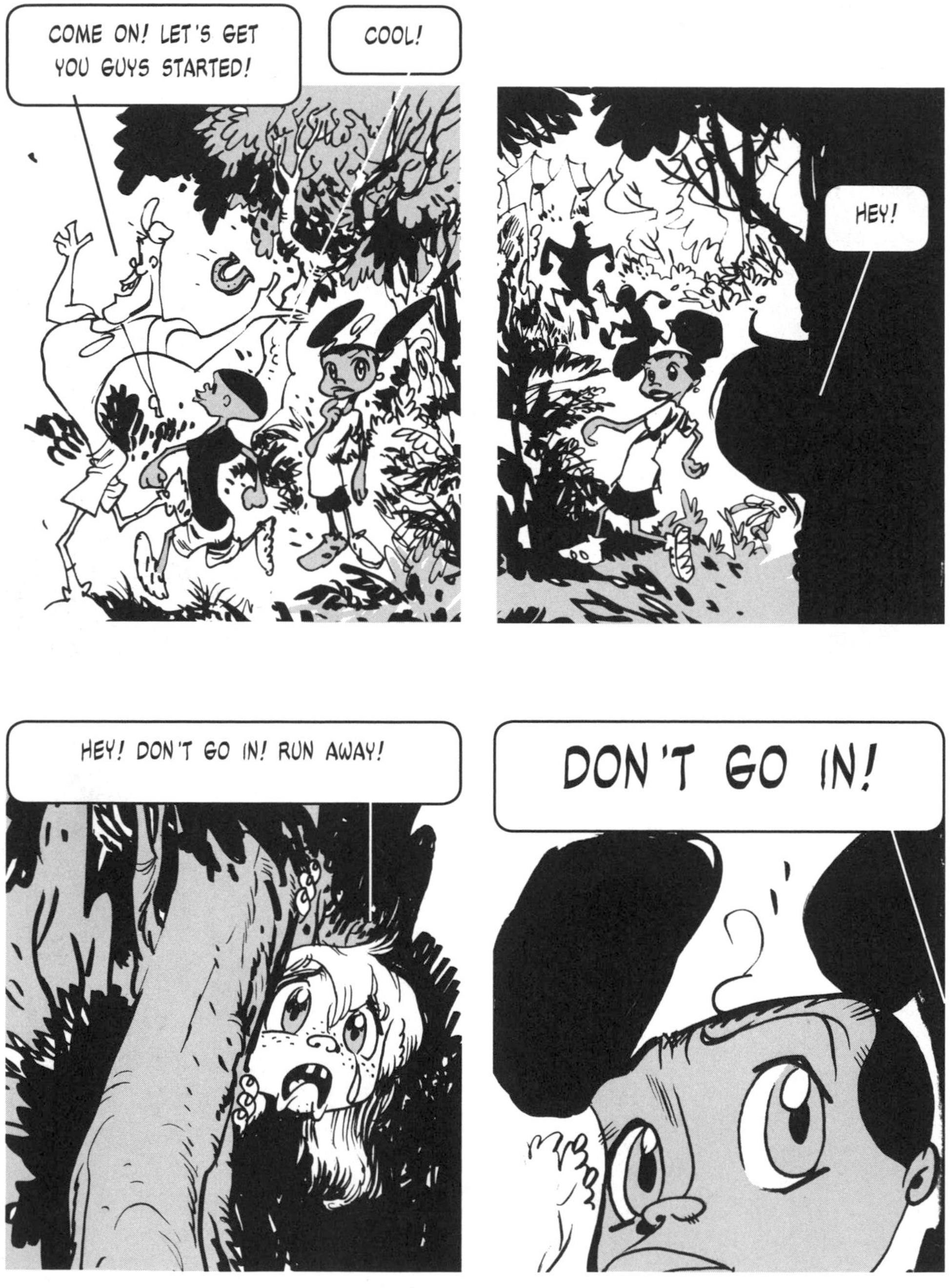
COME ON! LET'S GET YOU GUYS STARTED!
COOL!
HEY!
HEY! DON'T GO IN! RUN AWAY!
DON'T GO IN!

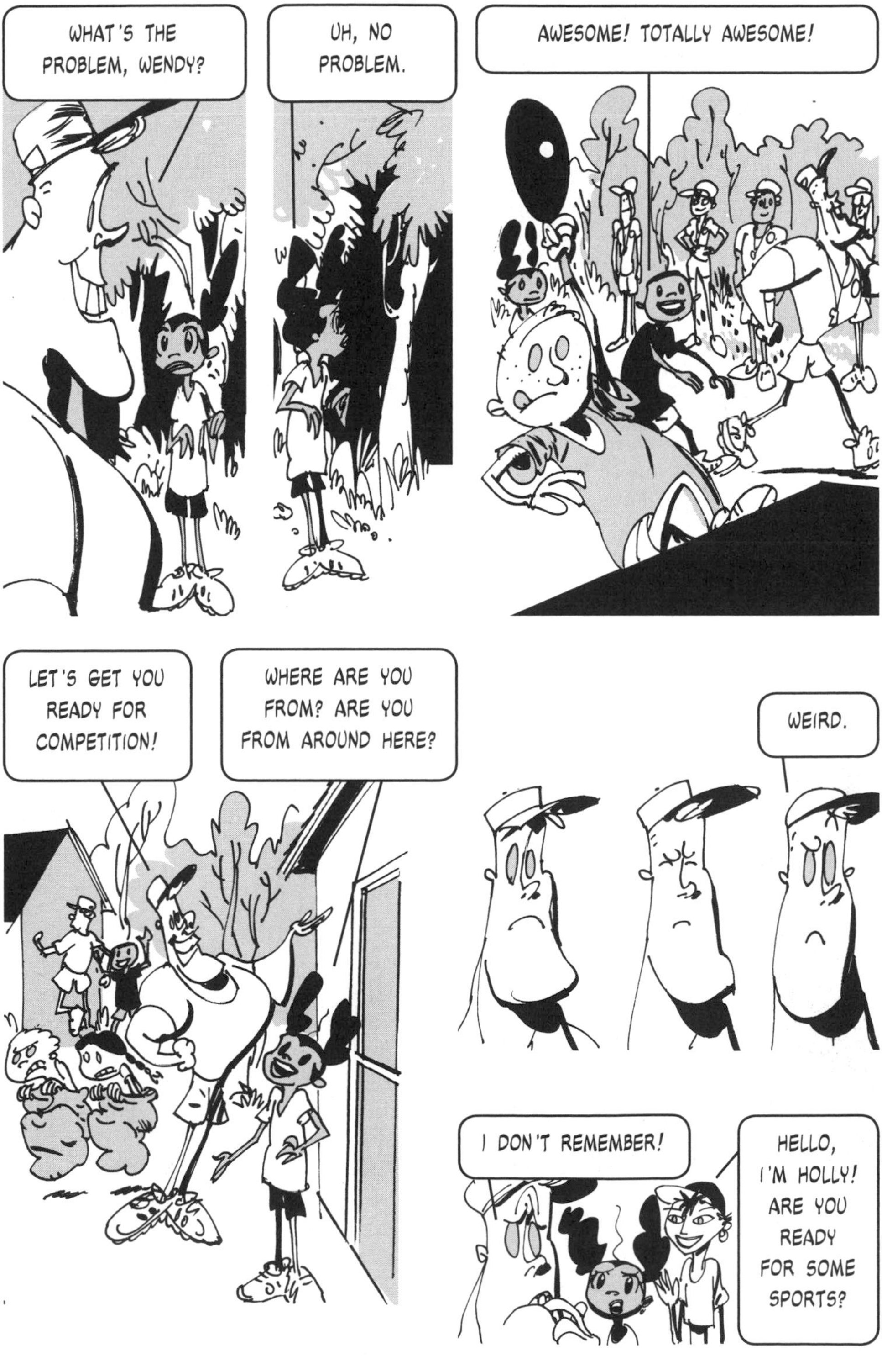
WHAT'S THE PROBLEM, WENDY?
UH, NO PROBLEM.
AWESOME! TOTALLY AWESOME!
LET'S GET YOU READY FOR COMPETITION!
WHERE ARE YOU FROM? ARE YOU FROM AROUND HERE?
WEIRD.
I DON'T REMEMBER!
HELLO, I'M HOLLY! ARE YOU READY FOR SOME SPORTS?

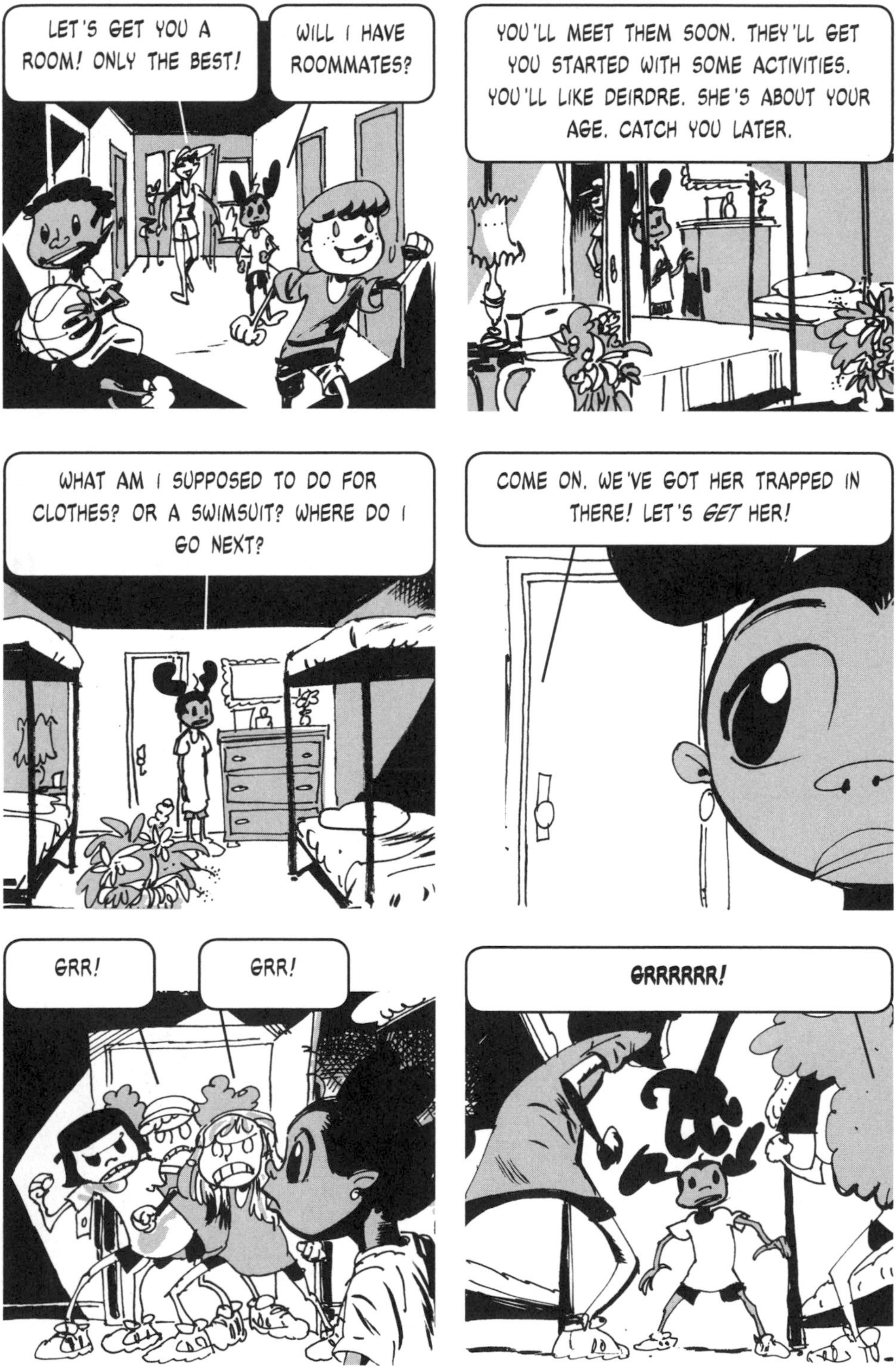
LET'S GET YOU A ROOM! ONLY THE BEST!
WILL I HAVE ROOMMATES?
YOU'LL MEET THEM SOON. THEY'LL GET YOU STARTED WITH SOME ACTIVITIES. YOU'LL LIKE DEIRDRE. SHE'S ABOUT YOUR AGE. CATCH YOU LATER.
WHAT AM I SUPPOSED TO DO FOR CLOTHES? OR A SWIMSUIT? WHERE DO I GO NEXT?
COME ON. WE'VE GOT HER TRAPPED IN THERE! LET'S *GET* HER!
GRR!
GRR!
GRRRRRR!

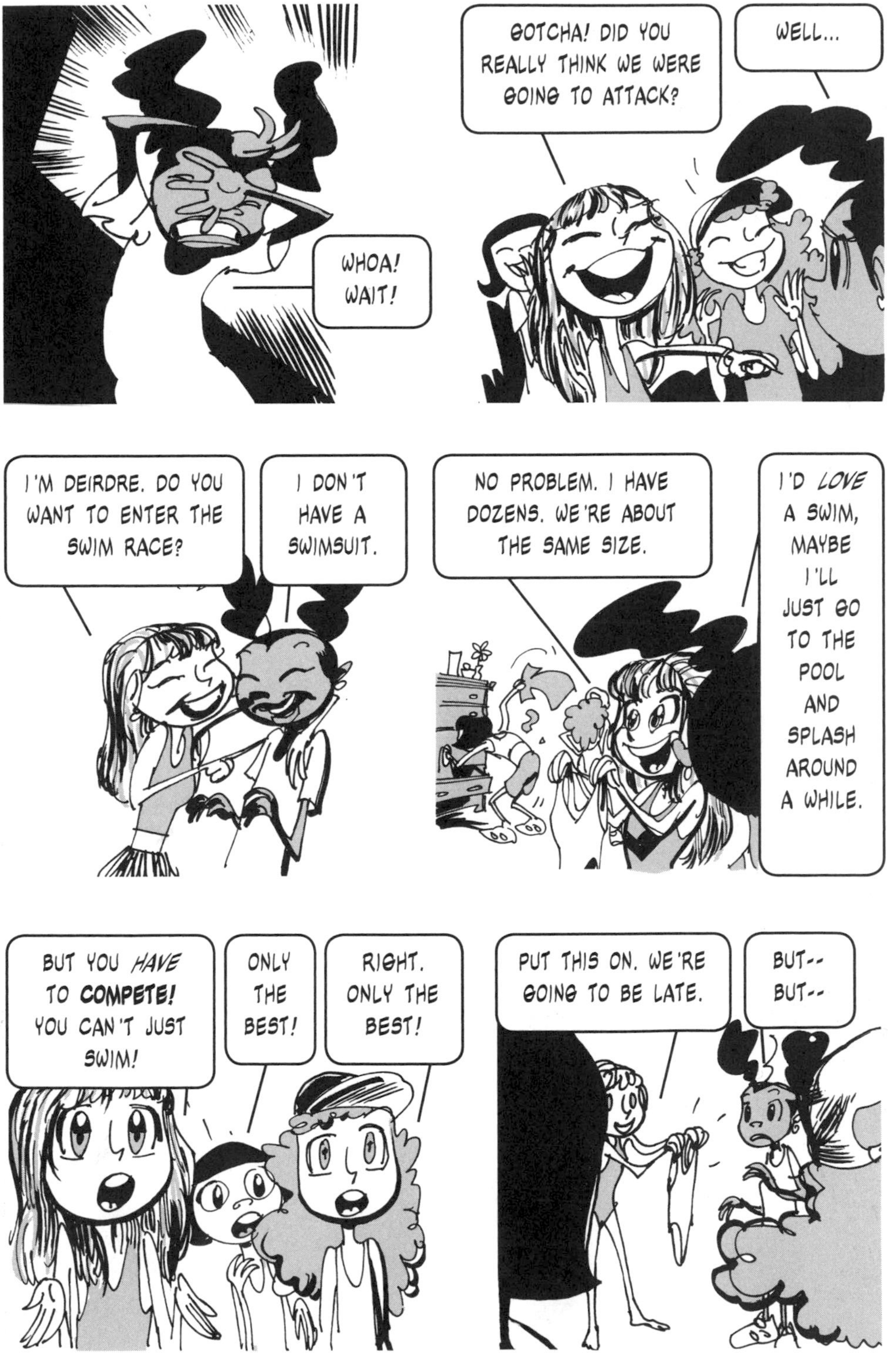
WHOA! WAIT!
GOTCHA! DID YOU REALLY THINK WE WERE GOING TO ATTACK?
WELL...
I'M DEIRDRE. DO YOU WANT TO ENTER THE SWIM RACE?
I DON'T HAVE A SWIMSUIT.
NO PROBLEM. I HAVE DOZENS. WE'RE ABOUT THE SAME SIZE.
I'D *LOVE* A SWIM, MAYBE I'LL JUST GO TO THE POOL AND SPLASH AROUND A WHILE.
BUT YOU *HAVE* TO **COMPETE!** YOU CAN'T JUST SWIM!
ONLY THE BEST!
RIGHT. ONLY THE BEST!
PUT THIS ON. WE'RE GOING TO BE LATE.
BUT-- BUT--

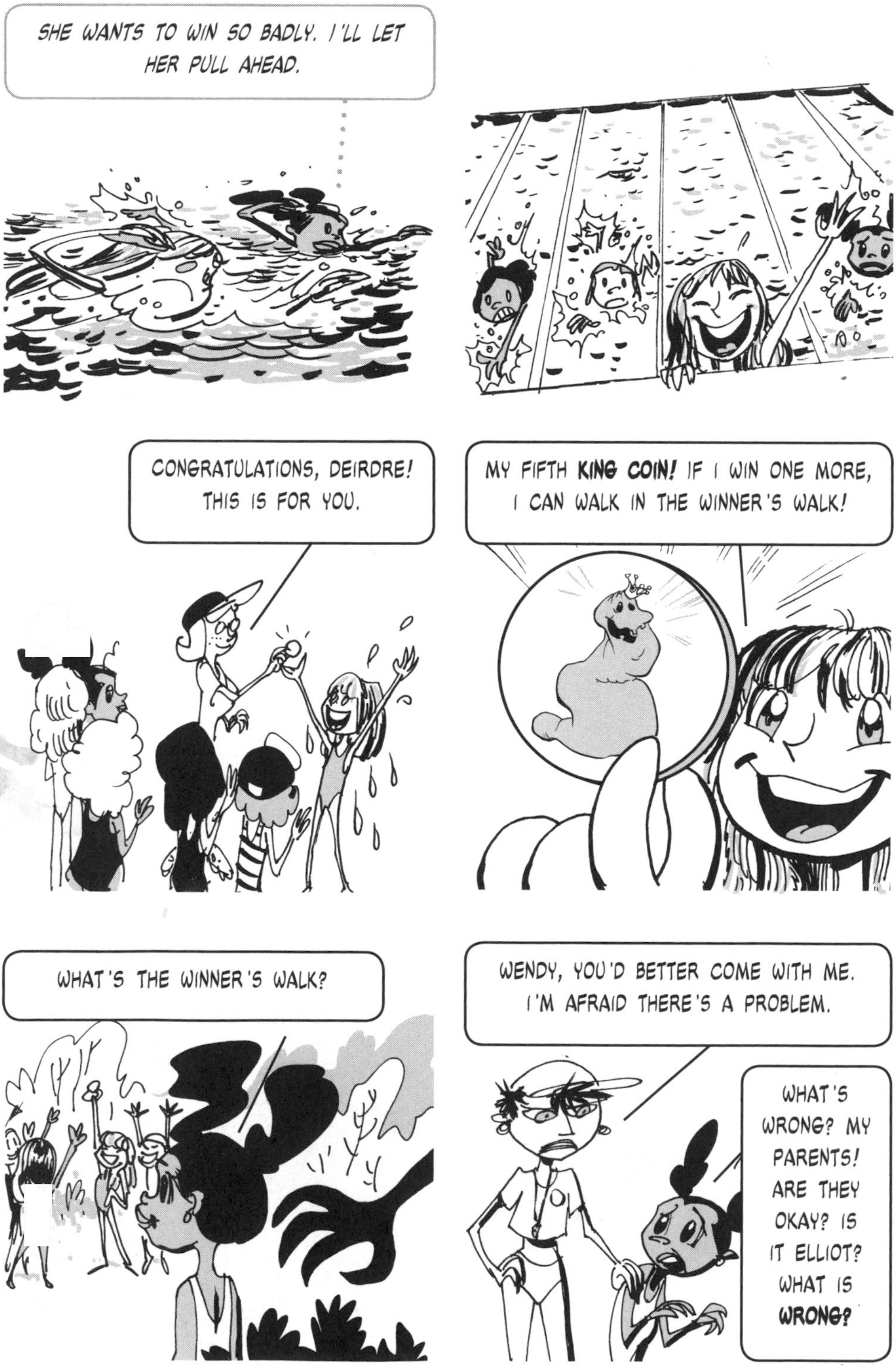
SHE WANTS TO WIN SO BADLY. I'LL LET HER PULL AHEAD.
CONGRATULATIONS, DEIRDRE! THIS IS FOR YOU.
MY FIFTH KING COIN! IF I WIN ONE MORE, I CAN WALK IN THE WINNER'S WALK!
WHAT'S THE WINNER'S WALK?
WENDY, YOU'D BETTER COME WITH ME. I'M AFRAID THERE'S A PROBLEM.
WHAT'S WRONG? MY PARENTS! ARE THEY OKAY? IS IT ELLIOT? WHAT IS WRONG?

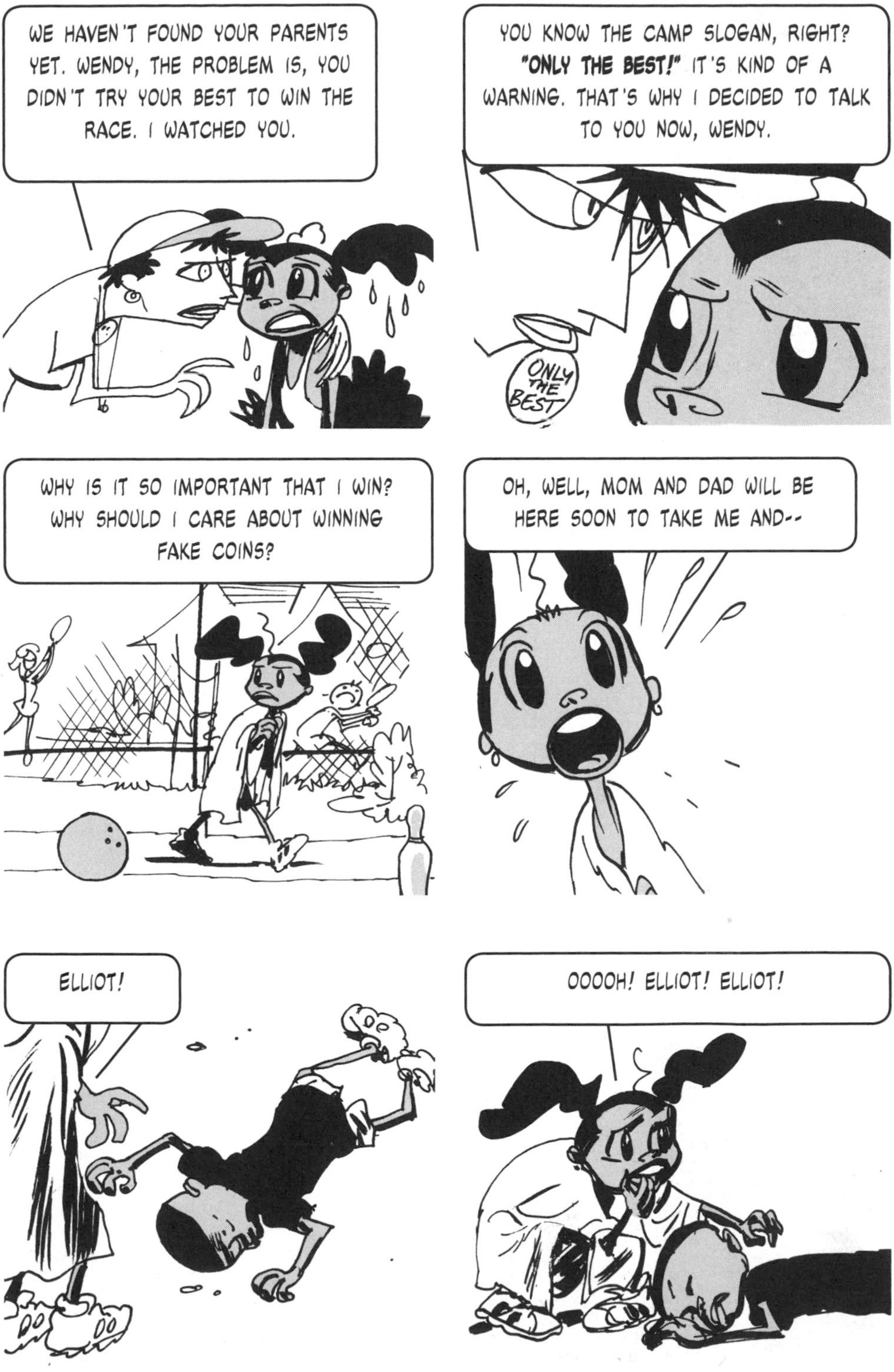
WE HAVEN'T FOUND YOUR PARENTS YET. WENDY, THE PROBLEM IS, YOU DIDN'T TRY YOUR BEST TO WIN THE RACE. I WATCHED YOU.
YOU KNOW THE CAMP SLOGAN, RIGHT? "ONLY THE BEST!" IT'S KIND OF A WARNING. THAT'S WHY I DECIDED TO TALK TO YOU NOW, WENDY.
ONLY THE BEST
WHY IS IT SO IMPORTANT THAT I WIN? WHY SHOULD I CARE ABOUT WINNING FAKE COINS?
OH, WELL, MOM AND DAD WILL BE HERE SOON TO TAKE ME AND--
ELLIOT!
OOOOH! ELLIOT! ELLIOT!

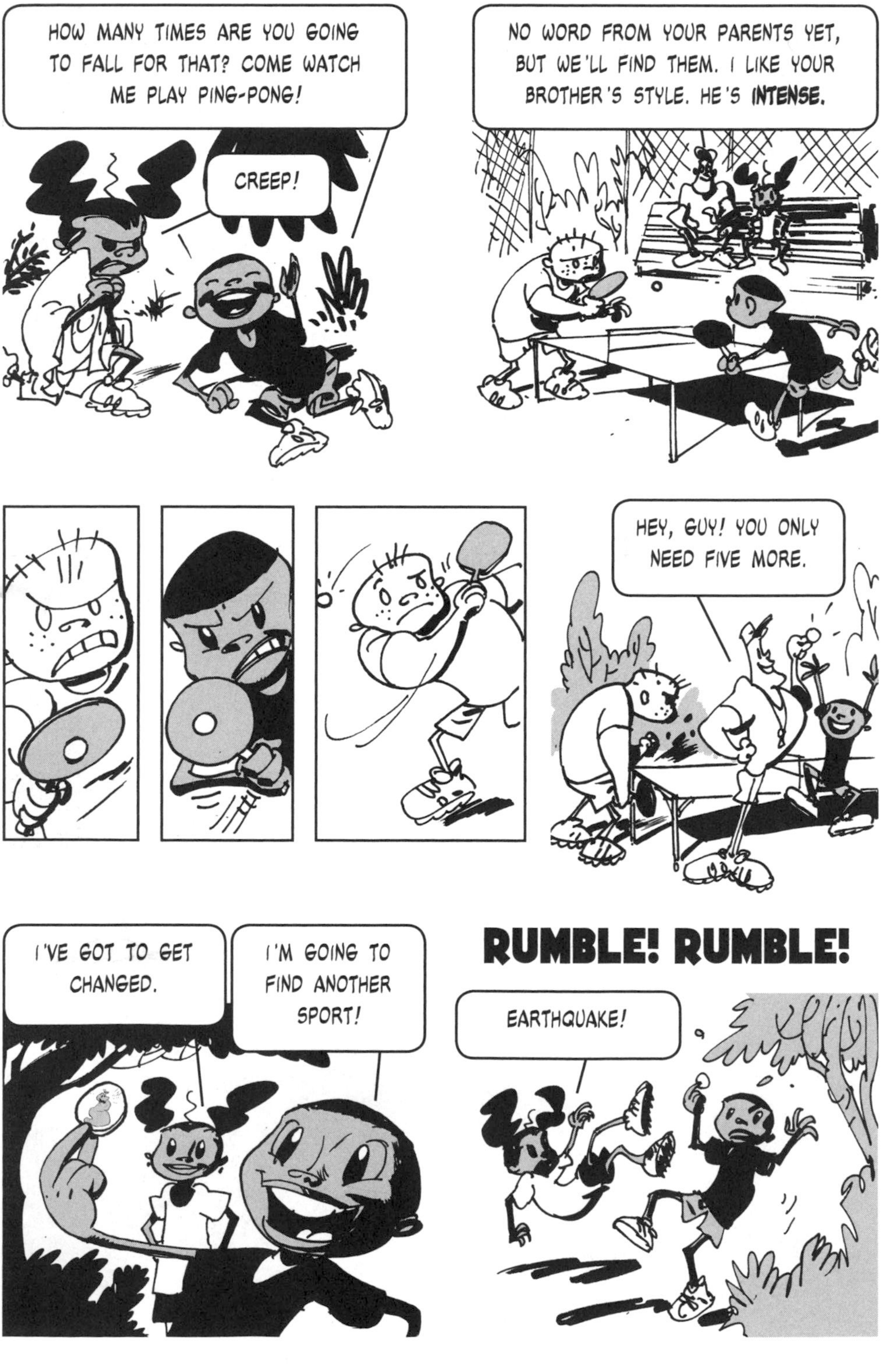
HOW MANY TIMES ARE YOU GOING TO FALL FOR THAT? COME WATCH ME PLAY PING-PONG!
CREEP!
NO WORD FROM YOUR PARENTS YET, BUT WE'LL FIND THEM. I LIKE YOUR BROTHER'S STYLE. HE'S **INTENSE.**
HEY, GUY! YOU ONLY NEED FIVE MORE.
I'VE GOT TO GET CHANGED.
I'M GOING TO FIND ANOTHER SPORT!
RUMBLE! RUMBLE!
EARTHQUAKE!

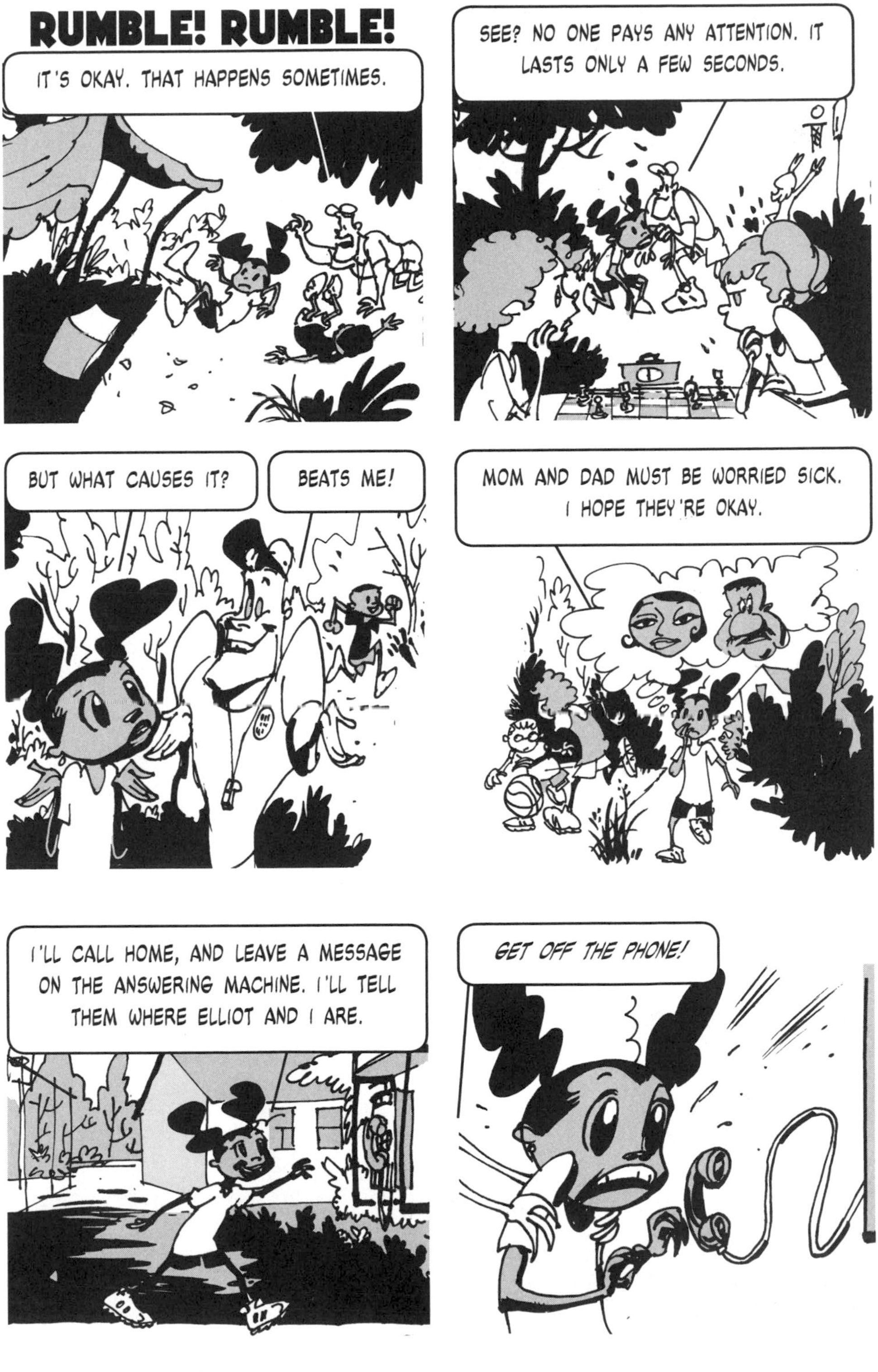
RUMBLE! RUMBLE!
IT'S OKAY. THAT HAPPENS SOMETIMES.
SEE? NO ONE PAYS ANY ATTENTION. IT LASTS ONLY A FEW SECONDS.
BUT WHAT CAUSES IT?
BEATS ME!
MOM AND DAD MUST BE WORRIED SICK. I HOPE THEY'RE OKAY.
I'LL CALL HOME, AND LEAVE A MESSAGE ON THE ANSWERING MACHINE. I'LL TELL THEM WHERE ELLIOT AND I ARE.
GET OFF THE PHONE!

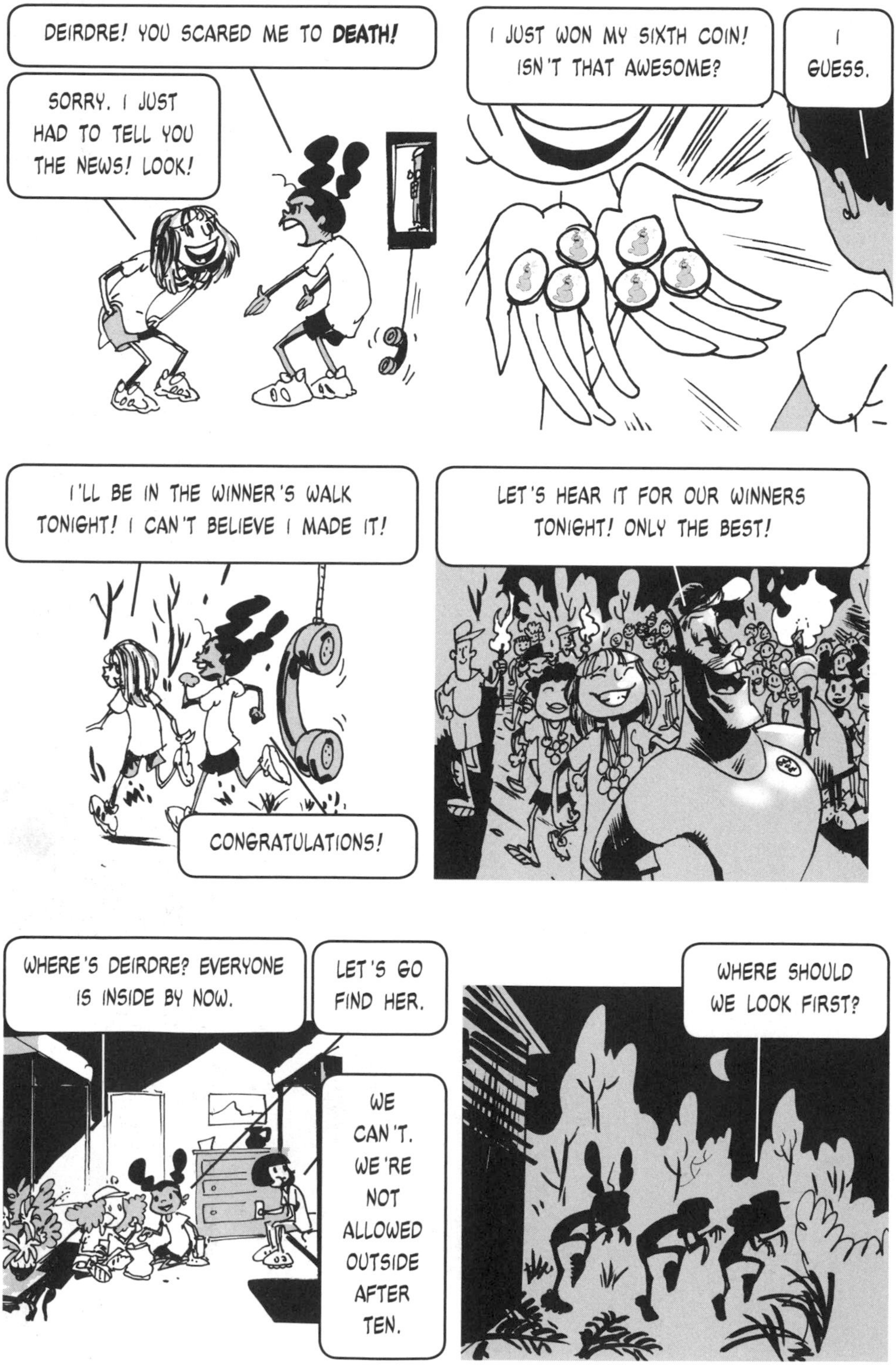
DEIRDRE! YOU SCARED ME TO **DEATH!**
SORRY. I JUST HAD TO TELL YOU THE NEWS! LOOK!
I JUST WON MY SIXTH COIN! ISN'T THAT AWESOME?
I GUESS.
I'LL BE IN THE WINNER'S WALK TONIGHT! I CAN'T BELIEVE I MADE IT!
CONGRATULATIONS!
LET'S HEAR IT FOR OUR WINNERS TONIGHT! ONLY THE BEST!
WHERE'S DEIRDRE? EVERYONE IS INSIDE BY NOW.
LET'S GO FIND HER.
WE CAN'T. WE'RE NOT ALLOWED OUTSIDE AFTER TEN.
WHERE SHOULD WE LOOK FIRST?

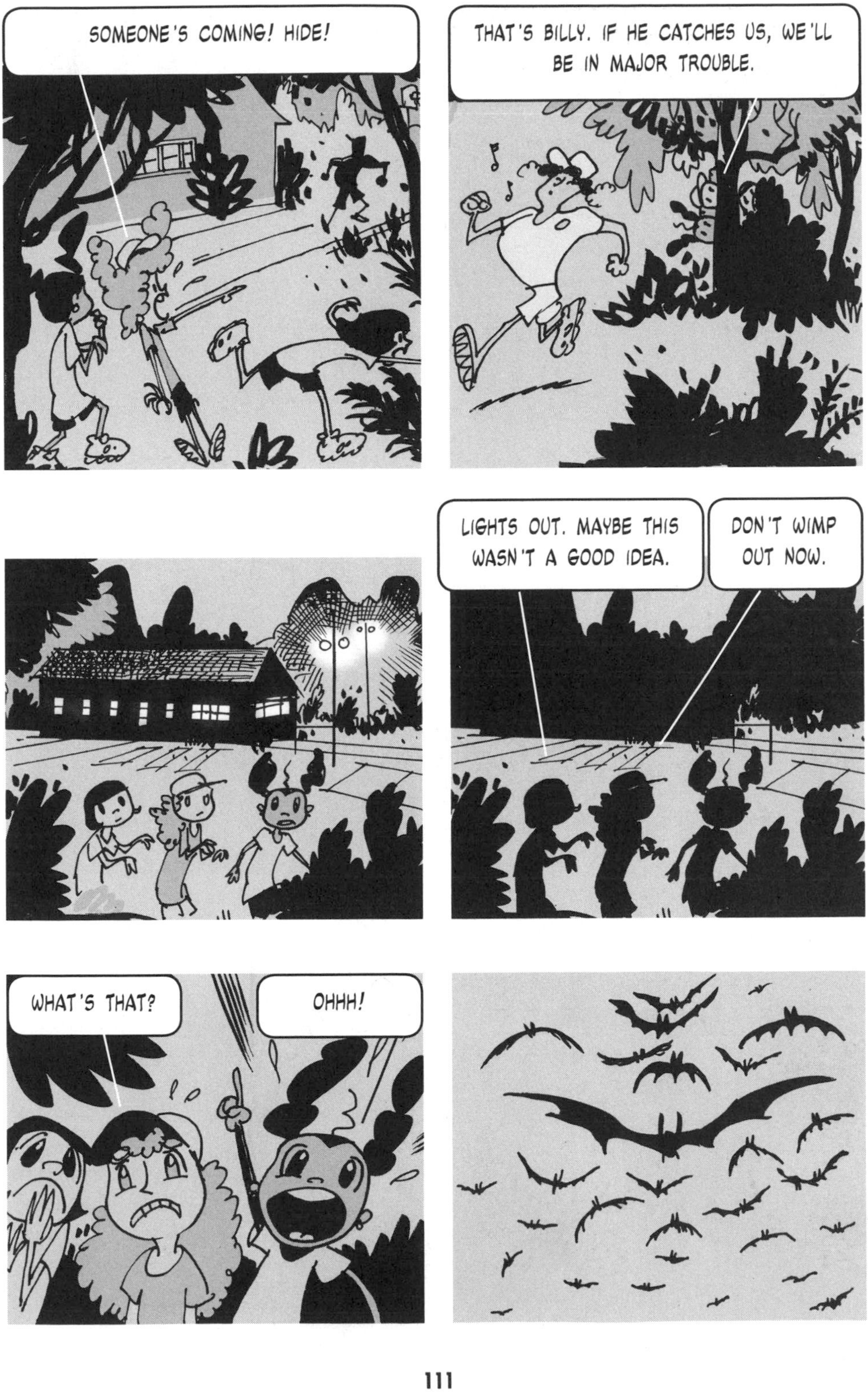
SOMEONE'S COMING! HIDE!
THAT'S BILLY. IF HE CATCHES US, WE'LL BE IN MAJOR TROUBLE.
LIGHTS OUT. MAYBE THIS WASN'T A GOOD IDEA.
DON'T WIMP OUT NOW.
WHAT'S THAT?
OHHH!

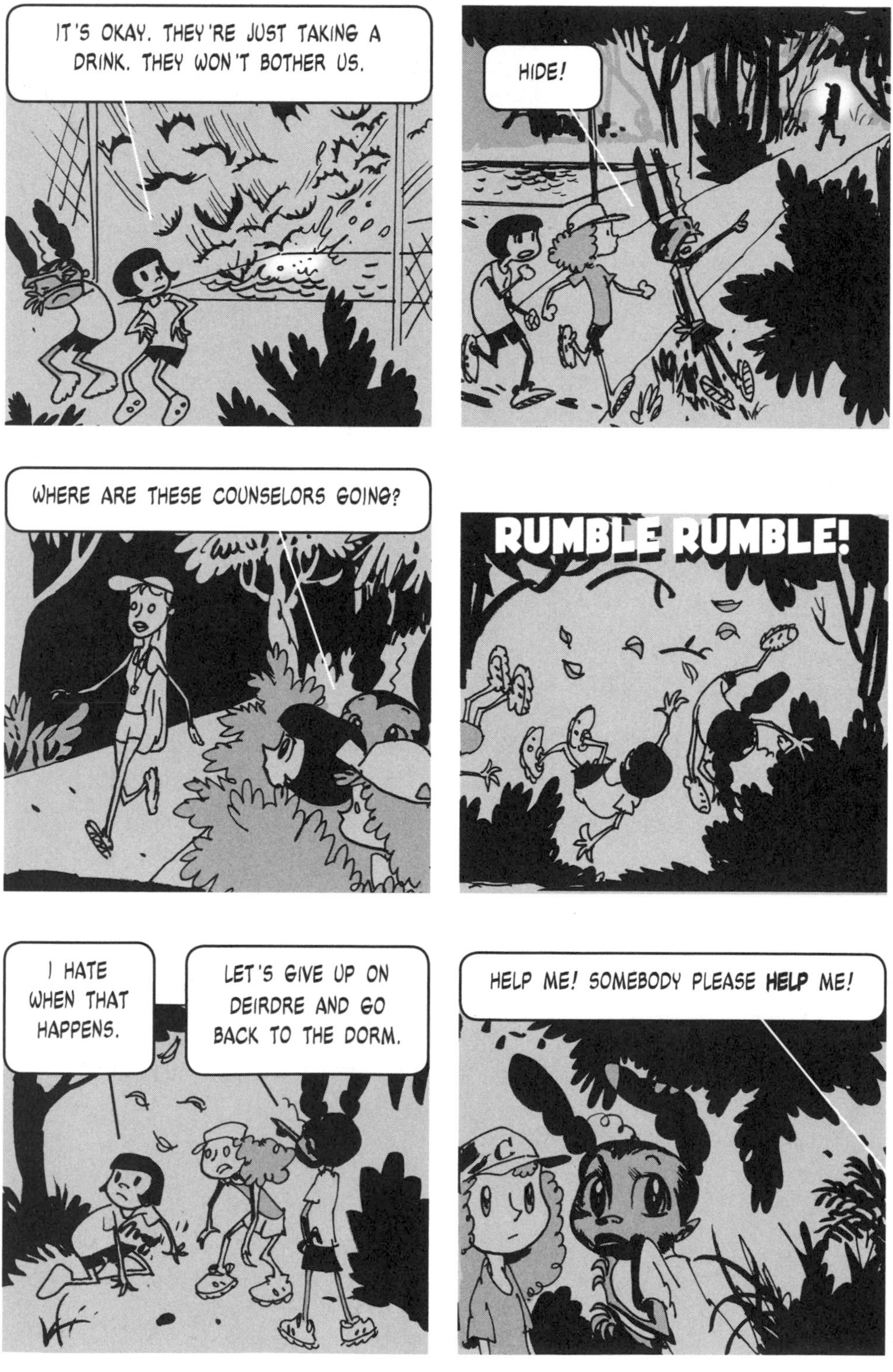
IT'S OKAY. THEY'RE JUST TAKING A DRINK. THEY WON'T BOTHER US.
HIDE!
WHERE ARE THESE COUNSELORS GOING?
RUMBLE RUMBLE!
I HATE WHEN THAT HAPPENS.
LET'S GIVE UP ON DEIRDRE AND GO BACK TO THE DORM.
HELP ME! SOMEBODY PLEASE **HELP** ME!

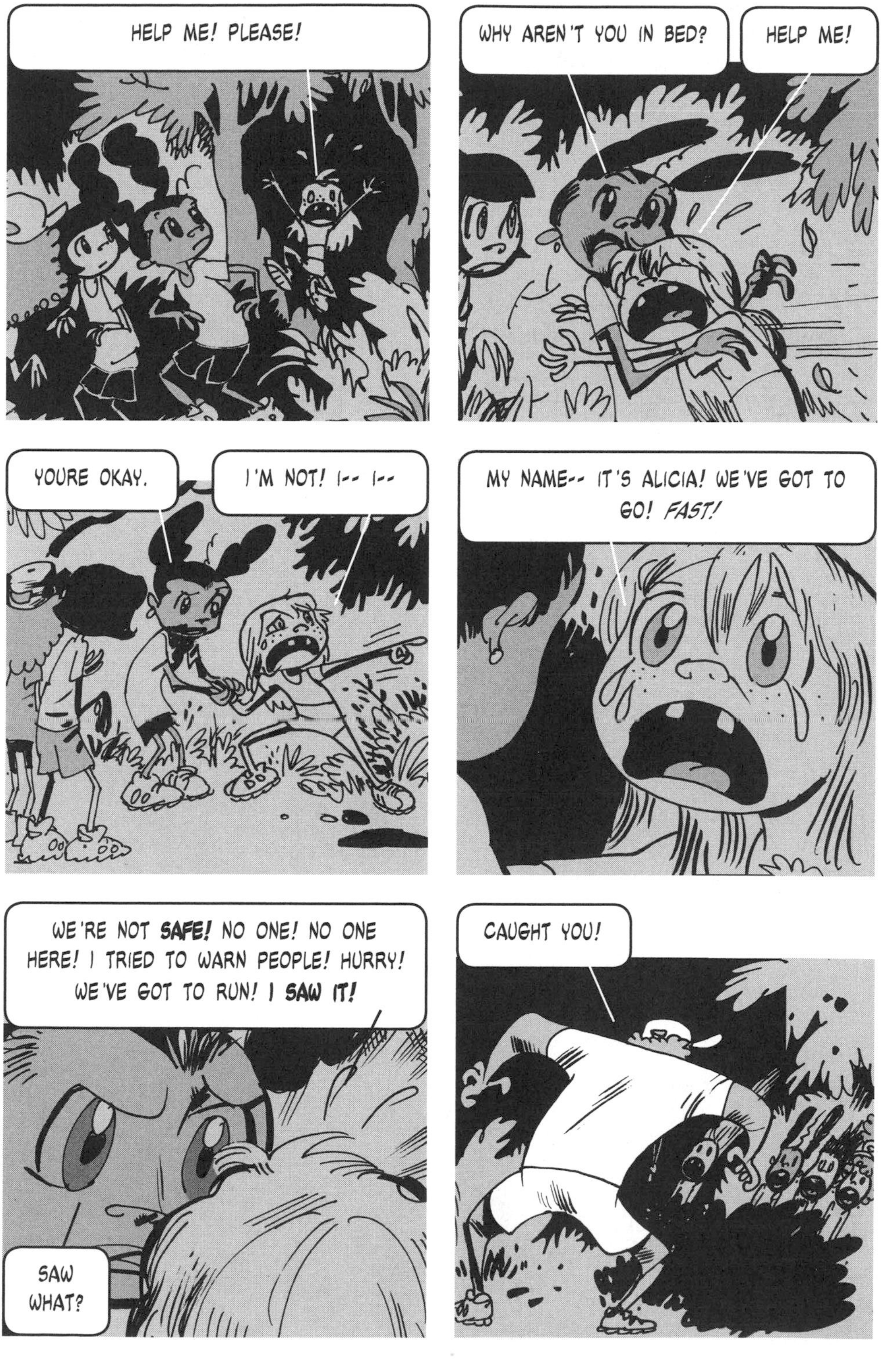
HELP ME! PLEASE!
WHY AREN'T YOU IN BED?
HELP ME!
YOURE OKAY.
I'M NOT! I-- I--
MY NAME-- IT'S ALICIA! WE'VE GOT TO GO! *FAST!*
WE'RE NOT **SAFE!** NO ONE! NO ONE HERE! I TRIED TO WARN PEOPLE! HURRY! WE'VE GOT TO RUN! I **SAW IT!**
SAW WHAT?
CAUGHT YOU!

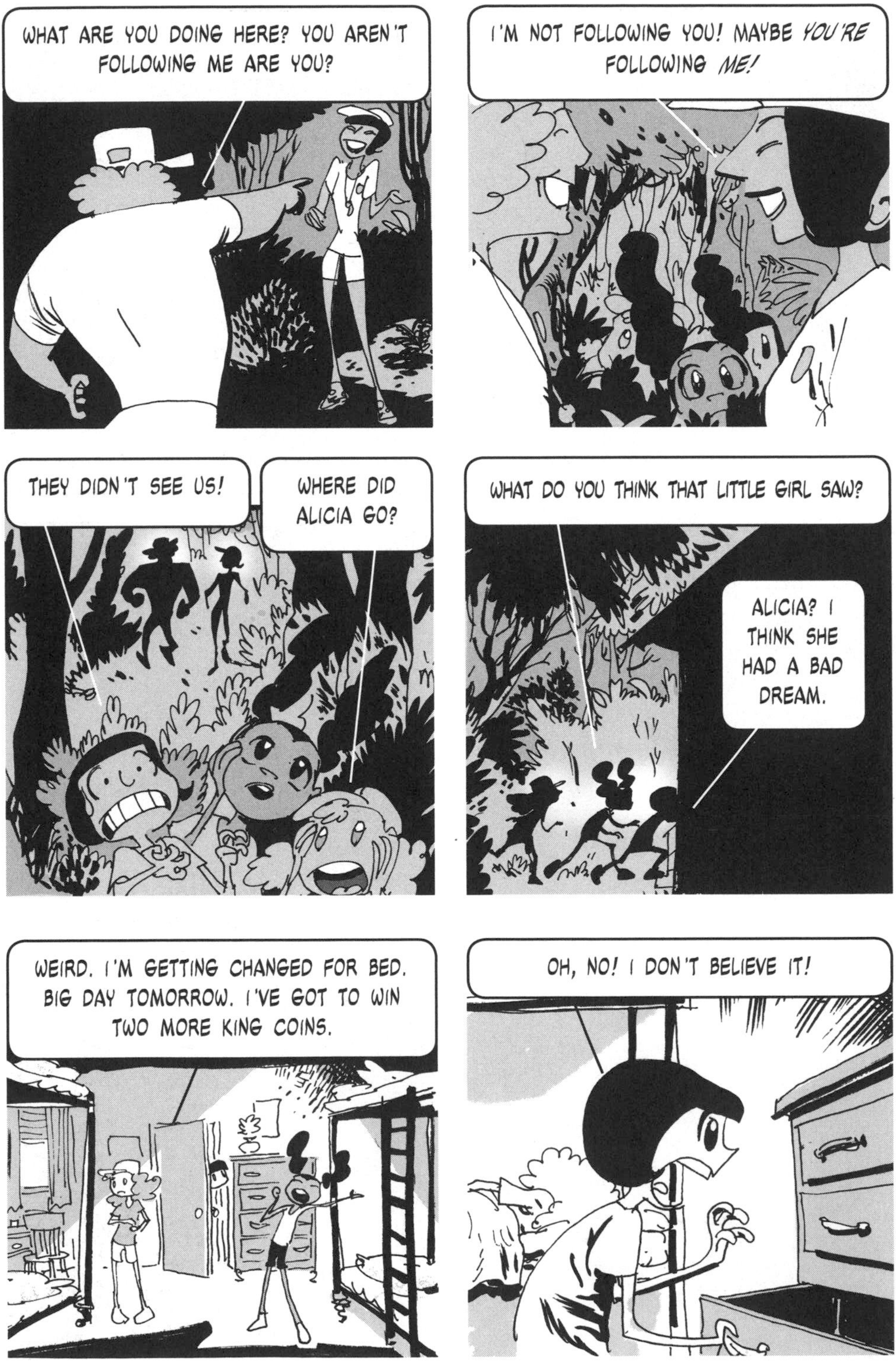
WHAT ARE YOU DOING HERE? YOU AREN'T FOLLOWING ME ARE YOU?
I'M NOT FOLLOWING YOU! MAYBE *YOU'RE* FOLLOWING *ME!*
THEY DIDN'T SEE US!
WHERE DID ALICIA GO?
WHAT DO YOU THINK THAT LITTLE GIRL SAW?
ALICIA? I THINK SHE HAD A BAD DREAM.
WEIRD. I'M GETTING CHANGED FOR BED. BIG DAY TOMORROW. I'VE GOT TO WIN TWO MORE KING COINS.
OH, NO! I DON'T BELIEVE IT!

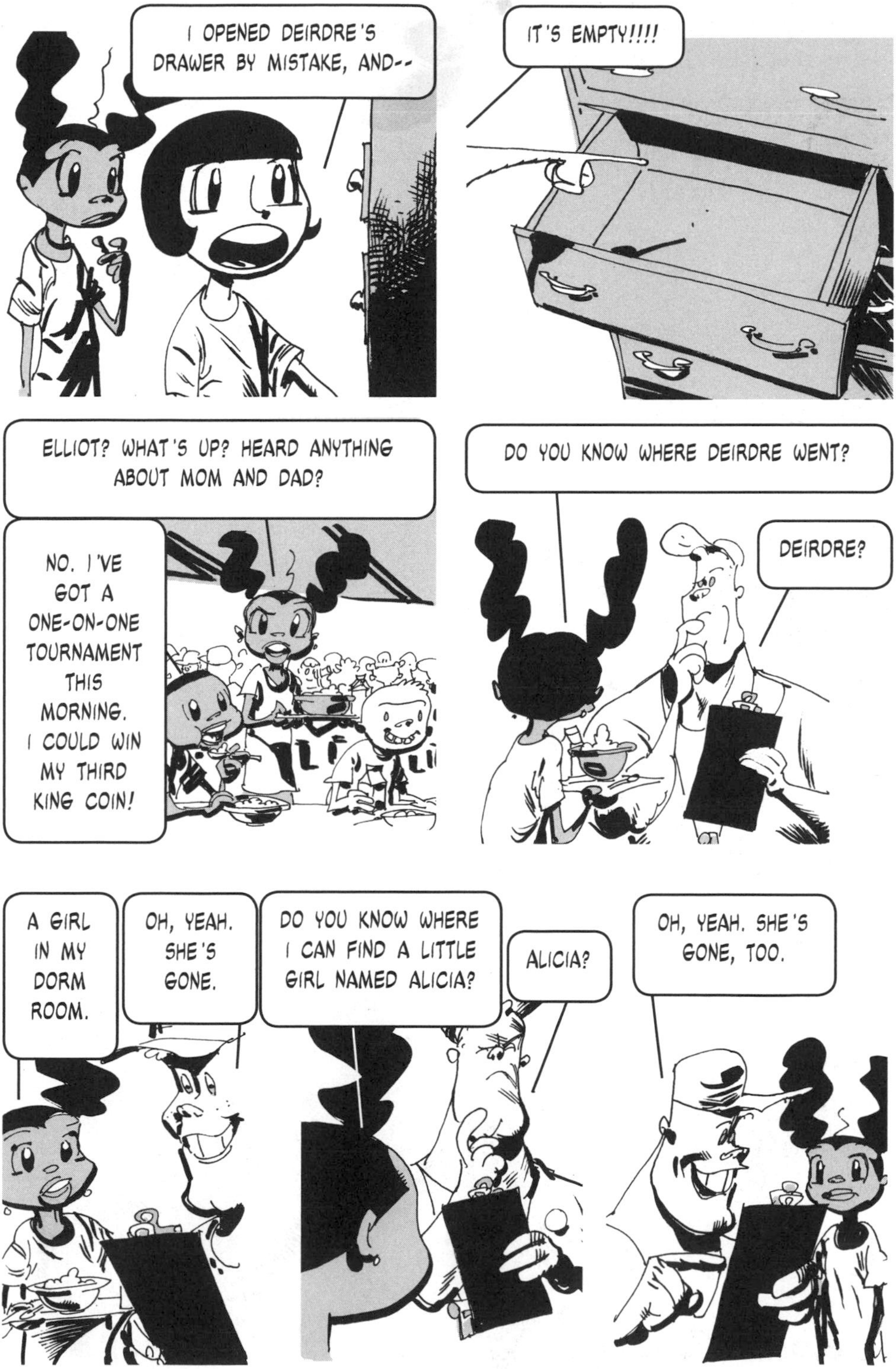
I OPENED DEIRDRE'S DRAWER BY MISTAKE, AND--
IT'S EMPTY!!!!
ELLIOT? WHAT'S UP? HEARD ANYTHING ABOUT MOM AND DAD?
NO. I'VE GOT A ONE-ON-ONE TOURNAMENT THIS MORNING. I COULD WIN MY THIRD KING COIN!
DO YOU KNOW WHERE DEIRDRE WENT?
DEIRDRE?
A GIRL IN MY DORM ROOM.
OH, YEAH. SHE'S GONE.
DO YOU KNOW WHERE I CAN FIND A LITTLE GIRL NAMED ALICIA?
ALICIA?
OH, YEAH. SHE'S GONE, TOO.

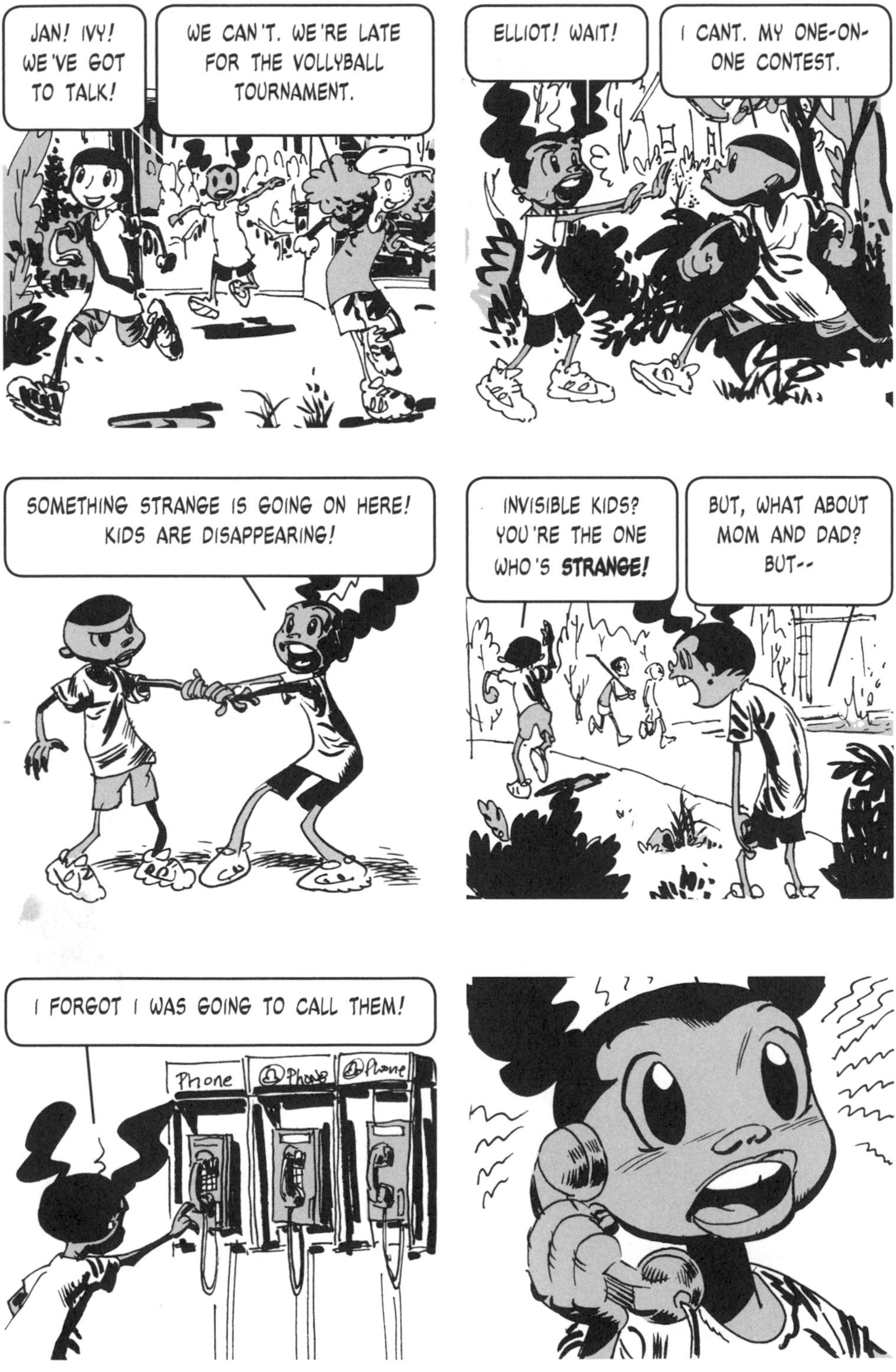
JAN! IVY! WE'VE GOT TO TALK!
WE CAN'T. WE'RE LATE FOR THE VOLLYBALL TOURNAMENT.
ELLIOT! WAIT!
I CANT. MY ONE-ON-ONE CONTEST.
SOMETHING STRANGE IS GOING ON HERE! KIDS ARE DISAPPEARING!
INVISIBLE KIDS? YOU'RE THE ONE WHO'S **STRANGE!**
BUT, WHAT ABOUT MOM AND DAD? BUT--
I FORGOT I WAS GOING TO CALL THEM!
Phone
Phone
Phone

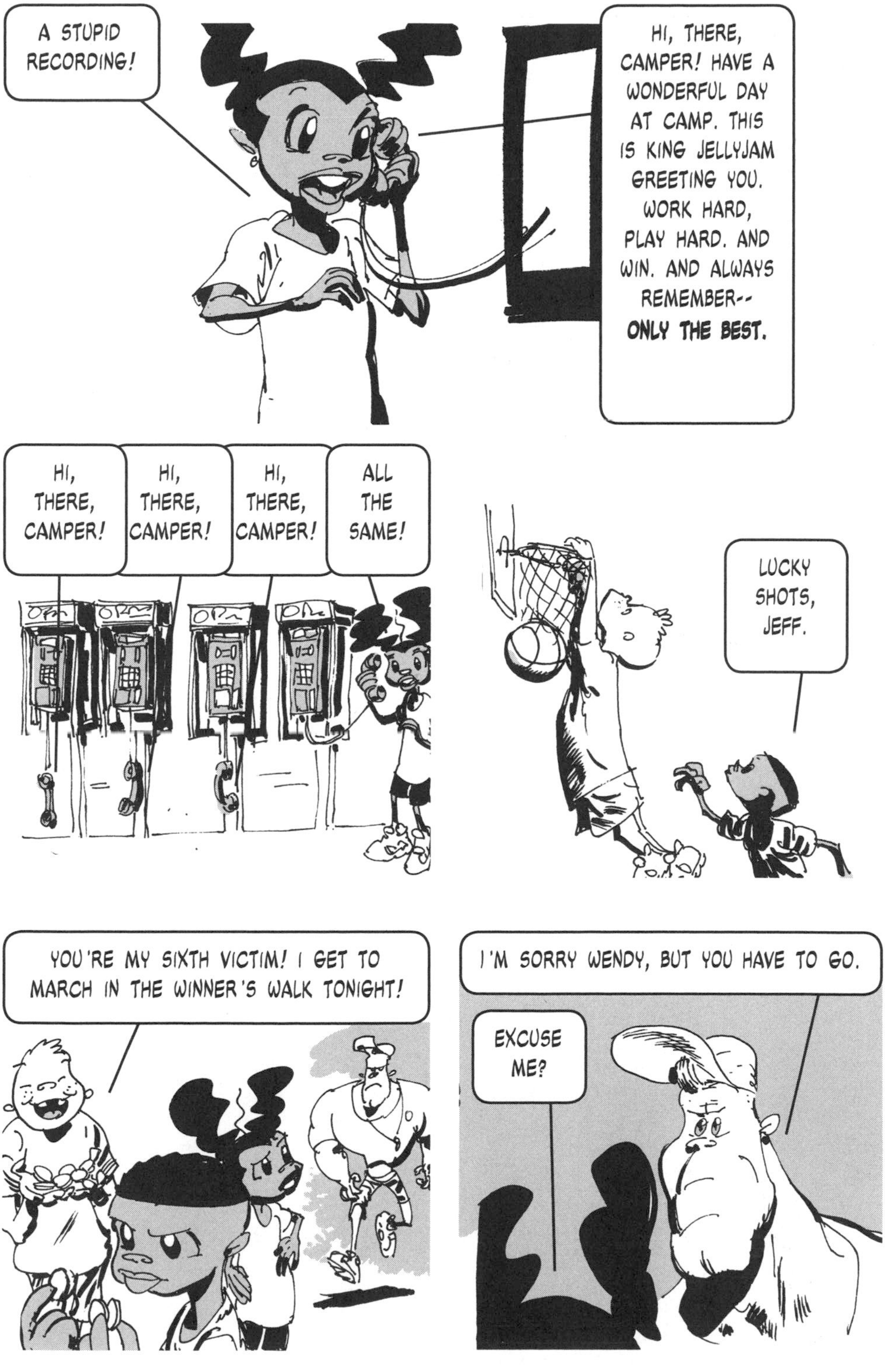
A STUPID RECORDING!
HI, THERE, CAMPER! HAVE A WONDERFUL DAY AT CAMP. THIS IS KING JELLYJAM GREETING YOU. WORK HARD, PLAY HARD. AND WIN. AND ALWAYS REMEMBER-- **ONLY THE BEST.**
HI, THERE, CAMPER!
HI, THERE, CAMPER!
HI, THERE, CAMPER!
ALL THE SAME!
LUCKY SHOTS, JEFF.
YOU'RE MY SIXTH VICTIM! I GET TO MARCH IN THE WINNER'S WALK TONIGHT!
I'M SORRY WENDY, BUT YOU HAVE TO GO.
EXCUSE ME?

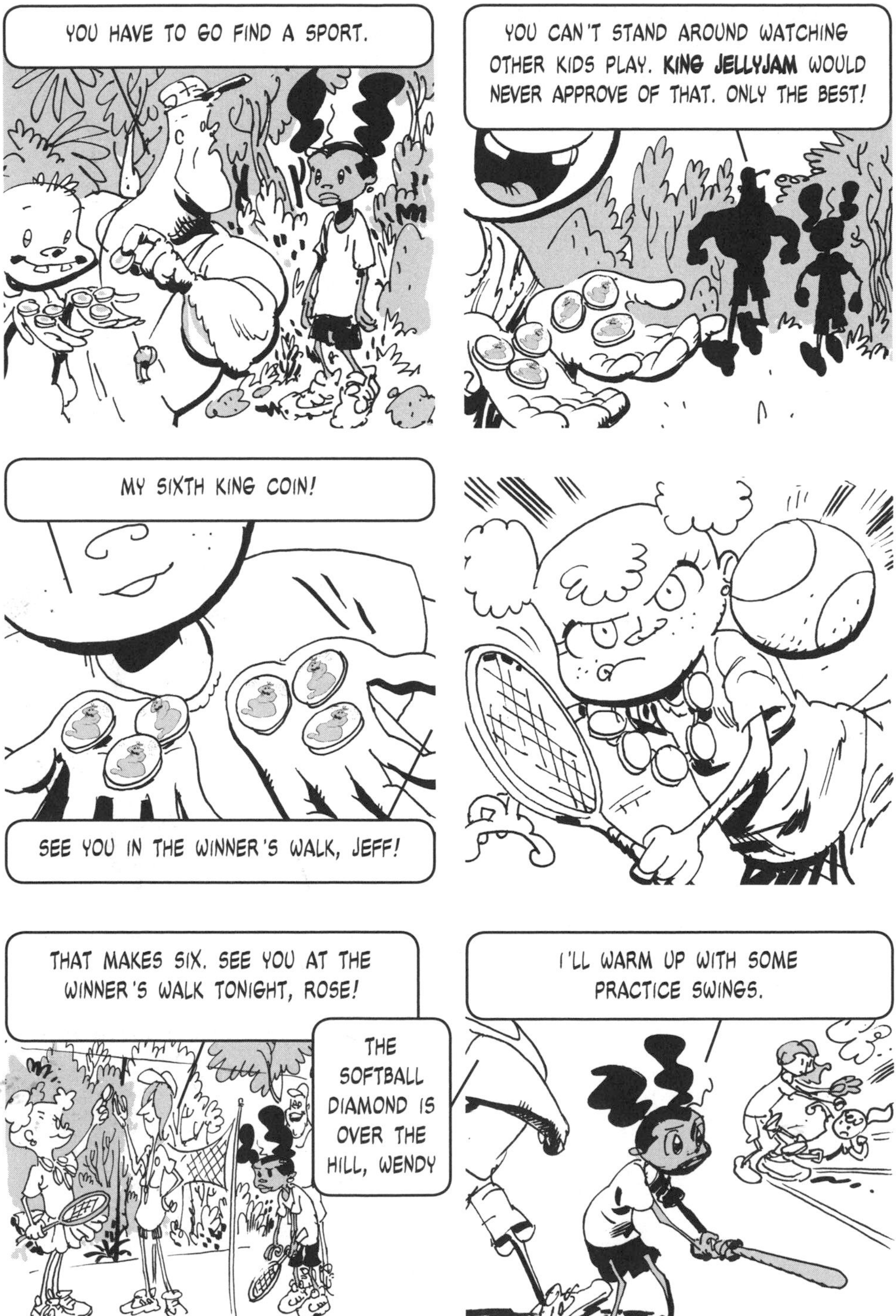
YOU HAVE TO GO FIND A SPORT.
YOU CAN'T STAND AROUND WATCHING OTHER KIDS PLAY. **KING JELLYJAM** WOULD NEVER APPROVE OF THAT. ONLY THE BEST!
MY SIXTH KING COIN!
SEE YOU IN THE WINNER'S WALK, JEFF!
THAT MAKES SIX. SEE YOU AT THE WINNER'S WALK TONIGHT, ROSE!
THE SOFTBALL DIAMOND IS OVER THE HILL, WENDY
I'LL WARM UP WITH SOME PRACTICE SWINGS.

THOCCCCK!

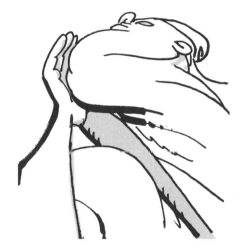

I LIKE THE WAY YOU CHOKE UP, BUT MAYBE WE COULD FIIND YOU A LIGHTER BAT.

THE WINNER'S WALK. THERE'S ROSE! WITH JEFF BEHIND HER.

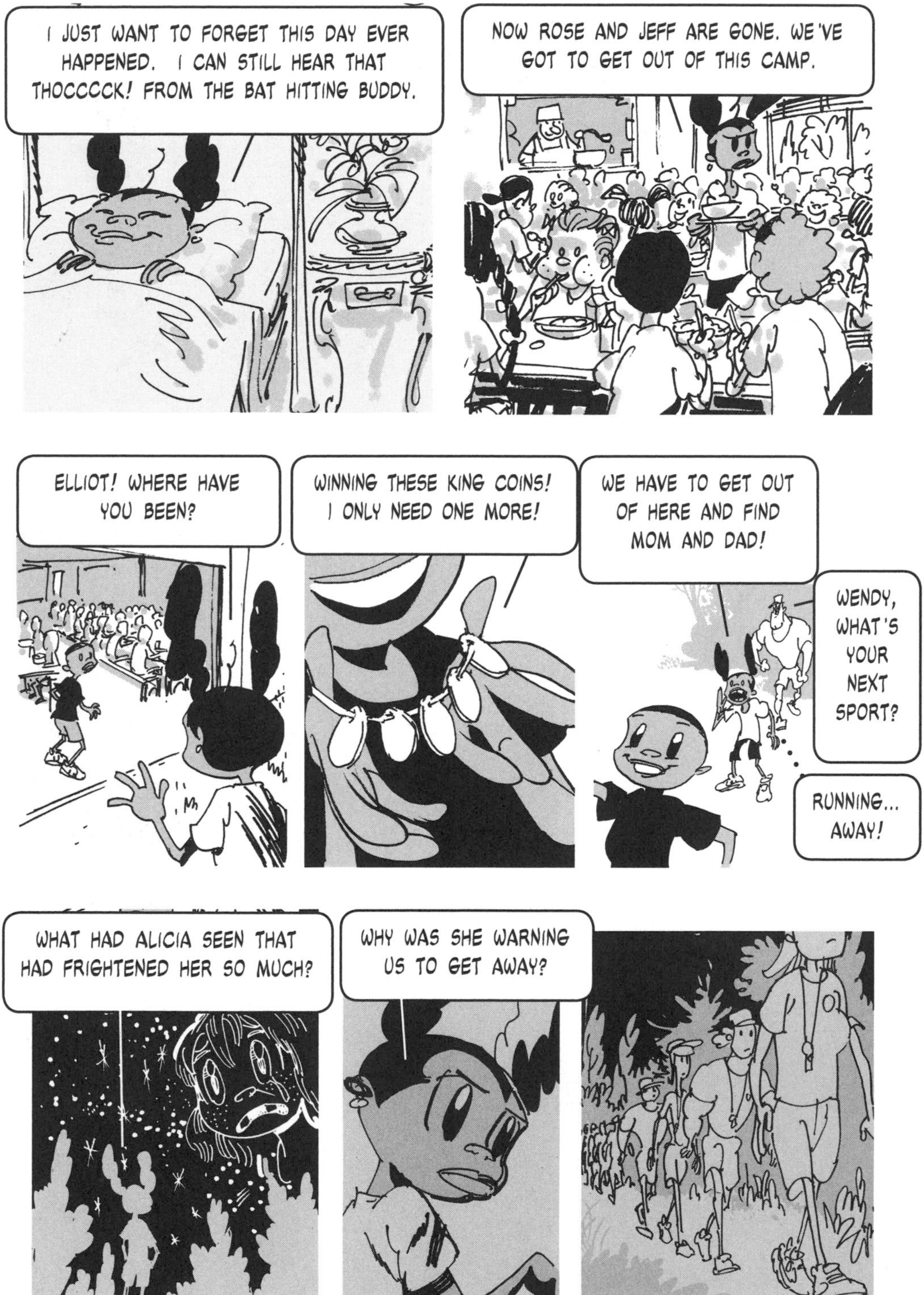
I JUST WANT TO FORGET THIS DAY EVER HAPPENED. I CAN STILL HEAR THAT THOCCCCK! FROM THE BAT HITTING BUDDY.
NOW ROSE AND JEFF ARE GONE. WE'VE GOT TO GET OUT OF THIS CAMP.
ELLIOT! WHERE HAVE YOU BEEN?
WINNING THESE KING COINS! I ONLY NEED ONE MORE!
WE HAVE TO GET OUT OF HERE AND FIND MOM AND DAD!
WENDY, WHAT'S YOUR NEXT SPORT?
RUNNING... AWAY!
WHAT HAD ALICIA SEEN THAT HAD FRIGHTENED HER SO MUCH?
WHY WAS SHE WARNING US TO GET AWAY?

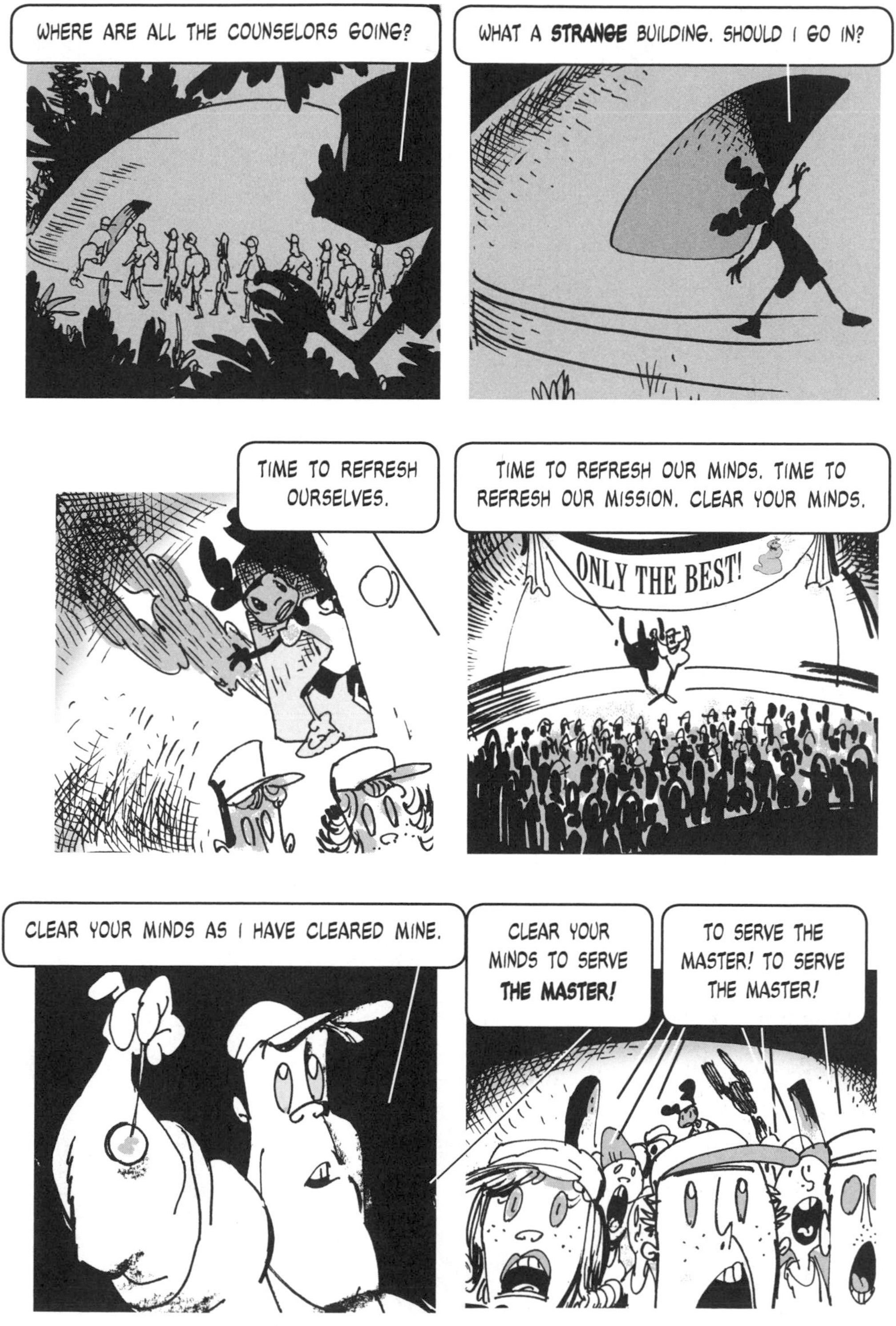
WHERE ARE ALL THE COUNSELORS GOING?
WHAT A **STRANGE** BUILDING. SHOULD I GO IN?
TIME TO REFRESH OURSELVES.
TIME TO REFRESH OUR MINDS. TIME TO REFRESH OUR MISSION. CLEAR YOUR MINDS.
ONLY THE BEST!
CLEAR YOUR MINDS AS I HAVE CLEARED MINE.
CLEAR YOUR MINDS TO SERVE **THE MASTER!**
TO SERVE THE MASTER! TO SERVE THE MASTER!

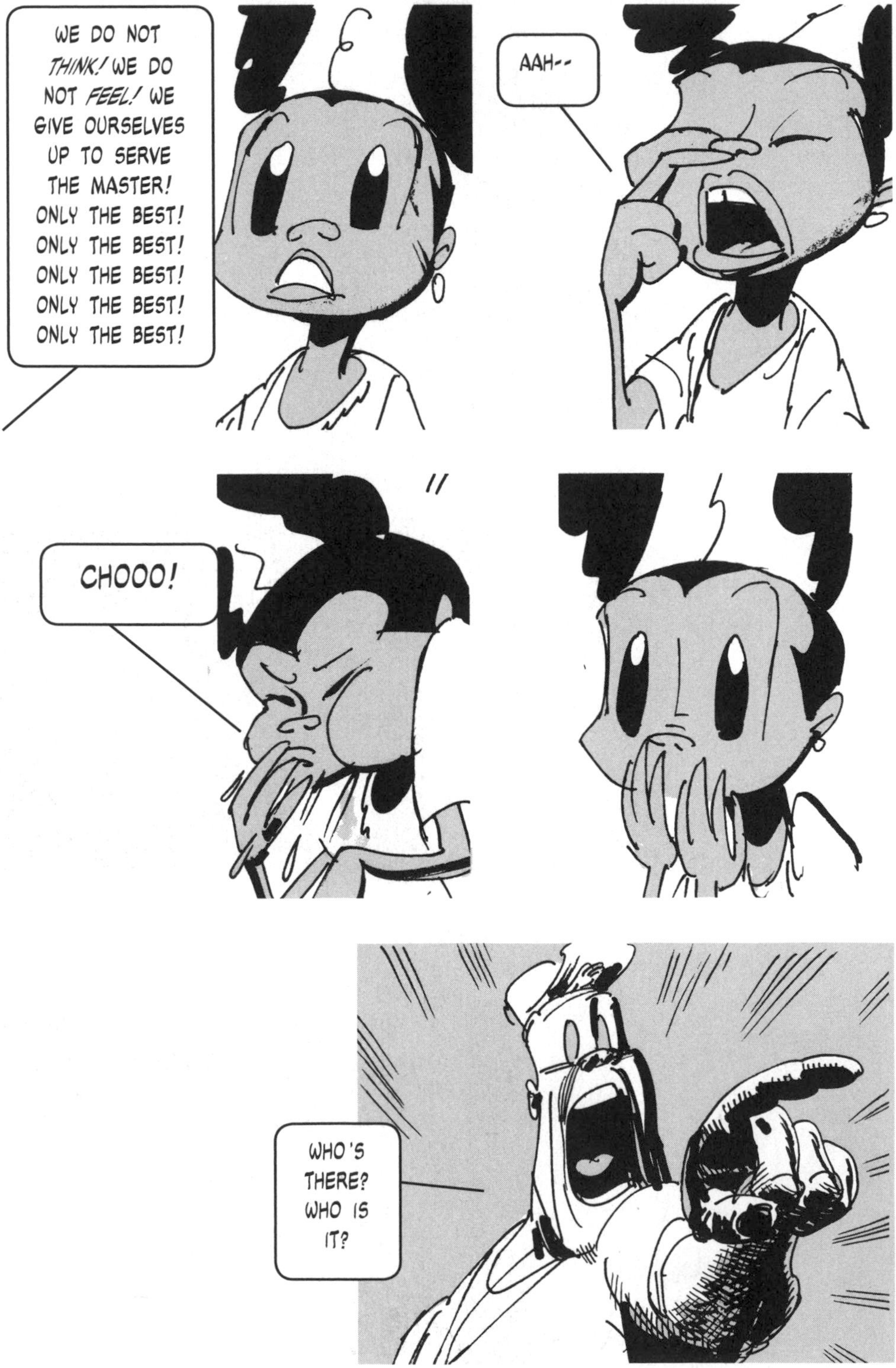
WE DO NOT *THINK!* WE DO NOT *FEEL!* WE GIVE OURSELVES UP TO SERVE THE MASTER! ONLY THE BEST! ONLY THE BEST! ONLY THE BEST! ONLY THE BEST! ONLY THE BEST!
AAH--
CHOOO!
WHO'S THERE? WHO IS IT?

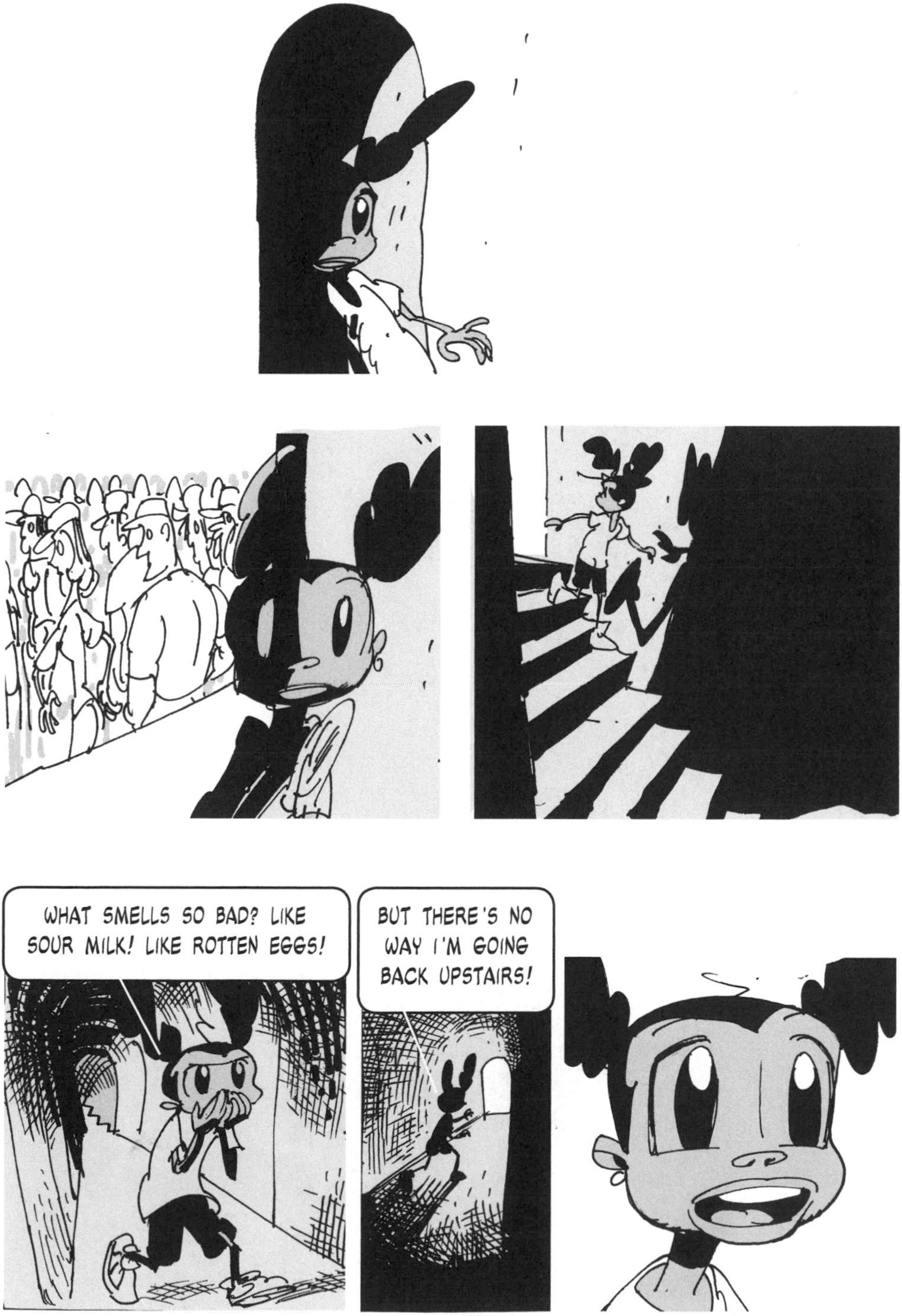
WHAT SMELLS SO BAD? LIKE SOUR MILK! LIKE ROTTEN EGGS!
BUT THERE'S NO WAY I'M GOING BACK UPSTAIRS!

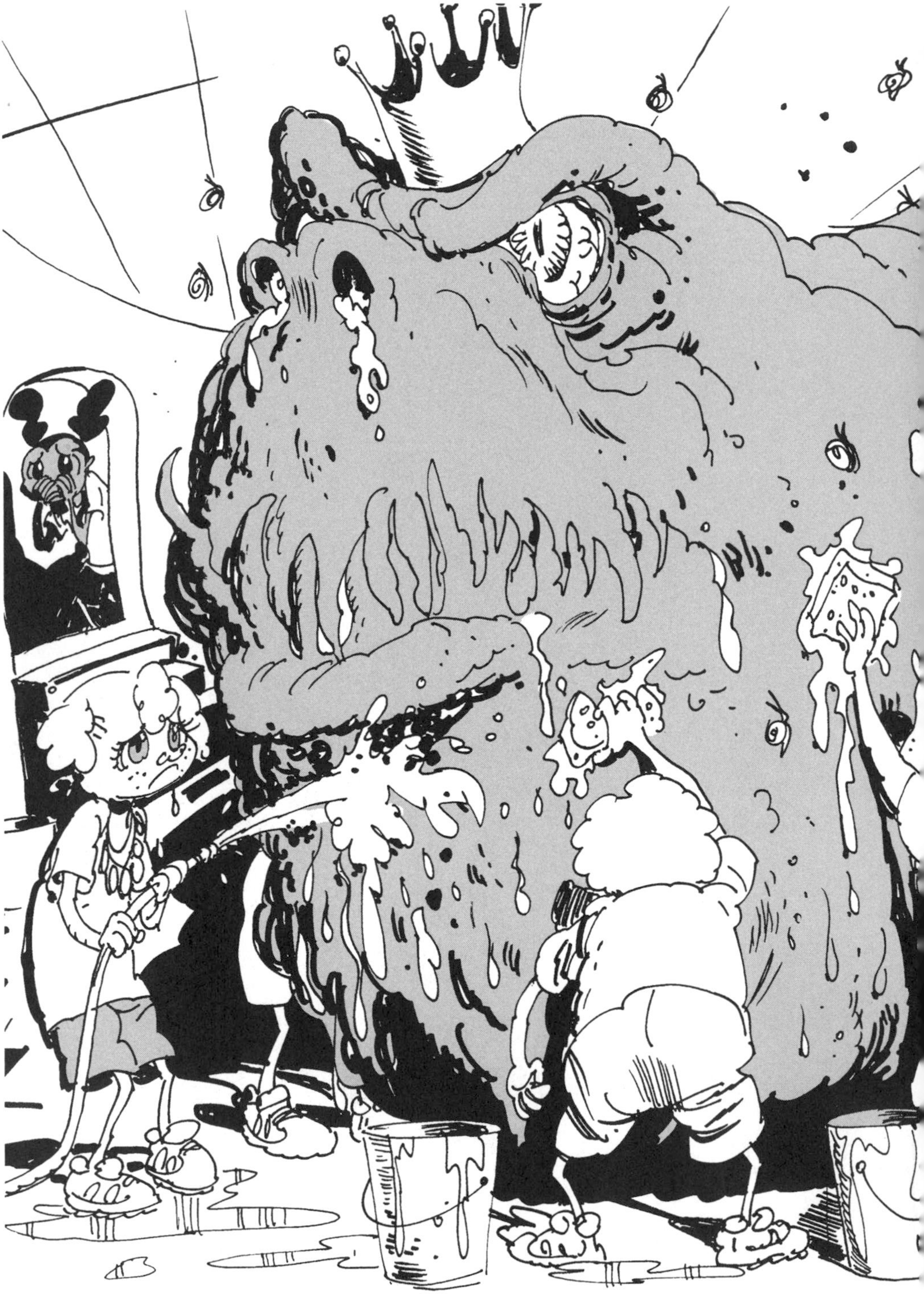

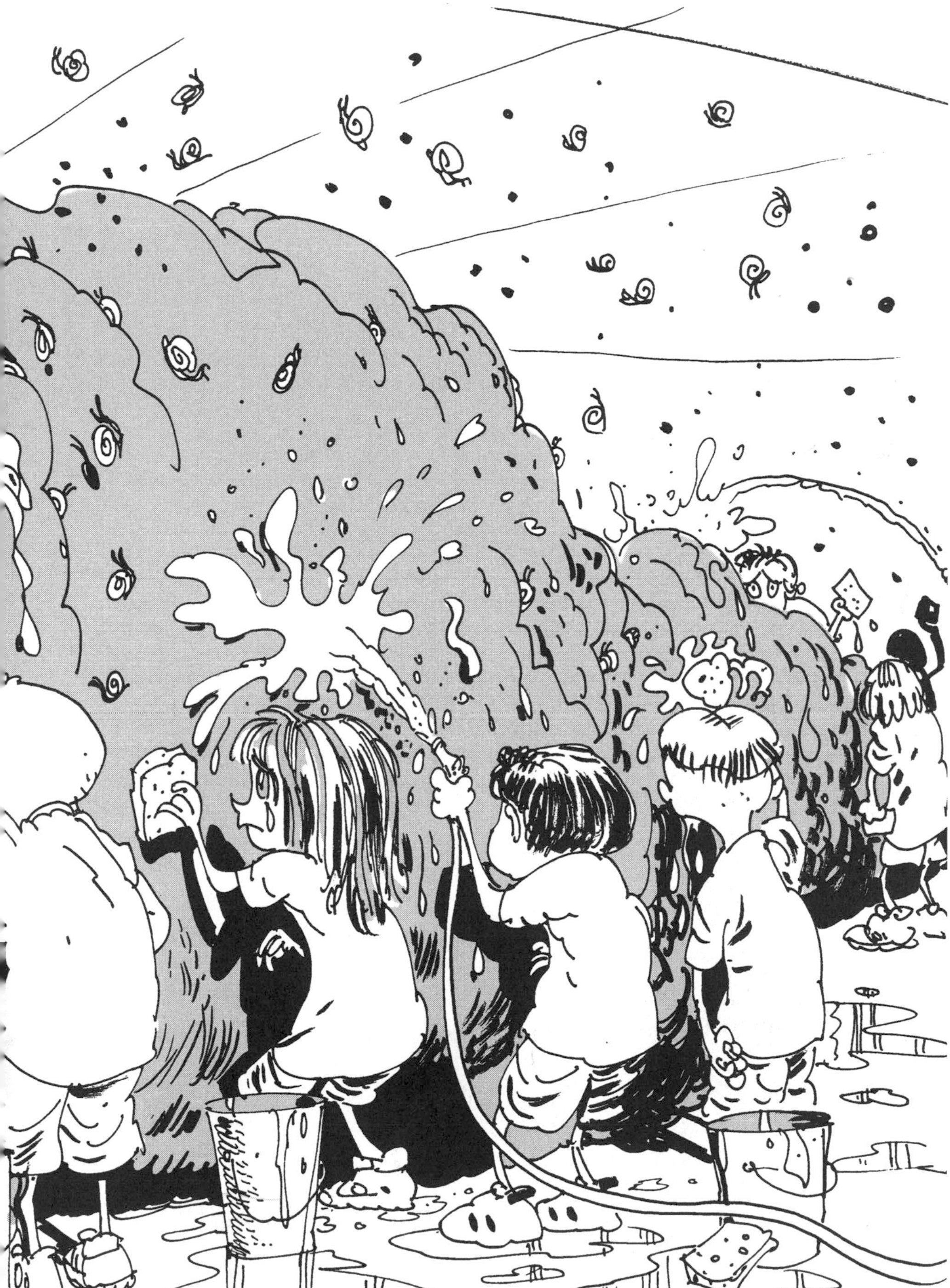

GET AWAY FROM HERE, WENDY! **RUN!**

DEIRDRE! WHAT'S HAPPENING?

ONLY THE BEST! ONLY THE BEST GET TO BE KING JELLYJAM'S SLAVES!

DON'T YOU SEE? THESE ARE ALL SIX-COIN WINNERS! KING JELLYJAM GETS THE STRONGEST KIDS! THE BEST WORKERS!

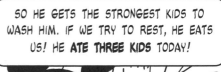

HE HAS TO BE WASHED ALL THE TIME! HE HAS TO BE KEPT WET AND HE CAN'T STAND HIS OWN SMELL. **HE SWEATS SNAILS!**

SO HE GETS THE STRONGEST KIDS TO WASH HIM. IF WE TRY TO REST, HE EATS US! HE **ATE THREE KIDS** TODAY!

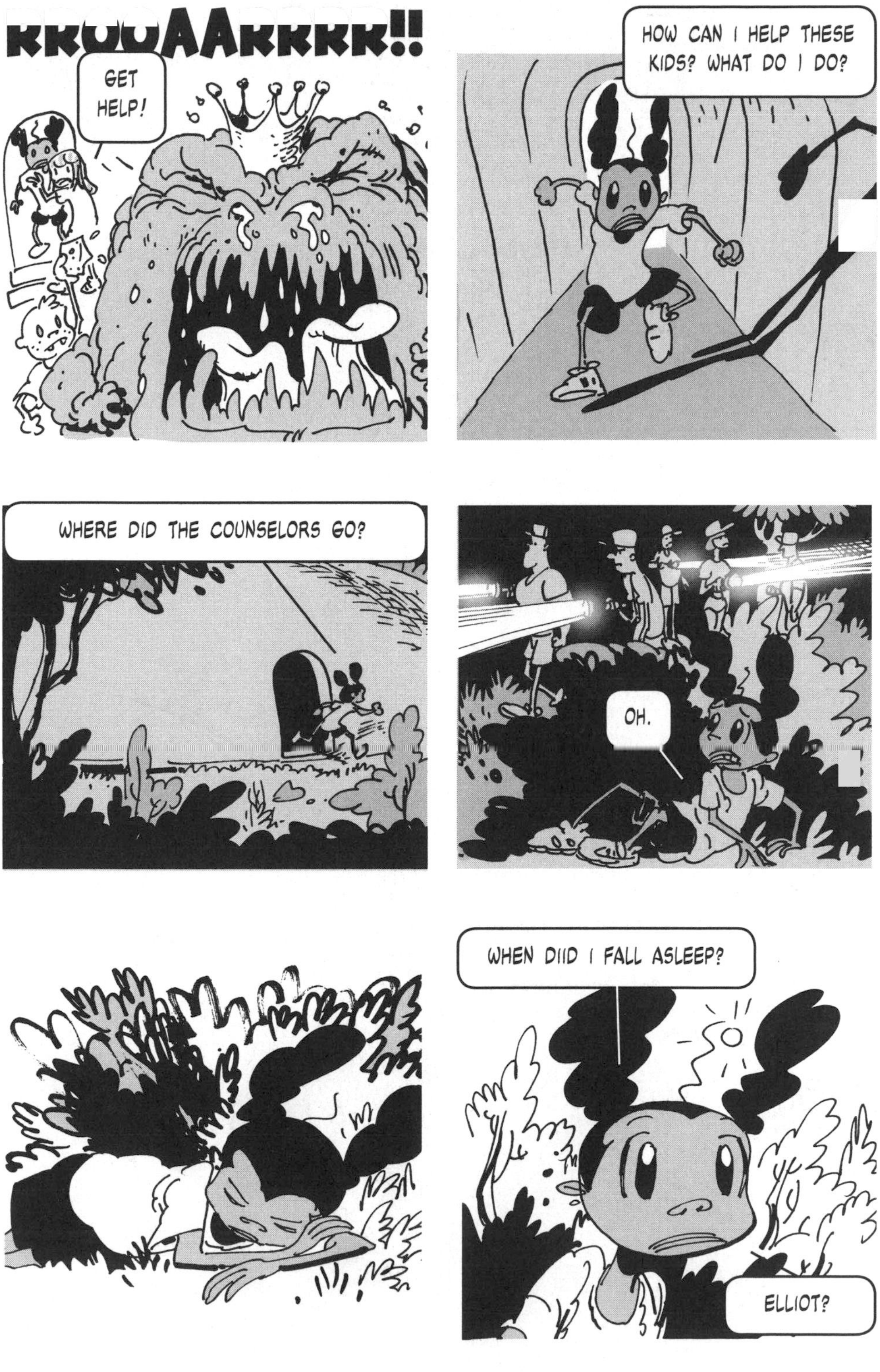
GET HELP!
HOW CAN I HELP THESE KIDS? WHAT DO I DO?
WHERE DID THE COUNSELORS GO?
OH.
WHEN DIID I FALL ASLEEP?
ELLIOT?

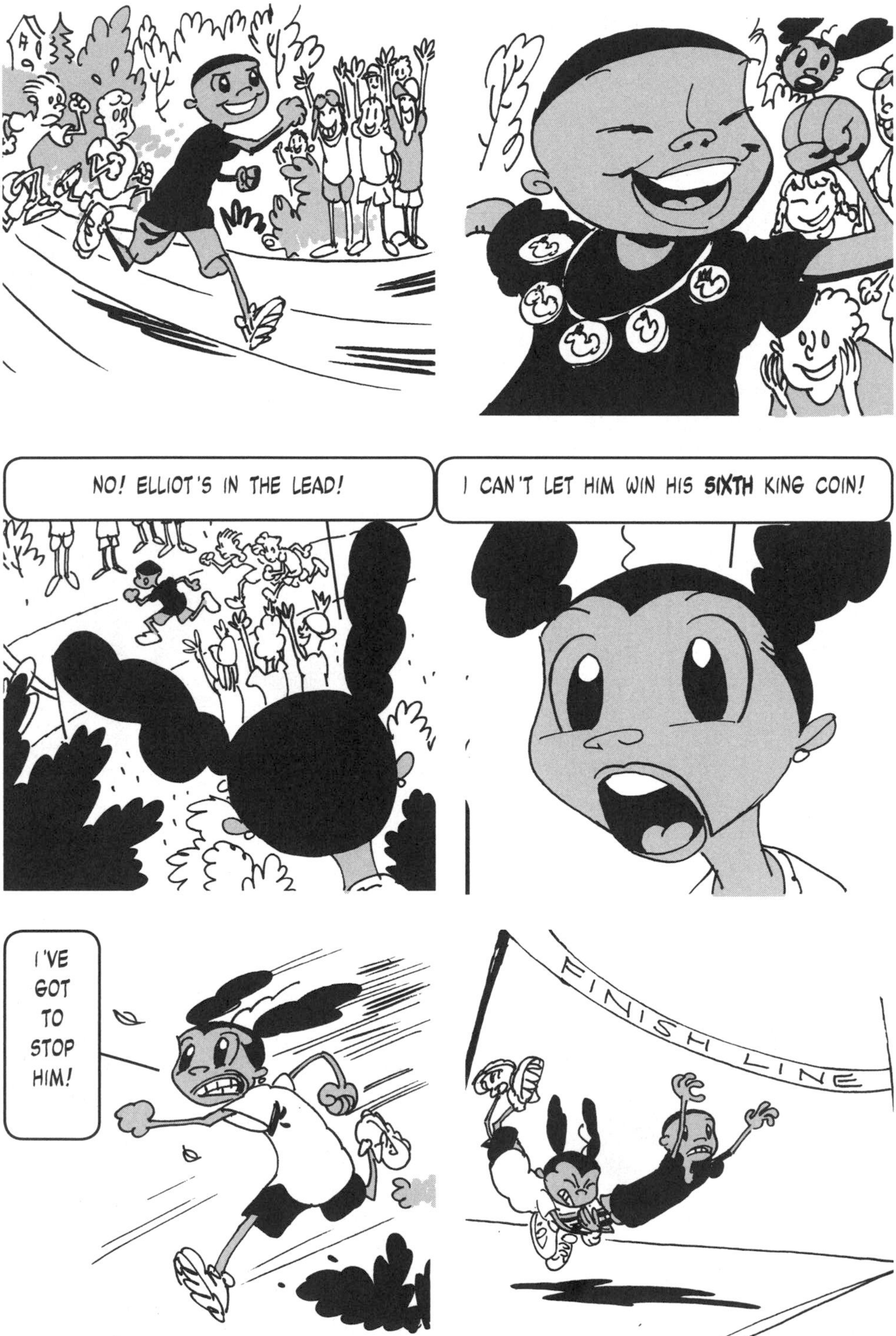
NO! ELLIOT'S IN THE LEAD!
I CAN'T LET HIM WIN HIS **SIXTH** KING COIN!
I'VE GOT TO STOP HIM!
FINISH LINE

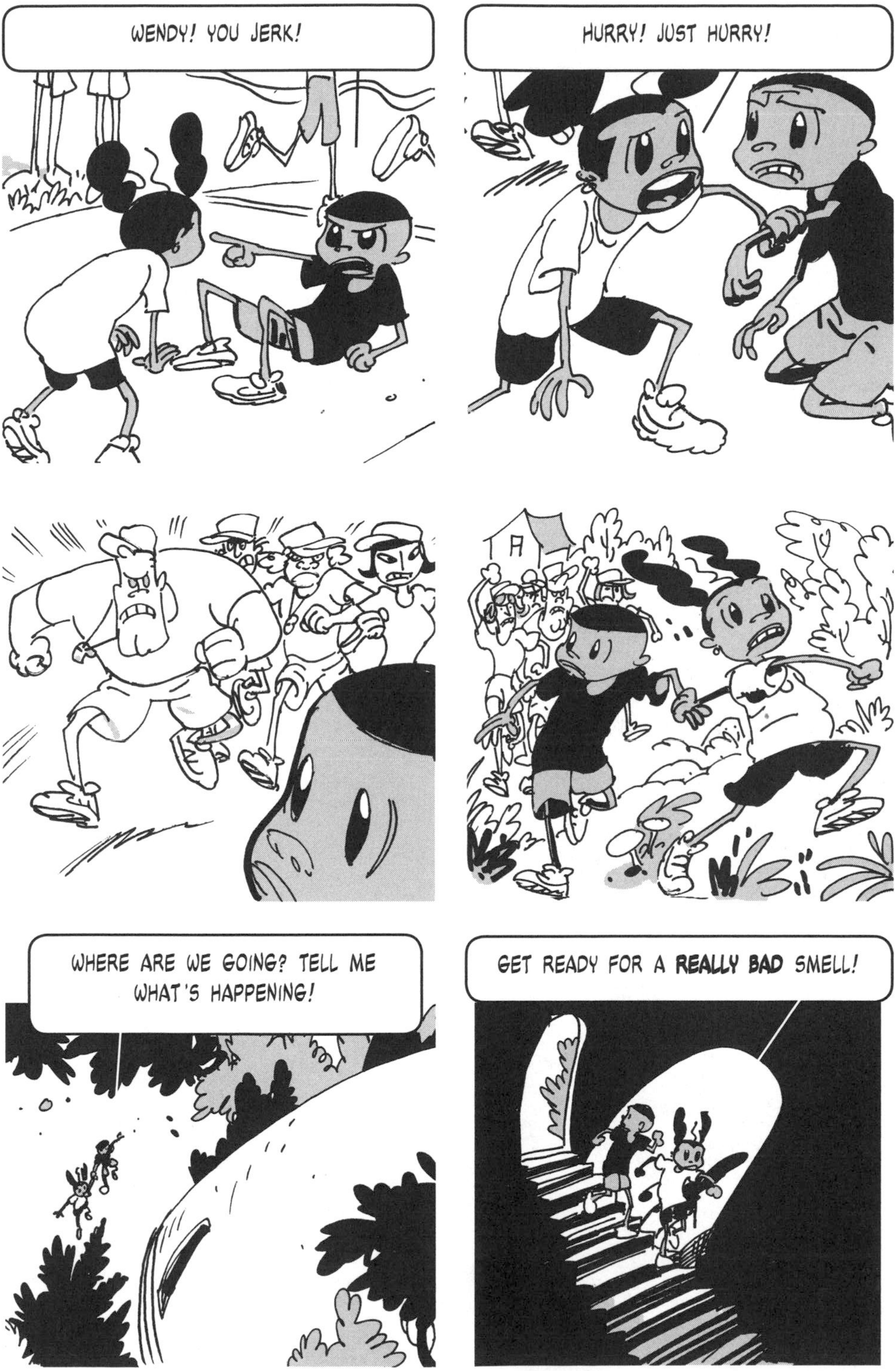
WENDY! YOU JERK!
HURRY! JUST HURRY!
WHERE ARE WE GOING? TELL ME WHAT'S HAPPENING!
GET READY FOR A **REALLY BAD** SMELL!

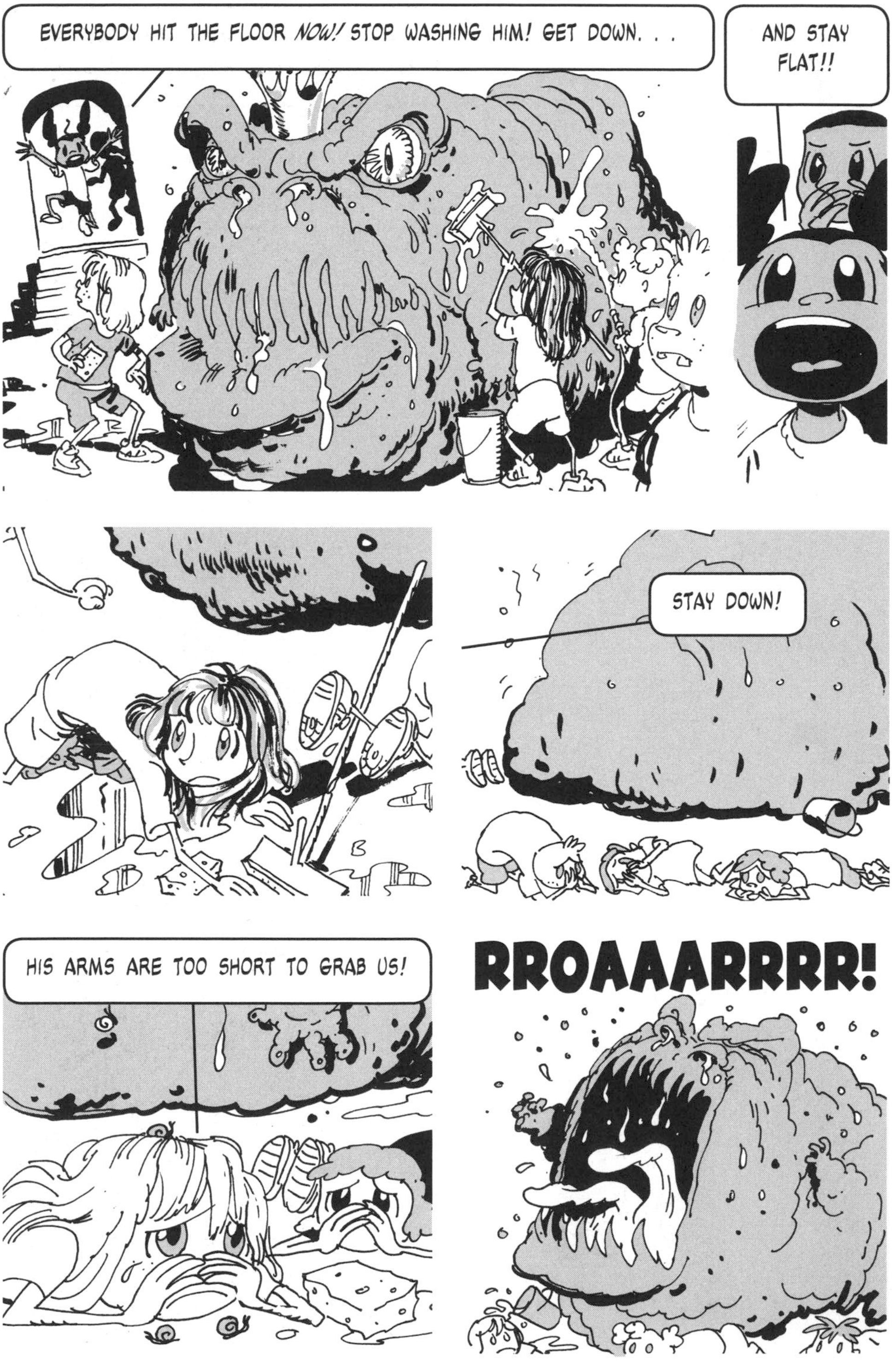
EVERYBODY HIT THE FLOOR *NOW!* STOP WASHING HIM! GET DOWN. . .
AND STAY FLAT!!
STAY DOWN!
HIS ARMS ARE TOO SHORT TO GRAB US!
RROAAARRRR!

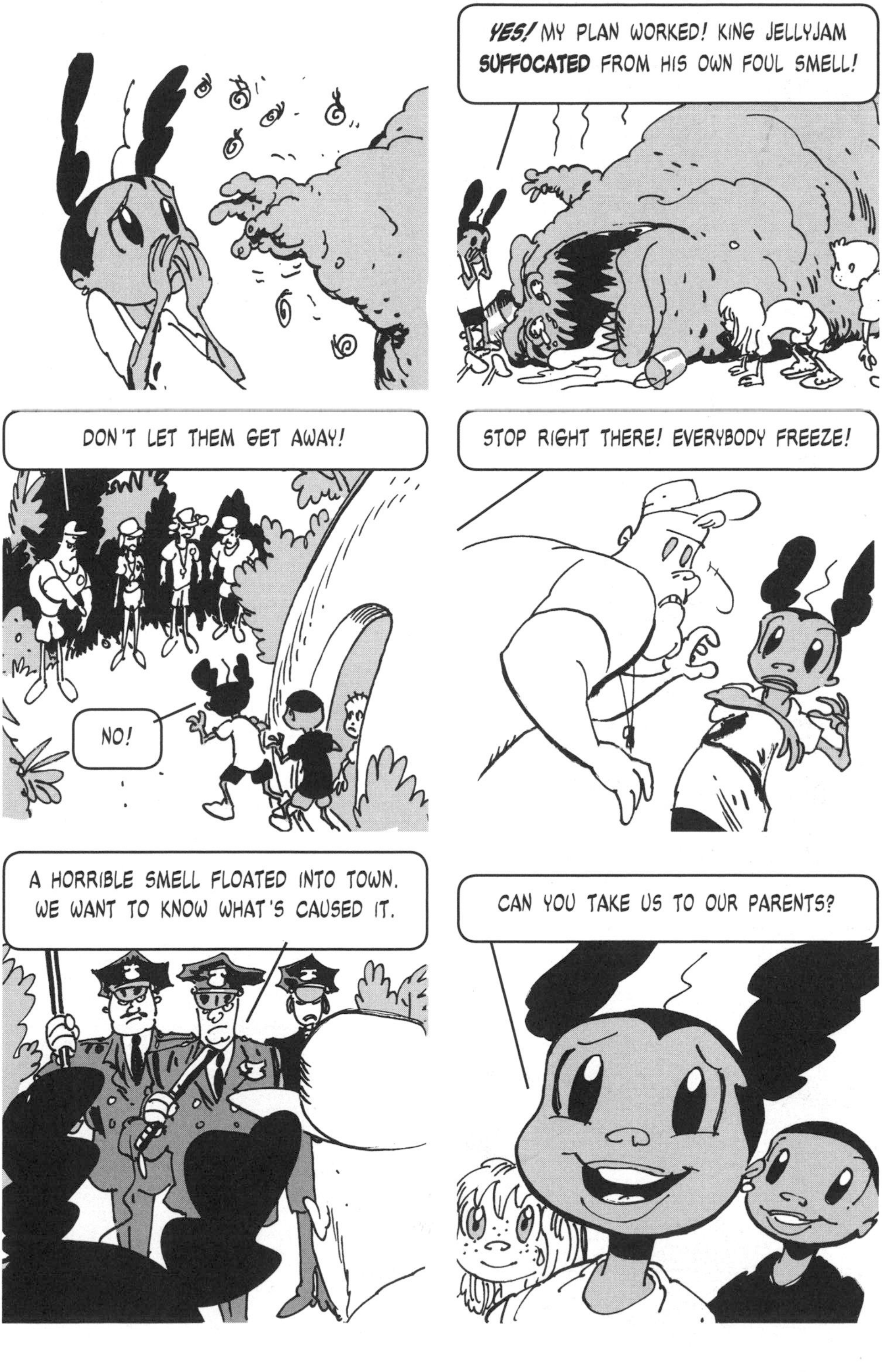
YES! MY PLAN WORKED! KING JELLYJAM SUFFOCATED FROM HIS OWN FOUL SMELL!
DON'T LET THEM GET AWAY!
NO!
STOP RIGHT THERE! EVERYBODY FREEZE!
A HORRIBLE SMELL FLOATED INTO TOWN. WE WANT TO KNOW WHAT'S CAUSED IT.
CAN YOU TAKE US TO OUR PARENTS?

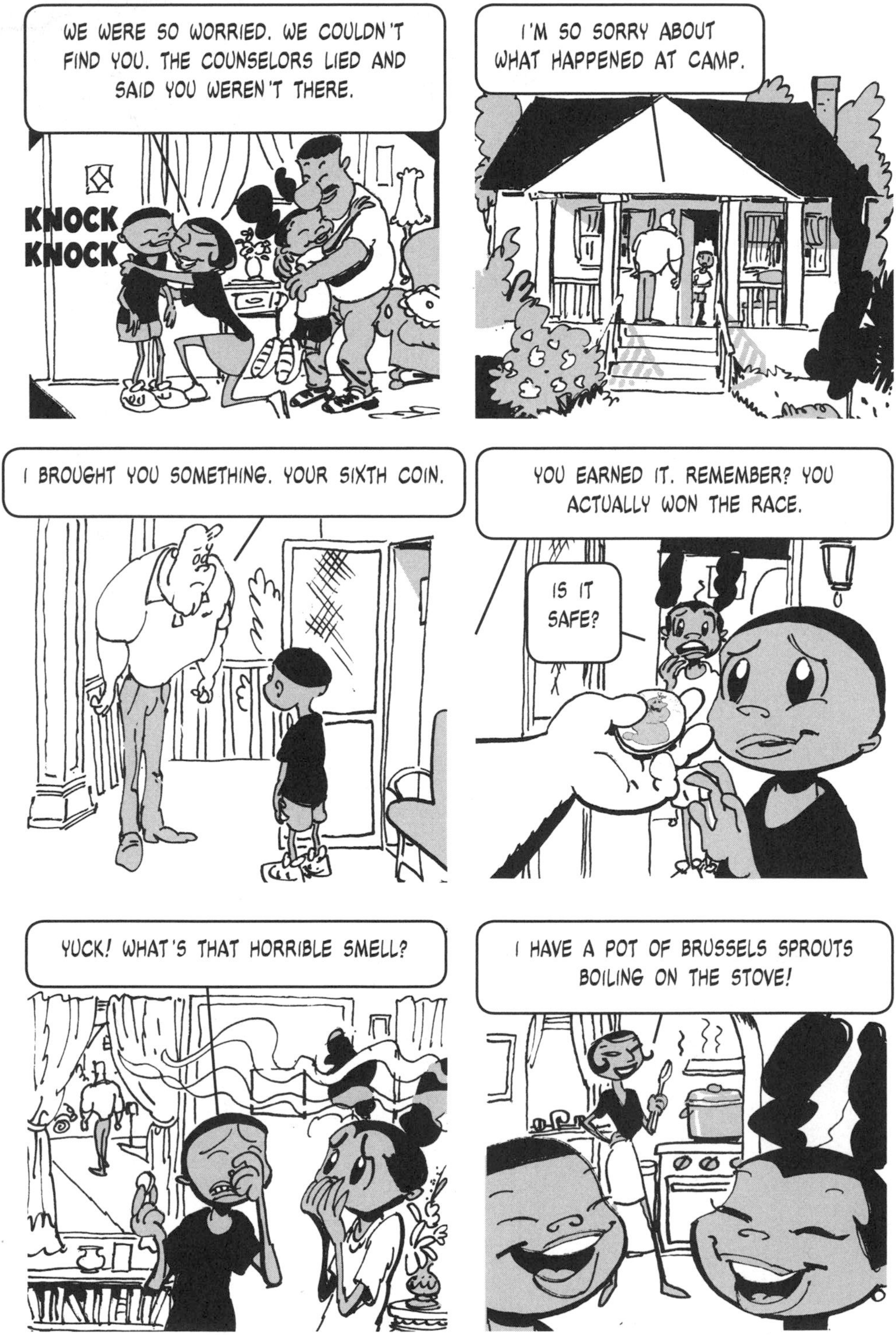
WE WERE SO WORRIED. WE COULDN'T FIND YOU. THE COUNSELORS LIED AND SAID YOU WEREN'T THERE.
KNOCK KNOCK
I'M SO SORRY ABOUT WHAT HAPPENED AT CAMP.
I BROUGHT YOU SOMETHING. YOUR SIXTH COIN.
YOU EARNED IT. REMEMBER? YOU ACTUALLY WON THE RACE.
IS IT SAFE?
YUCK! WHAT'S THAT HORRIBLE SMELL?
I HAVE A POT OF BRUSSELS SPROUTS BOILING ON THE STOVE!

MEET THE ARTIST

Dean Haspiel

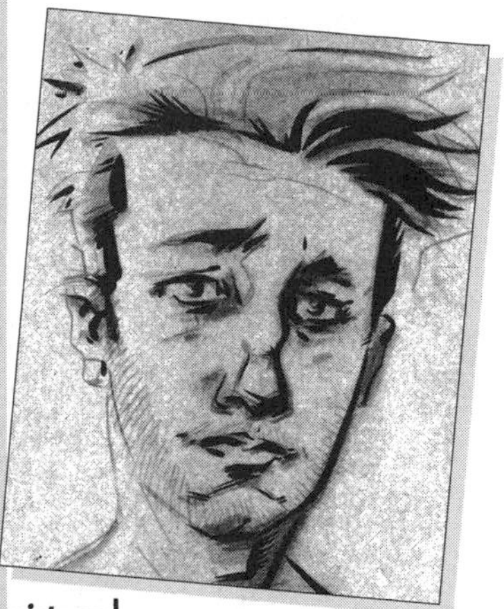

Dean Haspiel is a native New Yorker and the author of super-psychedelic romances and semiautobiographical comix. He was nominated for a 2002 Eisner award for "Talent Deserving of Wider Recognition" and a 2003 Ignatz award for "Outstanding Artist." He recently collaborated with Harvey Pekar on *The Quitter, The Escapist,* and Vertigo's relaunch of *American Splendor*. Dean's work has appeared in anthologies such as DC Comics' Bizarro Comics and Alternative Comics' *9-11: Emergency Relief,* and in comics such as *Captain America, X-Men, Spider-Man, Batman,* and *Justice League*.

Dean first adapted *Revenge of the Lawn Gnomes* into a script that broke down the story into pages and panels. He then sketched the main characters, such as Moose.

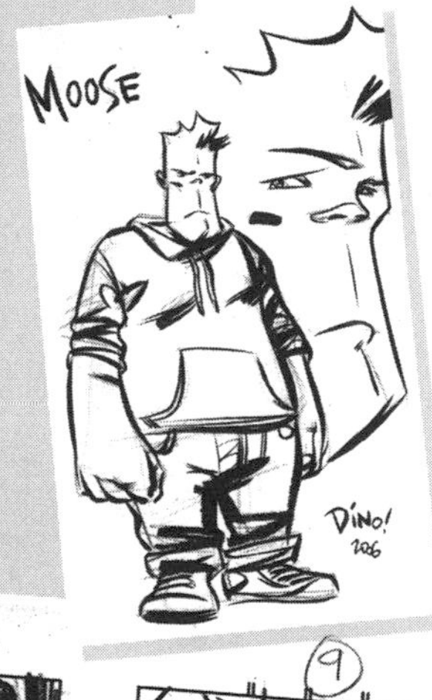
MOOSE

Character sketch

Next, Dean did thumbnail layouts. These rough drawings, based on Dean's script, showed what each page would look like.

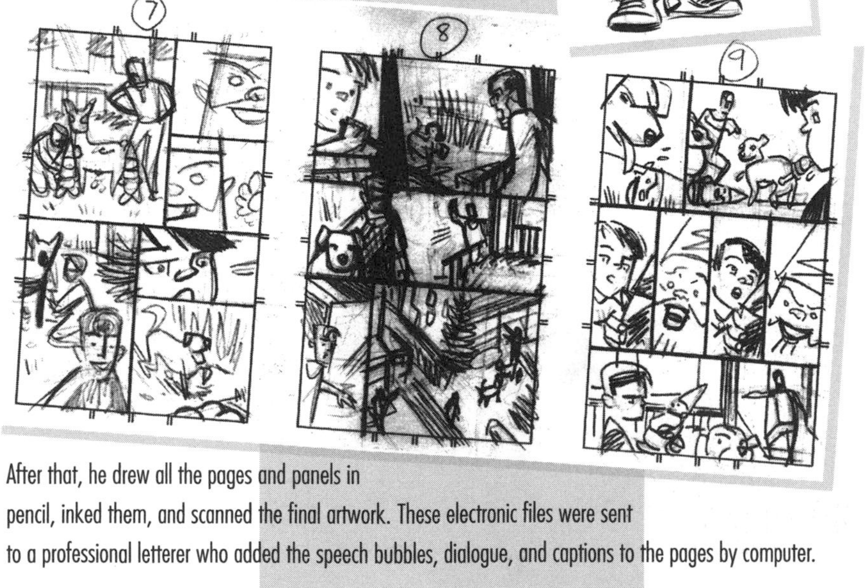
7
8
9

After that, he drew all the pages and panels in pencil, inked them, and scanned the final artwork. These electronic files were sent to a professional letterer who added the speech bubbles, dialogue, and captions to the pages by computer.

MEET THE ARTIST
Ted Naifeh

Since Ted Naifeh spent far more time drawing in class than paying attention, it's a good thing he eventually got good at it. Ted is the creator of the goth romance comic *GloomCookie* and the young adult series *Courtney Crumrin*, a tale of witchcraft, fairies, and monsters. His most recent successes are *Polly and the Pirates* and the *Death Junior* graphic novels. Ted lives in San Francisco, California.

Ted approaches comics in four phases. First, he sketches the entire book. This is where important decisions are made about pacing and layout.

Ted next draws the book in pencil. This is the first refinement stage, where things like expression and gesture are carefully drawn and redrawn till they're just right. He draws on single-ply drawing paper.

To ink, Ted tapes a sheet of two-ply Bristol board over the pencil drawing. He lays the work over a light table and uses Hunt #107 quills to ink. He also uses an old, scratchy brush to fill in the black areas with a distinctively rough, atmospheric style.

Finally, Ted scans the work into the computer and applies gray tones. This adds the final layer of mood to capture that spooky Goosebumps feeling. After that, a letterer uses a computer to add the dialogue and captions.

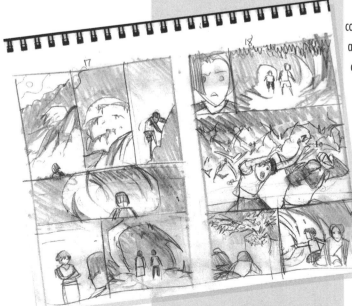

MEET THE ARTIST

Kyle Baker

Eisner award–winning artist Kyle Baker has drawn and written for comic books, newspapers, television, movies, and magazines, including NICKELODEON and MAD, for nearly a quarter century. His graphic novels include *Nat Turner, The Bakers*, and *You Are Here*. He was recently guest art director on the *Class of 3000* television show and is currently making animated cartoons of *The Bakers*. Kyle's most recent book is the one you're holding.

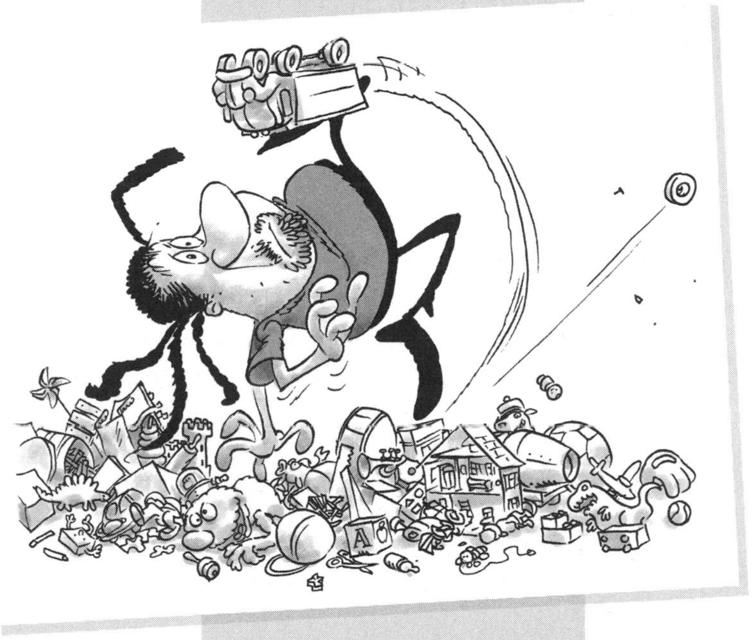

To create this Goosebumps graphic story, Kyle first read the original *The Horror at Camp Jellyjam* novel to his daughter Lillian. (Reading with your family is fun!) Then he drew the pages with markers. Each chapter of the original book corresponded to roughly one page of this comic, with more space given to action scenes because cartoons are about action! The drawings were then scanned into a computer, where the gray tones, speech bubbles, dialogue, and captions were added.

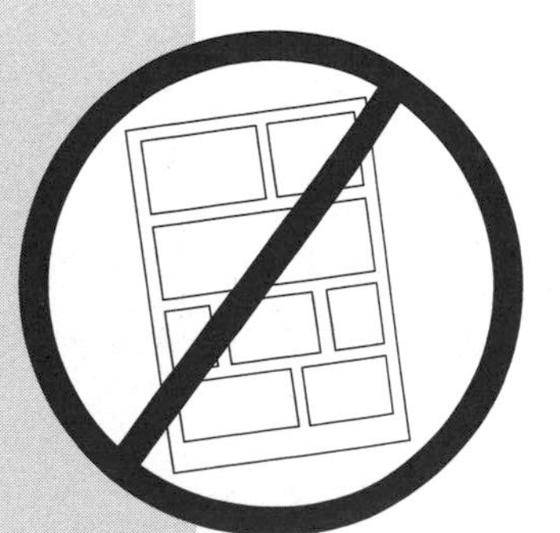

Kyle doesn't do sketches. He boldly jumps in and draws the art all at once.

MORE GHOULISH TALES FROM

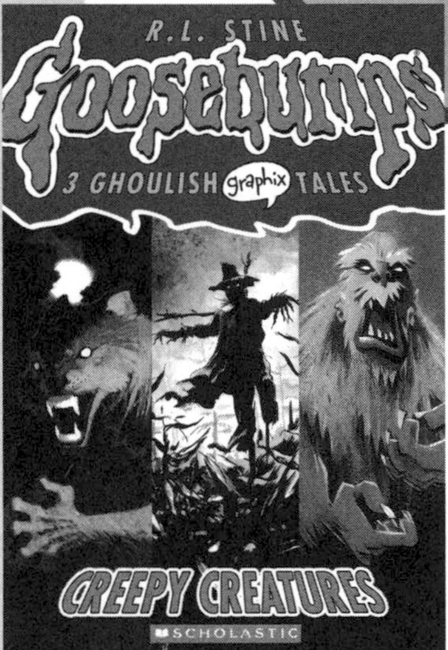
R.L. STINE
Goosebumps
3 GHOULISH graphix TALES
CREEPY CREATURES
SCHOLASTIC

Watch your back!

With his shadowy illustrations, **Gabriel Hernandez** creates the perfect atmosphere in ***The Werewolf of Fever Swamp***, a spooky story about a boy and his dog who go sniffing around in a lonely swamp . . . and wish they hadn't! Hernandez is the artist of The Thief of Always series.

Greg Ruth's beautiful work has been seen in the Heartland and Conan series. His eerie drawings in ***The Scarecrow Walks at Midnight*** turn a girl's visit to her grandparents' farm with her kid brother into one scary and dangerous summer vacation.

Scott Morse is the the award-winning author of more than ten graphic novels, including *Magic Pickle*. He brings his quirky sense of humor and madcap illustrations to ***The Abominable Snowman of Pasadena***, where a curious brother and sister unwittingly unleash a fierce—and *frosty*—monster in sunny California.

Goosebumps graphix

Come along for the ride...
Though it could be
ONE-WAY!

Jamie Tolagson, artist on The Crow, The Dreaming, and The Books of Magic series turns up the juice in **A Shocker on Shock Street**, the story of a brother and sister who land a dream job: testing the rides in a movie-studio theme park, where the special effects are REALLY special!

Or how about spending **One Day at Horrorland**? Award-winning artist **Jill Thompson**, creator of the Scary Godmother series, brings her quirky humor and madcap illustrations to this story about a family lost in an amusement park. Funny: there're no crowds, no lines, nobody around . . . to tell them the next ride might be their last!

The splashy, spooky fun of **Amy Kim Ganter**'s art is perfect for this story about two kids who find themselves in **Deep Trouble** while snorkeling. There's something dark, scaly and *very* fishy swimming along with them! Amy is the creator of Tokyopop's Sorcerers & Secretaries series.

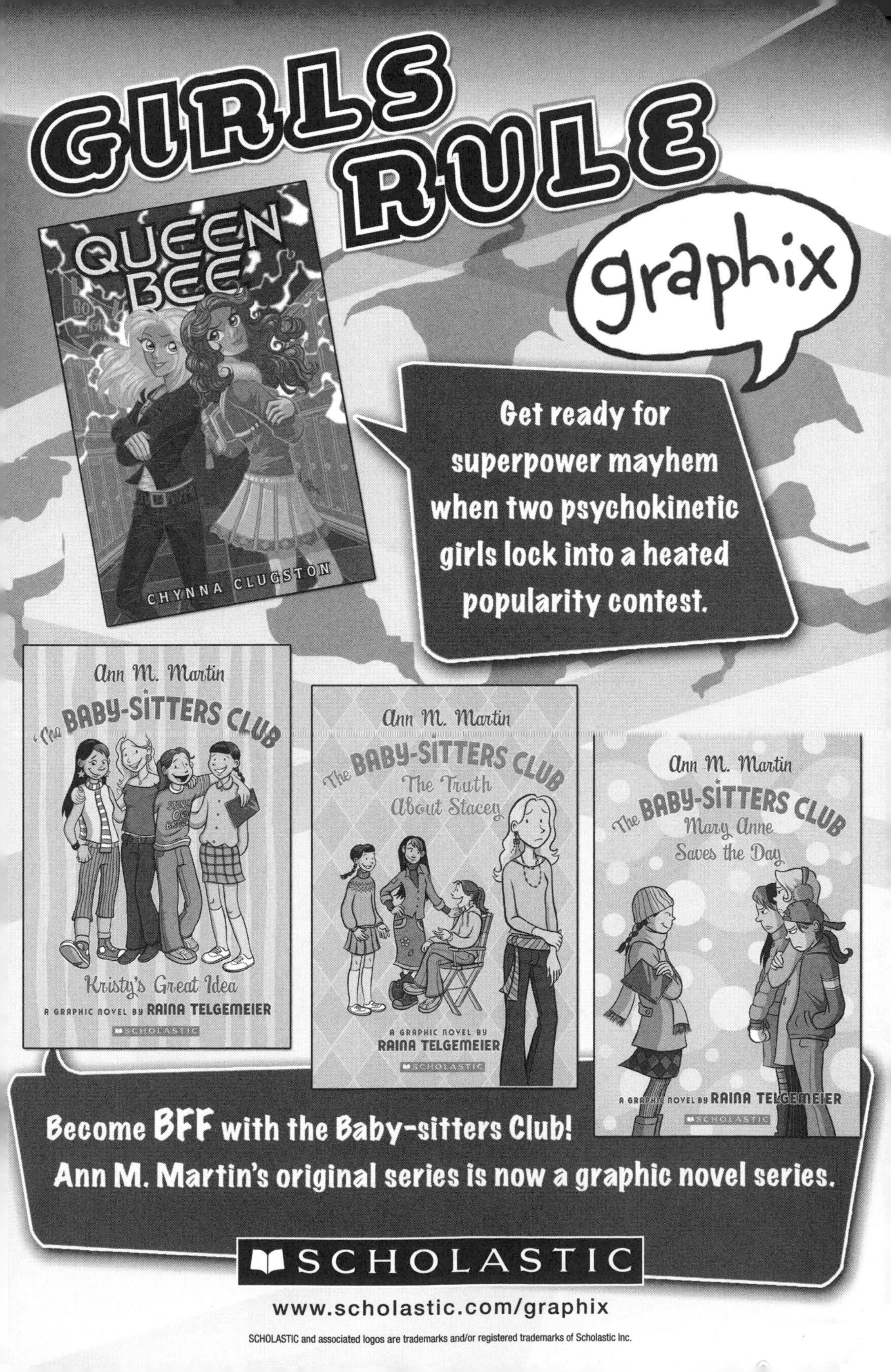
GIRLS RULE
graphix
QUEEN BEE
CHYNNA CLUGSTON
Get ready for superpower mayhem when two psychokinetic girls lock into a heated popularity contest.
Ann M. Martin
The BABY-SITTERS CLUB
Kristy's Great Idea
A GRAPHIC NOVEL BY RAINA TELGEMEIER
SCHOLASTIC
Ann M. Martin
The BABY-SITTERS CLUB
The Truth About Stacey
A GRAPHIC NOVEL BY RAINA TELGEMEIER
SCHOLASTIC
Ann M. Martin
The BABY-SITTERS CLUB
Mary Anne Saves the Day
A GRAPHIC NOVEL BY RAINA TELGEMEIER
SCHOLASTIC
Become BFF with the Baby-sitters Club!
Ann M. Martin's original series is now a graphic novel series.
SCHOLASTIC
www.scholastic.com/graphix
SCHOLASTIC and associated logos are trademarks and/or registered trademarks of Scholastic Inc.

There's something strange behind the basement door!

After the tragic death of their father, Emily and Navin move to a strange old house where a sinister creature lures their mother through a door in the basement. Desperate not to lose her, they follow, and discover a terrifying yet wondrous underground world inhabited by talking animals, a giant robot, and man-eating demons.

From Award-winning, Acclaimed Artist Kazu Kibuishi

Visit the Graphix web site at

www.scholastic.com/graphix

for more information about all
our cool Scholastic Graphix titles.

While you're there, be sure to check out
Goosebumps Graphix . . . **IF YOU DARE!**